John Bromley

THE ADVENTURES OF ARTHUR MULROONEY

Limited Special Edition. No. 4 of 25 Paperbacks

To Paul

I hope you enjoy reading this

— John

The author is now retired after working as a policeman, publican and having spent many years in overseas trade, involving sales, finance and shipping. He now lives in West Sussex where he enjoys working in the garden while continuing to write and is currently working on another novel. He also spends many hours walking his King Charles Spaniel in the Sussex Countryside.

To my wife, Patricia, for her patience and understanding while I write.

John Bromley

THE ADVENTURES OF ARTHUR MULROONEY

AUSTIN MACAULEY PUBLISHERS™
LONDON • CAMBRIDGE • NEW YORK • SHARJAH

Copyright © John Bromley (2019)

The right of John Bromley to be identified as author of this work has been asserted by him in accordance with section 77 and 78 of the Copyright, Designs and Patents Act 1988.

All rights reserved. No part of this publication may be reproduced, stored in a retrieval system, or transmitted in any form or by any means, electronic, mechanical, photocopying, recording, or otherwise, without the prior permission of the publishers.

Any person who commits any unauthorised act in relation to this publication may be liable to criminal prosecution and civil claims for damages.

A CIP catalogue record for this title is available from the British Library.

ISBN 9781528914376 (Paperback)
ISBN 9781528960885 (ePub e-book)

www.austinmacauley.com

First Published (2019)
Austin Macauley Publishers Ltd
25 Canada Square
Canary Wharf
London
E14 5LQ

Synopsis

Who is Arthur Mulrooney?

He arrives in the tiny coastal hamlet of Little Bridge soon after the end of the Second World War to see out the remaining years of his life with his friend Doctor George Wallace.

The once thriving fishing community is now reduced to a few aged residents, but it gives Arthur the anonymity and tranquillity he craves after a supposed life as a sailor.

The harbour community rely on the larger village at the top of the hill for their daily needs, and for most of the residents who are unable to make the trek, Arthur and George are their lifelines. It is the villagers who begin to question the real truth about Arthur's past, especially when he is drawn into the domestic abuse suffered by a young woman and her daughter. George warns him of the perils of becoming involved, but Arthur has a compelling need to help, with traumatic results.

In the meantime, Arthur's love of reading also places him within the humiliating grasp of Florence Merryweather, the driver of the mobile library, whose salacious humour is merely a cover for her true feelings, although an affront to his sensitivity.

All these characters are finally drawn together as the story reaches a dramatic conclusion and an ultimate sacrifice

Chapter One

As another wave battered the side of the small fishing vessel, the deck was once more washed with a flood tide of angry, grey foam. Anything not secured before the storm struck was swept away and lost in the roiling sea. At the helm, Captain Arthur Mulrooney braced his feet further apart as he fought with the wheel to bring the boat head on into the storm. He knew for certain that, if he failed, the next wave that broke over the deck would roll the vessel beyond the point of no return and the five-man crew huddled into the cabin below would have no chance to survive.

Despite the icy wind that howled in the ink black night and rattled the fragile windows of the wheelhouse, Arthur felt beads of sweat trickle from beneath the peak of his cap as, little by little, the boat began to respond to his iron determination and brute strength. He allowed himself a thin smile of congratulation as once again he had cheated the sea out of his life and those of the men who relied on him for their livelihoods, and their lives.

"And where are you today, Arthur?"

The words broke into Arthur's deep reverie, transforming his euphoric success into a disappointing reality. "What? Oh, sorry, George. I was miles away."

"Aren't you always?" George Wallace smiled benignly at his friend. "Where was it today?"

Arthur made no reply. Leaning against the weathered stone plinth that supported the rusted cast iron basket of the disused beacon, he continued to gaze longingly over the waters of the English Channel. He was standing, as he often did, at the end of the horseshoe-shaped harbour imagining the beacon beside him, and the identical one on the other side of the harbour entrance, alight and guttering in the wind as they guided the fishing fleet back into the safe embrace of the harbour.

But the fleet was long gone, together with most of the fishermen. And there was no wind whipping up the sea, just the late afternoon sun hanging low over the western horizon like a burnished copper disc that bathed the sea in an amber glow.

"I thought you might like a walk, before it gets too late," said George, knowing it would be several seconds before Arthur fully acknowledged his presence.

It had always been the same. Arthur would drift away into one of his daydreams at almost any time, even during one of their daily games of chess, but it was all part of his friend's complex character and, although sometimes annoying, a part he was prepared to accept. It was a small price to pay for companionship,

"I suppose so," replied Arthur finally, dragging his attention away from the sea and starting off at a brisk pace along the harbour wall.

"Slow down a bit," protested George, hurrying to catch up. "You forget your legs are longer than mine."

In fact Arthur's legs were a good deal longer. Although well into his seventh decade he was still a good six feet tall with a ramrod straight back that might have been the product of a career in the military. The top of his head was bald and tanned to the colour of old leather, but was surrounded by a thick tonsure of black hair which extended down to cover most of his face in a full beard. His size and appearance could well have had an intimidating effect on those who didn't know him, but to those who did, he was shy and introverted to the point of appearing rude, reluctant to speak even when spoken to. George understood this and expected little from his friend in the way of conversation, although he knew Arthur could get quite animated on certain subjects.

When they reached end of the harbour wall, George prayed that Arthur would take the more leisurely route along the shore and not the hill up to the village. For a man of his years that was an arduous enough journey when necessity dictated, not one taken for simple pleasure.

"Let's take the beach path," he suggested, pre-empting any idea Arthur may have had to the contrary. "It'll be a wee bit cooler in the trees."

George heaved a relieved sigh as his friend turned to their right, taking the footpath that ran alongside the narrow beach before winding its way through the forest of pines that rose gently away from the sea.

Although of a similar age to Arthur, George Wallace had neither the legs nor the stamina to match his friend's fitness, but it was only during these walks that he was able to drag Arthur out of his daydreaming and into an awareness of his surroundings. He did, however, sometimes wonder if it was worth the effort

As unseen seagulls screeched above the thick green canopy, the only other sound as they trudged between the trees was the crunch of dried pine needles beneath the thick soles of their brogues. With Arthur taking the lead they thread a path through the pines that eventually gave way to a greater variety of trees; silver birch, oak and beech, all interlinked with thick brambles that, to George's benefit, slowed their progress. The arboreal change also marked the border of the grounds belonging to Luxford House.

They emerged from the trees onto what a more perceptive eye would have recognised as a once well-manicured lawn interspersed with a variety of exotic shrubs and bushes. The only evidence left of these were some overgrown rhododendrons, a few woody rose trees and the inevitable brambles.

"Such a shame," mumbled Arthur, stopping and shaking his head, as he always did, to survey the sorry scene through his sad, dark blue eyes. "Something should be done about it."

"Of course it should, but who's got money to take on something like this. Not the government, they've got enough to worry about putting right what was destroyed in the war." George agreed with his friend's sentiment, but as a doctor his view on life was much more pragmatic. He had seen enough of suffering before, during and after the war to know what the priorities were. "The National Health Service was a start," continued Arthur," but there's still much to do. Come on, let's get a move on. It's getting late."

They picked their way across the thick, dried-out grass towards Luxford House which was in the same sorry state as the grounds in which it stood. Built in typical Georgian style with much of the façade hidden behind a tangled mass of ivy, it was difficult to appreciate that it had once been one of the most envied residencies in the county. Most of the small panes of glass were missing from the sash windows and there were holes in the roof. The fluted plasterwork on the pillars supporting the portico looked as though it had been used for target practice, and the steps leading up to the large oak door were broken and crumbling.

The last Lord Luxford had been killed in the First World War without leaving an heir and it had stood empty during the intervening years while various distant relatives squabbled over their claim. At the outbreak of the Second World War the government had asserted its claim to the property and over the next six years the house was used variously as a commando training establishment, home to naval intelligence and finally as an orphanage which closed its doors a year after the war ended.

Again Arthur shook his head sadly as he followed George down the sweeping gravelled drive to the two stone pillars from which once hung the ornamental iron gates. The gates were one of the earliest casualties of war.

By the time they covered the half mile back to the village of Upper Little Bridge, George was gasping for breath. Normally he would make the detour up to the small churchyard to visit his wife's grave before going down the hill to the harbour. Arthur was already heading in that direction when George caught hold of his arm.

"I think I'll give it a miss today. I'm sure Mary will forgive me." He patted his chest. "That walk has taken more out of me than I thought."

"You know best," replied Arthur blandly. "After all, you are a doctor."

George pointed towards the top of the hill and the rickety wooden seat on the small patch of grass between the road and the river. "Just a few minutes for me to catch my breath."

As George lowered himself gingerly onto the seat, Arthur stood staring at the view over the channel. The sun had changed to a deeper shade of orange as it dipped into the sea and Arthur appeared mesmerised by its brilliance, although George knew his friend was once more enticed away to some exotic place far beyond the horizon.

That small patch of grass and the hill that dropped down to the sea was like a no mans' land that separated the small harbour community and the population of the village, and while one relied on the other for most of its needs, there was little reason for the villagers to make the trek down to the harbour. But in its heyday as a thriving fishing port the roles were very much reversed and Little Bridge played an important part in the lives of those living in the surrounding area. Back then the village of Upper Little Bridge was much smaller, mainly home to workers on the vast Luxford estate, the principal employer in that part of South Devon. With the death of the last of that ancient family the estate was broken up into smaller farms and small holdings bringing more families into the area and the village at the top of the hill grew while the harbour community shrivelled into its present clutch of geriatrics clinging to a life that consisted almost entirely of memories.

It was into this dwindling, insular world that Arthur had drifted with barely a raised eyebrow from his neighbours who treated him less of an enigma and more as another piece of flotsam washed up on the tide. It was a world that suited Arthur, where he could remain largely invisible until life's circumstances forced him to make the journey up the hill.

"Ready?" said George after five minutes of staring at the back of Arthur's head. He pushed himself off the seat and walked stiffly over to where his friend was, still staring into the distance. "I don't know about you, but I'm ready for my tea."

It was a few moments before Arthur shook himself free of whatever occupied his mind.

"Sorry, what did you say?"

George chuckled. "Nothing, Arthur, I didn't say a word."

They started off down the hill accompanied by the mesmeric sound of gurgling water as the small river followed the line of the road on its way down to the sea. After the long, hot summer the water rolled down the hill at a leisurely pace, barely disturbing the gravel bed or its mud-lined banks. But after heavy rain, it took on an entirely different persona, angry and virile, roaring its way seaward and washing away the banks to cover the road in a slippery slick of red brown mud which made the hill virtually impassable to both foot and motor traffic.

At the bottom of the hill the road crossed the bridge from which the little port had taken its name. It had begun life as a narrow, wooden structure which had since been rebuilt in local stone and then widened about the time of the First World War to accommodate motor traffic. Now there was little reason for vehicles to make the journey down to the harbour, just the occasional visitor who thought the road led to somewhere more interesting or a tractor from one of the local farms on a mission to supply the harbour community when mud covered the hill.

Once over the bridge Arthur felt more at ease, where the almost motionless pace of life suited his anonymous existence, away from the scrutiny of those who took an interest in his past. His was a timeless world of make-believe, daydreams and books, a world beyond which little else existed. Of course it had not always been like that. Of course there had been a life before the harbour community had taken him into their embrace, but no one asked and Arthur was certainly not going to say because Arthur said very little to anyone, apart from George Wallace.

Past the decaying remains of the Lobster Pot public house were the two rows of tiny fishermen's cottages with their equally tiny gardens, some neatly tended, but most overgrown and as neglected as the empty cottages they served. There remained just a few aged remnants of the community to keep alive the memory and the spirit of the brave fishermen who had risked life and limb to bring home the fruits of the sea, and the hardy wives and children who waited to welcome them back. The children had long gone, either lost to the war or to a better life elsewhere, leaving behind the aged remnants which now made up the bulk of Arthur's acquaintances.

"Do you want to come in for some tea?" George shaded his eyes against the setting sun as he looked up to see if he had Arthur's attention.

Beneath the dark bushy brows Arthur's eyes were scanning the English Channel. "Where do you think that's going?" He pointed into the distance where George could just make out the dark outline of what appeared to be a freighter heading westwards into the Atlantic.

"No idea," he replied with a shrug of his shoulders. "Could be almost anywhere." He gave a smile that went unnoticed. "Anywhere you want it to be Arthur, that's the beauty of imagination. "

"No," said Arthur in his usual serious tone.

"No what?"

"No, I won't come in. I've got my book to finish before tomorrow."

"In that case I'll see you in the morning for a game of chess." George sat on the wall of his cottage watching Arthur as he walked to the far end of the harbour and turned up the narrow path to the second row of houses. He sighed deeply, realising, as he often did, how deeply he appreciated the company of the man who had helped him salve the grief of losing his wife.

Chapter Two

Enid Gulliver danced her jig, hopping from one foot to the other as she waited outside her cottage for George Wallace to approach. With her hair pulled back in a neat bun and her slight frame tightly wrapped in a floral pinafore, the doctor thought she looked even smaller and more pinched than she had the day before. Whether from years of anxious waiting for her husband to return from the sea or just from a naturally nervous disposition was hard to say, but Enid found it virtually impossible to remain motionless during her waking hours, even when George stopped to ask after her husband.

"As well as might be, doctor," she replied in a high-pitched staccato voice that matched the rhythm of her movements. "No more, no less in my opinion, but that's not to say he's no worse."

George smiled inwardly at the medical evaluation of a man crippled with arthritis who, on a good day, was only capable of managing a few steps. "Would you like me to look in on him for a few seconds?"

As her head bobbed back and forth her little rheumy eyes remained fixed on the doctor.

"Will it make him better?"

He shook his head gravely. "No, but I just thought…"

"Then there's no point troubling either of you." Her bony hand rummaged in the pocket of her pinafore and she produced a shilling. "You'll be going up top later, I expect, it being Thursday." Between the bobbing she jerked her head in the direction of Arthur's cottage. "I need a loaf and some milk."

"Of course, I'll tell Arthur to remind me his memory is better than mine."

Without another word Mrs Gulliver pranced up the steps to her front door and disappeared inside. Again George shook his head, although this time in amusement. The antics of Mrs Gulliver had never failed to amuse him.

Inside the compact living room of his cottage Arthur paced the floor as best he could, given the amount of space available for pacing. As he manoeuvred between the two bulky armchairs and coffee table he thought about having another cup of tea. He had already had two, one more than usual in the morning, but this was Thursday, which twice a month swamped Arthur with the conflicting emotions of joyful anticipation and dread. He had finished his book the night before and now George expected him to play a game or two of chess. How was he expected to concentrate?

He stopped in front of the large pine bookcase that housed his most prized possessions and tried to recall how he had managed to accumulate so many volumes. George was responsible for most of them. George knew a lot of people, especially ones who had a lot of books they no longer required and were keen to see them go to a good cause. George had been a good friend to him, an indispensable friend who had provided him with his present existence when it could have been much worse. Perhaps a game of chess was not such a great price to pay. But it was still Thursday; there was nothing George could do to change that.

"Good morning. I trust you slept well." George had let himself in through the back door and was standing in the doorway to the small galley kitchenette.

Lost in his disturbing thoughts Arthur spun round. "I didn't hear you come in, I was miles away."

The doctor gave him a benign smile, the corners of his mouth disappearing into the folds of his cheeks. "When are you ever anywhere else, Arthur?"

With a slowness that mirrored his reluctance Arthur took the wooden box of chess pieces and board from a shelf on the bookcase and put them on the little round table in the bay window, pulling the table out to allow George to take his place on the window seat. "Just one game, my heart isn't really in it today."

"All the more reason to give me a good game instead of letting me win all the time."

Through the thick growth of facial hair Arthur tried to look indignant. "I've never let you win. You're a better player than me and that's all there is to it." He waved his friend towards the window seat. "Just sit down and let's get it over with so we can go for a walk afterwards."

George shook his head vigorously. "Oh no, you sit there. I want you concentrating on the moves and not gazing out of the window like you usually do." He ushered Arthur towards the window seat before taking the straight backed chair opposite. "And as for going for a walk it's out of the question. Walking up that hill later is quite enough exercise for me."

"No one is forcing you to come. I'm quite capable of going on my own."

With a sideways look at his friend George gave a loud snort. "The last time I suggested that, you almost begged me to come with you. Besides, I've got some things to get for Mrs Gulliver and I want to look in on Mary." He finished setting up the chess pieces and patted the table. "Come on, you to start."

The game went the way it usually did, and despite Arthur going through the pretence of studying the board and taking an inordinate amount of time planning his moves the game was over in less than forty-five minutes.

"Well, I suppose that was a bit of an improvement," said George, raising a bushy speculative eyebrow. "Are you sure you don't want another?"

Before George could pursue the suggestion Arthur began collecting the pieces and putting them back in the box. "No, I think I'll go for a walk along the harbour until it's time to go up."

"Then we'll go up a bit earlier and I'll treat you to a pint." George sometimes took a perverse pleasure in watching his friend's discomfort, but there was no malevolence in it, just a devilish tease.

Arthur's response was to remain silent. He disliked the pub, not because he had anything against the occasional drink, but because it was a place where people felt compelled to talk to each other, whether they knew them or not, and Arthur had spent his time since arriving in Little Bridge diligently avoiding familiarity.

The hour or so he spent sitting at the base of the beacon, and watching with an envious fascination the coasters and great ocean going vessels as they made their way east and west along the Channel, passed in an apparent instance. George was calling him, pointing at his watch to indicate it was time to go. With a surge of mixed emotions Arthur turned reluctantly away from the sea and walked slowly back to where George was waiting for him.

"I collected your book for you," he said, holding out the volume on the wildlife of the Gobi Desert. "I thought it would save you the walk."

Arthur nodded his gratitude as he took the book and tucked it under his arm. "Perhaps we should give the pub a miss," he muttered in an attempt to sound indifferent to the idea. "We probably won't have enough time."

"Nonsense, there's plenty of time, and besides, I thought you would welcome a bit of Dutch courage." George chuckled to himself at the thought of the ordeal Arthur went through twice a month for the sake of literary stimulation.

Halfway up the hill George caught his friend by the arm and pulled him to a halt. "Just give me a couple of minutes to catch my breath," he said, bending forwards and breathing noisily.

Arthur took the opportunity to wander over to the river bank and allowed himself to be carried away by the hypnotic effect of the water as it gurgled and splashed its way down towards the sea. For a few brief moments he was engulfed in a calmness of mind he felt only when he escaped from the reality that was his life. It was with a feeling of annoyance bordering on anger that George brought him back to reality with a pat on the shoulder.

At the top of the hill they made another brief stop for George to recover before continuing into the village. To their right was the road that led to Luxford House and past that, leading into the village, was Mrs Metcalfe's little shop which, together with the pub, provided the life's blood of the community. Along the same side of the road, which could loosely be termed the high street, were a number of cottages of varying shapes and sizes and built as the original accommodation for the workers on the Luxford estate. Towards the end of the road, before it widened out into the main route out of the village, was the Dun Cow public house. Its grimy exterior gave little encouragement for a casual passer-by to venture inside, but with such trade virtually non-existent there was little incentive for the landlord to make any real effort. His was a captive clientele.

After the bright midday sunshine it was like stepping into a twilight world as Arthur followed George into the single bar with its heady atmosphere of stale beer and cigarette smoke. The furnishings were sparse, a few settles lining one wall, each with a small round table in front, and little else. It was the landlord's contention that seated customers were inclined to drink less than those standing, a theory based simply on an observation that it was only women who sat down to drink and women invariably drank less than men.

On a Thursday lunchtime at the height of the harvesting season there would usually be only a handful of elderly customers in the bar and this day was no exception. In fact there were only three or four that George could make out as his eyes became accustomed to the gloomy interior and he nodded an acknowledgement to each of them in turn and received the same in return. Arthur shuffled in behind, trying to make his large frame as inconspicuous as possible as he moved into a dark corner beside the door.

"A pint of mild then?" said George, leaning on the counter and addressing the empty space behind. He took out half a crown and tapped in on the sticky wooden counter top.

"No, just a half for me," replied Arthur, his deep voice reacting as though to a threat. "I don't think I'll have time for a pint."

"Suit yourself, but I'm having one. I need it after walking up that hill." He was about to tap again when the landlord made an appearance through the doorway behind the counter that led through to the kitchen. "Good afternoon, Joe, I was just beginning to think I'd have to help myself."

"Keep your hair on, Doc, I heard you come in. I was just getting a sandwich for old Bert there." He put the plate noisily down on the counter before shouting, "Here you go Bert, your sandwich."

Bert detached himself from his two companions and tottered unsteadily over, the hobnails in his boots echoing off the flagstone floor.

Joe returned his attention to his new customers. "So, Doc, what'll it be?"

Before replying George gave his friend a brief questioning glance. "A pint and a half of mild please, Joe. Apparently Arthur here seems to think he hasn't time for a pint.

With the landlord's attention drawn to him Arthur shrank deeper into his dark corner and silently cursed his friend for his insensitivity.

"I should have thought time was the one thing the two of you had plenty of," said Joe before breaking into a low chuckle. The folds of flesh beneath his chin rippled as he nodded his understanding. "It's got nothing to do with it being Thursday, has it?"

George joined in on the amusement. "I think it's got everything to do with it being Thursday."

Arthur could feel the hackles rising on the back of his neck He wanted to leave, but felt that would only serve to raise his profile even further. Why was George being so obtuse?

"Alright, I'll have a pint if it makes you feel happier, but don't blame me if I haven't time to finish it."

Moodily Arthur collected his pint and returned to the corner as George chatted with the landlord.

Joe Butler was a man in his mid-sixties, but not quite ready for retirement. He had been at the Dun Cow since the beginning of the war; after being bombed out of the public house, he ran in Plymouth. Originally from London, he was a tall man, although not quite as tall as Arthur, with a girth that suggested he had drunk as many pints as he had sold over the years. His large round face was clean shaven and threaded with purple veins, which were most prominent in his bulbous nose. He was dressed, as he always seemed to be, in blue serge trousers and matching waistcoat, both liberally stained with the hallmarks of his trade. His collarless shirt was once white with a thin brown stripe, although the white was now grey and the brown faded until the two colours now merged into one. His manner was typical of his calling, jovial for the most part but intolerant towards those he disliked. His attitude towards Arthur was still under review.

While Arthur sipped his beer in sullen silence George and the landlord continued to chat in apparent disregard to his presence, until they were interrupted.

"So, is one of you gents going to buy me a beer?"

The figure leaning against the counter where it butted up to the back wall of the bar had so far gone unnoticed by George, but now he stood up and rattled his empty glass on the counter top. As he came forward the doctor recognised him as someone he had seen around the village although they had never exchanged a word in conversation.

"Buy your own beer, Stan," said the landlord. "I've told you before about pestering my customers."

The man gave a gruff laugh. "Who's pestering? You know I always stand me round when I've got a few bob in me pocket." He was now standing close to George yet his dark, smouldering eyes were fixed on Arthur. "What about your friend there, he don't have much to say for himself but I reckon he ain't tight with his money."

"Right, that's enough of that." Joe lifted the flap in the counter and caught Stan by the arm as he barged past George. "No one's going to buy you a drink so you'd best be on your way."

He pushed him towards the door. "If you want to drink in here find yourself some work to pay for it. There's plenty about this time of year."

Stan's thick lips twisted into a sneer. "What would you know? I bet you ain't done a proper day's work in yer life." His attention returned to Arthur who looked down into his glass. "And what about him, he don't look like he's done much either."

Still holding Stan by the arm Joe pulled open the door and shoved him out. "I'm sorry about that, gents, he can be a nasty one when he's on the drink. I feel sorry for that wife of his. A lovely looking girl she is."

"I blame the war," said George, always prepared to take a benevolent view. "It's left a lot of men bitter."

"Well, after going through the Great War I don't know that I agree with you, doc, but I suppose it won't hurt to give him the benefit." He cocked his head at George's empty glass. "Are you stopping for another?"

George looked over at Arthur. His glass was still nearly half full. "I'm going up to see Mary shortly, but I don't think she'll begrudge me a small Scotch. What about you, Arthur?"

Arthur shook his head vigorously before taking a large swallow of his beer. "I'll finish this and wait outside." He nestled the book tighter under his arm. "Just in case it's early."

George and the landlord exchanged a knowing look. Both grinned.

Chapter Three

Florence Merryweather hunched her broad shoulders over the steering wheel and stamped down the brown brogue harder down on the accelerator pedal. The engine groaned and vibrated at the effort expected of it, yet it knew better than fail to respond. Florence Merryweather was not a woman to be ignored. Behind her the books clung to the wooden shelves as though their very lives depended on it as the converted charabanc bounced and lurched along the country road. She had a schedule to keep to and, as in the war, nothing short of death would prevent her from keeping to it.

Rather than sit at home brooding while her husband was enjoying the thrill of battle, she had volunteered her services as a driver, first as a chauffeur to various staff officers, but this proved too mundane and she graduated onto lorries, ferrying essential equipment from supply depots to the docks, and vice versa. It was possibly the happiest time of her life, away from the cloistered existence her husband had forced on her. She flourished in the company of men, giving as good as she got when it came to colourful language and ribald banter. The brash, earthy woman had emerged from the cocoon of a gentile existence and it had frightened the life out of her husband when he came home on leave. When he was killed in action towards the end of the war it was rumoured that he had thrown himself in front of a German machine gun rather than face surviving the hostilities and the prospect of her new-found liberation. She mourned his passing and the wasted years of virtual celibacy and then set about making up for lost time. A number of men had been left in her wake, discarded and exhausted, and little by little she had mellowed into the woman she was today with just one man the object of her desire. A desire whetted by the challenge it presented.

Framed by flame red hair beneath the brown trilby her florid face was tight with determination as she aimed the vehicle at Upper Little Bridge. For the number of people who use the mobile library in the village it was hardly worth the long drive, but the need to bring culture and enlightenment to the more remote areas of post war Britain, and to one person in particular, made it well worth her while.

Showers of dust and gravel thrown up by the speeding wheels of the charabanc threatened the wellbeing of anyone foolish enough to keep too close to the edge of the road as she entered the village, and when she skidded to a halt beside the green opposite the Dun Cow, it was accompanied by the smell of burning rubber.

Arthur smartly stepped back a few yards onto the green, consciously avoiding the beaming gaze of Mrs Merryweather through the open side window. The moment that had haunted his waking hours for the past weeks was upon him once again. The question of whether or not it was worth the torment was again raised and the answer just as vague. The object of George's amusement was for Arthur a constant source of anxiety.

"First in line as usual, Mr Mulrooney." Her voice boomed out over the green to the cottages beyond like an address system announcing her intentions. "Couldn't wait to see me, could you?"

Arthur cuddled the book to him as though it afford some little protection, like a silver cross warded off the unwelcome advances of a vampire. To Arthur his situation was not so dissimilar to that of Van Helsing.

As the engine spluttered into silence Florence Merryweather heaved her bulk out of the driver's seat and squeezed past the counter that had replaced the first row of seats. Arthur kept his distance while she opened the side door of the charabanc and positioned a set of wooden steps. He looked around anxiously to ensure there were no witnesses to the coming humiliation. Mrs Merryweather seemed equally anxious that there was, her thick, painted lips pushed forward into a pout as she stood hands on broad hips, daring Arthur to approach.

"Where is your good friend, the doctor?" It was more in the nature of a demand than a question. The lips spread into a salacious grin. "Oh, I see, didn't want to share me, did you? You're a devious little devil, Mr Mulrooney, that's what you are."

Behind his beard Arthur felt his skin burn, mostly with embarrassment but partly with anger. He had no idea why any woman would want to single him out for such demeaning treatment, and this woman in particular was worse than any beyond his imagining.

He chose not to respond to her, mainly because he could think of nothing appropriate to say. Edging slowly towards the door of the charabanc he prayed that she would retreat inside and allow him to pass unmolested.

"Oh, do come on, I'm not going to eat you," she boomed, finally mounting the steps and taking up her position behind the counter. She reached underneath and brought out two boxes of library tickets with the book slips tucked inside: beige tickets for fiction and green for non-fiction. She reached across for the book still tucked tightly under his arm, snorting loudly when he recoiled at the sudden movement. "For God's sake, Mr Mulrooney, I only want the book, not your body." She smiled wickedly. "Not yet, anyway."

He held the book at arm's length and she snatched it away before flicking through the tray of green tickets, and pulling his out she held it provocatively close to the ample breast. The burning in Arthur's cheeks threatened to incinerate him before he was saved by a woman who came up the steps behind him with a young boy holding on to her skirt. With a sideways look of annoyance at the woman Mrs Merryweather threw the ticket on the counter which Arthur quickly grabbed before scuttling off to hide amongst the shelves.

Once concealed from view and safe from her lewd insinuations he was able to breathe more easily and concentrate on the pleasurable, but increasingly difficult, task of finding a book he had not yet read. For Arthur the non-fiction section was a dwindling world of familiar titles, further limited by his sole thirst for knowledge of foreign lands and travel. George had constantly chided him in an attempt to broaden his friend's literary interests to include other subjects, and even fiction. The reaction had been that of a man asked to worship another god.

With flagging expectations he searched along the shelves, his fingers trailing across the spines like a blind man reading Braille. He was about to give in to his disappointment when that fearful voice reverberated down the length of the charabanc, rattling the windows as it did so.

"If you care to come down here, Mr Mulrooney, I have something for you."

As he cowered behind the shelf Arthur was painfully conscious that the woman and her son were staring at him through taunting eyes as he sensed their joy at his humiliation. Of course it was all in his mind, but for him it was real enough to make him feverish. Why was she doing this to him? What had he ever done to her?

Had he been brave enough to peer round the edge of the shelf he would have seen that Mrs Merryweather was waving a book in the air with a triumphant flourish. "I saved this just for you," she boomed.

With the woman and the boy still watching him with interest Arthur ventured a brief glance around the edge of the shelf. He eyed the book with the same suspicion as a mouse would the cheese on a trap, trying to assess if the prize was worth the risk.

She held the book close to her face and squinted at the cover. "The Mysteries of India," she said with a hint of seduction in her voice. "I'm sure it's one you haven't read."

He was sure as well and the temptation was almost overwhelming. He cursed himself for his cowardice and was about to be lured out when he heard George's voice from the bottom of the steps. Rather than viewing his arrival as a source of relief he convinced himself that it was to join in the humiliation. He retreated along the shelf.

"I hope you're not being difficult with him, Mrs Merryweather," George said as he came up the steps, searching the inside of the library for his friend. "You know how shy he can be."

As Arthur cringed she chuckled derisively. "A fine figure of a man like that frightened of a poor weak woman, he ought to be ashamed of himself." She directed her words down the length of the charabanc causing the woman with the boy to give Arthur a contemptuous grin. "How he survived all those years at sea is a mystery to me. I thought sailors are supposed to have a girl in every port."

"Not Arthur," said George in his friend's defence. "I think he went to sea to get away from women like you. He needs to be handled with kid gloves. Perhaps if you were a little less forward."

She glared at George as though hurt by the inference. "Are you suggesting I'm some kind of hussy, Doctor Wallace? That's quite hurtful to a sensitive soul like me."

If his situation wasn't so dire Arthur may have laughed aloud at her remark, but all George had so far managed to do was to cast him in the role of villain, not the victim.

"I'm just a naturally warm-hearted woman," she continued, showing George the book. "I saved this especially for Mr Mulrooney and that's all the thanks I get."

"In that case I apologise for my rudeness, and for any offence Arthur has caused you. I'm sure he didn't mean to, it's just the way he is." He turned to where Arthur was still in hiding. "Do come on out and show your gratitude, Arthur."

As if to ease the heavy burden of distress heaped upon him by both George and Florence Merryweather, the woman found the books she was looking for and, with her son still clinging to her skirt, she left the library. Sulkily, Arthur ventured out of his hiding place and walked slowly up to the counter, carefully avoiding the judgemental gaze of the other two.

Spurred only by the exciting prospect of the book he slid his library card across the counter as Mrs Merryweather held the volume seductively to her chest, tempting him to take it from her.

"For pity's sake, Mrs Merryweather, just give him the book," pleaded George, unable any longer to collaborate in Arthur's discomfort. "Arthur, thank Mrs Merryweather for her thoughtfulness and we can be on our way."

Arthur mumbled a word of thanks although he refused outright to retrieve the book from the warmth of her bosom, shuffling anxiously until she finally held it out for him to take. Once it was in his grasp he almost leapt down the steps to join George in the road.

"Come on," said George with undisguised annoyance as he took Arthur's arm and marched him along the road towards the far end of the village. "I don't know why you allow yourself to get into such a state when you know it only encourages her,"

"I can't help it. I don't know why she has to pick on me like she does."

George laughed at his friend's naivety. "You really don't, do you, Arthur. She does it because she likes you, any fool can see that."

Arthur blanched at the suggestion. "Don't be stupid. And even if you were right, I certainly don't like her. I just wish she would leave me alone."

"Then try being a bit more sociable and maybe she will."

They had passed the last of the cottages on the fringe of the village and turned up the narrow lane that led past the school to the small church. "I'll wait for you here," said Arthur, resting his hands on the low wall that surrounded the playground.

George nodded and carried on through the lychgate into the cemetery. Even though she had never lived in the village it had always been his wife's wish that she should be buried there, knowing that, when the time came, George would be joining her. For most of their married life they had lived in Exeter where George had his practice, and during that time had spent their summer holidays in the countryside surrounding Little Bridge. They both loved the area and had planned to retire there, but Mary had contracted pneumonia and died a year before making their dream a reality. Before her death, though, she had made George promise he would make the move, and so he had.

Now he stood at the foot of her grave in silent contemplation, trying to imagine, as he always did, how different his life would have been had she lived and how it would have affected his friendship with Arthur. What would she have made of him? At odds with the emotion that wetted his eyes he smiled at the thought. Mary was a plain speaking woman and would have told Arthur exactly what she thought. After a few more minutes of conversation George turned away from the grave.

He found Arthur where he had left him leaning on the wall and gazing at the school.

"It's not going to be finished in time," Arthur muttered, as much to himself as for George's benefit.

"They're calling it the baby boom," replied George, just as absently.

They were both watching the half dozen workmen who seemed to be in no particular hurry to complete the extension of old Victorian building that was the village school.

"It won't be finished before the new school term," repeated Arthur, as though it was a matter that should cause him some inconvenience.

George chuckled. "I can't see the kids complaining too much if it means a longer holiday. Better that it's finished properly and not rushed, I suppose."

Arthur found it hard to agree, but kept his opinion to himself. To him it was quite straightforward; there was a job to be done in a limited amount of time and all it required was enough men to make it happen. Such was Arthur's simplistic view of the world.

They walked back through the village absorbed in their own thoughts; George rarely had much to say after his visit to the churchyard. It was only when they reached the village shop that he remembered the shilling that Mrs Gulliver had given him.

"I have to pop in here," he said, holding up the coin. "Mrs Gulliver needs a few things."

Arthur scrutinised the shilling. "I hope she doesn't need much if that's all she's given you. Doesn't she know how much things cost now?"

George smiled and shook his head as he went up the steps into the shop. He had no idea how long it had been since Enid Gulliver had last climbed the hill, he only knew that the next time she made the journey it would probably be inside a coffin, as it would be for most of the old folk who lived down at the harbour. It made him wonder how long it would be before he was in that same situation. It was that thought that gave him the determination to make the most of what life he had left, and that Arthur should do the same.

Chapter Four

Rosie Jessop curled her fingers around the edge of the window sill and pulled herself up on tip toe. Even then she could only just give herself a limited view of the road outside. For a six-year-old she was small, as were many children of her age who lacked nourishment caused by years of rationing and shortages after the war. But she was a pretty girl with long fair hair that, when not tied into bunches, cascaded over her shoulders or fell across her pale, oval face. Her cornflower blue eyes were wide open as they searched the road, but it was fear and not excited anticipation that was reflected in the dusty glass.

She had no idea of the time. Even if the clock on the mantle shelf still worked she had not yet learnt what the numbers on the dial and those funny little arrows meant. But still she knew that soon daddy would be home, that he would be angry with mummy and angry with her. She never knew what it was she had done, or what mummy had done, to make him so angry, or why she had to be punished, it was just something that happened and was part of her life.

In the kitchen Daisy Jessop was no less agitated than her daughter, or her life no less miserable. Of course it was her own fault, she had been warned against marrying him and forced to ignore the warnings by a rebellious nature that knew better. Her parents had told her what sort of man Stan Jessop was, what everyone else had told her he was, and now, when it was too late, she knew they had been right. With both her parents dead, killed in the Plymouth blitz, and no other close relatives to offer support she felt trapped in a loveless, violent marriage. She could have endured it for herself, but it was often Rosie who had to endure the product of Stan's meanness and it was for Rosie that she reserved all her pity. The guilt Daisy had felt at having wished Stan had perished in the war had long since passed, only to be replaced with thoughts of wishing to kill him herself, if only she had the courage.

With the backs of her legs aching from the strain of standing on tip toe, Rosie lowered herself down from the sill and stood trembling, either from the effort or from trepidation. Then she heard the gate slam shut and let out a hushed, anguished cry as she ran to the far corner of the living room and crouched down behind the ragged armchair. It was no safe haven. If her father wanted to punish her it was the first place he would look, but for a few minutes at least she could create for herself a little world of pretence and block out her father's ranting until he came for her.

Daisy heard the gate too and her heart sank. Stan was supposed to be working. He had told her when he left the house that morning he had work on a local farm helping with the harvest. She had been foolish enough to believe him when most of what came out of Stan's mouth was lies. Even during his war service with the Royal Air Force, he had managed to remove himself from danger and hard work by inventing a back injury and serving his time as a stores clerk from where he ran a lucrative black market sideline. Not that Daisy had reaped any benefit from his dubious business acumen; any money he made had found a home in the pubs surrounding the camp or on the women who frequented them. It was only by the slimmest of margins that he talked his way out of a court martial and a lengthy prison sentence. But that was the one thing Stan Jessop was good at, talking. It had been his loquacity and her gullibility that had tempted her into his bed and into marriage, and a lifetime of regret.

As soon as he came into the kitchen she could smell the stale beer and cigarette smoke that followed him about with a nauseous permanence. Long before she came under the influence of his beery breath, his heavily lidded eyes told her where he had spent most of the morning, and what little money they had. Not wanting to engage with him she kept her head down and carried on with the washing she had in the sink, scrubbing on a stain on Rosie's dress that had long since disappeared. She heard his lumbering footsteps across the bare stone floor and felt the heat of his breath on the back of her neck. It was only when he slid his hands around her waist and onto her belly did she show any acknowledgement of his presence, flinching and turning her head away when he tried to kiss her neck.

She had never denied him the rights of a husband, even though the love had gone and the passion was one sided. His slightest touch was repugnant to her, and when he entered her she was forced to close her mind to him and try to place it elsewhere, anywhere. She had so far kept from him the existence of the baby now growing inside her because to do so was to admit to a further tie to the husband she so despised. It had been three months since her last period, and while she had not yet had the pregnancy confirmed for fear of Stan finding out, she knew it was there. Soon he would know too, when the few dresses she owned began to be too tight, or the morning sickness interfered with making his breakfast. How he would react when she did finally tell him was yet a further worry that joined all the others that plagued her life.

His thick, slavering lips left a slug trail of spittle on the side of her neck and shoulder as his mouth took full advantage of the bare skin provided by the thin cotton summer dress. Daisy dropped the garment she was washing into the water and squirmed sideways, pushing him away with her elbows.

"Stop it, Stan. Rosie's in the next room." She felt guilt at using her daughter for an excuse but it was the first thing that came into her head.

"What's she doing in the house on a day like this; ain't she got no friends she can play with?" The words had a ring of contempt. "That girl ain't right, hanging round you all the time."

There was an element of truth in what Stan said, but that was something else that Daisy blamed him for. With his threatening and abusive manner he had kept the two of them in virtual isolation. Daisy was not allowed to have friends and Rosie was so cowed by him, she used her mother as a social crutch.

Daisy wanted to say, 'What do you expect when she's got a father like you'. "There's nothing wrong with her, she just prefers to be here with me."

"Well, I'll be glad when she's back at school and out from under our feet." He renewed his advances but Daisy pushed him away, leaving soapy handprints on the front of his shirt. He grabbed hold of her wrists. "What's the matter with you, ain't a bloke allowed to show his wife a bit of affection?"

Not since the early days of their relationship had there been any affection between them, just a taking by one and a reluctant giving by the other. "There's a time and place, Stan," said Daisy through a mouth closed tight against his searching lips. "Leave me be and I'll get you some lunch."

With a strength she was unable to resist he pulled her close, his face an inch from hers. "I don't want no lunch and I'm sick and tired of you putting that brat before me." He pushed Daisy away, her back catching the edge of the sink. "It's time she was taught who's in charge of this house."

As he turned away with spite etched into his dark features Daisy made a grab for his arm. "No, Stan I'll go upstairs with you, if that's what you want, but leave her alone, she hasn't done anything." She placed her free hand round his neck and tried to kiss him, even though it sickened her. "Come on, she won't bother us."

He hesitated, weighing up his options before his mouth twisted into a cynical grin. There was no need for him to make a choice. "No, you can wait. The brat needs to learn a lesson."

"Please, Stan, don't. You can do what you want with me but please don't hurt our Rosie." She pressed her body into his, her blue eyes, seductive and pleading, staring up into his face.

"Always been yours since the day she was born, not mine. I don't even think I'm her father, you've only got to look at her to see that."

Daisy clung to him, trying to hold him back as he dragged her towards the living room door. "Of course she's yours. You don't really think I've been with another man, do you?"

He gave a harsh laugh, spraying her face with drops of spittle as he gripped her chin. "How do I know what you got up to while I was away fighting for king and country." He looked her up and down. "You were a good looking woman back then, before you let yourself go. And I could have had anyone, still could if I wanted. I stuck by you and that kid when I could have buggered off, so don't go getting any ideas that I owe you anything." He took her hands in a painful grip and pulled them off him. "You ain't that good anymore."

It was only fear of reprisals against her daughter that prevented Daisy from unleashing all the hatred and anger that welled up inside her as her eyes were drawn towards the paring knife on the draining board. If it was just her she could so easily have killed him in the moment of blind rage. But Rosie was now the focus of his venom and she was her priority.

"Leave her alone, Stan," she sobbed frantically. "It's me you're angry with, she's done nothing."

Deaf to her pleadings Stan pushed her away and went into the living room. A quick glance round the sparse furnishings was all it took to see where his daughter crouched trembling behind the armchair. She had clamped her tiny hands over her ears to block out daddy's anger, knowing it was all her fault even though she didn't know why. With her head tucked in tight against her chest she could sense him getting closer, and as the chair was dragged away a trickle of warm liquid ran down her leg and pooled on the wooden floor.

As nicotine-stained fingers gripped her upper arm she was yanked to her feet. She let out a little squeal of terror and clung to the back of the chair, frantically trying to save herself from the punishment she knew was to come.

"Stan, for pity sake, leave her be," pleaded Daisy, tugging at Stan's arm.

"The little brat's pissed herself again. You'd better get it cleaned up." He threw Daisy away from him with such force that she fell backwards onto the floor, sobbing helplessly. "She's going to be taught a lesson and you'd best not get in my way."

He dragged the screaming Rosie towards the bottom of the stairs while Daisy scrambled to her feet.

"No, Stan, I'm not going to let you. She doesn't deserve it."

She tried to place herself between him and the stairs but it was a futile attempt. With his free hand he backhanded her across the side of her face, snapping her head back. Before she could recover he punched her in the stomach. Rosie shrieked as her mother doubled over in pain, her little face streaked with tears and her face, a mask of uncomprehending horror.

"Mummy!" she screamed as she was dragged past her helpless mother and up the stairs. "I'll be a good girl, daddy. I promise I will."

Those were the last words Daisy heard as her daughter's bedroom door slammed shut. Unable to bear the sound of Rosie's pleadings she staggered through to the kitchen to fetch a mop. At that moment she loathed herself almost as much as she did her husband for being the weak woman she was, for failing to prevent her precious daughter's torment. It was then that she vowed to make it end. She had no idea how, but she would make it end.

Chapter Five

Tranquillity hung over the harbour of Little Bridge like a sea mist, shrouding the elderly residents with a serenity that eased them through the last years of their lives. For Mrs Gulliver, her husband and the handful of other old folk who had spent their whole lives in the cluster of cottages their world had gradually shrunk with their failing mobility and they now relied on the help of others to provide them with the necessities required to live. When George arrived amongst them they welcomed him into their bosom. Not only could he treat their ailments within the limits his skills alone could provide but he also had the legs to carry him up the hill. Once or twice a week he would collect from all of them a list of their requirements which he took up to Mrs Metcalfe's shop which she used to deliver in her dilapidated van, until it was finally defeated by the steep incline of the hill.

Long before his retirement and move to the harbour both George and his wife had been a part of their community. They had loved spending time amongst them, drinking with them in the Lobster Pot and listening to the endless tales that fishing folk loved to tell. It was during one such idyllic holiday that the pair formed the plans for the doctor's retirement. Sadly, events had intervened to sabotage their dream, but George had kept the promise he made to Mary and the harbour residents accepted him with open, sympathetic arms.

But for Arthur his arrival was greeted with little ceremony, just a bland acceptance that he was a friend of the good doctor and as such he was entitled to a place amongst them. He looked every inch the old sea salt that George presented him to be and no questions were asked of his previous life, which was just as well because Arthur was reluctant to talk about anything, and most particularly anything regarding his past.

It was mainly from the population of Upper Little Bridge that his arrival managed to raise the odd suspicious eyebrow or innocent question which he fended off by dropping his head or offering a well-practiced, single-word reply. Rarely did he venture up the hill alone. George was the buffer that protected his privacy and saved him from embarrassment, although even he could not prevent the shameless advances of Florence Merryweather.

Arthur shifted uncomfortably in his armchair, not from any fault of the chair itself but from the painful thoughts invoked by the book sitting on his lap. It was an interesting book; there was no question of that, more so because it was one he had not read before, unlike many of those he was forced to borrow from the library. There was no denying he should have been grateful to the woman for her consideration, but to be grateful implied a measure of indebtedness and that is what galled him, taking some pleasure from the read.

He was barely halfway through the first chapter before his mind began to wander and his gaze shifted from the pages and out through the small bay window to the sea beyond. Before he knew it, and completely outside of his control, he was leading an expedition through the hill country north of Simla. A tiger had attacked an English woman, leaving her alive but badly mauled and he had been tasked with the dangerous, but vital, mission to track it down and slay it before it struck again. That a nearby village had been terrorised by the animal for weeks, leaving a number of the villagers injured or dead, had so far proved to be an inconsequential item of news in the summer hill station. But now the beast had dared to lay its claws on a European, and a memsahib at that, and so its days were numbered.

With him Arthur had a small party of Pathan tribesmen and some native beaters. The Pathans were expert marksmen and fearless, the very men he needed for such a perilous undertaking, and he felt confident of his success, although he was aware of the danger that went with overconfidence.

There was a flash of white teeth as one of the tribesmen smiled triumphantly through his thick beard. He pointed at the ground. "Tracks, Sir Arthur! Fresh tracks."

Arthur nodded his agreement. He had already seen them, nothing escaped his eagle eyes. The undergrowth ahead of them was thick, ideal cover for the tiger, and he knew they would have to proceed with extreme caution.

He beckoned over the Pathan. "Mohammed, take half your men and circle round to the left and I'll take the rest to the right. Tell the beaters to give us fifteen minutes to get into position and then push forward making as much noise as they can."

In a clearing a hundred yards away Arthur listened to the clash of symbols and the wild cries of the beaters, his eyes scanning the line of undergrowth, his heart thumping with excitement. He knew that at any moment the tiger would break cover and they would have only seconds to bring it down before it attacked. It was now they were at their most vulnerable, when a missed shot could leave one of them dead. This was no time to fail.

The noise of the beaters had drowned out the approach of the beast and it crashed through the bushes barely twenty yards from him, giving him no chance to take careful aim. The beast was in the air, about to bring him down, as he squeezed the trigger. He faced death with a stoic calm.

"Arthur?"

"Mohammed?"

"What? For pity's sake, Arthur, where were you this time?"

The book fell to the floor as Arthur lurched forward in the chair. "I must have dozed off. You startled me coming in like that."

The look of fear on Arthur's face told a different story and George shook his head despairingly. "You weren't asleep, Arthur, you were daydreaming again." He bent down and picked up the book. "I presume it didn't involve Mrs Merryweather." He gave a devilish grin. "Or did it? And who the devil is Mohammed?"

Arthur looked away sheepishly. "No one! It doesn't matter." He snatched the book from George's hand. "I told you, I was reading my book and fell asleep."

George sat down opposite and assumed an expression of professional concern. "You've got to stop this, Arthur, living your life in one make-believe world or another. You need to make more of an effort to engage with real people in the real world." He took a deep breath and let it out in a long sigh. "I know some of the folk of Little Bridge can come across as aloof or rude even, but they probably see you as the same. You really should try talking to them more."

"Like that woman in the library van you mean," replied Arthur, resentfully.

"She's got a name, Arthur, Mrs Merryweather. And yes, I do mean her, and the others. If you want to make any sort of life here you've got to try to blend in." He patted his friend on the knee. "I don't mean to lecture you. I'm only saying it for your own good."

It was clear from the bland expression on Arthur's face that he was unconvinced by the argument. "The less I know about them the less they know about me, and that's how I prefer it."

"They'll only know what you want them to know, what you tell them. God only knows I've done my best to protect you but I think it's high time you started to speak up for yourself." Frustration was beginning to creep into George's voice; it was a conversation they should have had when Arthur first arrived. "Just tell them what they already know, that you were years in the merchant marine, and if they want to know more I'm sure someone with your creative imagination could make something up." He got up and went over to the bookcase for the chessboard and pieces. "Just try, Arthur, that's all I'm asking."

Sullenly Arthur nursed the book against his chest as though he was nurturing a young child. "I don't think I'm in the mood for chess."

"No, I don't expect you are." George put the chess pieces down on the table in the window and sat down again in the chair opposite his friend. "I'm not going to keep on apologising to you, Arthur, or for you. There's nothing wrong with daydreaming, I do it all the time." He forced a wistful smile, although the tear in the corner of his eye went unnoticed. "They usually involve Mary and what it would have been like if she was still here. But she isn't and I have to accept that despite the regrets. You have to do the same and stop regretting what might have been and be grateful for the life you have now. Stop trying to hide, the past is the past and it's done with. Just get on with living in the present."

When he had finished speaking George threw himself back in the chair not knowing if Arthur had even heard any of his words, let alone heeding them. Instead of embracing the chance of a new life in Little Bridge as George hoped he would it appeared his friend was shrinking ever further into anonymity. But he had tried and now there was nothing more he could do. It was up to Arthur.

As George ventured a glance across to the other chair Arthur's bearded features remained inscrutable. There was nothing to suggest the doctor's words had penetrated, or even reached him. Even when he spoke it was impossible to say. "You had better get the board set up if you still want a game. But don't expect me to take the window seat."

Chapter Six

Rosie Jessop pulled back the sheet that covered her and looked fearfully around her bedroom, searching the gloom for the bogeyman her father had told her came for naughty girls. And hadn't she been a naughty girl? That's why he had punished her and that's why he had punished mummy. Rosie had heard them in the next room before daddy started snoring and mummy began to cry. Eventually she had fallen asleep but the bad dream had woken her. The moon that glowed beyond the thin cotton curtain that covered the window bathed the room in a muted yellow eeriness. Rosie shrunk back under the sheet, her little body shuddering at the thought of what lurked beneath her bed, waiting to devour her for her wicked behaviour.

She lay there for several minutes, wide awake and afraid to close her eyes, yet equally scared of what she might see. In the next room the rumble of her father's snoring afforded her little comfort; she feared him as much as anything that hid in the shadows of her bedroom. If only mummy could be there with her, then she would be safe. Then they would both be safe. She had no idea how long it would be before dawn replaced the darkness, but the pain in her belly told her she needed a wee and the consequences of wetting the bed would be severe for both her and her mother.

Slowly, cautiously she pushed the sheet away from her face and sat up. The pot was always by the side of her bed and she felt for it with her foot as she swung her legs out. Fully expecting a hand to reach out from under the bed and grab hold of her ankle, she trembled with fright. There was no time to think about it, she needed to go and whatever threatened her from within the room could be no more frightening than what she could expect from her father if she soiled the sheets. As her eyes became more accustomed to the gloom she searched about for the pot. There was no sign of it, not on the floor, not where it should be.

She knelt down, one hand groping under the bed as the other clung tightly to the bed sheet as though it would prevent her from being dragged into the terrifying blackness beneath the bed. Her childish mind was racing through the possibilities of what might happen to her, although the most frightening prospect for her was that her mother might never know. She would be gone and no one would know where.

Suddenly the urgency of her bursting bladder wiped away all other fears and she scrambled to her feet. There was nothing else for it, she would have to face the demons her father had sown in her mind and go downstairs to the outside lavatory; either that or use the pot in her mother's room. Knowing how her father hated to be woken that seemed an unlikely option as she pulled open the bedroom door. Without allowing herself time for thought she hurried to the top of the stairs, her bare feet tripping lightly over the wooden boards. Her need to wee was desperate now and she held herself through her cotton nightdress to hold back the flow that was fighting for release. *Why hadn't mummy left the pot by the bed?* She asked herself that question as she took the stairs one at a time, but with an urgency that made each heavy step leak a little warmth into her hand.

Reaching the bottom she ran through the kitchen praying that the back door wasn't locked. Her free hand clutched at the handle which thankfully turned and the door swung open with its familiar creak. With no thought to what may be waiting for her in the pre-dawn gloom, and oblivious to the chill air that engulfed her, she ran past the open entrance to the coal shed to the lavatory which she reached just in time.

The relief she felt released her young mind to focus on her vulnerability, and as her bare feet touched the cold stone of the path she trembled. An owl hooted in the fields that backed onto the garden to be answered by the hoarse bark of a fox. Common sense dictated that she should run indoors and seek the safety of her bed covers, but either fright or guilt, or both, rooted her to the spot. To reach the kitchen door she must pass the coal shed with its pitch black interior and the demon that spent its nights there and lived on a diet of misbehaving children. That's what her father told her and what her mother had vigorously tried to refute. Of course Rosie believed her mother in everything and there was no demon or bogeyman. Was there?

The door to the coal shed had long gone, used for firewood during a particularly harsh winter a few years previous, and Rosie had always harboured the thought that something nasty lurked in that menacing interior. She had only ever ventured into there once before, when a ball she was playing with had rolled in there and her mother had been standing a comforting short distance away. Also then, the low late afternoon sun had spread an inviting hand far enough in to illuminate the dusty black floor and she was able to retrieve the ball with barely a glance into the scary corners.

She could not fathom what held her to the spot outside the lavatory, but something in the depths of her mind was willing her to face what terrors the coal shed contained. It was as though she was being invited to a trial by courage: if she went in there and survived then she would be vindicated of all the naughty things her father had accused her of and for what he had meted out all those cruel punishments. If she went in there and survived he would no longer be able to touch her in the way he did. If she went in there and was devoured by the demon how much worse could that be from the suffering she had already endured, and would endure in the future?

It seemed like an eternity that she stood there, her little body shivering with cold and the frightening vision conjured by her imagination. Slowly, so slowly she hardly noticed, she turned towards the open doorway which now seemed to beckon her in. Drawn with inevitability like a pin to a magnet, she shuffled forwards and was immediately struck by how much colder it felt inside. She was shaking violently now as the darkness enveloped her and a tightness gripped her stomach until she thought she would be sick. The inside smelt of damp and coal dust, but to Rosie the smell was of something far more sinister. If death had a smell this was how it would be. She could see no further than the length of her arms which she held out in front of her as she went further in towards one of the furthest corners where she assumed that anything evil in there would most likely live.

"Hello." It was a tiny voice in an immense void, echoing off the walls until it was almost deafening.

She reached the corner far sooner than she expected, the thick, sticky cobwebs entwining her fingers an instant before she felt the grimy brickwork. She recoiled with a squeal of horror, rubbing the clinging mass from her hands as she waited, tense with expectation, for something far worse to happen to her. When nothing did she turned back to face the doorway through half-closed eyes that gradually dared to take in the rest of the interior as they became more accustomed to the darkness.

"Hello," she said again, this time with a little more certainty. "I'll wait for you if you like."

She sank to the floor, her knees tucked up into her chest and the bottom of her nightdress pulled over her feet which were black and cold. As the minutes ticked away, her courage grew. Her father was wrong, there was no demon and she was not the wicked girl he would have her believe. She wanted to run back into the house to tell her mother, but something stopped her, an overwhelming sense of achievement. She wanted her father to know, she wanted him to find her there safe and well and to know that he was wrong. Sustained by that thought she fell asleep.

Daisy rolled over onto her side with her back towards her husband whose snoring had settled into a low, hollow wheeze, which was equally annoying. Facing the window she could see that the first traces of dawn had taken the edge off the darkness outside. It had been a long night where sleep had come in short bursts, disturbed by bad dreams in which she relived the torments of the previous day.

Instead of coming back downstairs after Rosie's punishment, Stan had gone for a lie down which reprieved Daisy from his earlier threat and allowed her the chance to rush to her daughter's side to give her the comfort she so badly needed. Rosie never spoke about what her father did to her and Daisy never pressed her, knowing it would be too painful for them both. All she saw was the distress in the child's eyes and the pale, tear-washed cheeks. The only comfort she could offer was to clutch Rosie to her chest and pray that she could find a way to free them both from all the hurt brought by her husband.

Thankfully Rosie was already in bed when Stan finally came down that evening, sparing the girl more of his abuse. Daisy was sitting in the living room sewing a button on one of her daughter's dresses, ready for the new school term which had been put back by a week due to the building work. As much as she missed not having Rosie at home, especially through the long summer holiday, school was the only place where she could be free from Stan's influence. It was also the place where she could make friends and form the social skills that had so far been slow to develop. Something else Daisy could thank Stan for.

He stood in the doorway, glaring at her through heavy, red-rimmed eyes. "Where's my fags?" His voice was thick, and he coughed up a ball of phlegm which he promptly swallowed. "I had fags when I went up and now they're gone."

"I haven't seen them," Daisy replied without looking up from her sewing. "You probably smoked them all."

"Don't be so bleeding stupid. I had a full packet when I went out this morning. How could I have smoked them all?"

Quite easily, thought Daisy, angry that he wasted so much of their meagre income on cigarettes and beer instead of providing the more pressing essentials needed by his family. "I told you Stan, I haven't seen them." She felt his presence by the side of her chair and smelt the tobacco smoke seconds before he grabbed hold of her hair and yanked her head up to face him. Unwilling to let him witness the pain in her scalp she glared back at him defiantly. "I told you, I haven't seen them."

"Then you'd best get over to the shop and get me some more."

As he spat the words at her the crusted saliva in the corners of his mouth repulsed her. What had she ever seen in him? The once darkly handsome face was now just dark with menace and hate. There was a time when she was prepared to accept that the war had made him into what he had become, but not anymore. He had used the war to serve his purpose, unlike so many men who had been used and abused by the conflict only to be spat back into society to do the best they could for themselves and their families. No wonder she despised him.

"I've no money for cigarettes and, besides, the shop's closed." Her determination not to be cowed by him was hanging by a thread as she returned his venomous gaze. "You'll have to wait until the morning."

He let go of her hair as he sat on the arm of the chair, his hand sliding round the back of her neck and over her shoulder. Her body stiffened to his touch and she did her best to ignore him, carrying on with her sewing. She could feel the heat of his stale breath as he leant in to kiss her neck.

"You haven't forgotten what you said earlier, I hope." His tongue raked the lobe of her ear and his hand reached down the front of her dress, cupping her breast. He pressed his lips to her ear. "I can do anything with you, that's what you said." With his free hand he snatched Rosie's dress off Daisy's lap and threw it across the room. "You can't say something like that and expect me to forget about it, even if you ain't the looker you once were."

Anger seethed from every pore of her body as she squirmed against his touch. "I asked you to leave Rosie alone. I begged you, Stan. I would have said anything to stop you hurting her but it doesn't mean I meant it. She doesn't deserve the things you do to her, and neither do I, and if I had somewhere to go I'd leave here tomorrow and never let you near either of us again." There, she had said it. Her heart was pounding against her chest and she knew Stan must have felt it as he continued to knead her breast. Now all she could do was to wait for him to take his revenge in the only way he knew how, with violence and pain. "So, just do what you want and get it over with."

She turned her face away with a resigned acceptance of what was to come. What more could he do to her that he hadn't already done. She cared nothing for herself; her only concern was for her daughter and the baby now growing inside her that she prayed would never know its father. He had long since stripped her of any self-respect and now all she had was pretence that she still retained some dignity.

Daisy readied herself for the blow that never came. Instead, Stan took hold of her chin and forced her to look him in the face. A leering smile greeted her which did nothing to offer her any prospect that she wouldn't have to pay for her outburst.

"Well, well, well," he said in a slow, malicious drawl. "So, you've finally said what you really think of me." He let out a dry, humourless laugh. "Not that it comes as any surprise, I suppose. The only thing that surprises me is that you've finally had the guts to say it. Anyway, it don't make any difference, like you say, you're stuck with me the same as I'm stuck with you, and all we can do is make the best of it." He bent forward and planted a long, slobbering kiss on her lips. When he had finished he got off the arm of the chair and dragged her to her feet. "So let's go upstairs and do that."

Daisy sat up in bed and spent a few minutes in the half-light reliving the previous evening. She looked down at the slumbering figure of her husband, renewing the loathing she felt for him that had hardly been diluted by the few hours of sleep.

Not content with taking her once he had made an unsuccessful attempt to repeat her ordeal and had slapped her across the face for his failure. The urge to take her pillow and force it across his face was compelling, and only a lack of faith in her strength prevented her. Gently she got out of bed and collected her clothes from the floor where they had been left when Stan had virtually stripped them from her the night before. She shuddered at the thought.

With her clothes tucked under her arm Daisy left the bedroom, closing the door silently behind her. She intended getting dressed downstairs, so as not to disturb Rosie or her husband, and then finish the chores that she had been prevented from doing. It was the time of day she enjoyed most, the peace and quiet of the early morning with only the dawn chorus to interrupt the quiet. In an hour she would get Rosie up and together they would prepare breakfast, even if it was only a slice of toast or a bowl of porridge. It was a special time when they could pretend there was no one else in their lives, before the magic was dispelled when Stan emerged from his bed.

Before going downstairs she couldn't resist a peek in at her daughter who she thought looked even more beautiful as she slept. Pushing the door open just enough to peer in she gave a little gasp of surprise at the sight of the empty bed. Then she realised that with all the upset of the previous day she had forgotten to put the pot in the room. The poor child must have gone down to the lavatory.

Tiptoeing along the landing and down the stairs, Daisy hurried to be with her daughter, worried that she may have been scared by the experience. By the time she had reached the kitchen there was no sign of Rosie, nor was there in the living room where she expected to find the child playing. The back door was still ajar and Daisy went out into the garden, not giving the coal shed the slightest glance as she went past to the lavatory. Finding it empty her heart gave an anxious lurch.

"Rosie? Rosie, where are you darling?" she called in a hushed voice for fear of disturbing Stan or the neighbours. She ran back into the house to check behind the armchair where Rosie usually hid from all the traumas of her young life. If she had been frightened that is where she would be. "Rosie, sweetheart, please answer mummy."

Her anxiety was turning to panic as she rushed about frantically searching for her daughter. Outside the first glow of the sun's rays was spreading across the fields at the bottom of the garden and Daisy was drawn towards them, even though there was no reason to expect to find Rosie there. The child had never wandered away from home on her own; she wouldn't even walk to school alone, insisting her mother took and collected her

Feeling sick with worry Daisy wandered back towards the house not knowing what to do. As much as she dreaded the thought she would have to wake Stan, not that he would care much what happened to Rosie. But she needed to share the burden of fear with someone and he was all she had.

For some reason that she would never be able to fathom she pulled open the lavatory door as though it was possible she had failed to notice Rosie the first time. Resisting the urge to empty the contents of her stomach she slammed the door shut and was about to go inside to rouse Stan when she was stopped by a sound. Unable to identify what it was, or where it came from, she spun round on the path, her tear-filled eyes searching for a glimmer of hope.

"Rosie, is that you? It's Mummy, baby."

Another muffled sound drew her attention to the doorway of the coal shed. Why had it not occurred to her to check in there? She knew why. Rosie had always been terrified of the place, thanks to Stan's threats and tales of demons. Daisy went inside and was struck by the same damp mustiness that had engulfed her daughter. It made her shudder, raising the doubt that Rosie would not have gone in there of her own accord. As her eyes became accustomed to the black interior she could make out the movement in the corner and the indistinguishable shape slowly evolved into the unmistakeable form of her daughter.

Daisy cried out with relief as she rushed forward to take the child in her embrace, crushing her daughter to her chest, despite the filthy grime that covered every part of her little body.

"Rosie, what are you doing in here? I was so frightened," Daisy sobbed as she picked her up in the confined space and carried her outside. "My poor baby, you must be frozen."

Rosie buried her head into her mother's neck. "I wasn't eaten, mummy. I'm not naughty, am I?"

The tiny voice almost broke Daisy's heart. "No darling, you're not naughty. You're my precious girl." Inside the kitchen she sat Rosie down on the draining board, although she couldn't bear to let her go. A flood of emotions surged through her; the overwhelming love she had for her daughter combined with the anger and hatred she felt for the husband who had infected the child with so much of his poison. "You could never be naughty, never," she gasped through the tears. "Now, we had better get you cleaned up before…" No, she should stop fretting about what her husband would say or do.

Rosie had the appearance of an infant Victorian chimney sweep. Her arms, face, feet and nightdress were all covered with grimed-in coal dust and her hair was matted and streaked with black. Daisy filled a saucepan with water and put it on the stove to heat while she stripped off the nightdress and stood Rosie in the sink. Were it not for the lingering and frightening pain of losing her daughter, the sight of the child would have been comical; the pale pink body with its contrasting extremities resembled a scene from a vaudeville act. But slowly and by small degrees the relief of finding Rosie safe and sound, albeit in a filthy condition, teased away at the trauma until both mother and daughter were reduced to fits of hushed giggling. But the spectre of Stan was still there.

Chapter Seven

Queenie Butler was the antithesis of her husband in both form and sociability. Her short, thin body appeared even more diminutive next to her husband when she made one of her rare appearances behind the bar of the Dun Cow. The narrow face gave prominence to an aquiline nose and the small, grey eyes perfectly matched the colour of her tightly permed hair. She was not so much an unfriendly woman but she presented an impression to her customers that she would prefer to be elsewhere.

The one exception to her aloofness was George Wallace and she couldn't wait to apprise him of the details of her latest complaint. Queenie Butler was a slave to so many ailments, most of which defied medical science and under normal circumstances would have rendered her dead. Of course her husband didn't understand the extent of her suffering, only Doctor Wallace could, and she took every opportunity to seek his professional advice.

Having missed the good doctor on his last visit she was anxious not to do so again, having recently discovered that she had lost the feeling in her left hand.

"Joseph, make sure you call me the instant he comes in," she had ordered her husband one morning.

"If he comes in," Joe reminded her. "He's not one of our customers you can set your watch by, but if he comes in I'll call you, dear." He had smiled to himself at the thought of the doctor humouring her with another imaginative diagnosis.

"Of course he'll be in," Queenie had snapped back indignantly. "It's Thursday, isn't it, and he always comes up with that strange friend of his when the library's due. I don't know about you but I can't take to that man at all; there's something not right about him."

Joe had shrugged off that last remark. There were very few people his wife took to, although he had to agree with her assessment of Arthur Mulrooney. And she was right about the library being due and the likelihood of the doctor turning up with his friend.

George was puffing hard as he made heavy work of the hill. A few yards ahead of him Arthur appeared to be breathing normally, although his face was lined with the usual anxiety that came with the visit of the library, and Florence Merryweather.

Summer had slipped almost unnoticed into autumn, the weather was still balmy during the day and it was only the nights that had succumbed to the change of seasons. The last two weeks had passed without incident, but with a rapidity that seemed to increase with age and now, too soon, Arthur was trudging up the hill to face another period of torment that may or may not result in success.

"Do you mind if we sit for a minute, Arthur?" They had reached the top and George was already staggering over to the bench beside the river. "I don't want to turn up at the pub wheezing like a worn-out set of bagpipes."

"I don't know why we have to go to the pub at all. We could just stay here until the library comes." Arthur stood by the edge of the river watching the clear water roll lazily over the rocks. The gurgling of the water had a mesmerising effect and he found himself being drawn into another daydream, until George spoke again.

"You may not have to, but I do. It's my only chance for some intelligent conversation and sociable company. And a pint of beer." The sharpness of his tone was tempered by the hidden smile that crept across his round face. "If you think I nearly kill myself on that hill just to hold your hand in front of Mrs Merryweather then you're sadly mistaken."

Arthur turned slowly away from the river, his sensitive nature stung by his friend's remarks. "I'm sorry you feel that way, George. I didn't realise I was such a bore and a burden to you." Behind the thick beard his face was a picture of embarrassment and pathos.

George allowed himself a few moments to savour his friend's discomfort before bursting into a fit of laughter. "For goodness' sake, Arthur, all the time we've known each other and still you don't know when I'm teasing you." He got up off the bench and went over to him. "I'm sorry, old chap, I should have realised you would take it the wrong way." He patted Arthur on the shoulder. "Come on, let's go and have that drink."

As soon as the pair entered the atmospheric interior of the bar, Joe Butler leant across the counter to confront George. "Just a word of warning, doc," he said in a hushed voice, "the wife wants you to look at her hand."

George responded with a knowing nod. "I see. Serious, is it?"

"Isn't it always? I'm sorry, but if I don't tell her you're here I'll never hear the last of it." He raised his eyes apologetically before going through to the back and calling his wife. "Let me get the pair of you a drink to make up for it," he said when he returned.

George held up a hand. "That's not necessary, Joe. I owe Arthur here a drink for upsetting him earlier. I know he'll only have the one so if I don't buy it for him now he won't get it at all."

"Fair enough, but just so as you know, the offer's there. Two halves of mild then?"

"I'll have a pint off you, landlord, if you're feeling generous." From his corner at the other end of the bar Stan Jessop straightened up and slid his glass across the counter. "After all, I am one of your best customers."

"No one's feeling generous, especially where you're concerned, Stan Jessop." Queenie Butler emerged from the kitchen behind the counter and gave him a withering stare. "And a good customer is one who spends in here, not time. It's a shame you don't put as much effort into doing some work."

"And it's a shame you don't put more effort into minding your own business," he sneered in reply.

"That's enough of that. I think it's time you left." Joe squeezed past his wife and took the glass from the counter. "Go home, Stan, and sort yourself out. Come back when you've got money you can afford to spend."

Stan snorted derisively, a grin creasing his face. "What sort of a man lets a woman tell him what to do?" He jerked his head in the direction of George and Arthur. "And what about them, what have they ever done?" He lurched towards them, jabbing his finger close to Arthur's face. "I did my bit for king and country, what were you doing, sitting on your arse?"

Arthur flushed. This was the very confrontation he always expected and feared.

"We did our bit in the Great War," intervened George, placing himself between them. "Arthur was in the merchant marine and I spent three years in field hospitals in France, so don't ever think we don't deserve our retirement."

Arthur had never seen his friend so angry and a wave of guilt enveloped him. How would he have coped if George hadn't been there? The thought left him cold.

"All right, Stan, you've had your say, now on your way before I have to bar you. And you wouldn't want that." He watched as Stan sauntered belligerently to the door. "I'm sorry about that, gents, he can be a nasty piece of work when he wants to."

"Never mind him, Joe, just get these two their drinks while the doctor takes a look at my hand." Queenie pushed her husband out of the way and waved her arm across the counter. "You don't mind, do you, doctor? I'm worried it might be the start of something serious."

As Joe shook his head in despair George peered over his glasses at the hand hanging limply in front of his face. "If you're that worried you should really see your own doctor, Mrs Butler. As I've told you before it's a breach of medical etiquette for me to get involved."

"I know all that, Doctor Wallace," she snapped impatiently, "but that new doctor over in Cottingham is barely out of school, and it's such a drag going all the way over there when you're here, on the doorstep as it were."

Reluctantly, George took the hand in his and gave it a perfunctory examination, bending the fingers, squeezing it and turning it over several times. "Is it always this cold?"

She nodded with an exaggerated look of alarm on her face. "Always. What do you think it is?"

George let out a long sigh, prolonging her concern. "Poor circulation. It affects us all as we get older."

As the landlord placed the drinks on the counter he found it hard to conceal a grin. "I told you it was nothing to worry about. Now leave the doctor to enjoy his beer in peace."

Disappointed by the diagnosis she snatched her hand away. "Perhaps I will go and see my own doctor after all and get a second opinion, just in case."

George nodded sagely. "Best be on the safe side." He winked at Joe as he took a large swig at his beer.

With Stan Jessop gone and Queenie withdrawing to the kitchen, the pair were able to enjoy their drinks in peace, although Arthur was still smarting from the confrontation. It was almost with relief that he heard the roar of the engine as the charabanc sped into the village and screeched to a halt outside. He quickly finished his drink and rushed out after offering a terse word of thanks to the landlord.

"He's a strange one right enough," commented Joe. "Can't afford to be like that in a small place like this. It don't matter in somewhere like Plymouth or Exeter, but not here."

"You would rather he was more like Mr Jessop then?" replied George, annoyed.

"Well, you know where you are with someone like Stan, but that friend of yours is a bit of a mystery and folk round here don't like that. Maybe if you had a word with him, Doc, get him to be a bit more friendly."

George shrugged dismissively. "Arthur's his own man; you can't turn him into something he's not. I've tried." He finished off his beer and gave the landlord a resigned smile. "Now I had better go and rescue him from the clutches of Mrs Merryweather."

Arthur stood at a respectful distance while Florence Merryweather climbed out from behind the steering wheel and put the steps in place. As she straightened up she turned on Arthur, her florid face set in a stern expression.

"You had me worried, Mr Mulrooney," she barked. "When I drove down the road and couldn't see you waiting there I thought you had stood me up." She marched over to where Arthur was waiting. He prayed the ground would open up and swallow him as she glared at him through narrowed eyes. "You're not going off me, are you?"

Arthur shrunk away from her as she bore down on him. "I'm sorry, I…"

"Still chasing the men I see, Flo Merryweather. I thought you would be past that by now."

The voice came from behind the charabanc and stopped the librarian in her tracks as a glimmer of recognition flashed across her face. Arthur heaved a sigh of relief and craned his neck for a glimpse of his saviour.

The woman was tall, slim and elegant-looking with shoulder length auburn hair tied back with a brown ribbon. She was dressed in a smart, two-piece suit and a blouse tied at the neck in a bow. For what seemed like several seconds the two women stood staring at each other with the usually garrulous Mrs Merryweather apparently stunned into silence by the surprising sight of a familiar face.

"Dotty Sawkins!" she finally roared. "Well I never. What on earth are you doing here?"

She rushed forward like a charging bull, any thought of Arthur swept away. As George appeared round the other end of the charabanc he looked on the scene with bewilderment. Expecting to find his friend fending off more unwelcome advances and set to go to his aid he now found himself wishing he had stayed in the pub. With his eyes fixed on the two women vigorously embracing each other he wandered over to where Arthur was still recovering from his brush with death.

"Who's that?" asked George.

Arthur shrugged and shook his head. "I don't know, but I'm extremely grateful to her."

When the woman was finally able to break free from her friend's exuberant welcome she looked across at Arthur with an apologetic smile. "I'm sorry," she said, her cultured voice, breathless. "I didn't mean to interrupt anything."

Arthur simply smiled back politely, unable to express his gratitude in words.

"Let me introduce you," said Florence, dragging her friend by the arm towards the two men. "This is my old friend from the war, Dorothy Sawkins. We drove lorries together, amongst other things." She gave the woman a knowing wink. "And now, would you believe it, she's going to be the new headmistress at the village school." She gave the poor woman a resounding slap on the back. "Isn't that marvellous?"

Arthur exchanged a glance with George and the two of them smiled back benignly. For Arthur anything that threatened to bring Mrs Merryweather to the village more than once a fortnight could never be considered marvellous.

"Marvellous," replied George, as though reading Arthur's mind. "I never had much to do with your predecessor, but I always thought her a bit of an educational dinosaur. I'm sure you are just what the school needs, Miss Sawkins."

The headmistress held out her left hand. "It's Mrs actually, Doctor... I'm sorry, I'm not good with names. But he was killed in the war so technically I'm single, in case you were interested." Her brown eyes twinkled mischievously.

"Dotty Sawkins, you're worse than me. I'm sure Doctor Wallace has no such inclination. Have you, Doctor?"

Taking it all in good humour George laughed. "I'm flattered that you should even think that, Mrs Sawkins. Perhaps if I were twenty years younger."

All this time Arthur was watching the exchange in sullen silence. Wasn't it bad enough that there was one woman plaguing his life without the prospect of another permanently located in the village? He was just thankful that so far he had been spared further embarrassment from the librarian. The relief was short lived.

"Well, as much as I would like to I can't stand here chit-chatting all day. I've got a library to see to and I know Mr Mulrooney can't wait to rummage through my wares." To Arthur's horror she slipped her arm through his and led him into the charabanc. He went meekly, like a man going to his execution. "Come along, Mr Mulrooney, let's see what we can tempt you with today."

Mrs Sawkins watched them go. "Your friend doesn't seem comfortable in the company of women," she said to George. "I know Florence can be a bit overbearing, but she's well meaning. If the truth be told I think she's lonely and this is her way of coping with it."

"Arthur isn't good in any sort of company, and someone like Mrs Merryweather is his worst nightmare." He gave a sigh. "The trouble is I think she genuinely likes him and if he wasn't so shy they could be good friends. "

"Well, we are what we are, I suppose." She watched as Arthur was led into the library. "He has the look of a man who has led an interesting life and seen many things." She gave George a questioning look. "I'm not usually wrong about people; please don't disappoint me, Doctor."

George gave a cautious nod. "Well, he did spend some years in the merchant marine."

The Headmistress smiled seductively. "Then he must have seen more of the world than most of us could hope to. Some of the children at my school will never venture much further than Devon let alone this country, so perhaps if they can't get out to see the world then we could help bring the world to them. Maybe we could persuade your friend to come to the school and talk to the children and, who knows, it might be of benefit to him as well. What do you think?"

George was unsure what to think. If he had read her right, what she was suggesting was out of the question. "It's a commendable idea, but I don't think he would be up for anything like that. I've seen him get tongue-tied asking for something in the village shop." He shook his head. "You can ask him, but I know what his answer will be."

"I rather hoped you would speak to him," she said, a pleading expression on her face. "I'm sure if anyone can convince him it would be you."

George was old and wise enough to know when he was being patronised, although he knew it was for the best of intentions. "I'll ask him, but don't expect too much." He nodded in the direction of the library. "Now, I had better go and rescue him from your friend."

"Yes." She looked thoughtfully up the road in the direction of the school. "The new term starts on Monday and there's still so much to do." As she began to walk away she looked back over her shoulder. "It was nice meeting you and your friend, and I hope to see you both again soon."

Chapter Eight

Arthur thought he was still dreaming. He had been dreaming. He was being chased through the backwoods of northern Canada by a pack of hungry slavering wolves, but when they had finally cornered him against the sheer face of a cliff they were no longer wolves but a hoard of baying children led by a leering Mrs Merryweather in a fur coat.

He had gone to bed dwelling on the frightening suggestion that he should stand up in front of a classroom full of school children and talk about his worldly experiences, a suggestion he had immediately dismissed out of hand. Even so the memory of his conversation with George had lingered long after the two had parted company the previous afternoon and he had settled down for the night annoyed that his friend had even bothered to mention the idea to him.

Now he sat up in bed wondering if it was that awful nightmare or something else that had woken him. He blinked his eyes open and stared into the gloom of his bedroom, trying to decide what time it was. Picking up his watch from the bedside table he held it up into the thin shaft of moonlight that filtered through the small window. It was then that he knew what had woken him. The hammering on the door reverberated through the cottage that sent Arthur jumping from the bed. Without bothering to put on his dressing gown and with his heart threatening to explode from his chest he almost fell down the narrow staircase. When he threw open the door he must have presented a scary sight to the small boy who took several steps back. Arthur looked at him with incomprehension, wondering if he was still in the throes of a dream. "What do you want?" he blurted out as the boy tried to recover some bravado.

"You Mr Mulrooney?" The boy was about ten or eleven years old and was wearing a worn-out jumper over his pyjamas and a pair of sandals on his otherwise bare feet. "The doctor wants you. Said to say it was urgent."

Arthur was still trying to make sense of it all as the boy started to retreat into the darkness that surrounded the harbour. "What is it all about?" he called after him.

"Urgent, that's all he said." Then he was gone.

It took Arthur just a few minutes to throw on some clothes and by the time he reached George's cottage the doctor was coming out, following the boy who was carrying his bag. "What on earth is going on?" asked Arthur breathlessly as the three hurried along the harbour towards the hill.

"Sorry to drag you from your bed, Arthur, but there's an emergency up in the village and I didn't fancy tackling that hill on my own." He was already breathing laboriously from his exertions and the shock of being so violently awakened from his sleep. "I hope you don't mind."

Now that he was wide awake and more aware of the circumstances that had dragged him from his bed in the early hours of the morning, Arthur found that he didn't mind at all. In fact he found the experience to be invigorating. The cool breeze that drifted in off the sea smelt fresher than it did through the day and he breathed deeply at the fresh air to clear his head.

"What sort of emergency?" he asked, keeping pace with the doctor as they started up the hill.

George was already struggling and his reply came in short, sharp gasps. "Don't know. Boy said it's his... next door... neighbour."

After that nothing more was said as the two men tried to keep pace with the boy who led them to the top of the hill and across the green. Heavy dew had settled on the grass and the damp attached itself to the bottoms of Arthur's corduroy trousers until they flapped around his ankles like wet cardboard. By the time they reached the far side and the rows of houses that bordered the green, both men were close to exhaustion, especially George, and Arthur fully understood why his friend needed his company.

They followed the boy to the bottom of one of the lanes that had houses on both sides and ended at the edge of a field. The boy pointed to the last house on the left. "It's that one, Mister," he said flatly, handing the doctor his bag.

As George looked up at the house a face appeared at the bedroom window where a light glowed dully inside. Then it was gone, only to reappear a moment later when the front door was thrown open.

"Took your bleeding time," growled the man who George and Arthur immediately recognised.

"I shouldn't be here at all," snapped back George angrily. "If it's an emergency you should have phoned for an ambulance."

"Oh yeah and what would have happened then? They would have carted her off to hospital." As George tried to enter the house Stan Jessop barred his way. "You do what needs to be done then bugger off back to where you belong." He jerked his head towards where Arthur was standing on the path. "And what's he doing here? He ain't no doctor."

"He's just here to keep me company, that's all." George made another attempt to enter the house. "Now, where's the patient?"

"Upstairs, at the front," grunted Stan taking his arm away and pointing at Arthur. "But he ain't coming in."

As the doctor and Stan disappeared inside Arthur went out to wait on the pavement and when he looked up to the bedroom window there was another face looking down at him, the face of a terrified small child that a few seconds later was dragged away by her father. Arthur winced as a cry of anguished pain broke the quiet of the night and he felt a surge of sympathy for George and pity for his patient. Anyone associated with Stan Jessop was deserving of his pity and he found himself thinking of the child and how it must be to have such a father. A memory from his own past flashed unnervingly through his brain.

It must have been nearly an hour before George emerged from the front door looking drained of strength and emotion. Arthur went back into the garden to meet him only to come face to face with Stan who had followed the doctor downstairs.

Before Arthur could speak Stan had grabbed the doctor by the shoulder and spun him round. "Call yourself a bleeding doctor." He jabbed a finger into George's face. "That was my son she lost just because you couldn't get here on time."

"There was nothing I could have done, even you should realise that, you stupid man." George looked up at the bedroom window. "And your wife should be in hospital where she belongs,"

"You heard her, she won't go. Anyway, what good would that do her now? You've made sure of that." He roughly pushed George away from the front door. "Now piss off and leave us be."

"There's no need for that. I'm sure the doctor did everything he could," said Arthur, stepping forward in defence of his friend.

Stan glared at him through heavy, bloodshot eyes. "Who asked your bleeding opinion, are you a doctor too?" Before Arthur could react Stan had come at him and slammed a fist into his face. "I ain't going to tell you again, piss off, the pair of you."

Arthur went sprawling heavily backwards onto the small patch of grass that was the front garden, narrowly missing the pointed wooden fence. While George bent to help him up Stan went back inside and slammed the door shut

"I'm sorry about that, Arthur. Are you all right?"

"It's nothing," replied Arthur, shakily, as he licked a trickle of blood from his bottom lip. "I've had worse."

As they walked away neither of them noticed the small pale face watching them from the bedroom window. "I can't help worrying about that poor woman and that daughter of hers, stuck with a brute like that. She must have been suffering for hours and he left it until it was too late to do anything about it."

"Shouldn't she be in hospital?"

"Of course she should. I tried to make her but she refused to go, and I doubt if he would have allowed it anyway. She's terrified of him, it's easy to see that."

"Is there nothing you can do?" asked Arthur as they trudged back across the green.

"I can't force her to go to hospital and what goes on between a husband and wife is up to them. I know what I would like to do, especially to that husband of hers." George sighed loudly. "All I can do is to phone the midwife and get her over in the morning to sort everything out. Other than that my hands are tied."

They stopped at the telephone box on the other side of the green and while George made the call Arthur paced around muttering to himself angrily, frustrated with the way they had been forced to leave things. For someone who had spent years assiduously protecting his anonymity this sudden involvement in the affairs of others was both alien and unsettling. When George had finished his call they walked back down the hill in a brooding silence that only ended when they reached the harbour and George invited Arthur in for a cup of tea.

"If you don't mind," replied Arthur, "I think I would rather be on my own."

Instead of returning to his own cottage, Arthur turned and walked around the harbour wall to contemplate his life while resting against the comforting solidarity of the beacon and gazing out over the sea. He was still there when the first glow of dawn tipped over the eastern horizon.

***

"How long have you known?" It was not so much a question as a demand. Stan Jessop had his fingers round his wife's throat as she lay helpless in bed. "How long have you known you was pregnant?"

Too weak and distraught even to care what he did to her she peered up at him through tired, half-closed eyes. "It doesn't matter now, does it?" she whispered, her voice strained with mixed emotions.

Since she had first discovered she was pregnant she had been unable to identify her feelings. The joy she should have felt was not there. The baby had not been conceived as the result of a loving union between two people who waited with unrestrained anticipation for a successful outcome. No, the baby was the result of a brutal assault made under the guise of a husband's conjugal rights over a submissive wife. As much as she would have welcomed the arrival of another baby, a brother or sister to Rosie, Daisy could only see the event as a further tie to a husband she loathed and from whom there seemed no escape. So it no longer mattered to her that the baby was gone, and any grief she felt was tempered by the relief that the child would never be subjected to the same abuse that had been heaped on her daughter. Of course she couldn't go to hospital. There was little enough she could do to protect Rosie while they were all under the same roof, and Daisy dared not even think about what would happen to the child if she were not there.

"It was a boy, wasn't it?" hissed Stan through gritted teeth. "It was a bleeding son and you and that bastard of a so-called doctor killed it."

Daisy turned her head away. She had given no thought to whether it was a boy or a girl. The doctor hadn't said and she didn't even know if it was possible to tell at such an early stage of pregnancy. "Yes, it was a boy," she said with little satisfaction at the lie.

Chapter Nine

The events of that night had affected Arthur more than he could understand. For the next couple of days they played on his mind when he should have been lost in the pages of his library book or his latest adventure. Since arriving in Little Bridge he had totally immersed himself in the pedestrian pace of life of the harbour community and its cloistered protection to the complete exclusion of what went on up the hill. He was not stupid enough to believe that they were self-sufficient; of course they needed the village to survive, but he had so far managed to separate himself from its inhabitants. Now he felt that had changed. With his sore and swollen lip as a constant reminder and the outrageous invitation from the Headmistress he felt he was being sucked into a life he had neither sought nor wanted,

"Don't let it bother you, Arthur." He had said nothing, he didn't need to. Across the chess board George had no trouble seeing that his friend was even more distracted than usual. And he knew why. "I should never have asked you to come with me, but it's done now and you should forget about it."

"I have forgotten about it," he lied with undisguised annoyance. "Can we just get on with the game and not talk about it anymore. I'd like to go for a walk while the weather is still fine."

The game was over soon enough and Arthur couldn't wait to be out in the fresh early autumn air, virtually pushing George through the doorway of his cottage. A watery sun hung high in the clear blue sky and a stiff breeze rippled the surface of the sea inside the harbour wall. Arthur would have normally taken all this in, absorbing the pleasures of nature like a sponge. Instead he strode along the harbour, setting a pace that left George trailing in his wake. By the time Arthur had reached the footpath that ran parallel to the beach, George was several yards behind.

"Slow down, Arthur or go on your own," he wheezed, bending forward to catch his breath. "I can't keep up if you're going to carry on like that."

Arthur glanced over his shoulder, apparently unaware of his inconsideration. "Sorry, George, I didn't realise." He waited for his friend to catch up, which took a good deal longer than the distance suggested. "I wasn't thinking."

A thin smile creased George's flushed features as he mopped his brow with a handkerchief. "Oh, you were thinking, but obviously not about me." He gripped Arthur's arm as he recovered from the exertion, gulping in great mouthfuls of air. "You've done nothing but think about that night ever since it happened so don't try to tell me otherwise,"

Arthur's silence suggested the truth of the statement as he continued along the path, but at a more considerate pace. They had turned away from the beach and were amongst the pine trees before he spoke over the loud crunching of the summer-dried needles. "I was thinking, I don't belong here, I should move."

George thought he had misheard and pulled Arthur to a halt. "I'm sorry, Arthur, what did you say?"

When Arthur failed to meet his gaze he knew he had heard perfectly well. It was as though an unbridgeable gulf had suddenly split their friendship. "I don't belong here, George," he repeated in a low voice that resonated with sadness.

George took hold of Arthur's arm and shook it vigorously until his friend's eyes met his own. "You didn't belong anywhere, Arthur, that's why you came here in the first place. Where on earth would you live if it wasn't here?" He refused to let go or move until he had had his say. "For God's sake, you're too big and ugly to hide behind me for the rest of your life. Sooner or later you're going to be noticed and the more you try to stay hidden the more obvious you become. The best way to be anonymous is to be the same as everyone else."

Beneath the thick eyebrows Arthur blinked, his sensitivity stung by the outburst. He went to reply, but even though his lips moved no words came out. He pulled away from George's grip and carried on through the trees.

"That's right, walk away," George called after him. "Is that how it will always be with you, one little upset and you up sticks and leave."

Arthur had gone several more yards before he stopped and turned, his face set in a questioning expression and his big hands held out in supplication. "You don't understand. How could you? You've no idea what it is like being me."

George thought he detected a tear trickle from his friend's eye, but he was too far away to be sure. Even so it was enough to soften his heart. "Of course I don't, I've never pretended to. But I'm your friend and I'm only telling you what any friend would, that running away isn't the answer to anything." He made an expansive gesture with his arm. "This is the most perfect place for you as it is possible to be if only you would make more of an effort to embrace it, and the people who live here."

Arthur's eyes narrowed. "Like that man the other night?"

"It's just one person. There will be a Stan Jessop everywhere you go. He's just a bully and like all bullies he's a coward. The only way he wins is if you let him, by running away. He has no more interest in you than he has in anyone else. It's just that you stick out by being different."

There was a grassy knoll to one side of the track and Arthur lowered himself onto it. "You think I should make more of an effort. I know that, and I know you're right, but what can I do? I can't change what I am."

"No, you can't, not overnight." George joined him on the knoll, shifting to avoid a hard tuft of grass. "But you could start by giving some thought to what that new headmistress said."

Arthur stared at him, horrified. "No, definitely not! I'll try to be more accommodating as far as the villagers are concerned, but you're asking too much if you think I could stand up in front of dozens of children and talk on something I know nothing about. No, it's out of the question."

"And you won't even think about it?"

"There's nothing to think about, George, and you should have told her that." Arthur turned his attention to the tree tops as though something had suddenly grabbed his interest.

George sighed. "I did tell her. I said you would be far too scared to do it. It's a shame. I was hoping to be proved wrong for the second time in my life."

Arthur's head snapped round and he raised a sceptical eyebrow. "Only the second time?"

George gave him a sorrowful smile. "Yes, the first time was when I told Mary she would outlive me. It was the day before she died."

A lump caught in Arthur's throat, even though he was sure he was being manipulated. He had never met his friend's wife, but George had spoken of her in such endearing detail that she was almost as much a friend as the doctor himself. How his friend had endured the loss Arthur could only imagine and it thrust upon him a sense of shame. His own tragic memories, although many years earlier, were still raw, and still a barrier he hid behind. Perhaps George was right. Perhaps it was time to ease himself into a wider society. Perhaps.

As they continued their walk both men had sunk into their own separate thoughts, dwelling on what had been said, and unsaid. When they crossed the tangled lawns of Luxford House that were even more overgrown since their last visit Arthur still felt compelled to comment on the sadness of the neglect and decay suffered by the old building and how useless it made him feel.

"What good is it to keep worrying about things you can do nothing about when there are plenty of other things you could be doing?" It was not meant as a rebuke even though George realised Arthur would take it as such. "We may be old Arthur but we can still be of some use."

They passed through the stone pillars and Arthur looked reflectively back down the sweeping drive towards the house. "Perhaps even that will have a use someday."

***

"Come along, Rosie, you can't be late on the first day back." It was not so much Rosie's fault as her own that they should already have left the house, Daisy conceded. A little more than three days earlier she had lost the baby she was carrying and had since found the smallest of exertions tiring. "Let's go before daddy comes down."

The fact that Stan had taken every opportunity to blame her, and everyone else, for the loss of the son he was certain she was carrying had washed over Daisy like all the other abuse he had heaped upon her over the years. Any grief she felt had been shared with Rosie alone and between them they had managed to resume something close to normality, focusing on the start of the new school year. Anything more than that Daisy kept hidden from her daughter.

They crossed the green and melted into the throng of children, the younger ones with their mothers and the older ones alone, as they converged on the school gates. The new headmistress was waiting for them just inside the gate, smiling and nodding a welcome as the children said their goodbyes and filed in, some returning the smile while others looked back anxiously, determined not to cry.

Rosie had no such determination. Standing at the periphery of the circle of women she clung to her mother's skirt, her thin legs shaking nervously. "I don't want to go, mummy. Can't I stay with you?" Tears filled her pleading eyes.

Conscious that other eyes were upon them Daisy stooped down and folded her arms around Rosie's body, pulling her close. "I don't want you to go either, darling, but you have to otherwise mummy will be in trouble and you wouldn't want that, would you?" She stroked her daughter's head and kissed her lightly on the cheek before whispering in her ear. "Remember how brave you were when the doctor came to see mummy?" She paused as Rosie sniffed and nodded against her mother's shoulder. "Well, that's how brave you have to be now. Mummy will be waiting for you at lunchtime and you can tell me all about your new teacher and all the lovely things you've been doing." She bit back on her own tears as she held Rosie at arm's length and smiled bravely. "Off you go now, there's a brave girl."

Hesitantly, Rosie turned away and a second later she was lost in a sea of assorted drab-coloured garments as she made her way through the crowd and towards the gates. Daisy stood and watched until Rosie was safely in the playground and being ushered into the lines forming in front of the school door. There was another heart-rending moment for both mother and daughter as Rosie turned back just before going inside and raised her hand in an anguished wave. And then she was gone.

Holding her emotions in check Daisy backed away from the dispersing crowd of mothers before any of them could engage her in conversation. Since Rosie had started school the year before, Daisy had never attached herself to any of the small cliques that formed amongst the mothers, not because she was by nature unsociable but more because Stan had bled her dry of self-confidence and self-esteem. Whenever she left the house he would question her on who she had met and what had been said and why she had been so long. But if all that was not bad enough, far worse was the deplorable fact that she had allowed it to happen and for it to continue. All the promises she had made herself over the past few years that she would put an end to the misery that was her life and that of her daughter had come to nothing. The occasional courage that surfaced was just as quickly snatched away by an inexplicable notion that Rosie needed a father when so many children had been deprived of that benefit by the war. Had her parents still been alive or she had the support of a wider family she would not have hesitated to break free from his shackles and make a proper life for herself and her daughter, but she had no one and so the days passed into months and the months into years and she could not see it ever being otherwise.

Any hope she had that Stan would still be in bed when she arrived home was dispelled the instant she stepped through the back door. He was sitting at the kitchen table glaring straight ahead through the greasy strands of hair that hung down over his face. He was dressed in just a vest and trousers with bracers that hung down by his sides. From the heavy-eyed look on his face it was clear he had not long been awake, although too soon for Daisy.

"Where have you been this time of morning?" he grunted without looking at her.

"You know where I've been," Daisy replied at the very limits of her defiance. "It's the first day of term."

She felt his eyes follow her as she went over to the sink and tensed as the chair scraped over the stone floor. His breath on the back of her neck confirmed what she feared.

"I might have known you'd put the brat before your own husband." His hand slid over her shoulder and down onto her breast. "Do you know how long it's been that I've gone without? I woke up this morning and you weren't there." His hand tightened on her breast until she winced with the pain. "And then I came down here and what do you think I found?" His other hand gripped her shoulder and spun her round to face him. "No bleeding breakfast on the table, only an empty fag packet." He licked away the crusty whiteness at the corner of his mouth before running his tongue round his lips with undisguised salaciousness. "I ain't too bothered about breakfast and I can do without a fag for an hour, I suppose, but I won't put up with you getting away with all your other wifely duties." He thrust his hand into the softness between her legs searching through the thin layers of her clothing, his dark eyes wild with lust. "I think I've been patient long enough, don't you?"

Daisy released a little whimper through lips pressed tight together. It was not so much the lingering soreness from aborting her barely formed baby but the sickening thought of allowing him the use of her body to which she now considered he had no right. But what did that matter to someone like Stan Jessop.

"No, Stan, it's too soon." She twisted away as his lips sought hers. "I'm frightened it's going to hurt."

His mouth twisted in anger and he raised a threatening fist. "It'll hurt a lot more if you don't, and not just for you." The menace in his voice combined with hot fetid breath to send a shudder of fear through Daisy's body. "So, what's it going to be?"

What he did to her was no longer of any consequence, but the thinly veiled threat to Rosie was real enough, and the choices open to her, limited. With seething hatred burning the tears in her eyes she gave an anguished nod.

Throughout the ordeal she thought of nothing but revenge. She had no idea what form it would take, or when it would happen, but it was all she had to salve the degradation and the pain. Somehow she would be free of him. Somehow.

***

George was wheezing badly as the two men reached the end of the lane that led from Luxford House to the village. The short, gasping breaths he was forced to take had made conversation virtually impossible, not that it had bothered Arthur who had more than enough crowding his thoughts to want to speak. He had taken to his heart much of what they had talked about, although putting into practice George's advice still remained something of a challenge. If he was to integrate more into the life of the village it would have to start small and grow by infinitesimal stages.

At the junction with the village high street, Arthur stopped, much to his friend's relief. "I have to go to the shop. Are you coming with me?"

George shook a weary head and flapped a limp hand in the direction of the small patch of green at the top of the hill. "I need to sit. I'll wait for you there," he gasped laboriously.

Arthur took a few hesitant steps and turned to look back at George's slowly retreating figure. "Are you sure there's nothing you need? We won't be coming up again for a few days."

When George gave no indication that he had even heard, Arthur trudged the short distance to the shop. It was typical of every shop in every village up and down the country, stocking most of what was needed to sustain a modest standard of living within the limits of the continued rationing. On a wooden stand outside the shop were boxes of misshapen vegetables, grown locally and still bearing the hallmarks of their origins, mud, caterpillars and a variety of other rural wildlife. It would be many years before the population would be treated to the sterility of perfectly formed, pre-packed vegetables.

Inside, the shop was a disorganised treasure trove of tins bearing the first stages of rust, boxes collapsing under the weight of others, bundles of firewood stacked in front of the counter and in a corner of the shop where the sun never reached was a range of dairy produce, milk, butter, cheese, eggs and a small selection of fresh meat and sausages. But most notable was the smell which was not unpleasant yet indescribable, a mixture of everything that had been stocked in the shop and absorbed into its fabric over the decades of its life.

The owner, Mrs Metcalfe, was a tall, angular woman of advancing years with a thin face and hook nose that supported a pair of round, wire-framed spectacles. Her grey, silver-streaked hair hung loose to her shoulders, although she occasionally tied it back with black ribbon, possibly as a reverential memorial to her husband who had died some ten years before. It had been a happy marriage and his death had soured her previously milder disposition, leaving her tetchy and unpredictable. On a good day she could be pleasant and chatty, but during her darker moments there was no room to engage in polite conversation.

It was this latter side to her nature that suited Arthur best, to make his purchase with barely a word exchanged between them, and it was what he prayed for as the bell above the door announced his entrance. The woman at the counter with her back to him half turned in his direction as he stood behind her, but Mrs Metcalfe showed no acknowledgement whatsoever, which he found encouraging.

"That's four and eight pence," she said to the woman who was putting some items into a shopping bag perched on top of the firewood.

The woman pulled a purse from her coat pocket and poked around inside while Mrs Metcalfe sniffed back her impatience. Arthur thought the woman appeared nervous, for which he had some sympathy, and after a few seconds of searching she emptied the contents of her purse onto the counter,

"I'm not sure I've got enough," she said timidly as the shopkeeper's deft fingers flicked through the assortment of coins.

"Four and two pence," Mrs Metcalfe said abruptly when she had finished counting. "Six pence short."

The woman flushed and was even more agitated. "I'm so sorry. I'm sure I've got it indoors, I can drop it in later if you like."

"I've heard that before. Leave it 'til later and soon it gets forgotten. You'll have to leave something and come back for it." There was little room for compromise in the shopkeeper's tone.

Flustered, the woman began looking through the shopping bag. "I'll leave the bread, I'm sure I can do without it."

"It's all right, take this." It was as though the voice was detached, belonging to someone else, and Arthur found himself holding out a six pence piece to the woman who looked round, her face flushed with embarrassment.

She managed a weak smile. "No, it's all right, I couldn't."

Before Arthur had the opportunity to insist she had put the loaf on the counter and rushed from the shop, leaving him exposed to the judgemental glare of Mrs Metcalfe.

"I was just trying to help," he said, defensively.

"It would take more than six pence to help that poor woman," she replied, tossing her head dismissively. "She would rather take home her no-good husband's cigarettes than put bread on the table. It's shameful, that's what it is."

Apart from common courtesy nothing passed between them, but when Arthur left the shop he proudly felt that he had taken the first small step into village society. How much further he was prepared to go remained to be seen, but he knew where his next obstacle lay and to overcome that would be a real test of his resolve. For now, though, he allowed himself a modicum of smugness.

Chapter Ten

In a matter of weeks, two in fact, from one library visit to the next, the weather had turned from the margins of summer to decidedly autumnal. Westerly winds swept squalls of rain off the Atlantic and up the English Channel, depositing the contents of dark clouds along the South Devon Coast. The season had arrived with a suddenness that took everyone by surprise, even those whose livelihoods depended on a propensity for reading nature's signs.

For Arthur it heralded a time of year that gave free rein to his imagination, when the wild, black sea and howling winds conjured up limitless opportunities for adventure. It was a time when every sailor faced the wrath of the oceans and survived with his courage, and his life, intact. *And what times they were*, thought Arthur.

Unusually, George had allowed him to sit at the small table facing out of the window, to witness the rain bouncing off the yellowed glass and the wind whipping up an anger in the waves that recoiled against the harbour wall.

More unusually, and to Arthur's concern, his attention was drawn away from the panorama outside and onto the strained look on his friend's face. It was as though the heavy burdens of life had been transferred from his shoulders and onto those of the doctor. The round face that usually exuded an air of positivity was now creased with worry, and when he made his play he moved the chess pieces in a disinterested, desultory fashion. Arthur let it pass for as long as he was able before speaking.

"There's something troubling you, George, and please don't insult me by saying it's nothing because, clearly, it's not nothing."

Slowly George looked up from the chess board and tried to smile, but it eluded him. "That's just the thing, Arthur, it is nothing. At least nothing that you or I can do anything about."

"That's not good enough. It's one thing having to put up with my own shortcomings without adding yours to it as well." With his concern growing Arthur leant across to scrutinise his friend more closely. "You're not ill, are you?"

George shook his head with a resigned sadness. "I wish it were that simple."

Arthur sighed impatiently. "For goodness' sake, George, you're beginning to sound like me and I don't like it. Just tell me what it is."

"So, now you know what I've had to put up with all this time." He managed a dry laugh before he resumed a look of worry. "You're going to think of me as a stupid old man, and that's the nub." He peered at Arthur through his glasses. "We're getting old, you and me,"

A mix of relief and confusion crowded into Arthur's mind. "Of course we're getting old. Is it something you've only just realised?"

It was George's turn to show impatience. "No, Arthur, you don't understand." He sat back into the window seat. "I saw Mrs Gulliver on the way to here this morning. She wants me to pick up a few things from the shop."

"Well there's nothing strange about that. She generally does ask you when she knows you're going up to the village."

A flicker of exasperation crossed George's face. "That's just the point I'm trying to make, she depends on us, like most of the others down here. What's going to happen to them when we can't get up the hill? Who's going to look after them, and us?"

"What's brought this on, George? You've never mentioned it before, why now?"

George shrugged as he turned to look out of the window. "The time of year, I suppose. You don't think about things like that when the sun is shining, but winter's coming and that climb up the hill isn't getting any easier." He paused and took a deep, thoughtful breath. "And that other night, when I was called up to the woman with the miscarriage, Mrs Jessop. It nearly killed me and by the time I got there I was far from my best."

Arthur held up a hand to stop him. "Don't you dare start blaming yourself for that. You're retired, George, for pity's sake. You should never have been there in the first place. If all this has got anything to do with what her husband said..." Angrily he slapped a hand down on his thigh and looked his friend directly in the eyes. "Stop fretting over what that stupid man said. I doubt the outcome would have been any different if they had called an ambulance, like they should have done in the first place, so put that idea out of your head."

"You're right, I know, but it isn't only that. It doesn't change the fact that sooner rather than later we're not going to be able to look after ourselves down here." He turned again to gaze wistfully out of the window. "It all seemed so easy when I first moved here, so perfect that I never gave much thought to the future; it seemed so far away. Now, all of a sudden, the future has arrived and it frightens me."

A silence settled over the cramped living room of Arthur's cottage as the two men sunk into a thick mire of despondent contemplation. All thought of continuing their game of chess was forgotten, George had ensured that even though Arthur needed little encouragement. It was a silence that continued long into the morning and only ended when Arthur got up to free his leg from the stiffness brought on by sitting too long on the hard chair.

"I'll make some tea, shall I?" he said, flexing his leg before hobbling through to the kitchenette.

"Yes, that'll put everything to rights," replied George before realising how heavily his voice was loaded with sarcasm. "I'm sorry, Arthur. I didn't mean it like that."

After putting on the kettle Arthur stood in the doorway scratching at the hair behind his ear. "I know, but we can't simply brush it under the carpet and hope it goes away. We need to give it some thought."

***

A few hours later the pair was starting up the hill, helped along by a stiff breeze that was blowing in off the sea. Thankfully, the rain it had brought earlier had ceased, leaving the sky a mottled pattern in varying shades of grey. For both of them it had been a relief to escape the brooding silence inside the cottage, even if it was replaced only by the sounds conjured up by nature, for neither spoke until they had completed half the hill when George began to chuckle.

Considering the depressing mood that was still hanging over them like a storm cloud, Arthur found his friend's sudden levity misplaced. "What on earth do you find amusing?"

With a rasping breath George found it difficult to reply and clutched at Arthur's arm for support, dragging him to a standstill. It took several moments before he could speak and during that time he grinned up at Arthur, much to his friend's annoyance. "I'm sorry, Arthur," he said finally, "but it just struck me as funny."

"What did?"

George gulped in the moisture-laden air. "What were you thinking about, just now as we came up the hill?"

Arthur's eyes narrowed beneath thick brows. "What do you think I was thinking about? The same as you probably, what we were talking about this morning of course, but I don't see how you could find it amusing all of a sudden."

"It's not, not at all." George's expression returned to the same solemn state it had been all morning. "But it sums up what I've been saying to you ever since you came to live here. There are far more important things to worry about than some of the trivial things you seem to fret over." He patted Arthur on the chest where the library book lay protected from the threatening elements. "What would you normally be worrying about now?" He paused as Arthur blinked thoughtfully. "Mrs Merryweather, of course!"

"And how do you know I wasn't thinking about her as well?"

"Because I know you better than you know yourself. You're only capable of worrying about one thing at a time and since our discussion this morning it certainly wasn't Mrs Merryweather. So, if anything good has come out of all this it's that there are more important things to worry about than your little foibles." A note of self-satisfied smugness had crept into his voice. "Anyway, you can thank me later. Right now you've got an appointment with the library."

With the exchange leaving Arthur in a state of agitation he started up the hill at a pace that left George trailing behind. He felt angry, although he was unsure who the anger was directed at. George could be irritating, infuriating even, but usually for the best of intentions. Realising that, the anger soon subsided and Arthur stopped long enough for George to catch up.

"All that business this morning, was it just an invention for my benefit?" He stared hard at George.

The doctor shook his head. "Not entirely. I still think it's something we should be very concerned about, even though I know there's not much we can do about it." He smiled weakly. "It only occurred to me that I could use it to advantage when we were coming up the hill. The thing is, has it worked?"

Arthur stared straight ahead as if pondering the question. "If you think it's going to change me overnight into something I'm not then no, it hasn't." He gave it some more consideration before continuing. "I'm not going to make you any promises I can't keep.

All I can say is that it does put things into perspective and I'm going to make more of an effort."

George slapped him on the back. "Well, that's as much as I could hope to expect." His eyes glinted mischievously. "Does that mean you're going to make a start this afternoon, with Mrs Merryweather?"

Arthur's response was a hoarse, choking cough with little more to add. George expected too much.

***

Florence Merryweather glared across the narrow divide of the library counter through the penetrating eyes of an inquisitor. With the wide brim of her brown felt hat pulled low over her forehead, casting half her face in shadow, she looked even more menacing. "Tell me the truth now, Mr Mulrooney, because I'll know if you're lying."

She placed her chubby hands flat on the counter and leant forward, making Arthur take a step back. "I don't know what you mean," he said with a little more firmness than would have been the case before his recent enlightenment.

The two men had arrived outside the Dun Cow at the same time as the charabanc slid to a halt on the other side of the road. Arthur had rather hoped his friend would stay with him but George had thrown back some feeble reason why it was more important for him to speak with the landlady about her latest debilitation and had rushed inside the pub. Now, as he faced the woman, Arthur felt a tinge of betrayal.

Balanced imperiously above the rust-red, rounded cheeks the eyes continued to search his face for an answer. "Don't play the innocent with me, Mr Mulrooney, I'm not a woman to be toyed with." The seriousness in her voice was unnerving and Arthur felt his limited resolve melting under her withering interrogation. "So, tell me, are you playing with my affections?"

"I'm not playing with anything." The words tripped over each other as they spilled from his mouth. He stretched out an arm and placed the book on the counter, "Please, can I just have my ticket?"

Mrs Merryweather snorted with all the threat of a charging bull, forcing Arthur to retreat further into the depths of the shelving. "So, there's no truth in the rumour that I've got competition for your affections?" she demanded with a bark.

"Oh, for heaven's sake, Flo, leave the man alone."

As the woman came up the steps Arthur peered round the shelf to see who owned the benevolent voice. When he recalled, it belonged to the new headmistress at the school; his gratitude was short lived. Whatever the librarian expected of him this woman expected more, although her motives were entirely more worthy.

"Talk of the devil and it's sure to appear." She never allowed the accusing mask to slip as she turned on her friend. "Dotty Sawkins, you've got a nerve showing your face here, pretending you're my friend when all the time you want to get your claws into my man here."

She swept her arm in Arthur's direction while Mrs Sawkins looked from one to the other with a mix of shock and confusion. "What on earth are you talking about?"

Florence Merryweather allowed the charade to continue for several more moments before collapsing over the counter, convulsed by outrageous laughter that rocked the charabanc on its creaking suspension. When she was able she took out a handkerchief and wiped the tears from her eyes before blowing her nose.

"You should see the look on your faces," she spluttered, waving the soiled handkerchief at them. "I can't remember the last time I laughed so much."

Dorothy Sawkins threw Arthur a look of sympathy before turning angrily on her friend. "The last time you humiliated another poor man, I don't doubt," she said. "I was hoping you might have mellowed with age, but I can see you haven't." She returned her attention to Arthur as he crept from the cover of the shelves. "I'm sorry, Mr... she thinks everyone is fair game to her warped sense of humour, but it seems you've been singled out for special treatment."

"It's Mr Mulrooney, and he's quite capable of standing up for himself," retorted the librarian, recovering some of her composure.

Mrs Sawkins prided herself on being a good judge of character and where Arthur was concerned she was convinced her friend was wrong. "I'm not going to insult him by disagreeing with you, Flo, but I think it's high time to put an end to your little games and treat the man with the respect he deserves."

As he skulked amongst the shelves Arthur debated on what was the most humiliating, the merciless teasing of Mrs Merryweather or his patronising defence by her friend. In the end he decided that neither contributed much towards his search for self-esteem, although he was sure Mrs Sawkins was well meaning while the other woman's motives were somewhat obscure. When the former sought him out he pretended to be engrossed in the task of finding a suitable book.

"I do apologise for my friend, yet again, Mr Mulrooney. She always was insensitive to the feelings of others but she seems to be getting worse with age." She spoke in a cultured low voice that had been honed over the years from calming infantile histrionics. "You really should try to ignore her and she'll soon lose interest. If that's what you want?"

If he was warming to her sympathy it was all wiped away by her last remark which cut through him like a knife.

"What I want!" Never garrulous at the best of times Arthur could find no words to express just how much it was not what he wanted. His expression, however, must have said it all for him.

Mrs Sawkins gasped, placing one hand on her chest while the other gripped his arm. "Oh, I do apologise. Now it's me who is being insensitive. Of course it's not what you want, I should have known that." Flushed with shame she let go of his arm and looked about her, anywhere but at him. "I had come here hoping to see you, to try and persuade you to come to the school and speak to the children about your travels, but I can see I've ruined whatever chance I may have had." She turned to leave him alone amongst the books before hesitating. "Would there have been a chance before I put my foot in it?"

There was something in the sorrowful look she gave him that tugged at Arthur's intransigence, begging it to relent. It was a strange experience that only George would understand, because it made no sense to Arthur.

"I don't know. I don't think so." He spoke without thinking about what he was saying, something else alien to his nature. "I really don't think I'm qualified to do something like that."

Encouraged by his response the Headmistress halted her retreat and even dared to take a step forward. "These are young children, Mr Mulrooney. Most of them have never been more than a few miles from this village, and those who teach them, myself included, only pass on knowledge that we've borrowed from books. I went to France once, just before the war, and that's the extent of my knowledge of the world. Where you have been, and what you've seen, can't be learnt from books, and the knowledge you can pass on to those children will be absorbed far more than anything we can teach them." She stopped, almost breathless, like she had just completed a well-rehearsed speech. The smile she gave him was more relief and apology than satisfaction. "I hope that didn't sound too much like begging, but I really do care about those children. They haven't had the best start in life, what with the war, rationing and all that, so I'll do whatever I can to improve the quality of their education." She studied his face, looking for any sign of conciliation as she pressed her hands together. "What do you think?"

What he thought he couldn't say. That she had touched him with her words was undeniable, as was the merit in what she suggested. But could he do it? Could he stand up in front of those children and pass on all he had learnt? The very thought of it frightened him beyond imagination, yet here he was gracing the notion with some consideration.

He was about to speak when Mrs Sawkins held up her hand. "Please, just think about it, and if you think you can do it come up to the school and we can discuss it further. I imagine it's been some time since you've seen the inside of a school and it may not be as daunting as you remember." She gave him a nod of gratitude and was gone.

Arthur found his interest in finding a new library book had been superseded by a multitude of disparate thoughts that crashed through his brain at an alarming rate and in the end he picked up a book simply because he could no longer apply his mind to the task. Even the comments made by Florence Merryweather when she date-stamped the book washed over him like the ripple on a pond rather than the usual tidal wave of humiliation.

When he met up with George a few minutes later he had a compelling urge to tell his friend everything in order to free his mind of the burden, but in the end he said nothing in case the balance of the argument raging inside him was tilted in favour of the school before he was ready to make that commitment. So he stayed silent.

Chapter Eleven

Daisy Jessop hovered on the periphery of mothers congregated around the school gates. She hated the thought of her daughter running the gauntlet of judgemental looks and comments whispered behind cupped mouths as she pushed her way through the crowd, but the alternative unsettled her more. That she knew most of the women, by sight if not by name, and she also knew, or suspected, that some of them had surrendered themselves to her husband's dubious charms. There had been many times when he had arrived home after a 'hard day's work' carrying the scent of toil suited more to the bedroom than the fields. That he had money in his pocket as a result disturbed Daisy rather more than his infidelity, although years had taught her the painful lesson that Stan's immorality had few restrictions.

Now, as she waited for the school bell to announce the end of lessons, Daisy berated herself for allowing such women to view her through critical eyes when the only thing she felt guilty of was weakness, and if she was mistaking criticism for pity that was equally demeaning. She longed to find the strength to face up to them, and her husband, and to rid her life of both. The bell rang and Daisy removed such thoughts from her mind. Rosie was all that mattered now.

The children poured through the doors and into the playground like a screeching, screaming flood tide that swept towards the gates in a surge of pushing and shoving, hair pulling and horseplay. Amongst it all was Rosie, and Daisy craned her neck for an early sight of her cherished daughter as the child battled to stay afloat in the rush for freedom.

There was hardly a minute that passed when Daisy didn't fear for her daughter's welfare, whether she was in school or at home. It may have been an unnatural fear where school was concerned, it was the time when Rosie should be learning social skills and a degree of self-confidence, but at home the threat posed by her father was very real. Ever since starting school the year before

Daisy had been concerned by her daughter's introversion and had done her best to coax the child into forming friendships with her peers, yet Rosie remained, as her mother did, on the fringe of a society that singled her out as being different.

Resisting the urge to press forward to meet Rosie as she emerged through the gate, Daisy raised an arm and waved frantically. When Rosie broke through the sea of legs she flew straight into her mother's waiting arms.

"Hello darling." Daisy pressed the child to her chest. "Did you have a good day at school?" When she straightened up and took Rosie's hand it was clear the day had been far from good. "What's wrong sweetheart, has someone upset you?"

Rosie looked up at her mother, her cornflower blue eyes defiantly denying the tears that threatened while her bottom lip jutted and trembled. It was not unusual for her to leave school at the end of the day marred by the experience, but her mood brightened as soon as she was reunited with her mother. Today though, Daisy suspected, was different.

Once they were clear of the dispersing throng of mothers and children, Daisy squeezed Rosie's hand and gave her an encouraging smile. "Never mind dear, we'll be home soon and we can play a nice game until daddy comes home."

The previous day Stan had announced that he had been offered a few days' work on a local farm. What had surprised Daisy more than the announcement was the fact that he had got out of bed early that morning and left the house. It had been a relief to have the house to herself and Daisy tried not to concern herself with the truth, only that his absence resulted in some much-needed income. Rosie and money; beyond that little else in her life mattered to her.

They had reached the green when Rosie suddenly finally found her voice. "Mummy?" She was looking up at her mother, her tiny face screwed into a mask of agonised confusion. "What's a freak?"

In the way of all children Rosie bombarded her mother with endless questions, quite often unrelated to the activity they were engaged in and just as often completely obscure. "A freak, dear, why do you ask?"

"Billy Johnson said I was a freak. Am I?"

"No darling, of course you're not." Daisy knew Billy Johnson, and she knew his mother. Mrs Johnson was one of the women she suspected Stan had bedded and her son was an ill- bred bully. "Why would he call you that?"

Rosie shuddered as she started to sob. They were standing exposed in the middle of the green with a chill breeze tugging playfully at Rosie's fair hair so that it brushed her cheeks and wiped away the first of the tears.

"He said I was a freak because I couldn't tell miss about my family." Her voice was frail and the words tumbled from her mouth in short staccato bursts.

Daisy stooped down and folded her arms about her daughter. "Why did Miss Turner ask you about your family?"

Rosie sniffed back on her distress and run a sleeve across her nose. "It's what we were talking about. Miss said families were important and we should talk about them." As she cast her mind back to the moment the tears flowed freely and she thrust her face into her mother's shoulder. Her next words were choked and muffled. "Miss made me stand up and tell the class about my family and I didn't know what to say." She convulsed and Daisy stroked the back of her head, smoothing down her hair. "I said I only had my mummy and daddy and Billy Johnson laughed and said I was a freak and everyone's got a nanny and granddad and uncles and aunts and brothers and sisters and I haven't got any of them, have I mummy?" It all came out on a single rush of air that left her breathless and sobbing.

Daisy held her tight, sharing in her humiliating experience while allowing the emotion to spill over into anger. She would be having words with Miss Turner. "Don't let it upset you, darling," she whispered into her daughter's ear. "It doesn't matter how big your family is, all that matters is how much they love you, and mummy loves you all the world." *And if Billy Johnson knew what his mother got up to he would keep his poisonous little mouth shut*, she thought. "And daddy loves you too," she added in case Rosie thought otherwise, although it was with rather less conviction.

For several moments they stayed where they were, the dampness from the grass bleeding into the hem of Daisy's skirt which clung to the back of her bare legs. She picked Rosie up and continued across the green towards home. With a suddenness that struck hard into her heart she realised just how vulnerable she was, they both were. When it came down to it there was only the two of them. Stan was no more a husband to her than he was a father to Rosie; he was a leech that had attached himself to them slowly sucking away their lives to feed his own warped idea of a marriage. If Billy Johnson had any cause to mock her precious daughter, and it was unforgiveable that he was allowed to do so, then it only served to increase the bitterness Daisy felt towards her husband.

***

Arthur started up the hill with all the enthusiasm of a man going to his certain death. It was testament to his determination to change that had persuaded him even to discuss the matter with George, let alone give it an infinitesimal degree of consideration. All he had done was to mention the conversation he had with the Headmistress for his friend to be convinced that the matter was settled. It wasn't even a conversation; she had spoken and Arthur had been forced to listen, that was all. Now, after only an hour of discussion he found himself bundled out of his own cottage by someone supposed to be his friend to take that solitary journey towards the gaping black jaws of some terrifying nightmare that lurked under the guise of the village school. What was it George had said as he ushered him out of the door? 'It can't do any harm just to go and see'. How many people had been told that never to return?

He reached the brow of the hill hardly noticing the spent energy. Had he given it any thought he would have attributed it more to anxiety that bordered on tenor than to his advanced years. As he passed the village shop he thought he caught a glimpse of a wave from the shopkeeper, although in his present state he couldn't be sure.

Despite the chill in the air small beads of sweat glistened like gems on his bald pate and he was conscious of the warm dampness that had seeped into the armpits of his shirt. All this before he had even committed himself to the persuasion of the Headmistress and his friend, the doctor. He could still say no. In fact he was certain he would say no; a certainty that gathered momentum the closer he got to the school,

The playground was deserted. It was that time between morning play and lunch when the classrooms buzzed with the satisfying sounds of learning. The new classroom, attached to the side of the old school building, blended in with the subtlety of a carbuncle on a naked foot. No effort had been made to match the bricks, with architectural elegance giving way to educational expedience. In those bleak, lean years after the war the country had a greater need of scholars than attractive buildings.

Arthur pondered all these things in the short time it took him to cross the playground and reach the double doors that led into the school. He had been offered the opportunity to make a contribution, albeit an insignificant one, to the education of future generations and the fact that he was considering denying them that small offering now seemed petty and selfish. Cowardly even.

Guilt now robbed him of the trepidation that had followed him up the hill and now, as he pushed open the doors, he was met by the heady scent of floor wax, plasticine and the bodily odours of a hundred children. He found himself in a wide corridor, the shiny parquet flooring blurred along its centre by an intricate pattern of grubby footprints. A few yards ahead the corridor turned to the left and Arthur walked cautiously forward, peering from side to side as though he expected at any moment to be ambushed by a hoard of marauding infants. For a moment he was living an episode from one of his daydreams from which the only escape was to retreat. Instead he reached into a leaking reservoir of resolve that lasted until he came to a door marked HEADMISTRESS. He lifted a hand to rap on the door before the sound of voices coming from inside the office stopped him. He stepped back, struck by a flash of indecision as the reservoir suddenly ran dry, but before he could turn away the door opened and an irate-looking woman hurried out, giving him a sideways glance as she passed. He thought he recognised her and believed he detected the same in her eyes before she was gone and he was left to reconsider his position.

"Well, this is a surprise." Mrs Sawkins had got up from her desk to close the door behind her visitor when she spotted Arthur hovering in the corridor. "Mr Mulrooney, I'm so pleased I persuaded you to come." She rushed out to usher him inside before he changed his mind. "I must admit I never thought… Please, take a seat." She waved her hand at the chair in front of her desk and beamed at him as they both sat. "So, you've decided you'll do it?"

Like a nervous child Arthur did as he was bid and sat with his hands clasped tightly in his lap while the Headmistress planted her elbows firmly on the desk and rested her elegant chin in cupped hands. She looked across at him with eyes that hinted at seduction, as a spider tempting a fly into its web.

"Not exactly," he mumbled, trying to avoid her gaze. "My friend persuaded me to come, but I'm not sure what it is you want me to talk about."

She continued to smile at him, confident it offered some reassurance. "I'm happy to leave that entirely up to you, Mr

Mulrooney. A man as well travelled as you must have many tales to tell, about the places you've been and the things you've seen." She sat back on her chair and stared thoughtfully at the desk top as though troubled. "As teachers it is our duty to follow the national curriculum to get these children through their eleven plus examinations, English, arithmetic and a basic general knowledge." Raising her head to engage with Arthur her expression was almost apologetic. "You must remember from your time at school how dry lessons were, listening to the teacher droning on and trying to stay awake. Having someone like yourself, talking to them with enthusiasm about their personal experiences can only be beneficial for the children, stimulating even."

Arthur blinked back at her, searching for an argument in his favour, but could find none other than an admission of fear. "I really don't think... I'm not sure... I'm not really cut out for public speaking." With his voice as weak and as pathetic as his excuses he was sure Mrs Sawkins would agree with him. "I'm sorry,"

For several seconds the Headmistress said nothing, simply studying him, reaching into his mind. "Of course. I understand how daunting it must seem." She raised her eyes reflectively. "I remember the first time I stepped into a classroom, I was terrified. What made it worse was the knowledge that the children could see how scared I was and I saw them as something to fear. I was tempted to run from the room until one of the children put their hand up to tell me that I was prettier than their last teacher and how pleased she was that I had come to teach them." She paused to swallow back a surge of emotion. "It's such a silly thing when I think about it now, but at the time it made me realise that I had a part to play in their lives, an important part. After that I stopped seeing them as a threat but as the reason I had chosen to become a teacher. It can be very rewarding."

Arthur waited to see if there was a further point to be made, but nothing more was forthcoming. "But I'm not a teacher," he said meekly, "and I've never wanted to be one."

"Do you dislike children?" she asked poignantly.

"Not at all," he replied adamantly. "But they do scare me a little."

She nodded in agreement. "Yes, they do have that effect sometimes. They can be quite cruel, especially to each other with their teasing and bullying of anyone they perceive as being a little different."

Her last comment struck a nerve with Arthur. He knew all about the consequences of being different. "All the more reason to stay out of their way then."

"No, Mr Mulrooney, all the more reason to engage with them and educate them. It's ignorance that makes bullies and it's up to us to make them see how wrong and hurtful it is, and that's where you can help. In your travels you've seen all manner of people first hand and so you can explain to the children that not all people are the same, that it's all right to be different, that it's normal."

Her argument was so persuasive and passionate Arthur found himself pondering on the subject of his first talk before common sense reined in his impetuosity. "I suppose I could give it a try," he conceded after a long consideration. "But I will need some time to think about what to speak on. A few weeks at least."

The Headmistress smiled with patronising gratitude. "I'm sure you'll find it a very enlightening experience, and so will the children. We'll start with a small group to see how it goes before we get too ambitious." She stood up and extended a hand. "Just let me know when you are ready and we'll make the arrangements. And thank you, Mr Mulrooney."

Arthur walked home in a dream-like state convinced he had indeed been seduced by the woman and her less-than-compelling argument. George, of course, would be delighted.

Chapter Twelve

The children were told little of what to expect on the Friday morning as they were ushered out of their classroom and into the school hall, only that it was to be a surprise.

But the greater surprise was to be reserved for Arthur. Since the meeting with the Headmistress in her office his mind had been in turmoil, ebbing and flowing on a tide of indecision. George, of course, had been effusive in his encouragement, especially on the occasions when Arthur admitted that his enthusiasm for the talk was flagging.

"This is as much to benefit you as those kiddies," the Doctor reminded him. "I know that when it's over you'll feel like a new man, rejuvenated."

"When it's over?" Arthur responded tartly. "I've got to get through it first."

They had had many similar conversations in the few weeks Arthur had to prepare himself for the ordeal, and the closer it got the more he withdrew into long, sullen silences. Even when the library rolled into the village the prospect of more humiliation at the hands of Florence Merryweather melted into insignificance by comparison. He suspected she had spoken with her friend, the Headmistress, because, when she took his book from him, her tone was subdued, more sympathetic than taunting, although she couldn't resist adding with a smirk, "I wonder if you would have given in to me so easily. "

Now the day had arrived with all the foreboding Arthur had anticipated. He had slept fitfully that night, plagued by the dream of baying hounds clothed in ragged dresses and Fair Isle jumpers snapping at his heels as he sought the inadequate refuge of a chair. The weather too was dull and laden with an ominous portent for anyone who read predictions in the elements.

"Would you like me to walk up the hill with you?" enquired George as he peered out from the window of Arthur's living room at the low clouds gathering out to sea ready to sweep inland the minute they stepped out of the door. "I could even come into the school with you, if you wanted."

What Arthur wanted was to change his mind about going regardless of any accusations of cowardice or disappointment for the children. They would probably be disappointed anyway, listening to him droning on about the wild life and natives of Australia. "No," he replied absently, scooping up a sheaf of papers from the table and glancing through them in a desultory fashion. "I need to think about what I'm going to say and I don't want you distracting me."

George chuckled. "For the past two weeks you've thought of nothing else. Surely, if you don't know now what you are going to say you never will." He gave his friend an encouraging pat on the back. "You'll be fine, Arthur. Just relax and use your notes when you have to." He eased him towards the door. "Now, off you go and think how much the children will be better off from the experience."

The children sat on the floor in a large semicircle around a solitary chair. There was the muffled noise as they shuffled with discomfort and boredom while waiting impatiently for the treat they had been promised.

Mrs Sawkins met Arthur at the school door and shook his hand in a warm welcome. "I must admit, I had my doubts as to whether you would actually come," she said, pulling him inside in case he might yet have a change of heart. "The children are waiting for you."

He followed her along the corridor, the low babble of small voices getting louder as they approached the door at the end. "What classroom are we in?" he asked for the want of anything more useful to say.

"Oh, we're in here," she replied casually, waving a hand loosely towards the end of the corridor.

When she pushed open the door Arthur looked upon the scene with the horrified expression of a condemned man getting his first sight of the gallows. Behind the thick growth of hair his features blanched and his legs wavered uncertainly.

"I thought it would be just a few children," he said shakily as the hall suddenly fell into silence and fifty pairs of eyes turned to stare at him as though he was an object of extreme curiosity.

The Headmistress smiled a weak apology. "It was just supposed to be year two, but Mrs Fraser is off sick and I was taking her year three. They were due for games in the playground and I'm afraid I'm a bit too old for rounders so here they are. I was sure you wouldn't mind."

Whether he minded or not it seemed a little too late to start objecting and Arthur merely shook his head. Having overcome their initial curiosity a hum of conversation had broken out again and Mrs Sawkins strode into the centre of the hall and raised her hand to silence them. "This is Mr Mulrooney, children, and he has kindly agreed to come here today to talk to you about..." She turned to Arthur with a questioning look.

Arthur was still grappling with the trauma of having to face so many children in one place. "Er, I... The wildlife and natives of Australia," he blurted out.

Mrs Sawkins returned her attention to the children who showed no signs of excitement by his announcement. "Well, that certainly sounds interesting," she said, trying to raise some small degree of enthusiasm. "Mr Mulrooney was a sailor for many years and he has travelled all over the world, and so he has come here today to talk to you about some of the things he's seen. So, children, why don't you say hello to Mr Mulrooney."

A disjointed chorus of welcome rippled around the hall as the Headmistress waved Arthur towards the chair. He went forward, head bowed, afraid that any eye contact with the children would attract awkward questions before he was fully prepared, if indeed he ever would be.

Only when he was seated did he realise just how close he was to the children. The nearest row was no more than a half yard from his feet and he sensed their eyes staring up at him as he pulled his prepared notes from his jacket pocket and straightened them out on his lap. At that moment he really did feel like a sailor, adrift on a rotting raft with the eyes of several circling sharks viewing their next meal. His hands were shaking and he felt breathless, both conditions exacerbated by the knowledge that his audience were reaching the limits of their tolerance, like a restless herd of cattle on the brink of stampede.

"Right now, children, settle down," said Mrs Sawkins as she went over to stand with the young teacher standing on the other side of the hall. They both looked expectantly at Arthur. "I think Mr Mulrooney is ready to start."

If Arthur was ready for anything it was to make good his escape, but instead he nodded bleakly across at the Headmistress, cleared his throat and stared down at his notes. "Well, I thought... if you don't mind... I would start..."

There was a general disturbance accompanied by a lot of shuffling and a hand went up on the far edge of the circle. "Excuse me, mister, but I can't hear."

"Nor me, mister," chimed another boy.

It was all going horribly wrong, much as Arthur had expected. "I'm sorry," he said, venturing a glance over the sea of faces. "I hope you can all hear me now." He returned his attention to the notes. "Now, as I was saying…"

"You wasn't saying nothin' mister." It was the first boy again and he was greeted with a ripple of laughter.

"Quiet children," shouted the Headmistress. "I'm sorry, Mr Mulrooney. Please, carry on."

"I want to tell you about the animals and people that live in Australia," continued Arthur, trying to exert a little authority into his voice, "because they are very different from the animals…"

"Kangaroos. Me dad said they got kangaroos."

"Billy Johnson, will you please keep quiet." It was the young teacher, Miss Turner, who reprimanded the boy. "One more word and I'll send you out."

Taking advantage of a break in the disruption Arthur tried to continue. "The reason they are different," he went on hesitantly after consulting his notes, "is because they live in a country that has…" He stopped when he felt a sudden movement around his feet.

Billy Johnson, prevented from venting his discontent verbally had enlisted his little coterie of like-minded mates in the back row to cause further trouble. Making sure the teacher's attention was elsewhere they began kicking out at the children in front of them until they shuffled forward out of the way, creating a wave of movement that ended with a few of the children pressed against Arthur's legs and those of the chair. One little girl in particular was now sitting on his feet and staring up at him, distress written into her pale blue eyes. When she caught his eye she turned away in panic at the milling children crowding in on her. Close to tears she tried to scramble to her feet but was prevented from doing so by the tangle of arms and legs that engulfed her.

The hall was descending into a scene of chaos and Arthur saw no point in trying to create any further interest in the wildlife and natives of Australia while the child was clutching frantically at the legs of his corduroy trousers. With no apparent means of saving himself he stuffed the notes into his jacket pocket and bent forward to lift the child out of harm's way and onto his lap. He expected no show of gratitude from the frightened girl, but neither was he prepared for the reaction that stunned the hall into silence.

The piercing scream reverberated off the glazed brick walls as the girl threw herself off Arthur's lap, trampling legs and fingers underfoot as she ran from the hall. Apart from the shouted protests of the injured children the hall was shocked into a stunned immobility, until the headmistress said something to Miss Turner who took off after the fleeing girl as the remainder of the children began to find their voices and a babble of excited conversation broke out before Mrs Sawkins called for silence and told them to sit still until they could be returned to their classrooms. Amongst it all Arthur remained seated, at a loss to understand what had happened and whether he was in some way to blame. Sensing a multitude of accusing pairs of eyes on him he shifted uncomfortably and looked to the Headmistress for some glimmer of vindication.

Her expression was more one of bemusement than sympathy as she came round the circle of children to be at his side. "I'm really sorry for this, Mr Mulrooney, but I don't think we should try to continue,"

Arthur sadly nodded in agreement, although he was sure she could see the relief on his face. "I was only trying to help her. I thought…"

"I could see that. I don't know what got into her." She helped to clear a path for him as Arthur got slowly to his feet. "I had better go and make sure she is all right." She looked stem-faced at the children, while reserving her severest stare for the row of boys at the back. "Just sit quietly until you are told to move. Any more misbehaviour and some of you will be punished, and you know who I'm talking about." She took Arthur by the arm and led him towards the door. "Perhaps it was a mistake to experiment with the younger children. Next time we'll try it with year three or four."

"Next time?" Arthur's astonishment was bordering on disbelief. "I thought after today you would realise the whole thing was a mistake."

"No, not at all. Today was just a setback, but next time you should come out fighting, grab their attention from the start. Children generally have a short span of attention and once you lose their interest you may as well give up. It's something we learn early on as a teacher."

Arthur was about to point out that he was not, nor had any aspirations to be, a teacher but they had entered the corridor just as

Miss Turner was leading the girl by the hand into the headmistress' office.

"I thought she would be better off in here than back in the classroom," she said by way of explanation. "Just until her mother comes at lunchtime."

Arthur couldn't help noticing that the girl threw him a terrified glance before she disappeared into the office. He worried that Mrs Sawkins had seen it too. "Perhaps it was my beard that scared her," he said anxiously. "I suppose I do look a bit intimidating."

"Please don't go blaming yourself, Mr Mulrooney. I'll speak to her mother when she comes and explain everything to her. Don't you worry about it."

Arthur left the school grateful that the ordeal was over, even if it wasn't the success it could have been. He was even more grateful that nothing more was said about a second visit.

***

Daisy crossed the village green on her way to the school ignorant of the events that had reduced her daughter from her usual anxious self to her present sobbing, trembling state in the Headmistress' office. Had she known then all her thoughts would have been centred on getting to the school as quickly as possible to throw a protective cloak around her beloved child and smother her with love and reassurance. Instead her mind was focused on the more mundane aspects of her life, a workshy, brutal husband who kept her short of money, but more than adequately marked by the evidence of his marital demands.

For the past few weeks Stan had surprised her by the number of days he had gone out to work, although the money he had earned that found its way into her purse had come at a price. It was only the benefits that the money provided for herself and Rosie that had salved the shame of having to prostitute herself to his demands.

If Daisy felt any gratitude as she made her way to the school it was that the painful bruising on her arms and legs were well hidden beneath her autumn clothing. Fortunately Rosie had been in bed asleep by the time Stan had got home from the pub the previous evening and had been spared witnessing her mother's degrading humiliation.

The usual number of mothers congregated around the school gate and Daisy hovered around the perimeter as she waited for the children to emerge screaming into the playground. A few of the women turned their heads in her direction, some even giving a little nod of acknowledgement. They could so easily become her friends if she allowed them to be, or if she had a husband who understood the value of friendship. But for now they would have to remain virtual strangers.

As the bell sounded and the children flooded through the doors, Daisy's attention returned to her daughter and the precious hour they could spend together until the lunch break was over. She searched the streaming hoard seeking our Rosie's blond hair but saw only the faces of other children and the teacher who came with them who Daisy recognised as Miss Turner. Rosie had pointed her out previously and after speaking to the Headmistress about the bullying Daisy felt inclined to have more words with the teacher.

As the crush of women thinned, Daisy moved forward to confront the young woman while all the time watching out for her daughter. The two of them came together just inside the gate.

"It's Mrs Jessop, isn't it?" enquired Miss Turner before Daisy had the chance to speak her mind. "Rosie's mother?"

"Yes it is, and I…"

"Would you like to come with me? Rosie's inside." She turned away, expecting Daisy to follow.

"Why, what's happen? Is Rosie all right?"

Panic threatened to overwhelm Daisy as she followed on behind the teacher. Of course something had happen, why else had Rosie been kept in school? By the time they were inside the corridor she was breathless with trepidation, unable to ask the myriad of questions that crowded her brain.

"She's in here," said the teacher, opening the door to the Headmistress' office.

Barging the young woman out of her way Daisy forced her way inside where Rosie was sitting on a chair with Mrs Sawkins stooping by her side and doing her best to sooth the child. It was clear to see she was having little success; there was only one person Rosie wanted. She threw herself off the chair, catching the Headmistress in the face with her elbow as she rushed into her mother's arms.

As she hugged her daughter, to her Daisy looked anxiously from the Headmistress to the teacher. "What's happened to her, has she been bullied again?"

Mrs Sawkins pulled herself to her feet and rubbed the side of her face. "No, it's nothing like that. I don't know why she got so upset." She sat Daisy down with Rosie on her lap and explained as best she could what had happened. "He was only trying to help her. I'm sure he didn't mean any harm." She added when she had finished.

Miss Turner nodded in agreement. "That's all there was to it, Mrs Jessop. Mr Mulrooney picked her up to stop her from getting hurt."

Safe in her mother's arms Rosie quickly calmed and even managed a thin smile as Daisy kissed her lightly on the forehead. Whoever this man was Daisy was satisfied he meant her daughter no harm and that he was only acting in the child's best interest. If there was any blame she knew exactly where it lay.

"I'll take Rosie home now," she said in a quiet, emotionally charged voice as she stood up with her daughter in her arms. "I think I'll keep her home this afternoon."

"Of course, I think that's for the best." Mrs Sawkins placed a comforting hand on Rosie's shoulder. "We'll see you Monday morning."

Rosie stared back uncertainly. School had never been kind to her, but now it was another place where she felt unsafe.

Chapter Thirteen

"I'm sure you did nothing wrong, Arthur. Don't worry about it and stop blaming yourself."

"That's what the Headmistress said, but I can't help thinking I shouldn't have picked her up. You should have heard her, George, and seen the look on her face. She was terrified."

It was a few days after his disastrous debut as a public speaker that Arthur could give his friend the full details. The episode had upset him more than he realised, and when George had collared him on his return from the school all he would say was that it had not gone well which, on reflection, was a monumental understatement.

"Well, whatever it was that frightened her, I'm sure it wasn't you," said George with reassuring sympathy.

They were talking in the living room of Arthur's cottage having abandoned their game of chess after Arthur appeared even more distracted than usual. George had badgered him relentlessly until the truth had come out.

"Perhaps I should find out where she lives and go to see her parents, to explain everything," suggested Arthur tentatively. "And to make sure she's all right."

George puffed out his cheeks before letting out a long sigh. "I think I would be inclined to leave well alone," he replied in a professional tone. "If you want to do anything then have a word with the Headmistress; she's bound to have spoken with the mother and you can find out from her how the child is. Besides, you said she mentioned about your next talk so she can't be that concerned about it." He reached across the table and patted Arthur on the arm. "No, I think you're worrying unnecessarily."

Later that morning they took advantage of the early autumn weather to walk up to the village. Mrs Gulliver had given the doctor a short list of shopping she wanted from the village shop and George thought it would be an ideal opportunity to ease Arthur out of his brooding and to focus on other things.

Even though there was a damp chill in the air the sun had broken through the thin layer of cloud that had hung over the coast all morning and instantly brightened the mood amongst the two men as they trekked up the hill. George noticed the change in Arthur and smiled to himself. There was nothing Arthur liked more than to be out in the fresh air and the doctor felt it an honour that he was the only person who appreciated why. They had both proved to be the salvation of the other, despite their differing outlook on life.

"I've been giving some thought to what we were talking about the other day," said George with a casualness designed not you cause too much excitement.

Arthur looked round at him, his expression cautious. "What were we talking about?"

George cast his hand about him, taking in the hill and the river. "This, us," he replied cryptically. When Arthur still looked puzzled he went on. "About when the time comes that we can't manage the hill like the rest of those poor souls down there."

"I see," said Arthur, his eyes narrowing suspiciously. "And you have the solution, I take it?"

"I have an idea, but that's all it is at the moment." He stared vacantly into the distance. "I'm not sure it will come to anything, but I won't know unless I try."

"Are you going to tell me what it is?"

George shook his head. "Not until I've looked into it a bit further. Best not to raise any hopes."

Arthur let the matter rest, taking the pessimistic view that nothing would come of it, and they continued up to the village in a silence that was only broken by the noise of George's wheezing breath.

When they reached the top George took a moment to recover as he searched for Mrs Gulliver's list. "I'll leave this at the shop and pick up the shopping on the way back," he said. "I want to go down to see Mary if you don't mind."

Arthur didn't mind at all. He preferred the tranquillity of the little churchyard to the oppressing smoky atmosphere of the Dun Cow. He also preferred to be surrounded by those who were beyond caring about who or what he was, or where he came from. His only reservation came from the fact that to get to the church they would have to pass the school with all the recent memories that evoked.

He stopped at the lychgate to allow George a few minutes of private conversation with his wife. A weak sun cast a mellow haze over the cemetery that added to the peaceful scene, and imbued in Arthur a strong sense of contentment that when his time came he would be happy to accept this as his final resting place. He was still lost in contemplation when George made his way up the path to the gate.

"Mary sends you her best wishes," he said with a wry smile. "And she asked me to say well done."

Arthur cocked his head. "Well done?"

"For giving your talk at the school. She says well done."

"Did you tell her how badly it went wrong?" enquired Arthur, somewhat bemused.

George chuckled. "She doesn't need to know everything."

By the time they reached the school, children were streaming noisily across the playground at the end of morning lessons to make their way home alone or into the embrace of waiting mothers. While George remained apparently impervious to the sudden emergence of so much humanity, presumably still reliving the intimacies he had shared with his wife, Arthur cursed softly that he had so badly misjudged the time.

"We had better get a move on," he urged as they began to thread their way through the dispersing tide of women and children. "I expect Mrs Gulliver will be waiting for her shopping."

"Oh, I don't think there's any great rush," replied George, dragged back to the reality of the present. He scanned the scattered array of people until his eyes alighted on one woman in particular. "Isn't that Mrs Jessop over there? I must go over and see how she is."

Having never knowingly met Mrs Jessop, Arthur couldn't say it was her, he just wanted to escape the throng and return to the solitude of the harbour. "I really don't think we have time. And besides, I don't suppose she will want to be asked questions in front of all these people."

It was too late. George had already broken away from him and was making his way towards the woman, who was talking animatedly with the little girl who clung to her side. As George approached the woman she put a hand on her daughter's shoulder and the pair turned to walk away, as if anxious not to be spoken to.

"Mrs Jessop," George called after her, determined to be assured of her good health, "If I could just have a quick word with you."

Daisy hesitated and looked back over her shoulder. It seemed better to stop than to risk attracting the attention of the other women. "I'm sorry, but I haven't got time to talk. I have to get back for Rosie's lunch."

"I won't keep you a moment," said the doctor breathlessly as he caught up with them. "I just wanted to make sure you were all right after... well, you know."

"Yes, I'm fine," she replied, edging away, conscious of the curious glances they received from those passing by. "I really must be getting back."

George held his hands up in submission. "Yes, of course, I'm sorry to have delayed you. But if anything like that happens again you really must go to the hospital, regardless of what your husband wants."

By now Arthur was standing behind his friend and found himself staring hard, first at the woman and then at the child, both of whom he recognised, for entirely different reasons. As she backed away from them Daisy gave him a brief smile of acknowledgement as she too remembered their previous meeting, but the girl's reaction to him was far more disturbing. She let out a rasping gasp of fright and clutched at her mother's coat, moving to hide behind her legs.

Startled by her daughter's unreasonable response Daisy twisted round until Rosie's face was buried in her lap. "It's all right, love, there's nothing to be frightened of. I was just..."

"Don't let him touch me, please mummy," whimpered Rosie, her frightened voice muffled in the coat.

"Don't be silly, darling, no one's going to touch you." She stared at the two men, studying each face in turn for some clue to Rosie's sudden fear.

Arthur felt the guilt glowing like a beacon from his face. "I think it may be me that's scared her," he said as though admitting to some horrendous crime. "I expect the school has told you what happened on Friday. I really never meant to cause her any..."

"It was you?" interrupted Daisy, her hands cradling Rosie's head. "Yes, they told me what happened. You picked her up to stop her getting crushed. Is that all there was to it?"

"That's all," he replied, not sure if he read any inference in the question. "That's all it was."

George heard it too. "Of course that's all it was, Mrs Jessop. I hope you don't think it was anything more."

Daisy's expression softened and she shook her head. "I'm sorry, I didn't mean to imply… Perhaps I'm being a bit overprotective. "

"Perhaps," George cautioned her. "But I can quite understand it " He wanted to add, 'given the sort of man your husband is', but thought it best to keep such opinions to himself. He smiled down at Rosie who was peeking out from behind her mother's coat tail. "I know my friend here looks a little frightening, but he is completely harmless, I promise you."

"Yes, I can see that," said Daisy, trying to coax Rosie out from behind her while glancing agitatedly towards the green. "Anyway, I have to go. I'm already late."

Without another word from either of them Daisy took hold of Rosie's hand and marched her away. The two men watched them go, neither sure if they ought to be reassured by the meeting.

George lifted his cap and scratched his head. "Well, if there is anything wrong with them it's nothing we've done," he said, hardly comforted by the fact. "I've no doubt she'll get herself pregnant again and that child will grow up frightened of her own shadow while she's under the same roof as that father of hers."

"Well, there's nothing we can do about it, that's what you said. What goes on between a man and his wife has nothing to do with anyone else, isn't that right?" Arthur was speaking as though to himself, voicing aloud a private thought. "Until something terrible happens."

Although the words were quietly spoken the message they contained was not lost on George. He sighed heavily and repeated. "Until something terrible happens."

Daisy rushed her daughter across the village green to get home before giving her husband the excuse to ask awkward questions. He knew, almost to the second, how long it took to get from the school and there was no reason for it to take any longer. He had heard the excuses; that Rosie was late coming out or one of the mothers had stopped her for a chat, and many more, and he had dismissed them all out of hand.

Rosie's feet hardly touch the ground as her little legs tried to keep pace with her mother and by the time they reached the kitchen door her face was flushed. She didn't fully understand the need to hurry only that it had something to do with her father, that it made him angry if they were late. Everything made him angry and it frightened her. Perhaps it frightened mummy too.

When Daisy had left the house Stan was still in bed, having earned the right by working for most of the previous two weeks, and she prayed that he was still there as she quietly opened the door and led Rosie inside. The kitchen was empty and with a sigh of relief she took off her coat and helped Rosie off with hers before setting about making them both a sandwich. "We'll have ours and then I'll see if daddy wants anything," said Daisy as she sawed a couple of slices of bread from the loaf before spreading them with margarine. She raised her eyes to the ceiling and offered up a prayer that something nasty had happened to him as he slept. "That'll be nice, won't it?"

They sat at the kitchen table eating and chatting, Daisy questioning Rosie about her morning at school, anxious that the distressing episode of a few days before had been put behind her. It was the times they spent alone together that were most precious to Daisy and she knew her daughter felt the same. They had a special bond that had been forged from the abuse and isolation inflicted upon them. If Daisy had any cause to thank her husband it would be for that reason alone.

They had just finished eating and she was about to go up to the bedroom when the kitchen door was flung open. Daisy dropped the plate she was holding and it dropped noisily onto the table which made Rosie squeal with fright.

"I thought you were still in bed," said Daisy, her voice strained as she stroked Rosie's hair to calm her. "I was just going up to see if you wanted a sandwich."

"How thoughtful," said Stan vindictively as he stepped into the kitchen, his dark eyes matched only by his thunderous expression. "I'm surprised you've got the time."

He stood face to face with Daisy while Rosie cowered on the chair, not daring to move in case he noticed her.

"It's no trouble, there's plenty of time before we have to go back to the school." Daisy picked up the knife to cut the bread, pernicious thoughts entering her head. "I'll make you a sandwich, shall I?"

"You're not going to ask me where I've been?" he asked, his face twisted, sneering.

The smell of stale beer and cigarette smoke that clung to him constantly was no evidence that he had been to the pub and Daisy felt no inclination to question him when to do so had ended badly for her in the past.

"I've only got cheese. Is that all right?"

As if reading her mind his hand gripped her wrist as the knife cut into the loaf. "I'll tell you where I've been." He pressed his face to hers. "I've been watching you, talking to those old geezers, telling them our business." He allowed his foul breath to wash over her. "And then I went for a pint. That's where I've been."

"I don't know what you mean. They stopped and talked to me. The doctor just wanted to see how I was after... you know." She had no intention of letting her husband know what had happened at the school and the consequences that could cause. "I told him I was fine, that was all."

"Of course you did. What else could you tell him? But what about that mate of his, what's he got to do with it?"

"Nothing, he was just there with him. I hardly spoke to him."

"It didn't look like that to me." His eyes narrowed as he glared at her. "He ain't right, that one, so you just stay away from him. Stay away from both of them. If I see you talking to them again it won't be only you that suffers." He smiled evilly and kissed her hard on the mouth. "Now, make me that sandwich, and watch you don't cut yourself." On the way through to the living room he patted Rosie's head. "I hope you ain't been playing up."

Rosie looked tearfully up at her mother, terror etched into her young face. Everything her father said carried an undertone of menace.

When Daisy returned from taking Rosie back to school Stan was waiting for her in the kitchen, the bread knife in his hand and a menacing look set in his dark features. His mouth twitched as he took in the way she nervously avoided his gaze.

"I was going to wash up for you," he said, casually brandishing the knife in her direction. "Starting with this."

"It's all right Stan, I can do it." Stan had never washed up, or done anything about the house, and she knew for certain he was not about to start. She took off her coat and hung it on the back of the door. "Just put that in the sink."

"Why, afraid I might cut myself?" He drew the serrated edge of the blade across his hand, not heavy enough to draw blood, but hard enough for her to recognise the threat. "See, it's quite safe in the right hands, but imagine what it could do if I was a man of violence."

Daisy turned her back on him, not wanting to get involved in his mind games. But Stan hadn't finished with her. He stood behind her as she worked at the sink, one arm snaking round her waist and pulling her close, a situation she had been in so many times in the past. She knew what he wanted, what he expected and she resigned herself to the lascivious groping that made her skin crawl. What she didn't expect was the knife held to her throat.

He pressed his cheek to hers and his whispered words froze her blood far more than his touch. "You didn't really think I was going to leave it at that, did you? Like I said, I don't want you talking to those old geezers again. I don't want them sticking their noses into our business and I told them that, so the next time you see them, stay clear, for their sake as well as for you and that daughter of yours."

"Your daughter, Stan. She's your daughter too." Daisy's defiance surprised even her.

"She ain't mine, anyone can see that," he hissed, a spray of spittle peppering her cheek. "So it wouldn't matter to me what would happen to her if you weren't around to look after her." She felt the teeth of the knife against her neck and he chuckled mirthlessly as he allowed the knife to drop into the sink. "Now, I think it's time you showed me what a good and faithful wife you are, upstairs."

Chapter Fourteen

"Do you really think he meant what he said?" asked Arthur.

They were walking back down the hill, Arthur carrying Mrs Gulliver's shopping and both men brooding over the threats made to them.

"It's hard to say what men like that are capable of," replied George. "In my experience most bullies are cowards, so I'm more concerned about what he would do to his poor wife and daughter than to us."

Arthur was inclined to agree with his friend, for once. "I wouldn't like to see anything happen to them because of us so I suppose for their sake we should do what he says. I do feel sorry for them though, especially that little girl. Do you think the way she was with me has anything to do with her father?"

"I think it's got everything to do with him," replied George with absolute conviction. "She probably sees every man as being the same as him, something to be frightened of."

Arthur sunk into a sullen silence, made worse by a feeling of helplessness. A war had just been fought to rid the world of an oppressive tyrant, and here was another in their midst they could do nothing about. Life felt so unjust.

Enid Gulliver was waiting for them on the harbour side, hopping from one foot to the other in a disjointed jig. Her withered hands flapped loosely in front of her as she pranced up and down and her pale watery eyes looking more anxious than impatient.

"I'm sorry we were so long," said George, setting aside all thoughts of Stan Jessop. "It's entirely my fault, I paid Mary a visit."

She waved a hand dismissively in the direction of her cottage. "Not that," she said, eyeing the carrier bag Arthur was holding before giving her grey head a jerk. "Him, in there."

"Albert? Is there something wrong?" enquired George, his brow furrowed. "Do you want me to have a look at him?"

"I can look at him," she retorted. "Been looking at him for sixty years and what good has that done. Needs something doing."

George took the carrier bag from Arthur's hand. "I'll pop down when I'm finished here. Put the kettle on, I shouldn't be too long."

Arthur gave him a curt nod. He sometimes envied George, his knowledge and usefulness when he could only be a spectator. Perhaps it was time for him to make more of a contribution. But how? The talk at the school was supposed to be a start and look at how that ended. Whether he was prepared to give it another try was still shrouded in doubt.

He walked slowly along the harbour to his cottage, deep in contemplation and self-deprecation. He had long felt inadequate, but it had now become more than that; it was edging towards an unforgiveable cowardice. Everything George had said to him now rung with truth and perhaps it was time to emerge from the shadow of anonymity to take a more active role in the community that had taken him in. The prospect frightened the life out of him.

Once inside he took off his raincoat, shook it and hung it meticulously on the back of the kitchen door before filling the kettle and putting it on to boil. All the while he turned over in his troubled mind how his life could be more useful. He was still pondering the subject a half hour later when George let himself in. The tea had been brewing in the pot beneath the red and green knitted tea cosy for five minutes longer than Arthur considered proper.

"I thought you were only going to be a few minutes," he said sulkily. "The tea is probably stewed by now."

George raised a critical eyebrow. "There was a time, Arthur, when you would have asked me about Mr Gulliver before worrying about whether the tea is stewed or not. I know I wanted you to be a bit more assertive, but not at the expense of your more endearing attributes."

Arthur felt a flush of guilt. "I'm sorry, George, I wasn't... How was he?"

George sighed heavily. "As well as a man crippled with arthritis can be. There isn't much I can do for him except give him pain killers and some sympathy." He scrutinised his friend through narrowed eyes as Arthur poured the tea. "I know what's ailing you and it's nothing that a few tablets could ever put right."

"There's nothing wrong with me, it's just when you said..."

"That I wouldn't be long," interrupted George, unnecessarily irritated by his friend's pedantic interpretation. "But really, Arthur, does it matter that much in the great scheme of things. There's poor Mr Gulliver in constant pain and his wife trying to cope, and the Jessop woman with her daughter. God alone knows what she has to put up with." He jabbed an accusing finger in Arthur's direction. "And all you can worry about is the tea being stewed." The sofa complained noisily as he threw himself down on the aged springs. "Just give me that damned tea."

Sheepishly Arthur handed him the cup and saucer, the thin china rattling in his uncertain grip. "You're being a bit harsh, George, although I don't doubt I deserved it." He sat down in the armchair opposite, his head bowed. "But it's those very things I was thinking about before you got here that's made me angry, and frustrated." Holding the saucer in one hand, he clenched the other and thumped his leg. "That's what I feel, frustrated. Here we are, safe and sound, and all these things going on around us and there's nothing we can do."

"No, there isn't," breathed George angrily, his tea slopping into the saucer, "so there's no point in getting yourself worked up over it. Don't you think I want to make Mr Gulliver well, but I'm a doctor, not God, and until they find a cure for arthritis there's nothing I or anyone can do. And as for the Jessops… The only one who can do anything for them is Mrs Jessop herself. Until she gets away from her husband we can do no more for her than we can for the Gullivers."

Arthur sipped his tea in sullen silence. As usual George was right, and that's what stung more than anything. More than anyone he knew what it was to need help when none was available, and he knew also that George understood. He raised his head to look across at his friend and smiled weakly through the thick mask of hair. He nodded and George returned the gesture.

"I need to get on and finish my book before Thursday," he said quietly. "Preparing for that talk at the school has put me back."

"I think I need a bit of time to myself as well," replied George, smiling.

They parted, each certain what was going on in the other's mind.

***

Bolstered by a full pint of mild ale Arthur watched the approaching mobile library with less trepidation than he usually felt. Also, a new experience for him was the hour he had spent in the Dun Cow engaging in conversation with the landlord and, to a lesser degree, his wife who still viewed him with a mix of curiosity and suspicion. But it was progress, a small step towards his rehabilitation, as George had whispered to him before Arthur had made his excuses and left to meet the arrival of the library.

Even Mrs Merryweather appeared less intimidating as she gave him a salacious smile before squeezing her tweed clad bulk from out behind the steering wheel and throwing open the door.

"Good afternoon," he said with a brief nod, although he couldn't quite bring himself to meeting the probing eyes he knew were searching him for any sign of weakness.

"Well, that's an improvement," she replied, her voice sweeping over him like a stiff breeze that brought with it the threat of rain. She gave a little chuckle that sounded more like a gloat. "I knew it was only a matter of time before you gave in to my charms."

If she was expecting more from Arthur by way of conversation she was to be disappointed. He handed over the book and waited for the return of his ticket which she slid teasingly into his outstretched hand, allowing the tips of her fingers to slide gently across his palm. Feeling he had overstepped his familiarity with her, Arthur turned away and hid amongst the shelves, offering up a prayer that she focus her attention elsewhere. He shuffled along the rows of non-fiction gazing dispassionately at the all-too-familiar titles with little hope of finding something new.

It was the sound of another customer coming up the steps that encouraged him to concentrate his efforts on finding a book and make his escape while the librarian was busy.

"It's not for me," he heard the woman saying. "I want to take out books for my daughter."

"But you'll still have to enrol in the library. Here, fill this in and I'll make out your tickets while you look for the books. You'll find the children's section at the front."

Frantically, Arthur intensified his search, seeing an opportunity to get away while Mrs Merryweather was preoccupied, but the plan stalled as he debated the argument of placing self-preservation before literary enlightenment. Indecision proved to be his undoing when the customer appeared in front of him.

"I saw you come in on my way back from the school," she whispered nervously, clutching the pristine library tickets to her breast. "I wanted to talk to you, to apologise."

Arthur felt trapped, compromised. "It's quite all right," he muttered, forcing a smile he hoped would render her explanation unnecessary.

"The Headmistress told me how upset you were after what happened with Rosie and I wanted to let you know it wasn't your fault." The pained expression of Daisy's face was more than apologetic, like she longed to unburden herself of a terrible truth, although it was too subtle for Arthur to fully comprehend. "And my husband spoke to you, I think. He can be a bit overprotective towards Rosie and me, so I hope he wasn't too…" She didn't want to use the word 'threatening', although it suited the occasion.

Arthur held up his hand, and was about to tell her it was of no consequence when Florence Merryweather loudly cleared her throat immediately behind the already agitated Daisy.

"I believe I said the children's section is down there." She jabbed a chubby finger towards the front of the charabanc.

"Yes, I know, but I just wanted a word with Mr…" Her eyes met Arthur's and she sensed an understanding between them. "I just wanted to explain."

Arthur smiled and nodded, hoping to satisfy both women that their concerns had been allayed and that they could leave him in peace.

"I'm sorry to have bothered you," said Daisy while the librarian hovered like a predatory hawk. "I'll leave you to find your book."

As Mrs Merryweather escorted her down to the children's section Daisy, looked back over her shoulder and Arthur thought he detected that she had more to say, but his experience in the workings of the female mind was unreliable and he tried to dispel the notion. Even so he was sufficiently troubled to discover that his search for a library book had lost its importance.

Unwilling to be interrogated by Mrs Merryweather, or that she should heap any blame on Mrs Jessop, Arthur picked a book at random and made his way to the counter, catching Daisy's eye as he passed. Her lips moved, but only unspoken words were uttered which confused him even further.

"Are you sure you haven't read this before?" demanded the librarian as she took the book from him and snatched the ticket from his other hand. "Perhaps you should go and have another look," she peered over his shoulder to where Daisy was browsing in the children's section and added loudly, "undisturbed." It unnerved Arthur then when her attitude suddenly softened and she leant forward across the counter. "I heard what happened up at the school," she said in what passed for a whisper as her red hair mingled with Arthur's beard.

He stepped back, startled by her closeness as much as by what she said. "I don't think…"

"Oh, there's no secrets between Dotty and me," she said dismissively, "especially where you're concerned. Anyway, you shouldn't let it bother you. The child was obviously disturbed in the first place."

Arthur flinched, embarrassed by her insensitive comment, made more acute when he remembered Daisy was no more than five feet away. He glanced round, knowing she must have heard, which was confirmed by the look of anger and shame in her eyes, and in that moment it was an emotion he fully shared. Glaring back at Florence Merryweather he could find no words that would do justice to what he felt, and the humiliation she had heaped upon him in the past paled into insignificance against anything Daisy Jessop must be feeling.

With her pale cheeks streaked by the tears she was unable to hold back, Daisy rushed from the library, her head bowed. Arthur threw another bitter glance at the librarian and went in pursuit of the troubled woman.

"Was it something I said?" bleated Florence at the back of Arthur's retreating figure.

Aware of the risk to them both he caught up with Daisy and reached out to grab her arm before thinking better of it. "I'm sorry," he pleaded breathlessly as he kept pace with her. "She's a stupid woman and should never have said what she did."

Daisy sniffed back on her emotions, her eyes darting anxiously about her. "It's all right, it's not your fault," she replied. "Anyway, you should go. I don't want you getting into any trouble."

"I'm more concerned about you, and your daughter. I know there isn't much I can do, but if you ever feel the need to talk to anyone, well, you know…" He dropped back, allowing her to put some distance between them, shocking himself with his spontaneous offer. "If there is anything…"

Expecting her to continue across the green, Arthur was surprised to see her hesitate and waited to see if she had anything more to say. He ventured a little closer, all the while keeping watch for any sign of her detestable husband. The man had an unnatural knack of being where he was least wanted, which in Arthur's view was everywhere.

"I'm very grateful to you, and to the doctor," she said in a tremulous voice without turning to face him. "I just wish that…"

With her words trailing into silence she walked on, leaving Arthur to wonder at what was left unsaid. Deep in troubled thought he walked back towards the Dun Cow. He rarely felt the need to talk, but now he did and George would have to listen.

Chapter Fifteen

No one who knew the man would have raised an eyebrow at the degree and frequency of Stan Jessop's drunkenness. The only thing that would have shocked them was that he could reach saturation entirely from the contents of his own pocket. Those who used the Dun Cow, and any of the other hostelries within few miles of Little Bridge, would be familiar with his cajoling, bullying and begging ways, but now, tucked away in his favourite corner of his local pub, he was buying his own way towards oblivion, and Joe Butler was happy to take full advantage as long as he caused no trouble with his other customers. Not for the first time in recent weeks had Stan been spending money so liberally, but while the landlord was content to oblige him, Queenie took a more judgemental view,

"It's none of my business where he gets his money from, but I wouldn't mind betting that wife and child of his won't be seeing much of it." She spoke loud enough for Stan to hear, but whether he did or not her words had little effect.

"If he didn't spend it here it would only be somewhere else, and the chances are he would get himself knocked down on the way home," was Joe's reasoning as he refilled Stan's glass.

***

Daisy stared at the five-pound note trying to recall the last time she had seen one of the large white bank notes that she had found crumpled in his trouser pocket together with some loose coins. It came as no great surprise that he had money, or that he chose to keep it from her; there was nothing he could do that would cause her the smallest bit of wonderment. She pulled the creases from the note and held it up to the light, even smelt it before pressing it to her breast as she imagined all the things it could buy.

For most of the past month Stan had been working on a farm two or three miles from the village, at least that is what he had allowed her to believe, even though on many of the days he had returned home in the evening with little evidence of a day's toil. But Daisy had asked no questions, mainly because she didn't care. He had drip-fed her enough money to take care of their daily needs and then gone off to the pub to spend the rest of anything he had earned. More importantly, Daisy had been spared his abuse and, by and large, he had left her alone, lending more weight to her suspicions that he was satisfying his needs elsewhere.

For Daisy and her daughter it had been a month of comparative bliss tinged with a niggling concern. Throughout her marriage any silver lining that had drifted into her life had inevitably been enveloped in a Stygian cloud that had brought with it a downpour of misery.

Daisy stood by the side of the bed, one eye on her husband snoring resonantly beneath the patchwork counterpane and the other on the bank note as she debated the question of how much he would remember of the night before. The state he was in it was doubtful that he could remember anything at all. Daisy had heard him falling through the kitchen door and knocking over a chair on his way to the stairs. Pretending to be asleep through the noise of him stumbling about in the bedroom her main concern was Rosie who undoubtedly would have listened to him as she huddled beneath the bedclothes, trembling with fright at what he might do to her or her mother.

With his clothing thrown carelessly on the floor he had fallen into bed and, as much through habit than intention, his hand roughly groped her through her nightdress. But even before she had forced his hand away he was asleep, and Daisy had laid awake listening to his snoring and wondering for the thousandth time how her life had settled into its present state.

Now she looked down on him with unmitigated contempt while she held in her hand the means to provide for her and her daughter a small amount of succour. Was it worth the risk?

Daisy made a decision, and before she could give herself the chance to change her mind she shoved the loose change back into his trouser pocket and threw the garment back onto the floor. The five-pound note was still clutched in her hand, and as she backed away from the bed her mind was racing through all the possible outcomes of her rashness. Reason dictated that she was entitled to use the money for the benefit of her family. It was as much hers after all. But this was Stan, and reason played no part in the rights and wrongs of married life. To assume that he would be angry was a laughable underestimation.

Down in the kitchen Daisy knew it was still not too late. Stan would sleep through most of the morning, deaf to the comings and goings of his wife, and it would take only a minute to return her life to its miserable sameness. She paced the kitchen floor, torn painfully between cowardice and whatever five pounds could offer.

***

"Have you made up your mind what you're going to do?" asked George, the question coming out of the blue and in staccato gasps of captured air.

They had reached the top of the hill and George had stopped to catch his breath. It was a bright November morning, a watery sun giving the sea behind them a shimmering sparkle that had sent Arthur into a reverie of somewhere far away. George had recognised his friend's absence and knew better than to intrude, and with the hill taking its usual toll it had benefitted him to stay silent. But now, like the sea, the climb was behind them and George felt he could no longer avoid the question that had remained unasked for the past few weeks.

Arthur had continued absently for a few paces before George's words entered into his consciousness. He stopped and looked back. "Sorry, George, did you say something?"

The doctor took a few more deep exasperated breaths. "I said, have you given any more thought to what you are going to do?"

Arthur's face creased in feigned puzzlement. He had a good idea of what George meant. "About what?"

"You know very well what, about giving another talk at the school." He waddled up to where Arthur was waiting. "You can't keep putting it off. "

"I'm not putting it off," said Arthur with a degree of smugness. "I can only put it off if I had agreed to do it in the first place. And I didn't."

"You're putting off making a decision, that's what I meant and you know it. It's not fair on the Headmistress, or those kiddies to leave things up in the air like this." They continued walking slowly towards the village shop. "Just tell her yes or no."

Arthur let out a poor excuse for a laugh. "I don't think the Headmistress would want a repeat of what happened last time, and as for the children..." He pictured himself as the butt of infantile humiliation as he sat amongst them trying to capture their interest and imagination, and failing miserably.

They reached the shop with the matter still unresolved and Arthur was happy for it to remain so.

Mrs Metcalfe gave them a brief nod as she finished serving the woman at the counter, giving George the time to find the various shopping lists he had been given by the elderly residents of the harbour. Arthur spent the time studying the back of the customer's head, certain in the knowledge he recognised her.

"That's one pound nineteen and eight," said Mrs Metcalfe in a tone that questioned whether the woman had the means to pay the unusually large amount. "Are you sure you will be able to manage all that?"

"Yes, quite sure, thank you." The woman moved to one side of the counter as she fumbled in her purse and took out the five-pound note. There were two full carrier bags of shopping standing on the stack of firewood. She offered up the note. "I'm afraid I've only got this."

As Mrs Metcalfe took the note and rubbed it between forefinger and thumb Arthur exchanged a curious glance with George whose expression said 'mind your own business'.

It was also clear to both men that the shopkeeper was struggling to contain her surprise, and her suspicion. She tucked the note into her overall pocket before opening the till, all the while trying hard not to ask where the money had come from. "I'm sure I've got change."

Avoiding the three pairs of eyes she knew were looking at her Daisy put the change in her purse and hoisted the two heavy bags off the firewood, the string handles cutting into her fingers. "Thank you, Mrs Metcalfe," she muttered, almost apologetically, before turning away from the counter and into the path of the two men.

"Are you sure you can manage?" asked Arthur, the words coming as an involuntary reaction to the strain visible on her face.

Her eyes flicked briefly in his direction and there was a hint of a smile. "Quite sure, thank you."

One of the bags caught Arthur's leg as she pushed past, clearly anxious to be on her way.

"Well, I never thought I would ever see the likes of that," said Mrs Metcalfe, her incredulous gaze following Daisy as she struggled across the road and onto the green. She took out the five-pound note and studied it again before waving it in front of her other customers. "I've never known her to have more than a couple of bob in her purse let alone one of these."

"Life is full of surprises, Mrs Metcalfe," said George, although he shared the shopkeeper's curiosity. "But it's not for us to question the good fortune of others."

"The good fortune! I bet it was more than good fortune that put money like that in her purse." She folded the note neatly in half and put it reverently in the till. "Now, gentlemen, what can I do for you?"

As George handed over the shopping lists Arthur's attention was focussed on Daisy who was weaving an unsteady path across the green, pulled in different directions by the weight of the shopping. He saw her put the bags down and massage the circulation back into her fingers before flexing her back and continuing the trek homewards.

"I know what you're thinking," whispered George, bending his head close to his friend, "but it's not worth the risk to both of you."

"I know, but look at her. I can't just leave her to…" Before he could be talked out of it he started towards the door. "I'll be back to give you a hand."

George watched him striding purposefully across the grass and prayed the good turn would pass without regret. His old eyes scanned the green and beyond for any sign of Daisy's husband, although there would be little he could do if the man made a sudden appearance.

"Strange," said Mrs Metcalfe with a casualness that disguised any underlying insinuation, "that your friend always seems to be on hand when that woman needs help."

Resisting the urge to question her George returned his attention to the reason that had brought him to the shop in the first place now that Arthur had disappeared from his view.

"I can manage," Daisy insisted, looking anxiously about her.

Now that he had caught up with her Arthur became acutely aware of the trouble he could cause the two of them, just by talking to her. "I couldn't just let you struggle with those bags," he said, joining her in scanning the surrounding area for any sign of her husband. "Let me carry one of them to the end of your road."

Slowly and reluctantly she allowed him to take one of the bags from her, flexing her white, bloodless fingers. "Thank you, you're very kind," she said timidly, "I didn't realise just how heavy they were."

Arthur was beginning to realise it too and wondered how she had managed to get as far as she had. "Perhaps you shouldn't have bought so much," he said for the want of anything more useful to say.

Daisy remained tight lipped as they resumed their course towards the rows of houses that bordered the far side of the green. *How could a man like Mr Mulrooney,* she thought, *understand the circumstances that had brought them together so unexpectedly that morning?* There should have been nothing exceptional about a woman buying more shopping than she could easily manage, or a man gallantly stepping in to help her. Why should there be?

As they neared the end of her road she prayed Stan was still sleeping. There was already a price to pay when he woke up and remembered the five-pound note that was in his trouser pocket the night before, without finding her in the company of the man she had specifically been forbidden to associate with. How could anyone understand the unhappy complexities of her married life?

From where Daisy stopped and put down her bag she could see her bedroom window and the curtain still drawn across. But that meant nothing. Stan would never have thought to open the curtains when he got out of bed; such menial tasks were the preserve of women, not men, and at any moment he could make an unwelcome appearance.

"I'd better take them now," she said to Arthur. "It's best you didn't come any further."

Arthur nodded and put the bag down on the pavement. He sympathised with the unnatural fear she had of her husband, suspecting him capable of violence against both sexes. "I understand," he replied, following her gaze. "I wouldn't want to get you into any trouble." He went to turn away before hesitating. "If there's ever anything I can do please don't…" His words trailed off as he realised there could be no substance to his offer. What could he possibly do to help the poor woman? He gave her a weak smile. "Well, you know…"

He hurried away, leaving Daisy to continue the short journey home to face whatever reception awaited her. He tried not to think about it as he returned to meet George.

Chapter Sixteen

From her seat at the front of the class Rosie was first to the door when the bell rang for lunch. Urged along by the press of classmates behind she almost ran to the door with the euphoric relief that came with the release from purgatory of school life. It had been a miserable morning, made worse by the antics of Billy Johnson who had delighted in pulling her hair during the mid-morning break and reminding her of how friendless she was. And all that after a night's sleep disturbed by fear and vivid dreams.

She had heard her father stumbling into the kitchen immediately beneath her bedroom and the crash of the chair he had sent flying. His heavy tread on the stairs as he bounced off the walls and the familiar creaking of the floorboards on the landing outside her room had sent her seeking the protection of the bedclothes. She remembered trembling with fright as he had fallen against her bedroom door and the thought that he was coming for her, to inflict on her his special punishment. She had shrunk further beneath the covers when she heard him falling into bed, her young mind unable to comprehend the abuse he inflicted on her mother. All these things she had thought about in the classroom that morning and now all she wanted was an hour with her mother, to be told how much she was loved and, most of all, to feel safe.

As soon as she reached the fresh autumnal air in the playground her bright blue eyes searched the array of faces beyond the gate for her mother's welcoming smile and the wave that said 'Here I am, my darling girl'. But by the time she had reached the gate there was no sign of the smile or the wave, and panic struck Rosie with more force than a lightning bolt.

It was not a fear of finding her way home alone that sucked the blood from her cheeks, she could walk it with her eyes closed. No, it was far worse than that. Only something unthinkably serious would prevent her mother from meeting her and Rosie's young brain struggled to cope with the possibilities. She pushed her way through the circle of women around the gate, her eyes darting from side to side, willing the familiar sight of her mother to come into view, but by the time Rosie broke free of them it was clear her worst fears had been realised. For the first time since starting school her mother had not come to meet her.

She began to run. Blind to everything around her she sprinted down the road and onto the green. She didn't even know she could run so fast, as her feet barely touched the ground, and not until she reached her front gate did she slow down. All the thoughts she had shut out of her mind during the race came flooding back with frightening clarity and Rosie became aware of the tears that had been rolling over her flushed cheeks all the way home. She was almost too afraid to open the gate because she knew with absolute certainty something bad had happened to her mother.

***

Stan had woken in the darkened bedroom remembering only that he had been drinking the night before, which should have come as no surprise. He had no recollection of arriving home, getting into bed or whether he had satisfied his lust before falling into a deep, drunken sleep. With no idea of the time he lay on his back staring up at the ceiling through the slits of his heavily lidded eyes. He licked the dryness from his lips with a tongue that felt like it was coated in fur and cursed his wife for not anticipating his needs.

He rolled over onto his side and groped about on the floor until his hand found one of his boots which he hammered against the bare boards. "Get me a cup of tea, and bring up my fags you stupid cow." It was not the harsh demand he would have wished, more a hoarse croaking sound that had lost much of its volume.

Falling onto his back again he lay there with his eyes shut while he waited for his order to be obeyed. But when he opened his eyes again after an indeterminate length of time, during which he may, or may not, have fallen asleep, nothing in the room had changed.

He hawked to clear his throat and shouted again. "Where's that bleeding tea and me fags, you lazy bitch? Don't make me come down." Satisfied with the level of threat it contained he settled down to wait, but not for too long. He had been more than patient already.

Minutes passed and still nothing, no sound from downstairs. With his patience exhausted and his anger reaching its limit he threw back the covers and sat on the edge of the bed, shivering against the sudden chill of the room. He snatched up his trousers and cursed vehemently as coins fell from the pocket and rolled across the floor. Struggling into his trousers he scrabbled about on his hands and knees collecting up the money before going down to repay his wife for her lack of consideration and obedience,

He reached the bottom of the stairs as Daisy was coming through the back door, breathing heavily under the weight of the shopping and using the last reserves of energy to lift the bags onto the table. So fatigued was she that her husband remained unnoticed as he stood silently in the hallway watching her with an expression that was then more curious than threatening.

It was only when he moved towards her did Daisy let out a little gasp that spelt fear as well as surprise.

His bloodshot eyes flicked from Daisy to the carrier bags and she could almost hear the question he was yet to ask. Without speaking he poked at the top of the bags, peering inside before picking out the packet of cigarettes which he waved in her face. Doing her best to ignore his presence she slipped off her coat and hung it behind the door, but when she turned back to the table he was there in her face.

"Where did it come from?" he asked in a voice that held menace in its quietness.

"From the village shop," replied Daisy, feigning a misunderstanding of the question while conscious of the thunderous pounding in her chest.

"Not that, you stupid bitch," he sneered, jerking his head at the shopping, "the money to pay for it."

Daisy considered her reply carefully, although there was nothing she could say that would satisfy his vicious mind. She turned back to her coat and took her purse from the pocket, and, returning to the table, she emptied out the contents. "I found a five-pound note in your trousers and used it to buy food. That's the change." She raised her eyes from the money to meet his gaze with as much defiance as she could manage. "There was nothing left in the larder."

"So you thought you would just help yourself to feed you and that brat." His thick lips curled into an evil sneer. "And all I get is a packet of fags."

Conscious of her vulnerability Daisy began unpacking the shopping. "Not just for us," she said, carrying some of the food across to the larder, "for you as well."

"So that makes it all right to steal money from my pocket, does it?" He rounded the table, trapping her in the larder. A stubby finger prodded her chest, forcing her to retreat until she was wedged between the shelves that lined both sides of the larder. "That – money – is – mine," he breathed, emphasising each word with another jab that was more violent than the one before.

"You may have earned it, Stan, but it belongs to all of us, not just to waste on drink." Daisy knew her defiance would bring its rewards and she held out her hands to fend him off. "I would have asked you for the money if I thought you would have given it to me, but I knew you wouldn't. We have to eat, and we can't, not on the little you give me."

She had her hands pressed against his shoulders, trying to keep a little distance between them, but against him resistance would only be temporary. Spite oozed from every pore of his dark, drink-infused face as he forced her against the back wall of the larder with the sharp edges of the shelves cutting into her back.

Taking a warped pleasure from the pain and anguish evident in her expression his lips parted in a snarling grin. "You didn't think you could take what's mine and get away with it, did you? If I let you get away with this who knows what it would be next."

She turned her head away to avoid the foul breath that made her gag. "You've been taking what's mine ever since we've been married," she replied, her voice shaking with fear and raw emotion. "When did you ever ask what I wanted every time you took me?"

Stan let out a dry, mocking laugh. With one hand clamped round her throat, the other cupped the soft mound between her legs. "This is mine. It became mine as soon as you married me. It belongs to me just the same as you do." He allowed his hand to roam freely over her body as if to prove the point, disregarding her attempts to squirm away from his brutal touch.

In the confined space of the larder it was impossible for Daisy to fight back without causing herself more harm on the sharp edges of the shelves. But the alternative was to succumb to his abuse as she had done for most of her married life. Whether or not this was the right time to fight back would only be decided once it was over; the choice she had to make was if the consequences warranted any satisfaction to be gained by her defiance.

Without giving it any further thought she used all her strength to push him away and force herself out of the larder. Taken by surprise Stan staggered back, but any advantage Daisy had gained was brief as he recovered in time to pin her by the arms and propel her backwards into the cupboard.

Daisy let out a shriek of pain and angered hatred when the side of her head caught one of the shelves and she blindly lashed out with a clenched fist which struck him harmlessly on the shoulder. She heard him laugh scornfully at her ineffectual retaliation before he backhanded her across the face and slamming her head again onto the shelf. The cry of agony was cut short by a black mist of semi-consciousness as her legs crumpled beneath her and she collapsed onto the floor. She had a vague recollection of being manhandled out from the confines of the larder and into the kitchen before the darkness enclosed completely.

Rosie was too young to fully understand what she was seeing except that it was distressing enough for her to run screaming from the room and seek refuge beneath the covers on her bed. How long she lay there, rigid and traumatised, she couldn't say; time meant nothing as she tried to shut out of her mind the horror she had witnessed. But despite all her efforts, vivid pictures of her mother lying dead on the bed flashed into vision, bringing with them the frightening reality of being totally alone.

In the next room Daisy tried to lift her head from the bed, but when the agonising throbbing increased in intensity she allowed it to fall back again. Gingerly the tips of her fingers explored the side of her head. Her hair was sticky and matted and she winced as a sharp stab of pain shot through her when she felt her scalp. With the curtains still closed the room was bathed in an eerie gloom, and as Daisy's eyes roamed about her she slowly became aware of her surroundings. But how she had got there she had no idea. Her whole body was trembling and chilled and she clutched the unbuttoned cardigan she was wearing across her chest which was bare and tender to the touch. Again she raised her head off the bed, this time fighting against the pain to make sense of her circumstances. She was naked from the waist down, although she was still wearing her dress which was pushed up and ripped at the bodice.

Little by little her memory began to re-establish itself, an image of herself trapped in the larder and Stan's leering face hovering over her as she fell to the floor. Everything after that was blank, although it needed no memory and little imagination to know what had happened after that. As she sat up every muscle and joint screamed at her to lie back down, but now she had something else to occupy her tormented brain. Stan had taken his revenge and it was little more than she should have expected, but the damage to her body and her dignity was something she could endure, that she had endured for years. With no idea of how long she had been unconscious Rosie now became part of the nightmare. *Could it be lunchtime yet, or had it already passed? Was Rosie waiting for her outside the school and if not where was she?* Then an even more terrifying thought occurred to her, that Stan had continued taking his revenge against her precious daughter. Her whole focus now was on Rosie; she must find her and make sure she was safe.

Daisy picked her knickers up off the floor where Stan must have thrown them, a further reminder of his spite. Had he taken her or given up on his attempt? In her comatose state she had no idea, and preferred not to know. As she dressed herself she heard movement outside the bedroom door and immediately convinced herself he had returned to complete her humiliation. A fierce determination burned in her chest; she would suffer no more hurt.

The door slowly opened and Daisy got up, moving to the far side of the bed, as if it would provide a barrier to his intentions. She clutched her hands against her chest and glared at the door, drawing a ragged breath ready to scream her defiance. But the face that appeared cautiously round the door was not of her vengeful husband but of her frightened daughter. Daisy allowed her breath to escape in a show of overwhelming relief before realising she must have presented a disturbing sight to the poor child.

Instead of rushing to her mother's side Rosie stayed by the door, not daring to venture into the room and it was left to Daisy to walk unsteadily round the bed. "It's all right, darling, mummy fell over, but it's nothing to worry about." She held out her hands and slowly Rosie came to her, tears streaming down her pale cheeks. "Come and give mummy a cuddle."

As Daisy slumped down onto the bed Rosie stood in front of her staring up at her mother's damaged face. "I thought you was dead," she said, her little voice shaking with emotion. "I saw you on the bed and I thought you was dead."

What little colour remained in Daisy's features drained away as she imagined the trauma her precious daughter must have suffered at the sight of her lying on the bed, her clothing dishevelled and her face bloodied. She reached out and took the child in her arms and pulled her close, determined that this would be the last time her daughter would be made to suffer as a result of

Stan's actions. How she could promise that she had no idea, but somehow she had to make it happen.

Chapter Seventeen

Are you sure you're going to be all right?"

Arthur's expression was tinged with resentment. "I'm not a child you know, George. And I still don't know why you can't tell me where you are going. Why the big secret?"

The two were sitting in the small bus shelter at the top of the high road waiting for the bus that ran twice daily and would take George to the nearest station from where he could catch the train to Exeter.

Behind his glasses George's eyes twinkled mischievously, reflecting the small pleasure he took from teasing his friend. "I told you, it's nothing of any great importance and I'll tell you all about it when I get back!'

"Tomorrow."

"Yes, tomorrow. I'll stay with a former colleague of mine tonight." His expression hardened as he shuffled round on the rough wooden seat to see the concern on his friend's face. "And I don't want you fretting over me either. I'm quite able to look after myself."

"I know you are," replied Arthur curtly, still annoyed at the secrecy with which George had surrounded his trip. Any further thoughts were interrupted by the sound of the bus approaching at a sedate pace into the village. He checked the time on his watch. The bus was late and it occurred to him that had Mrs Merryweather chosen another career path it would probably have been early. He stood up as George did the same. "Well, here we are then. I hope you have a good trip," he said grudgingly.

George smiled. "I will. And don't go getting into any mischief while I'm gone."

Arthur waited while his friend took his seat and the bus pulled away, and as it did so, he was struck by a sudden feeling of loneliness, and a fear that one day he may have to face life alone. Since his arrival in the village this was the first day they had spent apart and his shoulders slumped as he trudged slowly back towards home.

Mrs Metcalfe had her face pressed to the window for a better view of the road and as soon as she spotted Arthur she pulled back, trying not to appear too obvious. As he drew level with the shop, Arthur had a sense that he was being watched and glanced across as the shopkeeper pretended she had just noticed him, beckoning him over with her hand. He hesitated, unsure if he was willing to exchange self-pity for frivolous gossip. He had barely spoken more than a few words to the woman in the past and the fact that she seemed keen to speak to him now raised only a mild interest. She probably only wanted to know where the doctor had gone, and he was about to ignore her and continue on home when she wrapped her knuckle urgently on the glass. Reluctantly, he sauntered across the road and Mrs Metcalfe met him at the shop door.

Her small eyes seemed to bore into his brain as she peered down at him from the top step. "I saw the two of you go down earlier and wanted to catch you on the way back," she said, glancing furtively down the road. "Doctor Wallace not with you?"

"No, he caught the bus," he replied cautiously. "Did you want him for something?"

Mrs Metcalfe shook her head dismissively. "No, it was you I wanted to speak to." She stepped back from the doorway. "Won't you come inside?"

Certain there was nothing she could say to him that couldn't be said outside he stayed where he was. "Well, I'm in a bit of a hurry actually," he lied. The last woman who had wanted to speak to him had dragged him into the embarrassing episode at the school.

Mrs Metcalfe huffed impatiently. "I don't want to shout. It's about Mrs Jessop." She cupped a hand to her mouth as she came back out onto the top step. "I was a bit concerned. I thought you might know something."

It may have been the accusatory note Arthur thought he detected in her voice that prevented him from walking away; it even made him edge a little closer to the shop door. "Know something about what?" he asked nervously. "I hardly know the woman."

"Well, you seemed to know her well enough to help her with her shopping yesterday."

There's that tone again, thought Arthur, moving nearer still. "It was common courtesy, nothing more," he said indignantly. "You said you were concerned, has something happened to her?"

The woman gave a disappointed sigh. "I was rather hoping you could tell me." She glanced cautiously down the road before fixing Arthur with a steady gaze. "She said she fell, but it looked to me more like she'd been hit, the state of her face."

Arthur felt an involuntary flutter of pity for the young woman that quickly turned to a feeling of guilt. Suppose that husband of hers had seen him carrying the shopping? What if his interfering had led to a beating? He turned his head and looked anxiously across the green, half expecting to see the vengeful figure of Stan Jessop bearing down on him. The fact that there was no sign of the man afforded Arthur little relief; the damage had already been done.

"It's not really any of our business," he said, unable to meet her gaze as he shuffled away. "Now, I really must be going. Good day."

He could sense Mrs Metcalfe's eyes burning into the back of his head as he walked towards the top of the hill. Certain she suspected him of knowing more than he had told her only added to his guilt. Of course Mrs Jessop's injuries could have been caused innocently, but in his heart he knew differently. He knew what her husband was capable of, and knowing that created in Arthur a greater feeling of impotency. There was really nothing he could do.

Instead of going straight down the hill to the harbour, Arthur went over to sit on the bench that in the past had been such a boon to his friend. But as he sat there, his bearded chin supported in his cupped hands, Arthur's thoughts were not of his friend and the mysterious trip to Exeter but of a domestic situation of which he now felt part, albeit unwittingly. George had warned him, and if he had been there at that moment he would be wagging a chubby fore finger into his face and delivering a severe lecture.

Arthur let out a long sigh. George and his wisdom were not there and it was left to him to wrestle with this problem alone. But it was only a problem if he allowed it to be. As George had pointed out on more than one occasion, that as much as he regretted the poor woman's situation, there really was nothing they could do.

"I suppose she told you."

The sudden intrusion into his deliberations made Arthur start and he leapt to his feet. "I'm sorry, I was just…" He should not have been shocked by the appalling sight that Daisy Jessop presented, but the purple swelling around her eye and the puffy cheek that made her whole face appear lopsided was far worse than he expected. With a trembling finger he pointed at her disfigurement. "Is that because of me? Did he see us together?"

She shook her head and tried to smile through the obvious discomfort. "No, this was something else I did. It was nothing to do with you."

"Whatever you did, it doesn't give him the right to…"

Daisy held up a hand to stop him as she sat on the edge of the bench while Arthur looked about him anxiously. "It's all right, he's not likely to see us. He's working over near Draybourne, at least he's supposed to be, so he won't be home before he's drunk as much of his wages as he can."

That was of little comfort to Arthur who continued to scan the surrounding area as he sat beside her. Next to him she looked so small and pathetic that he felt a responsibility towards her. "Is there nowhere you can go to get away from him? Don't you have any family?"

"There's no one. And I've no money." She kept her face turned away from him, but Arthur sensed the sadness in her voice. "If it was just me it wouldn't matter, I could put up with anything, even homelessness. But I've got Rosie to think of and she's the most important thing to me."

For a reason he couldn't fathom, Arthur felt a responsibility towards her, that he was in some way that cause of all her worries. "I wish there was something I could do to help," he said with equal sadness.

Daisy found the courage to face him. "You're a kind man, Mr Mulrooney, I can see that, but there's really nothing you can do." She stared reflectively at the iron grey sky above the harbour. "I can just imagine what my mother would say if she were still alive, 'You made your bed and now you lie in it'." She gave a sharp, bitter laugh. "She warned me about Stan, but I thought I knew better and now I'm paying the price for my stubbornness. I've no one to blame but myself, but I've got Rosie and she's the one good thing that's come from my marriage." Those last few words caught in her throat and she gave a little sob. "She doesn't deserve a life like this." It was as though she was talking to herself, thinking out loud, and was suddenly aware of Arthur's presence. She reached out and gripped his arm. "I'm so sorry, I didn't mean to burden you with all my problems, you've probably enough of your own."

Arthur patted the hand that still clutched his arm. Although such familiarity was alien to him the gesture seemed natural, almost comforting. It also brought home to him with a harsh realisation that any problems he faced were trite and insignificant compared to those of this young woman and her daughter. He found himself probing possibilities, seeking answers on how he could help. He was being dragged into a situation in which he should not become involved. Impotency almost overwhelmed him as his thoughts drifted back over a lifetime of distressing memories.

He broke free of her grip and stood up. "I'm sorry, I wish there was something I could do to help."

Daisy jumped up and fixed him with her watery eyes. "Please, don't apologise. I should never have said what I did." She looked agitatedly back towards the green. "I have to go. Rosie will be coming out of school soon and I daren't be late." She started to walk away, but after a few yards she stopped and turned back, smiling weakly. "Thank you."

Arthur stayed where he was, watching her until she disappeared from his view. He couldn't rid himself of the conviction that he could do something to help, that there was something within his power that would relieve the unfortunate woman and her daughter of the miserable burden she carried. But what? George would tell him there was nothing and to put such ideas out of his mind and George would have been right.

For Arthur, as he walked back down the hill to his cottage beside the harbour the place had never seemed less welcoming. The home he had made where he had previously been content to see out his days had now become a hostile place and all because he had allowed himself to share the pain of others. The country had suffered six years of war, but for some there was still no peace. He had never needed George more than he did at that moment, but stopped short of cursing him for his untimely desertion. "I just hope it's important," he muttered to himself as he crossed the bridge at the bottom of the hill.

Chapter Eighteen

Whatever Arthur felt he needed to worry about, for Daisy the danger faced by her and Rosie was altogether more real and immediate.

After leaving Arthur at the top of the hill she went to collect Rosie from school, expecting to spend a few hours enjoying the company of her daughter before Stan returned home and subjected them to whatever torment suited his mood.

With a light drizzle now settling over the village, and the dark clouds hanging low over the English Channel threatening heavy rain in the next hour, Daisy felt her depression harden into despair. The only comfort she had to look forward to was the sight of her precious daughter emerging from the press of children flooding through the school gates.

Despite the scarf that covered her head Daisy was conscious that her injuries would attract the unwelcome and judgemental attention of the other mothers who already considered her something of an oddity to be pitied. She remained detached from the crowd that circled the gates. Even so she sensed a few unguarded glances in her direction, and imagined comments passed behind cupped hands. It all served to highlight how miserable and friendless her life had become, and was likely to stay for as long as she was tied to Stan.

Any further regrets that plagued her life were suddenly swept away as she caught sight of Rosie searching amongst the pressing crowd of adults for her own mother. Unwilling to attract undue attention by calling out Daisy, waved a hand until Rosie saw her. Straightaway the child broke into a sprint along the gravelled lane towards her. Stooping down, Daisy held out her arms, ready to welcome her daughter into her loving embrace while concealing the pain she felt behind a broad smile.

Never before had she seen Rosie run so fast, like she was escaping some threat and she smiled as she raised a hand to wipe away the drops of water that dripped irritatingly from the rim of her scarf onto the end of her nose. At that very moment a piercing shriek rent the sodden air. Daisy gasped in horror as she leapt to her feet and saw Rosie sliding outstretched across the rough surface of the lane.

As some of the other women turned to see what had happened Daisy rushed to her daughter's aid, sobbing with distress at the sight of blood that was already oozing from the cuts to Rosie's hands from which small shards of gravel were protruding. Rosie was screaming from shock and the stinging pain as Daisy gently lifted her to her feet. The anguish increased when they both saw the similar damage to her knees, and the blood that was running freely down Rosie's legs and pooling around the top of her socks.

For several seconds Daisy was immobilised with the same shock that had overwhelmed the child until she noticed one or two of the women taking a few tentative steps towards them. The last thing she wanted were strangers fussing around with feigned offers of help so they could ask awkward questions about her own injuries. She swept Rosie up in her arms and hurried away in the direction of home.

"It's all right my darling," she said in an emotionally strained voice, "mummy will make it all better."

Rosie's response was to cry out with increased ferocity at the pain that made her entire body tremble until Daisy carried her into the kitchen and set her down on the draining board. Never comfortable at the sight of blood, especially when it belonged to someone as special as her precious daughter, Daisy found it almost impossible to put on the brave face that was needed to calm the child. Nor could she see any practicable way of making it better.

"I'm sorry darling," she said, gulping back some tears as she wet a tea towel under the tap and dabbed at the blood running from Rosie's knees.

The girl cried louder and kicked out as the rough cloth dislodged some of the gravel from the deep cuts. Trying to inspect the damage to her hands was even more distressing as Rosie clenched them into tight fists and screeched at her mother to stop. Daisy's attempt to remain calm was rapidly dissolving into panic as she frantically searched the kitchen cupboards for something to dress the wounds. There was nothing, but she knew that already. Knowing she had to do something she pulled her most worn tea towel from a drawer and tore it into strips before bracing herself for another bout of anguished resistance.

"I'm sorry, sweetheart, but mummy has to bandage your hands and knees, so please try and be a brave girl for me." She kissed Rosie on the cheek as she coaxed her hands open and loosely wrapped the cloth over the cuts. Rosie screwed up her face into a tight grimace as her mother lifted her off the draining board. "I'm going to take you down to see the doctor. He'll make it all better."

Ignoring the rain that was now falling steadily Daisy half ran and half walked across the sodden green towards the top of the hill. With Rosie's face buried into her shoulder as she vainly tried to protect the child from the worst of the weather Daisy had not even considered what she would do if the doctor was not at home.

With the wind gusting off the sea the rain stung her face, adding to the misery of their situation and Daisy let out a great sob of relief and exhaustion when she finally reached the bottom of the hill and the meagre amount of shelter afforded by the harbour wall. It was only as she crossed the bridge that the realisation struck her that she had no idea which of the cottages belonged to the doctor, and on a day like this it was unlikely that there would be anyone stupid enough to venture out that she could ask. As a premature dusk began to settle over the harbour despair returned with a vengeance.

If there was any consolation for Daisy it was that Rosie had stopped crying and was peering over her mother's shoulder at the unfamiliar surroundings. Walking along the harbour, Daisy's eyes searched each of the cottages, praying for some divine intervention that would point the way. Her arms were aching almost beyond endurance as the child got heavier with every step she took and she knew that she was unable to carry her any further. She put her down on a low wall in front of one of the cottages.

Ever alert and unable to settle in one place for more than a few seconds, Enid Gulliver drew back the net curtain and peered out of the window at the swirling mist that swept in off the sea. There was nothing in particular that she expected, or wanted, to see, but it had been some time since she last looked out of that window and it was now due her attention. What she didn't expect, or want, to see was someone she couldn't recognise standing out on the harbour and what looked like a child sitting on her wall. It wasn't unusual for strangers to wonder down to the harbour before realising their mistake and retreating back up the hill, but not at this time of year and certainly not in weather like this. As the stranger looked in her direction, Enid darted back from the window, certain that she had been seen. That certainty was ratified a few seconds later by a soft rap on her door.

Enid clutched her bony hands to her chest, pulling at the front of her pinafore as she danced a jig around the furniture while deciding if she should answer the door. She wasn't comfortable with strangers; she was only just coming to terms with the arrival of Mr Mulrooney. While she was still wrestling with the dilemma there was another, more urgent knock on the door. Enid's head bobbed back and forth with indecision until she reached the bottom of the stairs.

"There's someone at the door," she called up in her trill voice to where her husband lay, virtually bed bound by his arthritis.

"Well, I can't answer it, you daft woman," he shouted back down, more bemused than irritated. "Hadn't you best see who it is?"

"It's a woman."

"Then see what she wants."

Enid gave a few pirouettes before finally tip-toeing to the door and gingerly opening it just enough to peer out into the settling gloom.

"I'm so sorry to trouble you, but I was hoping you could tell me where the doctor lives."

Enid's beady eyes fixed on the woman. "Why?"

"My daughter's been hurt," said Daisy, turning to look at Rosie still sitting on the wall. "I didn't know what else to do."

Enid opened the door a little further for a better look at the woman and child. She jerked her head to the right. "He lives down yonder, but it won't do you or the lass no good going there,"

Daisy found her tolerance wearing thin. "Why is that?"

"Because he's not there."

"Do you know where he is, or when he'll be back?" If her impatience showed the woman gave no sign of acknowledging the fact.

"Yes," replied Enid flatly as her head continued to bob back and forth.

At the end of her tether, Daisy went to turn away from the door. "I'm sorry to have troubled you," she said curtly, before adding sarcastically, "thank you for your help."

"Tomorrow," Enid said cryptically as Daisy prepared to lift Rosie off the wall, bracing herself for the long, exhausting walk up the hill. "But if you try three doors down, his friend lives there.

Not saying he'll be much help mind, but he might be better than nothing for the little mite."

Daisy gave her a nod and a weak smile of thanks. Of course she knew who the woman was referring to, and if the circumstances were not so dire she would have ignored the advice and started for home. But tiredness overwhelmed her and Rosie needed attention, and anyone was better than no one. It could do no harm.

No harm! As she hurried along the harbour with Rosie in her arms she knew exactly what harm it could do if Stan found out, and not just for her. But Rosie was all that mattered, whatever the risk.

Nervously she tapped on the door. Through the little bay window a dull light glowed, casting an arc of amber light into the sodden air outside. Her heart raced as she heard the heavy tread of footsteps from inside before the door opened.

Daisy took a step back when Arthur's initial expression showed rather more concern than surprise.

"Mrs Jessop!" he said after a short hesitation. He moved out from the shelter of the doorway. "What's happened? Why are you here?"

"I'm sorry, I didn't intend coming here, but the woman down there said the doctor was away and I didn't know what else to do." The words came out in a breathless rush. "It's Rosie."

"I expect that was Mrs Gulliver you saw," said Arthur, moving away from the doorway and waving them inside. "You're soaked. You had better come in and tell me what's wrong."

The chance of getting out of the rain and relieve the strain on her arms was more welcome to Daisy than Arthur could possibly imagine, and as she entered his small living room and glanced around an immediate feeling of warmth and cosiness swept over her.

Arthur pointed to the sofa. "Put your daughter down there and take your coats off. I'll hang them up in the kitchen." When he returned Daisy was kneeling on the floor next to Rosie and he noticed for the first time the child's bloodied knees and roughly bandaged hands. "It looks like she had a nasty accident. I can see why you came looking for George."

Daisy looked up at him and nodded, her face taut with anxiety. "She fell over outside the school. Her hands and knees are quite badly cut and I didn't have anything indoors to put on them, and I think there's still some pieces of gravel in the cuts. I shouldn't have come, but I didn't know what else to do. I couldn't just leave her like she was." The words washed out in a flow of pent-up emotion, but there was a reassuring compassion in Arthur's expression that had a comforting effect. "I'm sorry, I shouldn't be troubling you with all this. I'll take Rosie home, I'm sure I can find something."

As she pushed herself up off the floor Arthur held out a hand to stop her. "You stay there." He went over and took his raincoat from a hook on the back of the door. "I've got a key to George's cottage and I know where he keeps all his medical stuff. I'll be back in a minute and we'll see what we can do between us." Rosie had been watching him closely, unable to decide if she should like him or not, and she looked down when he gave her a friendly smile. He wondered if she remembered him from that morning at the school. "Anyway, I'll be back shortly," he added as he left.

While he was gone Rosie appeared more engrossed with her strange surroundings and less concerned by her injuries. She peered cautiously round the room, taking in every detail before letting her curious gaze settle on the oversized bookcase crammed full of more volumes than she imagined anyone could read. What she thought of it all was difficult to decipher, but for Daisy it was a relief that her daughter was able to focus on something other than her own plight. More than that, though, it was comforting to share the care of her daughter with someone who felt like a friend. It was a new and pleasing experience.

Within ten minutes Arthur was back, wet but with a triumphant grin splitting his thick beard. "I think I've got everything we need," he said, pulling various pieces of medical accoutrements from his coat pockets and laying them out on the table. He shook his raincoat out over the kitchen floor before returning to the table and sweeping his hand over the items. "Bandages, gauze, antiseptic cream and tweezers." He picked up the last item and brandished it in the air. "To extract any pieces of gravel," he explained.

Up to that point Rosie had been content to quietly follow his movements around the room, but at the sight of the shiny implement she sucked in an apprehensive breath and began to sob fearfully.

"There's some warm water in the kettle," said Arthur, quickly concealing the tweezers and retreating to the kitchen. "We'll need to bathe those cuts before we do anything else."

While he was out of the room Rosie looked pleadingly at her mother through tearfully red eyes.

"It's all right darling, Mr Mulrooney is going to help us make it all better. It might hurt a little bit so I want you to show him what a brave girl you are." She gently took Rosie's bunched and bandaged fists in her hands and kissed each of them in turn as Arthur came back with a bowl of water and a cloth. "Shall we just let him have a look?"

Frightened eyes moved from her mother on to Arthur as he set the bowl down and knelt down beside them. Remembering the last time he put his hands on her he held back from trying to remove the makeshift bandages and turned to Daisy. "Perhaps we should just leave them and hope they get better on their own and not turn poisonous. I've seen what can happen to the smallest graze, though, if it's not treated straight away. The hand turned black and dropped off."

Rosie's mouth gaped open in a silent scream as she reached out for her mother. Daisy glared at Arthur, horrified by his insensitive remarks before comprehending his psychological approach to a delicate situation.

"I'm sure it won't come to that, Mr Mulrooney," she said, giving him a furtive wink, "but we'll know soon enough if Rosie lets us take off the bandages and you can have a look." Her face was set in a serious expression as she looked at her daughter. "The sooner we do it the better, I suppose."

Rosie clamped her eyes shut tight as she let out a little squeal and held out her hands, slowly uncurling her fingers. Arthur gave Daisy a satisfied nod and began gently removing the strips of cloth with a light-fingered deftness. He wet the cloth and dabbed at the wounds, stopping each time Rosie flinched and cried out. Daisy could hardly bring herself to watch, sharing in the pain of her daughter as the child screwed her face with each touch. Certain that she would have been unable to treat Rosie's wounds without breaking down she was overcome with gratitude for Arthur's help. It was not as if she had a husband she could depend on at times such as this.

With a gentleness that was at odds with the size of Arthur's hands and thick fingers he wiped away the drying blood to reveal the real extend of Rosie's injuries. Thankfully, the tweezers were not needed, any pieces of gravel were easily brushed away, and when he had finished cleaning he applied a little of the antiseptic cream, which again made the child wince and bite into her lip.

Apart from that, though, Daisy couldn't help noticing how calm her daughter appeared, with no sign of the previous fear she had displayed in Arthur's presence as she watched him intently while he made little pads of the gauze and bandaged them in place.

"There," he said, struggling to his feet when he had finished. "What do you think, Mum, will she live?"

Rosie's eyes widened as she looked to her mother for some confirmation of her fate, but Daisy was still lost in amazement at the change in her daughter. Rosie had always shown an unnatural fear of strangers, especially men, for which Daisy laid the blame firmly at Stan's feet. Since the death of her parents this was the closest either of them had been to having a friend in their lives and it was an experience that filled her with confused trepidation. For anyone else a new friend would be a welcome addition in their lives, but for Daisy nothing was that straightforward. All she could manage was a reassuring smile. "Why don't you say thank you to Mr Mulrooney."

"Perhaps not up to George's standard," said Arthur, recognising the child's reluctance as he stood back to admire his work, "but I think it will do."

Rosie hunched with coyness, sinking deeper into the soft cushions of the old sofa as she inspected the dressings on her hands and knees.

"You were really brave, my darling," said Daisy, sitting down next to her daughter and placing an arm around her shoulders, "but you really should say thank you."

Rosie raised her cornflower blue eyes to study Arthur, trying to determine her feelings towards him. Arthur seemed to understand and removed himself to the kitchen with the bowl and cloth while mother and daughter carried on a whispered conversation. He could imagine what was being said.

When he returned, Daisy was looking anxious and not a little embarrassed. She got up to meet him. "I told Rosie her father will be angry if he finds out we've been here," she said in a hushed voice. "I've always taught her it's wrong to lie, but I don't want you getting into trouble just for helping us. I don't know why he's like he is and I'm sorry…"

Arthur placed a hand on her arm. "You don't need to explain, and you don't have to lie on my account. You've done nothing wrong, just what any mother would do for their child." He looked down at Rosie as she stared back at him. "You both deserve more."

"She might not tell you herself, but I know Rosie is grateful for what you've done." Daisy smiled weakly. "And she knows that she doesn't need to be scared of you anymore." She took Rosie's hand and helped her off the sofa. "We had better be getting back."

The sympathy he had previously felt towards Daisy and her daughter was nothing compared to the pity and compassion that swept over him. Although not prone to spontaneous demonstrations of affection he wanted to take them both in his arms in a protective embrace, to show them they could depend on him. But his surprise at his own feelings was eclipsed by the shock he felt when Rosie suddenly wrapped her arms round his leg in a tight hug. When he looked down, he found her gazing up at him.

"Do you want to be my granddad, Mr Rooney?" she pleaded in a clear, positive voice. "All the children at school have a granddad except me."

Daisy almost choked on the emotion that drove up from her stomach. "Don't be silly, darling, Mr Mulrooney can't be your granddad, you know that." She tried to prize Rosie away from Arthur's leg and force her into her coat. "Come along now, we have to get home."

"But he can be my pretend granddad, can't he?" she said, her eyes never leaving Arthur's face. "Please say you can."

Daisy and Arthur exchanged glances, hers apologetic, his incomprehensible. "I'm so sorry," she said, "I don't know what made her say such a thing. I'm sorry." She hurriedly put on her own coat.

"It's quite all right," Arthur assured her. He put a hand on Rosie's head. "If I could be anyone's granddad I would be proud to be yours. And if it's all right with your mother then I would be happy for us to pretend." He bent down until his face was close to hers and said quietly. "But it has to be our secret. Can you do that?"

Rosie looked to her mother for consent before nodding enthusiastically.

"That's settled then," he said, holding out his hand. "Shall we shake on it?"

As she took his hand her head darted forward and she kissed him on the cheek.

Daisy quickly took her daughter's hand and pulled her towards the door. "We really have to go," she said to Arthur, although what she really meant was rather more than that. "Thank you so much for all your help and I'm sorry for what Rosie said." She ushered her daughter out into the damp evening air before adding, "I'm sure she will have forgotten all about it by the time we get home."

"I hope not." Arthur muttered to himself, remembering with deep regret, an episode from his past. "I really hope not."

Chapter Nineteen

By the time she crossed the green towards home Daisy was physically and mentally drained, as well as being soaked through by the rain that seemed to increase with every muscle straining step. She had hoped that Rosie would have walked some of the way, particularly up the hill, but she had cried out every time Daisy had tried to put her down until in the end it was less stressful to suffer the pain.

While she had been at Arthur's she had been cosseted in the cosy surroundings and his calming influence and her only concern was for her daughter's welfare. But Rosie would recover; in a few days the only reminder would be a collection of scabs to be picked at, while life with Stan would be the same as it ever was, one great scab that would never heal.

Clearing the sodden grass, Daisy could endure the strain on her arms no longer and set Rosie down at the end of the lane leading to their house. The child took a few stiff-legged steps, accompanied by little squeaks of complaint, but Daisy's attention was drawn elsewhere. She was peering through the darkness for some sign that Stan was at home, waiting for them with anger fuelled questions and accusations. She could see no light on, but that meant nothing. Stan often sat in the dark, knowing his sudden appearance unnerved her. Also, his erratic work ethic meant that they were not only frequently short of food but without electricity as well.

With her heart already pounding with exertion Daisy feared it would burst as she went through the gate with Rosie dragging along behind. During the trek up the hill she had tried to rehearse what she would say and had given up when she realised it would mean nothing unless Rosie supported her explanation, and Stan knew how to get his daughter to tell the truth. Daisy shuddered as the thought crossed her mind. At the kitchen door she was close to collapse and had to wait a few moments to gulp in mouthfuls of damp air which caught in her throat and made her cough. She pushed open the door and took in the silence, which was almost as intimidating as Stan's presence, until she switched on the light and convinced herself that the house was empty.

"Let me help you, darling," she said breathlessly as Rosie fumbled with the buttons of her coat, "then you can go and play while mummy makes tea. You must be starving."

As Rosie limped off up the stairs to her bedroom Daisy was surprised to find herself thinking, not of her husband and his interrogation, but what her daughter had said to Arthur. It had been so unexpected and out of character. Rosie's chronic shyness and fear of strangers had held back her social development to such an extent that she found it difficult to form friendships, even at school surrounded by her peers. This had been a constant concern to Daisy and she worried what would happen to the child should anything happen to her. Stan could never be relied upon to be the father Rosie needed and deserved.

Her thoughts were still pondering on this new relationship and its implications for the two of them an hour later when she heard the heavy tread of Stan's footsteps at the back of the house. They had already eaten and Rosie was playing in the living room prior to bedtime while Daisy washed up when he threw open the kitchen door.

Fearful that her accident had somehow been her fault and that she would be in trouble Rosie had scurried to her hiding place behind the armchair. There she squatted down, wincing at the pain as the skin tightened over her knees and she trembled with fright.

"I didn't know what time you would be home," Daisy said, trying to hold her voice steady as she took a plate of sausages and mash from the oven and put it down on the table. "It should still be warm."

Slowly unbuttoning the old raincoat he wore Stan took it off and threw it over the back of his chair, spraying drops of water across the floor. His dark, glowering eyes never left her as he dragged back the chair and sat down. "Where have you been?" he grunted through the first mouthful of food.

Daisy stood at the sink with her back to him, knowing he could read the guilt in her face.

"Nowhere! I don't know what you mean."

Stan snorted like an angered bull, spraying food back onto the plate. "You know damn well what I mean, you lying bitch. I came back earlier and you weren't here, so I'll ask you again. Where were you?"

"I was probably at the school collecting Rosie." He knows, she thought, feeling her cheeks flush. "What time was that?"

"It don't matter what the bleeding time was, you weren't here and I want to know where you were."

Daisy jumped as he thumped the handle of the knife hard down onto the table. Slowly she wiped her hands on a tea towel and turned to face him, telling herself she had done nothing wrong. "Rosie had an accident when she came out of school. She fell over and cut her hands and knees. We didn't have any bandages or anything like that and they were bleeding badly so I took her down the hill to see the doctor."

She watched nervously as Stan continued to stuff food into his mouth and she began to feel that he believed her and that nothing more would be said. He finished eating and she took away his plate, washing it in the sink while he stayed in his seat. It was only when she had dried the plate that she heard the harsh scraping of the chair against the stone floor and felt him close behind her.

"So, where is she then?" he asked, the rank smell of stale beer wafting under her nose and alerting her fears. When sober Stan was unpredictable enough, but he was even more volatile with drink inside him. "Is she in bed? I'd better go up and make sure she's all right."

As he strode down the hall towards the stairs Daisy struggled to decide on what best to do. It was tempting to let him go upstairs, let him find Rosie's empty bed, lose any interest he had in his daughter and go for a lie down and sleep until the morning. Or, he would feel deceived and take his spite out on the two of them.

"She's in the front room, playing," called out Daisy impulsively. "But just leave her be, Stan, don't go upsetting her just before bedtime."

He turned back, glaring at his wife before his lips parted in a sardonic grin. "I ain't going to upset her, I just want to make sure she's all right, like any good father would, I want to make sure that old sod of a doctor has taken good care of my girl." His grin spread into a broad smile. "Don't you think I ought to care?"

Daisy didn't bother to reply, there seemed no point. For the whole of Rosie's short life he had never shown more than a modicum of concern for his daughter. She followed him into the front room in an effort to protect the child from any more suffering.

Knowing Rosie would be hiding from him as she always did Stan went straight to the armchair. He was still smiling; there was some satisfaction that she feared him, that's the way it should be. Dragging the chair to one side he bent over her as she cowered in the corner, whimpering. Before he could lay a hand on her Daisy squeezed past him and swept Rosie up in her arms, relieved that she had not yet wet herself and give Stan the excuse to punish her.

"Put her down there," he demanded, jabbing a finger at the armchair. "I want to have a look at her."

Although Rosie clung to her mother's neck Daisy reluctantly sat her down and pulled herself free of the tiny trembling hands. "It's all right, my darling," she said soothingly, "daddy just wants to look at where you've hurt yourself."

Unconvinced by her mother's assurance Rosie sobbed and continued to shake as her father leant forward and made an exaggerated show of inspecting the dressings on her wounds. When he prodded her knee she cried with pain and kicked out, narrowly missing his face.

"So, you went to see the doctor?" he asked her, thrusting his face into hers. Rosie's lips trembled and she looked up at her mother.

"I've already told she did," said Daisy with as much indignation as she could muster. "Who else do you think put those bandages on?"

Stan continued to pick at the dressings while Rosie squirmed in the chair against his touch. After about a minute, which seemed to last an eternity, he finally stood up and sniffed loudly. "Well then, you'd better get her up to bed, unless you want me to take her."

Daisy breathed a sigh of relief, hoping he wouldn't notice. "No, I'll take her, then I'll make us a cup of tea."

Mother and child were as eager as each other to escape his menacing presence and Daisy plucked her daughter from the chair and hurried upstairs, ignoring the plaintive sobs as Rosie's knees banged against her. But once inside the bedroom Daisy could relax a little into the protective, caring mother she had always been, lavishing kisses on Rosie's injuries as she removed her clothing. When Rosie was in bed Daisy lay down beside her, first reading her favourite story and then waiting until she fell asleep.

Finally Daisy got up off the bed. She would willingly have stayed there all night, close to her daughter and free from Stan's groping hands and rough, misguided passion. She tip-toed towards the door, carefully avoiding the loose floorboards, but as she pulled it open she stiffened with shock and took a step back, causing what sounded like a deafening creak. Stan was there, standing in the doorway. She turned, anxious that Rosie had wakened, and was relieved to see she hadn't stirred.

"You frightened the life out of me, I thought you were still downstairs," she said in a hushed, shaky voice. He refused to move out of the way as she tried to push past. "Let me go down and put the kettle on before we wake her."

He took a firm grip on the top of her arms and eased her away from Rosie's room and towards their own bedroom. "I think I'm entitled to a bit more than a bleeding cup of tea," he breathed into her face. "Don't you think you owe me that?"

"Perhaps later, Stan," she replied, despite her dry mouth, as she tried to resist his efforts to force her into the bedroom. "I need to go down and tidy up a bit. I didn't get a chance earlier, what with everything else,"

He cocked his head to one side as though considering her excuse. "Oh yeah! All that time down at the doctor's getting our little girl sorted out."

The note of sarcasm in his voice didn't go unnoticed. "Come on, Stan, I don't want to disturb her. She's had a tiring day and needs her sleep."

"And what about me, what about what I need?" The grip on her arms tightened, making her wince. He jerked his head in the direction of Rosie's room. "She's the only one you care about, just like I don't even exist."

It was developing into the argument they had had a thousand times in the past, and one over which Daisy could only ever hope to claim a moral victory. "That's not true, Stan, and you know it. Just because I don't give into you every time you snap your fingers." She fought harder to stop him from throwing her onto the bed. "If anyone's treated badly in this house it's me and Rosie, not you."

With one final effort that took him by surprise she shook herself free of his grasp and ran from the room, along the landing and down the stairs. But any relief she felt that he hadn't immediately chased after her quickly turned to panic when she realised he could easily take his spite out on her daughter, until she heard him following her down the stairs.

As he strode into the kitchen she turned to face him. Although his heavily lidded eyes smouldered angrily, the measured tone of his voice when he spoke was unexpected, catching her off guard. "I was in the pub earlier, waiting for you to come home." He sat on the edge of the table, his eyes following her as she tried to appear busy and unconcerned. "That old biddy of a landlady was going on about all her complaints, and about that doctor friend of yours." Daisy sensed his intimidating gaze as though he was searching for a reaction which expressed itself through a feeling of nausea. "Saying that he was never around when she needed him."

"She can't expect him to be at her beck and call, not when he's retired," she replied calmly, while wondering what he knew. "And not in weather like this."

"And not when he's busy looking after our little girl?"

Daisy gave him a vague nod of acknowledgement, although she didn't trust herself with any words of agreement. With her back to him she heard him slide off the table and braced herself for the anticipated assault when he would force the truth from her.

"One of the old blokes in the pub, a nosey bastard by all accounts, said he heard the doc had got the bus to Exeter this morning and wouldn't be back for a day or two," he went on in the same even tone as he moved close to Daisy until she felt his hot breath on her neck. "Wish I knew what I know now, I could have put him straight, couldn't I?"

Her whole body shook with an involuntary spasm. *He knows and he's playing with me*, she told herself with absolute certainty. The only question that plagued her mind was what to do next. She knew that to deny anything would only serve to dig a deeper grave for herself.

Nimbly she ducked around him and went into the front room. "I'll just pick up Rosie's toys while the kettle boils."

She could have left the toys where they were, but she needed to keep busy, and away from Stan's clutches while she worked on her response. In the end she concluded that only the truth would do and the rest would be up to him.

By the time she returned to the kitchen he was standing with his back against the sink as the kettle began to whistle on the hob. He said nothing, but the dark expression on his face screamed its threat. As Daisy went to pick up the kettle from the hob he grabbed hold of her wrist and lifted the kettle himself. Before she could react he had her hand clamped to the draining board with the spout of the kettle poised inches above.

She let out a gasp of panic. "Don't be stupid, Stan, let me go."

Daisy fixed him with a frightened, pleading look that had little effect. "So, was that bloke in the pub wrong or not?" he asked, allowing the kettle to tilt forward a little until a droplet of boiling water spilt on the back of her clenched hand.

Determined not to give him any pleasure from her suffering she bit into her lip to stop from crying out, although she knew her bravery would dissolve the next time the scalding water touched her flesh. She shook her head. "No, he wasn't," she admitted as the kettle tipped forward. "But I had to do something for Rosie. I couldn't just leave her like she was so I saw his friend and he offered to help. What else could I do?"

To her relief he replaced the kettle on the hob while he kept hold of her wrist, lifting her arm and twisting it backwards. "So, why lie to me?" he sneered as she whimpered in pain. "It makes me wonder what else you've lied about." He thrust his face into hers. "Well?"

"Nothing. Nothing else. I didn't tell you because I knew you would behave like this." She was close to tears, more from anger than from any punishment he chose to inflict on her. "If you weren't so unreasonable about who I see and who I speak to I wouldn't have to tell lies. Mr Mulrooney is a friend, the only one I've got because of the way you are." She blurted out that last accusation as desperate act of defiance, a determination to finally stand up to his bullying. Now she steeled herself against his response.

It never came, not immediately anyway, which was scant comfort to Daisy. A back-handed swipe across the face is what she expected, his usual reaction to her troublesome behaviour. It was violent and painful, but swift and quickly forgotten. She could cope with that. But the silence and waiting was the real punishment. He eyed the kettle. Steam still swirled from the spout, curling up into the chill air of the kitchen. Daisy stiffened as his cold stare returned to her, and she recognised that look, and what it meant.

Slowly he shook his head. "No, you're not much good to me with one hand, but it's no more than you deserve, you deceitful bitch." His eyes glinted evilly. "There's other ways you can make up for all your lies, either you or that little brat upstairs."

"You leave Rosie alone." She clenched her fist as she spat the words through bared teeth. "You can do want you want with me because you can't hurt me any more than you already have, but you touch Rosie again and I swear I'll kill you."

Stan let out a coarse snorted laugh as he began to drag her through the hall. "I think you would at that," he sneered, taking

140

hold of her other wrist and twisting her arm behind her back. "I'd better watch myself from now on."

Daisy stumbled as he pushed her up the stairs. Knowing what awaited her, or what awaited Rosie if she resisted, caused a knot to form in her stomach and a burning hatred towards the man who she was ashamed to call her husband. Again, her parent's advice echoed in her head and overwhelming regret engulfed her, but as they passed the door to Rosie's room the hatred and regret needed to be set aside for the sake of her daughter.

Inside her own room Rosie began to undress as soon as Stan released her from his grip. She did so with a total disregard to his presence; pretending he wasn't there made what was to follow more tolerable. She would close her mind to him, let him take what he wanted and afterwards allow the loathing to return with more passion. Before Stan could intervene, and in a final act of rebellion, she stripped naked, knowing how he enjoyed the dominance of ripping off her clothes before he humiliated her.

She lay on the bed, her legs spread wide and her eyes tightly closed. Feeling him climb onto the bed next to her she clenched her hands into tight fists as she waited for him to shift his weight on top of her and the pain as he tried to force an entry into her unreceptive cleft. It had been the same so many times throughout her marriage, leaving her feeling degraded and sore.

Feeling the movement on the bed she tensed and waited for the moment he took his pleasure. It would be harsh, frantic and, thankfully, quick. There had rarely been any tenderness or subtlety in Stan's lovemaking; it involved no foreplay or after-sex, just some urgent thrusting towards a noisy climax, after which he would fall into a deep and equally noisy sleep. But this time, instead of his weight bearing down on her she sensed him lean across her and before she could resist he took hold of her arm and forcibly rolled her over onto her front. Her face was buried in the pillow and she turned her head to the side in order to breath.

"You didn't think you were going to get away with it that easily, did you?" When she opened her eyes his face was close to hers and he planted a slobbering kiss on her cheek. "You didn't expect to get rewarded for all those lies?"

Reward! If she wasn't so consumed by anger and fear she may have found his remark humorous. Not since the very beginning of their relationship had sex ever been rewarding, when she was young and lacking in any experience and had been in awe of his attention. "What do you want from me?"

He moved out of her vision and she heard a gruff laugh as his hands gripped her hips and roughly jerked her forward onto her knees. "I thought it's time we tried something different, spice things up a bit. After all you're not the looker I married anymore." He slid off the end of the bed to stand behind her and seconds later she felt the hardness of his manhood probing between the cheeks of her buttocks. "I think I may enjoy this a bit more than you, sweetheart, but who knows."

Realising what he intended Daisy pulled herself free of his grasp and swung off the bed, snatching up her dress to cover her nakedness. 'You filthy bastard!' She wanted to scream the words, but thought of Rosie in the next room. "I don't even want you touching me let alone doing something like that. I only put up with you because I don't have a choice." Hurriedly, she threw on the dress, fumbling with the buttons, but when she tried to push past him he blocked her way.

"You put up with me?" He spat the words at her, his face twisted with menace. "The other way round more like. Look at the state of you, what bloke would give you a second look, only a mug like me." He cupped her chin in his hand and gave her a cynical grin. "Oh, I see! Maybe it's the old geezer down the hill, perhaps he fancies a bit of skirt and there you were willing to oblige. So, was that the price for looking after our brat?"

Daisy glared back at him in sickened disbelief. "You're disgusting. Only someone with a filthy mind like yours could think of something like that. That man has been a friend to me and Rosie, that's all. "

She made another attempt to get round him but he threw her back onto the bed with such force that she bounced off and landed heavily on the floor with a loud thud. She let out a shriek as a sharp pain shot through her shoulder as she hit the bare boards.

Stan stood over her as she dragged herself up onto her knees. "Get back on the bed; I ain't finished with you yet." Her half-buttoned dress gaped open at the top and she caught him leering at her bare breast. She gasped at the stabbing pain when she tried to cover up. "And don't try making out you're hurt either just to make another excuse to go running to your new friend." He leant over and yanked her to her feet. Afraid of disturbing Rosie she tried to stifle the agony that shot through her, but when he pushed her back onto the bed a sharp cry escaped her lips. "Shut your bleeding noise woman if you don't want to wake the brat." In an instant he was on her, pulling at the hem of her dress before launching himself on top of her.

She could feel his penis probing between her legs as she fought back with her one good arm, although she knew it was a battle he would ultimately win. It would have been best for her to give in to the inevitable and get it over with as quickly and as painlessly as possible, but his earlier attempt to degrade her had added a new layer to her resolve. She would stop him from using her as he pleased, somehow.

"Mummy?"

The small frightened voice at the door cut through the hostile atmosphere of the room with the sharp efficiency of a surgeon's knife.

"Get back to your bed," hissed Stan.

Taking advantage of the distraction, Daisy twisted onto her side and raised her head from the bed. "It's all right, darling, get back to bed like Daddy said and Mummy will be in shortly to tuck you in." As she tried to push Stan off her she was relieved to find he offered little resistance, allowing her to get up off the bed and pull down her dress.

"Later," he breathed. Even in the darkened room Daisy could read the vengeance etched into his face. "We'll finish this later."

Rosie was sitting up in bed when Daisy entered the room, her face half hidden behind the sheet she had clutched in her little fingers. Her eyes were wide with fright.

"It's all right, precious," whispered Daisy, sitting on the edge of the bed and pulling the child close to her. She tucked her other arm into her side in an effort to ease the stabbing pain in her shoulder. "Mummy's going to stay with you until you fall asleep."

The first fingers of an autumn dawn were feeling their way through the thin curtains at the bedroom window when Daisy awoke, still lying next to her daughter. She had no recollection of creeping under the covers, only the disturbing memory of what had driven her there in the first place. Carefully she sat up and peered down at Rosie still sleeping peacefully beside her. *How much would she remember when she awoke?* Daisy wondered.

As she slipped quietly from the bed she was reminded of her damaged shoulder, biting into her lip to stifle a whimper of agony. Creeping from the room she anxiously went to retrieve the rest of her clothes. Stan was still sleeping, lying on his back and snoring loudly. She stood over him, tempted by the spare pillow next to his head.

"You won't hurt us again, Stan," she mouthed, bending close. "I don't know how, but you won't…"

Chapter Twenty

What Rosie Jessop had said to him the previous day had played on Arthur's mind all night and was still with him the following morning. Now, as he tramped up the hill, he was still thinking about it when he should have been focussing on his other worry, George's mysterious trip to Exeter.

He had lay in his bed, listening to the rain that had returned with a greater intensity during the night, turning over in his mind what the child had asked of him, and the implications of what it would mean to all involved should he even give the idea any consideration. It was all too absurd and he ought to dismiss it out of hand. That's what George would say, and George was generally right. Despite that, he couldn't help wondering what it would be like, to be part of someone else's life that amounted to something more than just friendship. He reached the top of the hill, shaking his head dismissively. It had just been a childish whim, spoken in the heat of an emotional moment, and just as quickly forgotten.

The library book tucked under his arm almost slipped out, reminding him that he had other, more immediate, concerns in his life, Mrs Merryweather. As he walked along he debated on what he looked forward to least. The salacious attention he received at the hands of the librarian was bad enough, but at least he was used to it and was slowly developing immunity, although it was not yet complete. George was another matter though; it was something of an unknown which probably concerned him more. All manner of thoughts had crossed his mind, not least of which was that his friend was suffering from some serious complaint and had gone to seek specialist advice. The idea that he may lose him weighed heavily on his mind. And on top of all this were the Jessops. He had come to Little Bridge to make the most of his remaining years and now there was all this!

He stood on the edge of the green facing the pub knowing that, had George been with him, they would have been inside the hostelry with a drink in their hand. Instead he was bleakly staring down the road pondering on the probability of which would arrive first, the charabanc or the bus. That question was answered about five minutes later by the familiar roar of an engine being pushed to its limits by a driver who displayed the same cavalier attitude towards the sensitivities of machines as she did people. As the vehicle sped into the village great gouts of muddy water sprayed off the road as the wheels hit the deep puddles in the rutted road.

Before the charabanc got too close, Arthur retreated further onto the green, expectantly searching along the road for sight of the bus. Despite George's mocking attitude towards the strange relationship that had developed between himself and the librarian he still felt more comfortable with his friend at his side when he faced the woman. But, as in most of his dealings with his fellow man, Arthur resigned himself to disappointment.

He kept his distance until Mrs Merryweather had completed her routine of placing the steps and recovering the various paraphernalia that had been thrown to the floor by her erratic driving before squeezing her bulk into the tight space between the counter and windscreen. Only then did he venture inside.

"Mr Mulrooney, how nice to see you again." Her voice boomed out as she slapped a beefy hand down on the counter, shaking Arthur as much as the boxes of library tickets. Beneath her bushy brows her eyes narrowed imperiously as she leant closer to him. "Don't look so scared you silly boy. Wait until you see what I've got for you."

Arthur recoiled from her proximity and the seductive tone to her voice. He could think of nothing he wanted from her as he gingerly placed the book on the counter, fearing she would snatch him into her grasp as a spider would a fly.

His startled reaction must have amused her, as it always did, because she let out a snorting laugh. She shook her head. "Why are you so mistrusting, Mr Mulrooney?" As if to emphasise his shortcomings she squeezed back against the windscreen and reached under the counter, dramatically producing a book which she placed theatrically in front of him. "This is new. I kept it especially for you before anyone else could take it." She smiled jubilantly. "You won't have read it before."

If she was expecting an effusive demonstration of gratitude she was to be sadly disappointed. Arthur focussed on the cover, reading the title, IN THE FOOTSTEPS OF MARCO POLO. A barely perceptible quiver of anticipation tickled his insides, until a niggle of suspicion swept it away. She was right, it was new and he hadn't read it, but what did she expect in return.

"Thank you," he mumbled, the words tripping clumsily across his lips. He went to pick it up, but she took hold of his wrist, sending a wave of panic surging through him. She wanted payment.

He was almost relieved when she fixed him with her severest stare. "You naughty boy, you know you can't have it until it's been date-stamped. And I always thought you were a stickler for rules." She continued to hold him with her penetrating eyes until he was forced to bow his head in apologetic shame. For what seemed like an eternity she held on to his wrist until she suddenly threw her head back and the charabanc shook with her raucous laughter. Reduced to a shambling wreck, Arthur was on the point of leaving without the book when she whipped a handkerchief from the sleeve of her tweed jacket and dabbed her streaming eyes. "Oh, I'm sorry Mr Mulrooney, but I can't help myself sometimes. If only you weren't so sensitive I think you and me would get on like a house on fire."

Arthur had never quite understood the notion that a blazing building could in any way represent compatibility, although the woman in front of him was no less frightening than facing a raging conflagration. He hoped he had never given her any reason to believe she may be right.

Recovering her composure she flipped open the cover of the book and in what she probably perceived as an act of seduction she slowly picked up the date stamp and breathed on it heavily before impressing the flysheet.

"So, Mr Mulrooney, tell me what has been happening with you since the last time I was here. Not been getting up to any mischief, I hope." Her red painted lips trumpeted into an exaggerated pout which made her look like a feeding fish.

Even through his thick beard Arthur's cheeks glowed like a beacon. "Nothing! Why, what have you heard?"

Placing her hands on her expansive hips she gave an exasperated sigh. "For pity's sake, man, why do you have to take everything so literally? I wouldn't mind betting that burning your morning toast is probably the most exciting thing that's happened in your dull life." She pushed the book dismissively towards him. "Here, take it and be on your way. This is the last time I put myself out for you."

Arthur felt wretched, like a scolded schoolboy. Suddenly he was the culprit and not the victim. "I apologise," he mumbled, picking up the book and pretending to read the introduction. "The book looks very interesting, I'm grateful to you."

Whether genuine or not, her hurt expression remained firm and it wouldn't have been too much trouble for her to conjure up a few tears to teach him a lesson. "I know what you think of me, Mr Mulrooney, that I'm coarse and brash, a man eater." Through lowered eyes she studied him for a reaction, but got none, so she tried a long, self-pitying sigh. "But it's all show, you know, a façade to hide behind." She sighed again, this time punctuating it with a sob. "Deep down I'm just a weak, sensitive woman who has no man to look out for her, and I put up this barrier just to protect myself."

Moist, demure eyes blinked at him across the counter as Arthur continued to study the book Even though he felt she was playing him like a well-used violin he couldn't help thinking there may be a modicum of truth in what she had said. It was not unusual for a timid person to hide behind a screen of bravado. He did not pretend to be a student of human behaviour, preferring to take people at face value. So, was it time to re-evaluate his attitude.

Fortunately, he was saved from the dilemma when he heard the bus approaching at a more sedate pace than the charabanc. Hiding his relief behind a weak and sickly smile, he closed the book. "I have to go, I'm meeting Doctor Wallace off the bus." It sounded like a pathetic excuse as he jerked his head towards the door. "Thank you again for the book."

Before she had the opportunity to play further with his emotions he scurried down the steps and walked briskly down the road to where the bus had stopped. Without looking back he could feel her accusing eyes boring into him and he dared not contemplate what dangerous thoughts were going through her mind. The sight of George stepping down off the bus, however, set his mind off in a different direction and for the time being, at least, Florence Merryweather no longer existed.

"Well, I didn't expect a welcoming committee." George's expression, in fact, gave no sign of surprise as he extended a hand to his friend. "After all, I've only been gone a day."

Arthur casually waved the book in the air. "No, I was only up here for the library. I saw the bus coming so I thought we could walk down together."

"Of course," replied George, with a hint of scepticism in his voice as he gave Arthur a sideways glance, "but you don't mind if we stop in the pub first. I could do with a pint after that journey."

Arthur shrugged his shoulders. Anxious to question George about his trip, and to start reading his book, he would preferred to have gone straight home, but that was just him being selfish so he followed George into the gloomy, smoke laden interior of the pub.

There were no more than a half dozen customers spread around the small bar area and a noticeable lull in the muted conversations settled over the room as the two men entered.

George gave the other patrons his customary welcoming smile while Arthur tried to remain as inconspicuous as possible, which was difficult given his height. There was a knotting in his stomach when he caught sight of Stan Jessop glowering at him from the far corner of the bar.

"My treat," declared George cheerfully, oblivious to his friend's discomfort, "and you can tell me what's been happening while I've been away." He raised his hand in acknowledgement as Joe Butler appeared behind the counter from the kitchen. "Good afternoon landlord, two pints of your best mild if you please."

"Heard you were away," said Joe as he pulled the pints. "Just got back?"

"Yes, and pleased to be. I'd forgotten how noisy and smelly Exeter can be after living down here. Lots more cars on the road than I remember."

"No, can't beat the rich aroma of sea air and cow shit." Joe gave a loud guffaw until an icy stare and a rebuking snort from his wife silenced him.

With the landlord returning to the kitchen to face the wrath of his wife George raised his glass to Arthur before taking a large gulp of beer. "Ah, that's better. Now, how are things?"

"What things," Arthur snapped back testily. Why did everyone assume something had happened in his life that was worthy of sharing? "You're the one with all the news, dashing off to the city all of a sudden on some secret mission." He waited in vain for a response. "Well, are you going to tell me?"

Infuriatingly, George simply beamed back at him. "All in good time, and not in here."

Arthur sipped at his beer in sullen silence, conscious all the while that Stan Jessop was still staring in his direction. "We should be getting back," he said eventually with his glass only half empty.

"I think it's going to rain again soon and I don't want us getting soaked."

George peered out of the window, although it was impossible to see much through the grime covered glass. "It won't rain, at least not until later. You're in no particular hurry, are you?"

Since his life was totally devoid of any urgency Arthur felt it was pointless to offer an argument. "No, not really, it's just that I'm keen to get started on this…" His excuse was cut short by the sudden unwelcome appearance of Stan Jessop at his side.

"Sorry to interrupt, gents," he said with disarming cordiality, addressing himself to George, "but I just wanted to say welcome back, Doc. It's just a shame you weren't around yesterday when you were needed." He regarded Arthur with less friendly eyes. "Luckily your mate here was around to help us out, looked after my little girl good and proper, he did."

Mystified, George looked from one to the other for an explanation and as Arthur gazed uncomfortably at the floor it was left to Stan to oblige. "I suppose I owe you a drink for what you did, but as I'm a bit financially embarrassed at the moment perhaps one of you would do the honours." It sounded more like a demand than an invitation.

George stared pointedly at his friend. "Well?"

"I didn't bring any money with me. I didn't expect to…"

"Not that," snapped George, unsure which of the two men had irritated him most. "I want to know what went on while I was away."

Stan shrugged his shoulders. "No good asking me, Doc, I wasn't there. I only know what I was told, and that weren't much, so I wouldn't mind betting I don't know the half of it either." He gave Arthur a questioning look. "So, I reckon a drink might help things along."

George noticed they were attracting the unwelcome attention of the other customers and, in particular, the landlady who had been drawn out of her kitchen. "I think you were right, it is time we were going." He threw back the last of his beer and took Arthur by the arm.

"Not until I hear from him what he's been getting up to with my wife and kid," said Stan, putting himself between the two men and the door. His sudden move made Arthur start and the book slipped from under his arm and fell to the floor. Stan smirked as he kicked it away. "And I'm sure all these nosey bastards would too."

Angered more by the mistreatment of the book than the accusation Arthur shook his arm free and bent to retrieve the book. "I'm sure whatever your wife told you would have been the truth," he breathed, with more passion than George had ever witnessed in his friend. "Perhaps you should trust her more." Without waiting for George he pushed past the man and threw open the door, striding from the pub with the other occupants staring after him, disappointment clear in their expressions. Giving them all a reproving look George hurried after him.

Arthur's long legs and his brooding mood had carried him fifty yards along the road and he had reached Mrs Metcalfe's shop before George caught up with him, wheezing loudly from the exertion. The heated exchange that was about to follow already had an audience when the shopkeeper spotted them and decided the display of fruit and vegetables outside required her urgent attention.

"Now, would you mind telling me what's been going on," demanded George breathlessly, once again holding on to Arthur's arm to prevent him from moving any further.

Beneath the thick beard Arthur's jaw was set firm as he stared angrily into the distance, trying to assemble a suitable reply. He took a deep breath and compressed his lips. "I should have thought you knew me well enough to know it wouldn't be anything improper."

Conscious that Mrs Metcalfe was paying more attention to them than her root vegetables George led his friend at a more sedate pace towards the top of the hill. "I'm not accusing you of anything, you stupid man, I just want to know what that Jessop chap was talking about."

By the time they started their descent Arthur had composed himself sufficiently to give a calm and detailed account of what had taken place with Mrs Jessop and her daughter.

"And that's all there is to it?" pressed George when he had finished.

"Yes, that's all there is to it," repeated Arthur emphatically. "What would you like me to say, that I'm having some sort of secret tryst with Mrs Jessop like her husband is suggesting?"

George almost burst out laughing at the idea, but in deference to his friend's overly sensitive nature he held back. "Good grief, of course not! You're old enough to be her father,"

And the child's grandfather, thought Arthur. He had stopped short of telling George about that part of what had gone on the previous day. "I don't know why, but that man has never liked me, and I have to say the feeling is entirely mutual. He's a brutish oaf who doesn't deserve any wife, especially the one he's got."

"I quite agree, and from what you've told me there's nothing you could have done differently, apart from turning your back on that poor child and sending them away, and you haven't got it in you to do that. "

They had just crossed the bridge onto the harbour and Arthur was about to expand on his opinion of Stan Jessop when he suddenly stopped dead, causing George to bump into him. Coming towards them was someone they both instantly recognised, despite the scarf that covered her head. One arm of her raincoat hung empty and swung from side to side as she walked urgently up to them, her pretty face distorted by a mix of pain and relief.

"Mrs Jessop, what are you doing down here?" asked Arthur, instinctively looking about for some sign of her husband, even though they had left him in the pub not thirty minutes earlier.

"And what happened to your arm," added George, indicating the bulge beneath the front of her raincoat. "You had better come home with me so I can have a look at it."

"It's nothing," she said dismissively before turning to Arthur. "I only came to warn you that my husband knows it was you and not the doctor who looked after Rosie yesterday so, if you see him and he says anything it would only make things worse if you try to deny it for my sake."

George gave a wry smile. "It's a little too late for that I'm afraid, my dear. We've just left your husband in the pub and he made it clear to everyone in there what he thought about it." He reached out to gently pat her injured arm. "And I suppose this is the result of him finding out?"

She refused to meet his questioning gaze. "I fell, that's all. I'm sure it will be all right in a day or so. Anyway, I have to get back to meet Rosie out of school."

"It would still be best to let the doctor have a look, it may be broken," said Arthur, weighed down with a burden of responsibility for what he knew was no accident. "You can't be too careful, and there's plenty of time before school finishes."

"That's settled then," said George firmly, taking her by the good arm and leading her back along the harbour. "It will only take a few minutes."

George pushed open the door to his cottage and eased Daisy into the small, neat living room. "Let me help you with that," he said as she fumbled one-handed with the buttons of her coat. He slid it from her shoulders and laid it over the back of an armchair before casting a professional eye over the improvised sling she had fashioned from an old head scarf. "Well, I don't think I could have done a better job myself," he grinned, trying not to sound patronising.

He made her sit as he supported her arm before carefully removing the sling. Tenderly feeling the area around her shoulder he slowly flexed the arm, moving it around in various positions as she let out little gasps of pain accompanied by facial contortions. All the while Arthur watched in silence, suppressing a growing feeling of bitterness towards the man he knew was responsible for her injury. But he also accepted some blame for his part in her predicament even though, as George had said, there was nothing else he could have done. It was of little comfort, especially since George had also pointed out that what went on between husband and wife was beyond their sphere of interference.

"There doesn't seem to be anything broken," announced George when he had finished his examination, "but you may need to rest that shoulder for a few days."

Daisy made a face that suggested there would be little chance of that. "I'll do my best."

"Are you going to be all right?" asked Arthur, breaking his silence as the doctor helped her on with her coat,

Daisy raised her eyebrows as she gingerly rotated her injured arm. "It might take me a bit longer to do things, but I'll manage. I have to."

"I'm sure you will, but I wasn't talking about…"

"I know what you were talking about, Mr Mulrooney," she interrupted with a grimace, looking down at the floor to hide whatever it was she felt. "I know what you both must think of me, putting up with someone like Stan, but what choice do I have? I get precious little from him, but what I do get keeps a roof over Rosie's head and food on the table. It's not her fault she's got him for a father, so a few cuts and bruises are a small price to pay for those things. And it's not as if we have any other family we can turn to." As soon as those last words were uttered she remembered what Rosie had said how they may resonate with Arthur.

While Arthur was still considering how to respond, George saved him the trouble. "No one here is judging you, my dear. We know how difficult it must be for you, and you have our sympathies, for what good that will do. If there was anything we could do then you only need to ask."

As she made for the door Arthur knew it was neither sympathy nor hollow platitudes that would make life better for her, and when she gave them both a warm smile of gratitude he felt an overwhelming urge to take her in his arms and tell her everything would change.

"I know you both mean well, and it helps to know I have someone I can tell my troubles to, but it's my life and I have to cope with it the best way I can." With that she turned away and hurried off along the harbour.

The two men watched her until she was out of sight before Arthur spoke. "I don't accept that nothing can be done to help her," he said, his voice heavy with resentment. "Why can't she go to the police and tell them what he's like?"

George puffed his cheeks and shook his head. "And what do you think they would do? They would question him and he would deny everything, and when they leave he would take out his spite on her again. That's why they rarely involve themselves in domestic matters, it's just one person's word against another and if it doesn't affect anyone outside the house they prefer to turn a blind eye until something terrible happens." As soon as he finished he realised his mistake and spun round to face Arthur. "I'm so sorry, I didn't…"

"It's fine, George." Behind his back Arthur clenched and unclenched his hands, tormented by his memories.

Chapter Twenty-One

Stan Jessop lost no time in eliciting what sympathetic support he could from the small gathering in the pub. Had he any money in his pocket a pint all round would almost certainly have guaranteed a willing ear, but as it was he would have to rely on a persuasive tongue. Of course he would never openly accuse Mr Mulrooney of any impropriety regarding his wife, and far be it for him to suggest that his wife would even consider straying from the marital path, especially with a man old enough to be her father. No, he was far too fair minded for that. Unsurprisingly none of those listening were keen to offer a nod of agreement at his last remark, although there was a low murmur of assent at Stan's observation that Arthur Mulrooney was an odd sort of fellow who deserved to be viewed with a certain amount of suspicion.

"I'm not saying he's a wrong 'un," said Stan, leaning with his back against the counter and addressing the small crowd who had suddenly found his expanding opinions on the relative newcomer to their community far more absorbing than their own conversations, "but what do we really know about him? I mean, who would choose to come and live in a place like this unless they wanted to hide from something?"

"There's nothing wrong with this place," commented one of the customers, an octogenarian with no teeth who had lived in the village all his life and had probably never ventured more than twenty yards beyond its boundaries. "I like it here."

Behind an ingratiating smile Stan willed the old boy to drop dead. "Of course you do, and so do I, but we're the sort of men who belong her, men used to working the land." He chose to ignore a snigger of sarcasm from behind him as he continued. "You've only got to look at him to know he's never laboured a day in his life."

"Weren't he supposed to be in the merchant navy," one of the old men ventured. "Maybe that's why he came here, to be near the sea."

"Merchant navy, my arse!" mocked Stan, staring the man down. "I wouldn't mind betting the bloke don't know one end of a boat from another."

"I've always thought there was something a bit odd about him." Queenie Butler had been drawn out of the kitchen to add her weight to a developing piece of gossip. "Said the same to you more than once, haven't I Joe?"

Joe was reluctant to be drawn into the debate, especially if it meant agreeing with the likes of Stan Jessop. Also, as a landlord, he knew the value of sitting on the fence in all matters relating to religion, politics and his customers. "You say a lot of things, my love, but it doesn't mean they are all necessarily true."

Not to be deterred Queenie gave her husband a sour look and returned to the discussion. "I've never been one to pass judgement on anyone without good cause, but there's something about that man I've never been able to put my finger on. Not that I'm saying it's anything bad mind, but…"

"But something not quite right nevertheless. You're a very perceptive woman, missus, I've always thought that." Stan gave Queenie a patronising smile as he slyly slid his empty glass across the counter towards her. "I suppose that's what makes a good landlady."

Before his wife could demonstrate that she was not quite as perceptive as Stan would have her believe, Joe whipped the glass away and put it in the sink. "Time now gentlemen please. If you could just drink up." He noted with satisfaction the disappointment in Stan's face. If Stan thought he had found a gullible recruit to whatever malicious grievance he had, Joe would soon disabuse him of that. Later he would remind his wife that Arthur Mulrooney was a close friend of Doctor Wallace on whom she relied to solve the myriad medical complaints that constantly blighted her life. Joe smiled to himself as he watched the customers filing out the door with a smug looking Stan Jessop bringing up the rear.

***

It had started raining again by the time Daisy reached the top of the hill. Her shoulder ached, but she was relieved it was only bruised and not broken. But that was the only comfort as she scanned the road and village green for any sign of her husband. She shuddered when she thought of the consequences if he found out where she had been. She had gone down to the harbour knowing the risks, but Stan had gone off to work that morning and wasn't expected back until later. It was only right that she warn her new friend and the risk had seemed acceptable. She wondered if all women suffered as she did. Was the balance of equality in marriage weighted in favour of all men, or was it just her? Anyway, what was the point of worrying about such things? It was up to her to accept her situation or do something about it. But what?

She had reached the shop, and needing a few things before she picked Rosie up from school she pushed her problems to the back of her mind. Mrs Metcalfe ignored the bell that jingled above the door as Daisy entered, choosing instead to rearrange a display of canned vegetables on the shelving to one side of the shop. She had seen Daisy coming along the road and was curious to know, as Stan would be, why it was from that direction. And was that an empty sleeve hanging limp at Daisy's side? So, Mrs Metcalfe hid her curiosity amongst the tins of peas.

It was only when Daisy was standing in front of the counter did she drag herself away from the shelves, conspicuously not noticing the empty sleeve. "Mrs Jessop, what can I do for you?"

Daisy pulled her purse from her coat pocket together with a folded carrier bag. "I just need a loaf and some lard, please," she replied, putting her purse on the counter and shaking open the carrier bag. She gave the shopkeeper a wan smile. "I was going to make some chips for tea, but I'm not sure I will now. I'll see."

Mrs Metcalfe nodded wisely before her beady eyes widened in feigned shock. "Oh dear, you look like you've been in the wars. How did that happen?"

Daisy glanced down at the sleeve as though the fact surprised her too. "Oh that! I had a fall, it's nothing really, not broken." She placed the carrier bag on top of the stack of firewood in front of the counter and opened her purse one handed, shaking out the contents on the counter. "Can you take what you need?"

A little further along the road Stan turned up the collar of his coat and stepped out from the shelter of the pub doorway, marching hunched and purposefully towards the shop. He had been standing outside the pub since Joe Butler had bolted the door behind him, trying to decide if there was time to get home and torment his wife for an hour before she collected the brat from school. He was still undecided when he caught sight of someone who looked remarkably like his wife appear over the brow of the hill, watching her as she went into the shop. He hawked and spat onto the road; he had been far too lenient with her.

By the time he reached the shop the rain had soaked into the shoulders of his jacket, adding more fuel to his burning temper. Mrs Metcalfe saw him through the window as she was counting out Daisy's money and considered offering a word of warning, but instead, said nothing. He pushed open the door and stood dripping water onto the mat. Sensing his presence, Daisy turned to face him, unaware of what he knew but still bracing herself for some caustic remark. He took off his cap and ran his fingers through his lank hair, offering up a disarming smile.

"Afternoon, missus," he said, directing his oily greeting at the shopkeeper, "nice bit of weather we're having." He replaced his cap and held out a hand to his wife, his brow creasing with concern. "There you are, love, I've been looking for you." He placed a protective arm round her shoulders, making her tense as he faced Mrs Metcalfe. "I was worried about her, with her arm and that."

"I was just picking up a few bits before collecting Rosie from school." She took her purse from Mrs Metcalfe, wondering if the woman had been taken in by his act and deciding that she had.

Stan shook his head with apparent despair as he patted the bulge beneath Daisy's coat. "Can't be trusted, you know, always falling over or bumping into things. She's really going to hurt herself one day." He hid the menacing glance from the shopkeeper's view.

Mrs Metcalfe's expression gave no indication that she had recognised the veiled threat, but it had not been lost on Daisy. She picked up the carrier bag and gave the woman a brief nod of thanks before hurrying towards the door with Stan close behind.

Outside she half walked and half ran along the road in the direction of the school, conscious that they were being watched through the shop window. Before she had gone too far, however, Stan caught up with her and dragged her to a standstill.

"I don't suppose there's any point asking you where you've been all day." His face was almost touching hers, his expression, murderous. "You'd only lie to me like you always do."

She turned away from him, no longer caring what he did or didn't know. "I went to see the doctor. I thought my arm might be broken."

"But not just the doctor though. I don't suppose that weird friend of his was too far away?"

"Yes, he was there, but even if I said he wasn't you wouldn't have believed me. Anyway, I don't know what you've got against him; he's been really kind to me and Rosie."

He cupped her chin firmly in his hand and twisted her head back to face him. "Yeah, well men like that don't do anything for nothing." He cuffed away the rain that dripped from the peak of his cap. "And seeing as you ain't got any money it makes me wonder what he wants in return."

Daisy felt the hair on the back of her neck prickle and her stomach churned in disgust. It was the sort of remark she should have expected from him, but it was no less sickening to hear the words and proved once again, if proof was necessary, that he judged everyone by his own low moral standards. Too incensed even to reply she forcibly shoved him away and strode off towards the school.

"If you think this is finished with, you're wrong," he shouted after her.

Daisy laboured under no such illusion, it would never be finished with until she and Rosie broke away from his clutches and the two of them could live a life free from abuse and fear. That comforting thought lingered with her until she reached the school.

***

For several minutes after Daisy had left, Arthur sank deeper into a silent mire of despondency that lasted until George could stand it no longer. "For pity's sake man, will you stop brooding over something you can do nothing about? Of course I understand how you feel and that you want to help her, but Mrs Jessop's problems are her own and the more you try to interfere the more difficult you will make it for her. It's a sad indictment of the society we live in, but that's just the way it is." He studied his friend's brooding features. "It isn't anything more than that, is it?"

The creases in Arthur's brow deepened, and when he spoke, the words snapped with irritability. "What makes you say that, can't I show a bit of concern without there being more to it? Anyway, can you stand there and tell me you're not bothered by what happens to her and the child."

George shook his head with a despairing grimace. "There's a difference between being concerned and fretting over what you think you can do about it. Of course I feel the same as you, but I've seen enough of these situations to know how interfering generally makes things worse. Take my advice, Arthur, unless she asks for your help, steer well clear." He went through to the kitchen leaving Arthur feeling like a chastised schoolboy. "I don't know about you but I could do with a cup of tea. It's been a long, tiring day and I'm getting too old for any more stress in my life."

Arthur stood in the doorway, his head bent to avoid the low opening. "But not too old to go rushing off to Exeter on some secret mission," he said with more than a touch of rebuke.

"Oh, I wondered when we would get back to that," replied George, his red cheeks bulging with a smug grin. "I had rather hoped that with all the other excitement going on in your life you wouldn't mention anything about that today."

"Well, now that I have perhaps you would care to tell me what it was all about."

George stared at the kettle on the stove as though it would provide him with the answer. "No," he said after a lengthy consideration, "not today. There's been far too much drama since I got back." He faced Arthur and wagged a finger. "Tomorrow, I'll tell you tomorrow. In fact, I'll do better than that. If it's not raining I'll show you. Now, can we just enjoy a pleasant conversation without getting into an argument?"

Arthur gave a desultory shrug and went to sit down.

***

That night Rosie lay in her bed sobbing as she listened to the noises coming through the wall from the other room. She knew that daddy's special punishment was not reserved solely for her and that very soon mummy would be crying too. No matter how many times she had been forced to listen it would never harden her young heart to the pain. She shuffled over to make room in her bed, just in case.

Daisy felt the metallic taste of blood in her mouth as she bit deeper into her bottom lip. It wasn't just the pain, although the degrading act hurt far more than the usual rough, abusive sex she was forced to endure, it was the sheer hatred she felt towards him and the humiliating knowledge that she had been given little choice. Stan had made it horrifyingly clear what would happen to Rosie, so Daisy remained silent and made her plans.

Chapter Twenty-Two

Arthur woke up early the following morning feeling irritable, which was hardly surprising considering he had fallen asleep the night before in the same ill temper. All he had wanted from the previous evening was to immerse himself in the pages of his book and spend a pleasant night dreaming that he had accompanied Marco Polo on his trek into China, and more than once saving the life of the great adventurer, and so giving himself a place in history. But that had all been ruined, not just by George and his childish refusal to share the secret behind his trip to Exeter, which was annoying just by itself, but also by the nagging conviction that the suffering of Mrs Jessop and her daughter could not be eased by his intervention. He had lay awake long into the night restlessly turning over all the possibilities and reaching no laudable conclusion.

It was still dark outside when he got out of bed and dressed. Downstairs he put the kettle on, ready to embrace the belief that a cup of tea would dissolve the troubles that plagued his mind. He thought about breakfast, but decided he had no appetite, picked up his book, and put it down again. He went over to the little bay window and peered out, even though there was little to see in the pre-dawn gloom, except that it had stopped raining.

With another two or three hours still before he was due to meet up with his friend he decided he would go for a walk to try and clear his head. Just being outside always made him feel better, and as he stepped out onto the harbour and breathed in the salty air that blew in off the sea he felt some of the tension melt away. He strode along the harbour, slowing briefly as he passed George's cottage while he wondered if his friend had suffered a troubled night. The cottage was in darkness and Arthur concluded, with some resentment, that the doctor's conscience was probably clear. He marched on, determined that when the two of them got together later he would have walked any lingering angst from his system.

All was still with only the gentle lapping of the sea against the harbour wall breaking the silence. As he walked he conjured up an image, as he had done on numerous occasions since moving into the community, of how different it must have been in the heyday of the fishing fleet. The hustle and bustle of catches being unloaded, fish gutted and packed in ice, the shouted banter amongst the fishermen and their wives. Enid Gulliver and her husband would have been at the heart of all that activity, far removed from their current situation. That thought brought him abruptly back to the present, and having reached the bridge he realised he had been hasty in rushing from the house the way he had and that he had no idea of where he might go,

He leant against the low wall of the bridge and stared down at the river as it disappeared beneath him. After the recent rain the water rushed in a frothy brown torrent, carrying with it a variety of debris collected from the river banks on its journey down the hill. The turbulent current rushing angrily under the bridge reflected his own mood, but where the river diluted its anger as it merged into the sea there was no outlet for the swirling turmoil in his head. He sat on the wall, massaging his brow with the tips of his fingers, overwhelmed by a feeling of impotency. This was not how he imagined his life would be when he arrived in the small, insular community of the harbour. He had no wish to involve himself with their lives, beyond the occasional errands he was able to run, and it was the very privacy of their lives that he found most attractive. And it was his own privacy that he cherished most.

George had warned him, told him, of the dangers of becoming involved, which should have been sufficient, given his own experience, and as he sat on the wall vivid memories rushed back at him. He sat upright so suddenly that he almost threw himself backwards off the wall and into the river. His hands gripped the brickwork and he fell forward, gulping in air, his heart pounding against the wall of his chest. He slid down off the wall and stood on unsteady legs, all thoughts of walking gone. After a few moments of recovery he set off at a sedate pace towards home.

***

Daisy rolled onto her side in preparation of getting out of bed. She had no idea how long she had been laying on her back staring through the darkness at the ceiling. With all the thoughts that had been running through her mind it had been impossible to sleep for more than a few minutes at a time. Most, if not all, the thoughts had concerned Stan in some way or another, and more than a few had involved what she wanted to do to him. The idea of putting rat poison in his food and watching him suffer a long and miserable death appealed most but offered the least probable method of escaping detection. The more sensible solution would be an accidental death, a fall down the stairs or choking on his own vomit while in a drunken stupor, but while one did not guarantee his death, the other was more difficult to arrange. And what about Rosie? How could it possibly benefit her if her mother was imprisoned, or worse, for murder?

She sat on the edge of the bed, her head in her hands while Stan snored contentedly behind her. It was an unwelcome reminder of what he had subjected her to the night before and she wondered how much more she could hate him before she finally snapped. The thought terrified her.

It was too early to get up, yet being so close to her husband filled her with revulsion. She should have gone into Rosie's room once Stan had finished with her, but the state she was in would have been too distressing for her precious daughter to witness. Instead she had stayed in her own bed, allowing her loathing to mature.

Rosie was still sleeping soundly when Daisy peered round the bedroom door which was comforting, although she wondered how much the child had heard through the wall. She also wondered how much damage had been done to her young mind. A cold shudder ran through Daisy's body as she crept down the stairs.

***

George stretched, yawned and rubbed the sleep from his eyes. He groped for his glasses, put them on and peered at the clock on the bedside table. Six thirty. It was still early but he was too excited to go back to sleep so he climbed out of bed, put on his dressing gown and went to the window. Not that he expected to see much outside at that time of the morning, but he wanted to check on the weather, hoping the rain of the previous day had cleared away, if only for the morning. Even though dawn had not yet crept over the eastern horizon the stars that shone in the small expanses of clear sky were enough to give him hope. He smiled with satisfaction and, if he was honest, a small amount of smugness. He knew how much Arthur resented the secrecy behind his trip to Exeter, although George was sure when everything was revealed later his friend would be sufficiently impressed to forgive him. He was about to turn away from the window and go down to make a cup of tea when something caught his eye. A movement down on the harbour made him press his face closer to the cold glass, before drawing away quickly when he recognised the unmistakable figure of Arthur striding past his cottage.

He stood for a few moments in his bedroom, scratching his head, wondering where on earth his friend could be going at the time of the morning. Only one answer came back and it wiped away the reverie he was feeling. George's first thought was to get dressed and chase after him, but given the disparity of their levels of fitness, and Arthur's long legs, he knew his friend would be halfway up the hill before he left the house and he would have no chance of catching him. All he could do was to wait and pray that he was wrong and that Arthur was merely taking some early morning exercise.

Downstairs he went through the motions of making breakfast while his mind was elsewhere, turning over all the dangerous consequences of his friend's involvement with Mrs Jessop and her vindictive and violent husband. He shook his head at his own failure to convince Arthur of his folly and, more selfishly, that his plans for the morning had been ruined. His ill mood was broken by a sharp rap on the door.

"I saw your light on so I thought I would make sure you are all right," said Arthur, blinking at the light from the living room while George peered back wide eyed with surprise. "You're not ill, are you?"

"No, I'm not ill," snapped George, recovering his composure, "but I could ask you the same. Where do you think you were going this time of the morning?" He stepped aside, allowing Arthur inside. "I saw you going past a little while ago and I was worried you were going to do something stupid."

Arthur took off his coat and threw it over the back of a chair. "Like what? I couldn't sleep so I thought I would go for a walk."

"Well, it wasn't a very long walk," replied George curtly as he went into the kitchen to deal with the boiling kettle. "I was worried because I thought it had something to do with that woman and her child."

Arthur followed him. "At this time of day? What did you imagine I was going to do?"

George turned to face his friend, studying him in the brighter kitchen light. "If you don't mind my saying, Arthur, you look a bit off colour. You're not coming down with something, are you?"

"No, I'm fine," he replied, conscious that a few minutes before he felt close to collapse. "I just changed my mind about going for a walk, that's all."

As Arthur returned to the living room George busied himself making the tea, both men brooding with discontent. When he finally joined his friend George did his best to pretend that normality had returned to their strained relationship.

"What is it like out, do you think it is going to rain?" he casually asked as he poured the tea.

Arthur still eyed him with a degree of reserved annoyance. "Does it matter, or is it all to do with your big secret?"

"You really are in a foul mood, Arthur, aren't you?" After pouring the tea George sat back in his chair and studied his friend. "Who is it you are really angry with, me or yourself?"

"I don't know what you're talking about." Arthur picked up his cup and sipped the tea.

George gave an exasperated shake of his head. "Yes you do, and it's getting a little tiring. You've always been a bit of a moody bugger and I've put up with it because it's part of who you are, but since you've got involved with that woman you've got worse." His hard expression softened as he saw the sorrowful look on Arthur's face. "It wasn't meant to be a criticism, Arthur, it's good that you care, but there really is nothing you can do that will help."

Arthur's thoughts were hidden behind the tea cup as he continued to sip at the beverage that was too hot to drink. By small degrees he seemed to relax, settling back in the chair and nursing the cup in his hands. "So," he said finally, "when are you going to let me into your big secret?"

"When we've had some breakfast," replied George with a sigh of relief. "I'll make us some toast and then we'll go for a walk, and everything will be explained."

***

An hour later the two men had crossed the bridge with George leading them along the narrow path that ran between the beach and the pine trees beyond. With a number of low, dark clouds still threatening rain, night still reigned beneath the trees and it was only George's familiarity with their route that saved them from being mired in the thick undergrowth as they left the beach and headed inland up the gently rising ground. The thick carpet of damp pine needles felt like sponge underfoot, softening their tread into almost silence, and it was only when they left the belt of conifers and entered the area populated by the other autumn denuded trees did their way become clearer.

George stopped suddenly and held up a hand to prevent Arthur from lurching into him. "You don't mind if we stop a minute, I just need to catch my breath."

Arthur scrutinised the overgrown path ahead of them. "We're going up to Luxford House," he said, turning to George with an inquisitive look. "Why are we going there, what's it got to do with you going to Exeter?"

"All in good time, Arthur," he replied breathlessly, holding onto a low branch for support.

Arthur huffed impatiently, manoeuvring around his friend to take the lead. "You really are infuriating sometimes, George. Can we just get on with it?" He strode off through the undergrowth with George struggling in his wake to catch up.

When they reached the edge of the grounds the lawn and shrubs that had appeared sadly neglected at the end of the summer when they were last there now looked depressingly forlorn, which reminded Arthur of a long abandoned cemetery. By the time they had trudged through the long, wet grass the bottoms of their trousers flapped noisily against their shoes, spraying droplets of water in all directions.

Arthur stopped in front of the columned portico that covered the entrance and stared up at the once grand façade, his hands on his hips while he waited for George to join him.

"Well, here we are, so now you can tell me what it is we're doing here." He waited, his curiosity strained as George waddled puffing and panting past him and up the steps to the door. "For pity's sake, what are you doing?"

Ignoring his friend's demanding words George rummaged in his coat pocket and pulled out a key which he jiggled in the lock before it finally turned. With a triumphant grin spread across his flushed, chubby face he turned to face Arthur. "Are you going to just stand there or are you coming in?" With some effort he pushed against the heavy door and it swung slowly open, the ancient hinges complaining noisily. He beckoned to Arthur to follow him inside.

The marble tiled floor of the large entrance hall was largely unrecognisable beneath several years of accumulated dirt and grime, with many of the tiles cracked and broken from unsympathetic use by previous occupants. The wide mahogany staircase that swept up in an arc to the galleried landing was in an equally deplorable state, some of the ornate carving broken away and part of the balustrade completely missing. It was easy to see what an impression it must have made in its heyday, but now only served to highlight how far the deterioration had progressed.

Arthur stood next to his friend and looked about him with a feeling of sadness, the reason why he was there momentarily forgotten. He went to walk towards the staircase but George placed a restraining hand on his arm.

"I shouldn't if I were you, the stairs might not be safe. At least that's what I was told."

Arthur swung round to face him. "Who told you? What's going on, George, why are we here?"

Without replying straight away George walked across the hall and into one of the adjoining rooms with two wide bow windows that overlooked the front of the house. On the far side of the room a once imposing French-style fireplace dominated one wall, large chunks of the surround broken away with pieces lying across the hearth and over the floor.

"Look at that," said George, waving his hand at the fireplace and sighing heavily. "Just think what that must have looked like."

"I know, it's heart-breaking," agreed Arthur, picking up a piece of marble, "but you still haven't answered my question."

"You know, the last time I set foot in here was with Mary. It was a year after the war ended and the orphanage was just about to close. It was also the last time Mary came on holiday here, she died the following year." He stared reflectively at nothing in particular as though recalling that last time. Behind his glasses a tear blurred his vision, although the image of his wife in that room was crystal clear. "She loved this house and made me promise I would do what I could to save it."

"How did she think you could do that?"

George shook his head. "I don't know, but I knew she was dying and I made the promise." He forced a cough to hide the tremor in his voice. "But now, hopefully, I can make it come true."

Arthur's patience had reached its limits, but he stopped short of venting his frustration in deference to his friend's fragile emotions. In a corner of the room were some empty packing cases, left behind when the last occupants moved out. Arthur turned two of them over and swept away the dust with the sleeve of his coat. He indicated for George to sit.

George nodded his appreciation and sat down next to his friend and put on a brave smile. "I'm sorry, I didn't think it would affect me like that."

Arthur dismissed the apology with a wave of his hand, unable to meet George's watery eyes. "Then perhaps we should go, if it's going to upset you." He was sure that anything George had to tell him could be said on the walk home.

"No, I've dragged you up here and now that we are here what I have to tell you will make more sense." He waved his arm around the room in an expansive gesture. "It makes it all seem very real." Arthur fought to keep his curiosity and temper under control. George turned to face him, placing a hand on his knee. "Do you remember a conversation we had a wee while ago?"

Arthur's face creased into a look of unrestrained puzzlement. "George, we've had hundreds of conversations on any number of subjects so you'll need to be a bit more specific if you want an answer."

George leant closer, his expression tight with anticipation. "We were talking about what would happen to the old folk down at the harbour when they were too old and infirm to look after themselves." He patted his chest. "And we're not getting any younger so I suppose I'm including us as well."

Arthur nodded, although it made nothing any clearer. "But what has that got to do with us being here?"

"Everything," he replied with more than a touch of excitement. "Even before we spoke about it I had this idea, but after we talked I wrote to the county council. I told them about this house and how wrong it was that it should be left to rot. I suggested what it could be used for." He waited for a spark of comprehension to show on Arthur's face, but all he got back was a blank stare. "An old folks' home!" He said jubilantly. "That's why I went to Exeter. The council wrote back to say they would consider the idea once they had a look at this place so I went there to get them along a bit. It seems they like the idea and there's a good chance work will start in the new year." He sat back on the chest with a deep breath as though he had just unburdened himself of a weighty confession.

Arthur remained tight lipped for several seconds, his mind absorbing and analysing his friend's revelation. What appeared to be the suggestion of a surprised expression flashed across his face, mixed with a touch of annoyance. "Well, you kept that to yourself I must say," he said, slowly and deliberately. "It's an admirable idea, but I don't know why you couldn't have told me about it though." He stared thoughtfully for several seconds at nothing in particular. "Did you think I may have disagreed with you?"

"The thought never crossed my mind, Arthur. Why should it?" It was George's turn to reflect. "Unless you thought it could be put to better use."

"I don't know what you mean. I've said it's an admirable idea and I meant it. Apart from us lot down at the harbour there must be enough old folk in the area to fill this place several times over. No, George, you're to be commended. I'm just disappointed you didn't feel able to tell me about it before now. I may have been able to add some weight to the idea before you went to the county council,"

Unconvinced that his friend was not being entirely truthful, George smiled benignly, making no effort to voice his doubts as he got to his feet. "Well, now you know and I'm glad you do. Keeping secrets from your friends, whatever the reason, is exhausting, not to mention, deceitful." As they left the building and George locked the door he smiled again, this time to himself.

Chapter Twenty-Three

Stan was still sleeping when Daisy left the house to take Rosie to school. If the child had heard anything of her mother's ordeal the night before she showed no outward sign. But that was of little comfort to Daisy since Rosie was well practised in concealing her emotions.

"Did you sleep well, my darling?" Daisy had asked, desperate to be reassured.

In reply Rosie had simply nodded and continued to eat her breakfast in silence. It was the silence that said the most.

As they walked to school Daisy did her best to engage her daughter in conversation and was rewarded with a single-word reply or nothing at all. By the time they reached the school gates Daisy's love for her child was finally eclipsed by her hatred for her husband. Something had to be done.

After watching Rosie crossing the playground and finally disappearing into the school with the rest of the children Daisy started walking towards home, until she realised with startling suddenness that was the last place she wanted to be all the while Stan was there. Even if he wasn't, the place held so many unhappy memories for her that it no longer felt like home.

Instead of retracing her steps across the soaking wet grass of the green she kept to the road that led through the village. She had no clear idea of what she would do or where she would go, although the thought did occur to her that Stan would wake up to an empty house and that she would be interrogated of where she had been. But she was past caring, provided he limited his vengeance to her and not Rosie. She stopped in her tracks; there was no guarantee of that.

Inside her shop Mrs Metcalfe was listening to Queenie Butler giving a lengthy account of her husband's latest failings, but the sight of the woman standing in the road outside, apparently lost, proved to be more interesting and she stopped listening. Queenie's droning tailed away as she followed the shopkeeper's gaze out of the window.

"Isn't that Mrs Jessop?" Mrs Metcalfe took a step closer to the window. "Do you think she's all right?"

"Probably forgotten what she came out for," commented Queenie. "Happens to me all the time." She gave a little chuckle. "Mind you, a night with that husband of hers and I wouldn't even remember what day it was. He's bit of a bolshie bugger but I wouldn't mind betting he makes up for it in other ways."

"Queenie! How can you even think something like that?" Mrs Metcalfe backed away from the window when she caught Daisy looking in her direction. "Poor woman, I feel sorry for her." She came out from behind the counter. "I think I'll go and see if she's all right."

"I don't think she'll thank you for sticking your nose in. I don't know the woman that well but she strikes me as being someone who keeps to herself." Queenie dropped her purse into her shopping bag and slipped her arm through the handles. "I'd leave well enough alone if I were you," she added as the shopkeeper followed her to the door. She stopped in the doorway and tipped her head towards her friend. "But let me know if you find out anything."

As she walked back towards the pub Queenie took a sly glance over her shoulder to see Mrs Metcalfe on the edge of the pavement, apparently in conversation with the woman.

"It's none of my business, dear, but are you all right? I couldn't help notice you seemed to be in a bit of a dither." As she went to cross the road Daisy made to carry on walking, turning her face away. "Have you been crying? Perhaps you would like to come inside and have a sit down."

Daisy held up a hand to hide her face and carried on walking. "No, thank you, I'm fine," she lied.

As Mrs Metcalfe continued to watch Daisy changed direction and began crossing the green towards home with the feeling that she had been forced into a decision she should have made for herself.

"Why can't people mind their own business," she muttered to herself, even though she would have welcomed the help of anyone who could save her from her miserable existence.

Angry with herself, Daisy walked slowly around the side of the house and entered by the kitchen door. She was scared of entering her own home, knowing she would have to face the very person she should have been happy to be with, the person who would painfully remind her of the degradation she had endured the night before.

There was no sign of Stan, either in the kitchen or the living room, leading her to believe he was still asleep upstairs. She could go out again without him even knowing she had been there, even though she would have to face an interrogation later. Making up her mind she went back through to the kitchen and out of the door. With a bit of luck, Stan would sleep in.

The door to the outside lavatory opened a few inches, sufficient for Stan's dark, vengeful eyes to watch her go.

***

While Arthur strode along the lane back towards the village George breathed heavily a few paces behind, willing his friend to slow down. Not a word had passed between them since leaving Luxford House, partly due to the doctor's inability to talk while his lungs struggled to take in air, but mainly because Arthur's way of dealing with any new situation was to sink into a mire of silence. Although, at the time, George felt his reasoning was sound, he now wondered if he should have taken Arthur into his confidence. Whatever his friend's faults, George knew that failing to keep a secret was not one of them.

"Can we please stop for a breather?" George called out laboriously as the lane opened out onto the road through the village. He stopped, bent forward and gulped in air. "I need to pop into the shop anyway."

Arthur continued walking, but at a slower pace. "I'll wait for you at the top of the hill," he said without looking round.

While George went to the shop Arthur stood by the dilapidated seat, gazing out towards the sea, deep in thought. There was no denying the plans George had outlined for the house would be of enormous benefit to the community, something he would have been proud to be part of, given the opportunity, and he wondered if the good doctor had a reason not to tell him. He was still debating the point when something interrupted his thoughts, something that made him turn away from the view over the coast.

The figure crossing the green towards him was still fifty yards away but immediately recognisable. He watched her approach, his thoughts now set in an entirely new direction.

"Mr Mulrooney," Daisy said when she was close enough. "I wasn't expecting to see you, but I'm glad I have."

It wasn't a greeting filled with warmth or delight, but one Arthur sensed was led by need. "Has something else happed to the child?" he asked.

Daisy shook her head. "No, nothing like that." She stopped a few paces in front of Arthur and stared down at the wet grass beneath her feet. "It's nothing really, I just needed someone to talk to and you're the only one..." Her voice trailed away into an indistinct sob and she swallowed hard. "I'm sorry, I feel a bit stupid now that I'm here."

Arthur shared in her embarrassment; dealing with emotions was not something that came easily to him. Ideally, he would have taken her in his arms for a comforting embrace and whispered reassuring words, but despite her sharing some of her unhappiness with him they were still emotional strangers, and Arthur's natural reserve would do little to progress that.

"If it's something I can help with," he prompted, timidly.

Her head remained down. How could she possibly tell him of the latest outrage against her when she could barely admit it to herself? "It's nothing, really." She threw a quick glance over her shoulder and when she finally looked at Arthur there were tears in her eyes and her voice was weak and faltering. "I should be getting home, but I don't think I can, not yet."

She was sobbing freely now and her anguished expression begged for Arthur's intervention. He shuffled with uncertainty. "I'm just waiting for George. Perhaps we could all go down for a cup of tea, if that would help."

She nodded, managing a thin smile as she wiped away the tears with the back of her hand. "That would be nice." She considered the consequences but quickly dismissed them. What more could he do to her.

Before he had to worry about what to say next Arthur noticed that George had left the shop and was walking with uncharacteristic haste towards them.

"Mrs Jessop," he said with a note of concern, "we were just talking about you, Mrs Metcalfe and me." Not bound by the same restraints as Arthur, he reached out for Daisy's hand. "Have you been crying, my dear? Mrs Metcalfe thought you had."

"I've just invited Mrs Jessop to join us for a cup of tea, George," said Arthur to save Daisy the burden of a reply. He could see Mrs Metcalfe standing in the doorway of her shop watching them. "I'm sure we will all benefit from that."

Without another word they all set off down the hill in a conspicuous silence, broken only by the gurgling of the swollen river as it rushed towards the sea, until they reached the little bridge.

"We had best go to my place," suggested George with a knowing look at his friend. It didn't take a medical eye to recognise the fragile state of Daisy's nerves. "I've just got some fresh milk."

While Arthur took Daisy's coat and settled her into an armchair George put the kettle on before returning to the living room. "I think I've got a little whisky," he said, with a sly wink at Arthur. "Perhaps a drop in the tea wouldn't go amiss."

Arthur's brow creased into a frown. "I'm not sure it would be appropriate for Mrs Jessop to collect her daughter from school smelling of drink, but I won't say no myself. It's not often you're so generous."

"I'm just talking about a wee dram, Arthur, not half a bottle, and it's my medical opinion it would do Mrs Jessop more good than harm." He looked to Daisy for her response but she showed none. "Well, I'll leave it up to you, my dear,"

While George finished making the tea Arthur sat on the sofa opposite Daisy trying to find something useful to say. It was clear she was just as uncomfortable as him and it was a relief when George finally joined them. He set the tray down and fetched the whisky from a cupboard, pouring a drop into two of the cups before placing the bottle on the tray. "Just in case you change your mind." He sat down next to Arthur and stroked his chin reflectively as he studied Daisy as though seeking a diagnosis. "Of course you don't have to tell us, my dear, but sometimes talking about a problem makes it seem not a problem at all, but it's clear something is troubling you and I don't think you would be here unless you thought we could help."

Avoiding both men Daisy stared distantly at the tray. "I think I will have some whisky in my tea," she said weakly, "it can't hurt me any more than I've been hurt already."

Arthur exchanged a worried glance with George. Had he been mistaken about the cry for help hidden in her remark? "I take it you're referring to your husband?" he enquired cautiously.

Without replying she watched George as he poured a little whisky into her cup then pulled a face at the unfamiliar taste. She took a second, larger sip. "Of course," she said after several seconds, allowing the alcohol settle her nerves. Slowly she looked up and stared at the two men in turn. "Have you ever wished anyone dead?" she asked, purposefully.

After the initial shock George tried to manage a smile. "I think we have all had thoughts like that at one time or another, but it doesn't mean anything."

Arthur nodded his agreement, although he felt in her case it was more than an idle fancy.

"I mean it," she said, vehemently, emboldened by another sip. "There's hardly a day goes by when I don't think it. I've even thought of ways I could do it, and I think I would if it wasn't for Rosie."

"If things really are that bad then you ought to consider leaving him," said George, alarmed by her positive tone.

She glared back at him through anger-filled eyes. "And where am I to go? Do you think I would still be with him if I had any choice? I have no family and no friends, so how am I supposed to look after Rosie, let alone myself?"

"Have you tried talking to him, let him know how you feel?" suggested George for want of anything better.

Daisy let out a sharp, bitter laugh. "Do you know my husband, Doctor? Stan Jessop isn't the sort of man you talk to, the only argument he understands is violence."

Neither man could refute that, having witnessed the violence first hand.

With Arthur unable, or unwilling, to contribute anything further it was left to George to offer up a placating platitude. "I'm sure he would listen to reason, my dear. Perhaps if I were to talk to him?"

The look she gave him hardly did justice to the panic she felt. "No!" She almost screamed the word, startling the two men. "He doesn't even want me talking to you, or to anyone else, let alone about something like this." The whisky appeared to have lost its efficacy as she clasped her hands together to stop them from shaking. "I shouldn't be here, I should go."

George reached across and took hold of her arm. "You're in no state to go anywhere, my dear." He glanced round at Arthur before continuing. "I don't know what's happened between you and your husband, but I know the sort of man he is and can only imagine that living with him must be difficult."

Difficult! Daisy wanted to laugh. If only they knew. She fixed George with wide, tear-filled eyes. "You can't possibly imagine, and I can't begin to tell you what it's like, for me and my daughter." The anger in her words was clear until she took a deep breath. "I know you mean well, both of you, but there is nothing you can do." She looked down at the floor to conceal the resolute expression that flashed across her careworn features. "I really did mean it when I wished him dead. I know you'll think me wicked, but that's how I feel."

"It's not for us to judge you," said Arthur softly, finally finding his voice, "and it's easy to say things we don't really mean in the heat of the moment, but…"

"I do mean it," she interrupted forcefully, glaring at him. "I mean every word of it." Again she lowered her eyes, perhaps from shame. "You don't know what it's like living with him, what he's capable of. I can't even tell you." Slowly she raised her eyes, fixing both men in turn with a tearful, pleading look. "I know I can't ask this, but I want you to promise me something." She took deep breaths to steady an emotional surge. "I want you to promise that if anything happened to me you'll make sure Rosie is safe. You won't let her stay with Stan."

For several moments Arthur and George were stunned into silence and it was the latter who recovered first.

"I'm not sure we're in any position to make a promise like that, my dear," said George in a hushed voice, trying not to sound patronising. "Anyway, why would you think something bad might happen to you, has your husband made threats against you?"

Daisy's hands clenched into tight fists in frustration and she sobbed loudly. "I shouldn't have said anything, I knew you wouldn't understand. Why would you, you're men?" She got to her feet and wiped her eyes with the back of her hand. "I'd better go before I make an even bigger fool of myself."

As she turned towards the door Arthur rushed forward to stand in her way. "It's not that we don't want to help," he said, clearly upset by her distress, "that's not what George meant. We have no legal right to intervene and it wouldn't do either you or your daughter any good if we tried." He wished he could take her in his arms and offer some reassurance, but he was incapable of either and his impotence made him angry. "If you really think you are in any danger from your husband you should go to the police."

The look she gave him matched his own anger. "And what do you think they will do? It would just be my word against his, and we know who they'll believe. Besides, it's not just what he might do that worries me." With that she edged round him and opened the door before turning back to address both of them, her lips pressed into a thin, cynical smile. "Don't worry, I'm not going to do anything stupid. Just forget everything I said."

Before either man could respond she was gone, leaving them to wonder if there was any real substance in what she had told them. Arthur was rather more convinced than his friend.

"I'm worried about her, George," he said, scratching thoughtfully at his beard as he watched through the window at her scurrying along the harbour, "I think things are much worse than we believe."

George shrugged. "Well, we both know the sort of man her husband is, and I don't doubt he makes her life difficult, but it's a common enough problem." He joined Arthur at the window, although there was nothing to see other than a bleak, grey sky above a dark green sea. "A lot of men came back from the war changed by what they had been through, some hardly recognisable from the ones who went away, so it's not for us to pass judgement on them. All we can do is to give Mrs Jessop any support we can, which might not seem much to you, or her, but I'm afraid that's the best I can offer.

Arthur knew he was right, but it gave him little comfort.

Chapter Twenty-Four

Arthur sat up in bed, unsure if he had been dreaming or whether he had been asleep at all. Since the revelations made by Mrs Jessop a few days before he had not slept well despite trying to immerse himself in the adventures of Marco Polo. Whatever the adventurer had encountered as he journeyed to the mystical East, Arthur had found it hard to dismiss matters closer to home, like the plight of Daisy Jessop.

Now he sat in the darkness of his bedroom, waiting to discover if the noise had been real or imagined. The question was answered almost straight away with another loud hammering on the door downstairs.

He leapt out of bed and went to the window, throwing it open. A blast of cold, damp air hit him in the face, sweeping away any remaining traces of sleep. He blinked away the tears that formed and stared down at the harbour.

With a raincoat covering his pyjamas, George was beckoning to him with animated urgency. "Mr Gulliver has taken a turn for the worse," he said hoarsely, "I need you to go up and call an ambulance."

Arthur nodded his reply and in little more than a minute he was dressed and outside where George waited for him.

"Sorry, Arthur," said the doctor as they walked together along the harbour, "I didn't know what else to do. The poor man should have been in hospital months ago, but you know what they're like and I'm afraid they may have left it too late." They had reached the Gulliver's cottage. "If you wouldn't mind waiting up there for the ambulance to come and show them the way, I don't think they would find it otherwise."

"Of course," replied Arthur, turning up the collar of his coat and striding off along the harbour.

Once over the bridge Arthur started up the hill at a good pace, conscious of the urgency of his mission. After the feeling of uselessness that had hung over him for the past few days it was a relief to feel needed. If there was nothing he could do for Daisy Jessop at least his efforts may give Enid Gulliver a little more time with her husband. It was a good feeling and it drove him to greater effort up the steepest part of the hill, although by the time he reached the top he was forced to slow down in order to recover his breath sufficiently to make a coherent telephone call. His chest hurt as he sucked in the cold air, but he dismissed the pain as he walked the last few yards to the telephone box.

After making the call Arthur remained in the telephone box for several minutes, leaning against the door until he felt able to support himself. It would take the ambulance at least twenty minutes to reach the village and he resolved to spend the remaining time convincing himself that his life still had some purpose. Even if there was nothing he could do to ease the suffering of Mrs Jessop there were still the aged residents of the harbour who relied on him, and as he paced slowly back and forth across the wet grass of the green be began to fully embrace George's plans for the grand old house. That alone would be more than enough to occupy his thoughts in the coming months.

As he paced he became aware of the silence that surrounded him, broken only by the intermittent hooting of a distant owl or the barking of a fox, so when something else caught his attention it did so with a stark clarity. It wasn't the sound of an engine or the sight of headlights in the distance, both of which he was expecting, but something else much closer.

With no moon and dark clouds filling the sky his vision was restricted to no more than twenty or thirty yards, but whatever he could hear was coming in his direction. A fox or a badger, he thought, but they would have picked up his scent and shied away. The sound was definitely getting closer.

He was staring intently towards the dark outline of the houses that bordered the far side of the green when his attention was drawn to his right where the sound of an engine was accompanied by two pinpricks of yellow light. The ambulance was coming. He looked back in the direction of the original noise and was shocked to pick out a spectral figure emerging from the gloom.

Faced with the dilemma of what to do first, his attention switched back and forth between the approaching ambulance and the figure that appeared now to be motionless. Then, before it was too late, he remembered why he was there and went to the edge of the green to wave down the ambulance.

The driver pulled up beside him and wound down the window. "Are you the one who called us?" he asked.

Arthur nodded and pointed towards the top of the hill. "Yes, it's straight on and down the hill, over the bridge and along the harbour. The third cottage along."

"You don't want a lift then, mate?"

That had been his intention but something told him to stay. He looked back across the green to where the figure still waited. "No, I'll walk back down."

"Suit yourself," replied the driver as he began closing the window. "Second time in as many days, this place is getting popular."

Arthur ignored the remark, his mind was occupied elsewhere. He stood by the side of the road and watched the ambulance disappear down the hill before cautiously facing the figure who had not moved. He was too far away to make out who it might be, but one thing was certain, the person was small. A child? Why on earth would a child be out alone in the middle of the night? He looked about for any sign of someone else, and seeing nothing he moved slowly forward, anxious not to scare the child away.

"Hello," he said when he was close enough to be heard without shouting and frightening the child away. "My name is Arthur Mulrooney. Who are you?" He took a few more steps and when he was only two or three yards away he let out a gasp of recognition. "Rosie Jessop! Is that you?"

The child stood motionless, rigid with fear. Her arms were wrapped across her chest and her face was screwed tight against the cold. She was wearing an old dressing gown over her nightdress, although her feet were bare, almost covered by the wet grass.

"What are you doing here, where's your mother?" asked Arthur, stooping down in front of her. "Why aren't you at home in bed?"

Either too cold or too frightened to reply Rosie stared straight ahead as though Arthur was invisible, and when he reached out to her she shrunk away. But despite her timid reaction to him it was clear to Arthur that he had to do something. "Do you know who I am?" he said softly, standing up and slipping off his coat.

Rosie remained motionless for a while before eventually raising her head and nodding cautiously up at him. "You're my granddad." It was neither a question nor was it spoken with any certainty until she added timidly, "Are you my granddad?"

A lump formed in Arthur's throat and he felt emboldened to bend down and wrap the child in his coat. "Yes I am," he replied emotionally, "if you want me to be." Even through the thick folds of gabardine he could feel her trembling as he lifted her off the wet grass. "Now we must get you home to your mother."

She had not even settled into his arms before she started thrashing with her arms and kicking at him with her bare feet. "No! No!" she screamed as she squirmed to break free. "Not going home."

Unable to understand her panic Arthur clung on to her. "You have to go home; your mother will be worried about you."

"No!" she shouted frantically as she continued to struggle in his arms. "Mummy's gone away. I'm going to find her."

"Gone! Gone where?" Remembering the conversation with Daisy a few days before Arthur was confused, but more than that he was struck by a panic. Surely she would never leave her daughter, unless… "Has something happened to your mother?"

Rosie had stopped fighting him, but was sobbing too violently to reply so Arthur took the unavoidable decision to take her home knowing that, if her mother had really left home, he would be doing exactly what Daisy Jessop had begged him not to do. But he had no choice, and as he trudged across the green towards Rosie's home his mind conjured up a string of unpalatable possibilities.

When he reached the house it was in total darkness, a sign that Rosie had probably not been missed, that she really had sneaked out to look for her mother. As he knocked on the door there was a noticeable surge of anxiety in Rosie's trembling body, adding to Arthur's own discomfort. There was no response so he hammered harder on the knocker which, already loose, threatened to come away from the door. Eventually a dull light showed in the front bedroom and a few seconds later the window was thrown open.

"What the bloody hell do you want?"

Startled by the sudden aggressiveness of the voice above his head Arthur stepped away from the door and looked up. "It's Arthur Mulrooney, Mr Jessop, I've got your daughter here. I found her wandering about on the green."

Without any noticeable response Stan disappeared from view, leaving Arthur wondering if he would even bother opening the door, until he heard a heavy tread on the stairs and the bolt on the front door being thrown back.

Stan stood framed in the doorway dressed in vest and trousers with braces hanging loose by his side. His dark hair hung lank across his face, adding to his threatening expression. He made to snatch Rosie but Arthur stepped away, tightening his arms protectively around the child

"Give me the kid and piss off," hissed Stan, making another attempt to grab her before the coldness of the outside step made him change his mind. "Just give her here."

"Doesn't it bother you that she was out in the middle of the night and you didn't even know?" breathed Arthur, hiding his nervousness behind a defiant tone. "God only knows what would have happened to her if I hadn't been there."

Stan's puffy eyes narrowed. "And what were you doing there?" Something approaching a smirk curled his thick lips. "Or was this something you'd arranged with my bitch of a wife and you changed your mind."

"I don't know what you're talking about. And where is your wife, Mr Jessop?"

"That's none of your bleedin' business, just give me the kid and piss off." Stan reached out again, making Rosie whimper and bury her head into Arthur's shoulder. "Don't make me take her from you."

"Not until you promise that you won't hurt the child and you tell me where your wife is," insisted Arthur as Rosie clung to his jacket.

"I don't have to tell you anything, and what happens to the kid is nothing to do with you." This time he braved the chilling concrete and forcibly wrenched Rosie from Arthur's arms.

The child screamed and reached out for Arthur, and as much as it tugged at his heart he knew he had no right to object. Whatever Stan Jessop's shortcomings as a father he was still Rosie's legal guardian whether his wife was there or not.

"At least tell me where her mother is," pleaded Arthur. "Is she all right?"

Rosie sobbed loudly and looked pleadingly at Arthur as Stan stripped the coat from her and threw it at him.

"I told you, it's got nothing to do with you." He thrust Rosie into the hallway and went to push the door shut, stabbing a finger at Arthur. "You and that doctor stay away from me and mine or I won't be responsible."

With that the door slammed shut, leaving Arthur standing in the front garden wondering if he had made the right decision returning Rosie to her father and fearing something terrible had happened to her mother.

"There was nothing else you could have done," said George when Arthur had finished recounting to his friend what had happened. "If it's any consolation it was fortunate you were there at the time before the poor child became lost or injured."

"But you should have seen her, George, she was terrified of going back to him." Arthur sat slumped in an armchair in George's living room. "And I can't stop thinking about what her mother said a few days ago, and now she's disappeared."

"Not disappeared exactly," said George, giving his friend a comforting pat on the shoulder. "She's in the cottage hospital." He sat down opposite Arthur. "The ambulance driver told me they were called out here two days ago to attend a woman who had fallen down the stairs. It was Mrs Jessop."

Arthur's head shot up and he stared at George. "How bad was it, did they say?"

"Nothing broken apparently, but severe concussion. She'll probably be home in a day or so."

Arthur shook his head in disbelief. "Fell, or was pushed? It's a bit of a coincidence don't you think that straight after talking about something happening to her she falls down the stairs."

"We can't go jumping to conclusions, Arthur. But if it makes you feel any better I'll phone the hospital in the morning to see how she is. Perhaps I'll even go and see her, in a professional capacity."

"A good idea, I'll come with you." Arthur's dark mood seemed to brighten at the suggestion.

"No," replied his friend emphatically. "After what her husband said you should stay well away. Anyway, there's nothing she can tell you that she can't say to me, and I can check on Mr Gulliver at the same time."

"I'm sorry," said Arthur guiltily, "I haven't even asked how he is."

George sighed. "Not too good, it's his heart."

The two men sat in silence and after a while George began snoring gently, leaving Arthur to reflect on the night's events until a steel grey dawn crept over the eastern horizon.

Chapter Twenty-Five

Stan Jessop lost no time or opportunity to leech some sympathy for his domestic situation and the threat it posed to his precious daughter. It started that morning in Mrs Metcalfe's shop straight after he had deposited Rosie at the school gates.

"Ten fags, missus," he said, making an exaggerated show of searching his pockets for money he knew didn't exist. "And I'd better get something for my little girl's tea." He cast his eyes around the shop. "This is all a bit new to me, what do you suggest?"

Not quite as gullible as Stan would have liked, Mrs Metcalfe eyed him with a degree of suspicion. She had heard from Queenie Butler that Mrs Jessop had been taken off to hospital. Stan had already thought his distress worthy of at least one free pint, although there was little known regarding the circumstances.

"I don't know," she replied slowly as though she was giving the matter some thought. "What does she like?"

"Well, if I knew that I wouldn't have asked," he said with a heavy sigh. "Like I said, I'm a bit new at this, it's not easy when you've got so much else to worry about." He allowed his sorrowful eyes to linger on the shopkeeper. "I suppose you've heard what happened to my wife?"

She nodded sadly. She had also witnessed the Jessops arguing on the green a few days before when Stan had intercepted his wife as she was hurrying breathlessly from the direction of the hill. Although unable to hear what was being said it had been clear to Mrs Metcalfe that he was far from happy as he took his wife roughly by the arm and dragged her homewards. She could only speculate what had happened after that.

"Sausages," she said almost absently. "Children generally like sausages."

"A good choice, missus," he said with a strained smile. "A packet of fags and some sausages it is then."

"How many?" she asked, crossing over to the meat counter.

"What?"

"How many sausages do you want?"

He shrugged his shoulders. "I don't know, a couple for me and a couple for her, I suppose."

Mrs Metcalfe cut the sausages from a string and wrapped them in paper before returning to put them down in front of him. "Anything else?"

"Just them, and the fags."

She placed the cigarettes next to the sausages. "That'll be two and four pence then."

"Well, here's the thing, missus, my wife usually takes care of things like this. I hand all my wages over to her and she pays the bills. With her being laid up in hospital I don't know where she keeps anything, she might have even taken her purse with her for all I know." He went to pick up the items which Mrs Metcalfe kept in her grasp. "She'll be home in a day or two, so just stick it on her tab and she'll sort it out then."

Mrs Metcalfe's knowledge of Stan Jessop was more from hearsay than from personal experience, but it was enough to make her wary. "Your wife doesn't have a tab, none of my customers do. She doesn't buy what she can't pay for." She fixed him with a probing gaze. "I won't see the little mite go hungry, but I'm sure you can both do without the cigarettes." She snatched them away and put them back on the shelf then pushed the sausages forward. "You can pay me for those when she comes home. I wish her a speedy recovery."

With a sniff and a spiteful glance he picked up the sausages and left the shop, and an hour later he was in the pub having miraculously found enough money for a pint. Neither the landlord nor any of the customers were sufficiently moved to salve his misfortune with a free drink, and the landlord had even warned his wife not to overdo the sympathy.

"It ain't easy," he said as he grudgingly slammed the coins down on the counter and picked up his drink, "trying to earn a living and looking after a kid at the same time." He had told Rosie she would have to stay in school during her lunch break as he wouldn't be home from work in time to collect her.

"Well, you've got time to enjoy a drink at least," said Joe Butler, his words heavy with sarcasm. "It's not often we see your wife in here at this time of day."

"That's because women belong in the house and not in the pub." He smirked as he looked round at the other customers for support, but was met by an array of non-committed expressions. "Look at them, henpecked the lot of them. She's a good woman, my wife, and she knows her place, or at least I thought she did."

Queenie Butler had been hovering in the doorway to the kitchen listening to Stan's views on a woman's place and had only held her tongue because of the warning look she got from her husband. But now her interest had been whetted beyond endurance and she suddenly found a need to wipe down the counter.

"I can't say I know your wife too well, but she's always struck me as being the perfect wife and mother," she said casually, lifting Stan's glass and wiping away a ring of ale. "I can't believe she would do anything to upset you."

"And it's none of your business either, Queenie," warned the landlord.

"Of course not," she retorted, indignant at the suggestion, "and I'm certainly not one to pry."

"That's right, missus, the same as I'm not one to speak out of turn, especially with my wife laid up in hospital." Stan gave a sorrowful sigh and looked at her through baleful eyes. "And if it wasn't for what happened last night I would never have mentioned anything." He picked up his glass and took a long, slow drink, aware that he had attracted the impatient attention of the landlady. "Anyway, I've said enough, it was probably nothing."

Seeing his wife almost bursting with an anticipation that would almost certainly lead to a free pint, Joe Butler felt the need to intervene. "Then I expect it's time to go and see to your daughter," he said, waiting for Stan to finish his beer and taking the glass.

"She's staying up at school for her lunch. She prefers it, being with her pals." His sad eyes never left Queenie. "It's only my wife who insists on dragging her back home for her lunch every day."

"So you're stopping for another pint?" said Queenie expectantly,

Stan tipped his head to one side and gave her a regretful smile. "Afraid not, missus. There ain't many folk in the village who would lend me a sympathetic ear, but I reckon you're one of them, and if I had the price of a pint I would welcome the chance to tell the truth about one or two of them from around here, but sadly…"

Almost salivating at the prospect of gossip Queenie glanced along the bar to where her husband was shaking his head in disbelief. Torn between his wrath and allowing the source of the gossip to slip from her grasp she made her decision. "Let me treat you, Mr Jessop." She knew what it would take to pacify Joe later.

Stan puffed his cheeks, giving emphasis to his reluctance. "I should be going, but… if you insist."

"She doesn't," said Joe forcefully, glaring at his wife.

But she had already started to pull on the pump. "It would be a shame to waste it, Joe. I'll put the money in myself."

"Are you that desperate, woman, to pass on a load of gossip to all the other nosey biddies in the village just to make yourself feel important," Joe breathed angrily. "And you know damn well there's not going to be any truth in it."

"That's a bit unfair, guvnor," said Stan, appearing hurt as he almost snatched the filled glass from Queenie's hand. "When have you ever heard me speak bad of anyone who never deserved it?"

"I've never heard you say a good word about anyone either," argued Joe, for all the good he knew it would do.

"Well, we won't know, will we?" said Queenie impatiently, "Unless you allow Mr Jessop to speak." She turned her wide-eyed attention on Stan. "You mentioned something that happened last night?"

Stan took a long slurp from the glass, milking the suspense that threatened to cause the landlady an apoplectic fit. He leant forward across the counter as though about to impart a treasured secret. "I really shouldn't say anything, missus, but I know it won't go any further." He waited as she solemnly nodded her agreement. "I'm not accusing anyone, you understand, but when there's a child involved, you can't be too careful."

Queenie gave a sharp gasp. "Has something happened to your daughter?"

He glanced furtively around at the other customers before showing Queenie a pained expression. "That's just the thing, missus, I'm not sure, and I don't know what to do." He spoke softly, his words heavy with emotion and the landlady leant further across the counter until their heads were almost touching. He gave her a piercing look. "What would you do if you found your daughter in the arms of a man she hardly knows in the middle of the night? I tell you, missus, I'm beside myself with worry."

Queenie jerked upright with such suddenness that her husband, standing a few feet away, almost dropped the glass he was holding, then, just as suddenly, leant forward again. "What man, do I know him?" she asked, beside herself with anticipation.

187

Stan emptied his glass and slid it across the counter, shaking his head. "I don't think I should say any more. I mean, it wouldn't be right to point a finger at someone before I talk to the police. Anyway, I really should be going."

Queenie bit her lip to stop herself from squealing with excitement. This was beyond mere gossip, and hypnotised by the power that was within her grasp she took the glass and refilled it. "If this man is a danger to the children in the village then I think I… we have the right to know."

Unable to restrain himself any further Joe felt obliged to intervene. He glared first at Queenie and then at Stan. "I don't know what nonsense you're filling my wife's head with but I think it's gone far enough." He nodded at the glass in Stan's hand. "You've got her to give you a couple of free pints now you can finish that and get out, and I don't want to see you in here again unless you've got money in your pocket."

As Queenie looked distraught, feeling cheated, Stan turned to face the other customers who were now trying hard not to appear interested. "I bet you lot would want to know if there was some pervert preying on our kids."

No, Queenie silently begged him, if you have to tell anyone tell me. "Why don't you just tell me what happened, before you start a panic among all the mothers in the village." There was a pleading note in her voice. "After all, there might not be anything in it."

"Of course there's nothing in it," scoffed Joe. "I wouldn't believe anything that came out of that man's mouth."

Stan turned on the landlord, his dark eyes burning with contempt. "You might not like me, but I ain't one to do nothing when my kid's in danger, and there ain't another man in here who wouldn't do the same." He took a long drink and slammed the glass down on the counter. "I don't know what's been going on between them, but that old geezer who lives, down the hill has been sniffing around my wife, and I don't know how but last night my little girl ends up with him." He turned to address the customers who were now openly staring at him. "Why would she be with him if they hadn't made some secret arrangement, you tell me that."

"Are you talking about that friend of the Doctor?" asked Queenie, hiding her disappointment behind a screen of concern. "What's his name, Joe?"

188

"Mulrooney," replied Joe flatly, "and you can't go accusing him of anything, even if what you say has any truth in it, until he's had a chance to give his side."

"The evidence speaks for itself," insisted Stan, seeking support from his audience. "And if he can spirit her out of the house in the middle of the night what else is he capable of?"

There were a few nods of agreement but the only verbal response was from Queenie. "I've always said there was something strange about that man, haven't I, Joe?"

"You say a lot of things, woman, but it doesn't make it true," replied Joe, losing patience with his wife which he turned on Stan. "If you reckon he's guilty of anything just go to the police like you said instead of throwing around accusations."

Stan gave a derisive snort. "Don't think I won't if he tries anything else, but my little girl's been through enough, what with her mother stuck in hospital, and I don't want her questioned by some heavy-handed plod."

"Then I suggest you don't go saying any more, and that goes for the rest of you," said Joe, his threatening gaze sweeping the bar before settling on his wife. "You hear me, Queenie?"

She glowered with resentment although she said nothing before storming off into the kitchen.

"You won't be so pleased with yourself if something happens to my daughter," sneered Stan before finishing his drink. "It's a good job she's got me looking out for her." With a lingering aggrieved look at the other customers he left the pub.

***

"Well," asked Arthur before George was even through the door of his cottage, "how was she?"

Red faced and wheezing from the brisk walk down the hill George flapped a hand in the air. "Let me get my coat off first," he gasped, "and I could murder a cup of tea."

Arthur muttered something incomprehensible and went off to the kitchen. When George had hung up his coat he followed his friend, leaning heavily against the door frame.

"She's had a nasty bang on the head. Seems like she hit the wall when she fell down the stairs."

"Fell, or was pushed?" interrupted Arthur, sharply.

"She wouldn't say, but why would she? If he did push her and she told the police he would have been arrested leaving her daughter with no one to look after her." George sighed heavily. "The poor woman's beside herself with worry; she begged me to take her home, but she won't be up to it for another few days yet."

"Did you tell her about what happened last night?"

George shook his head emphatically. "No, of course not! What do you think she would have done if she knew? I told her you had seen the child and she seemed fine. I know it's not the truth, but it's what she would have wanted to hear."

"I suppose so," agreed Arthur reluctantly, "but did she say anything about what she had said before, about wanting us to look after her daughter if anything happened to her?"

"Not in so many words. She's confused and she's frightened; it's the first time she's been separated from her daughter for so long and for some reason she doesn't trust her husband to take care of the girl."

"Well, can you blame her?" asked Arthur, incredulously. "You know as well as I do the sort of man he is, and if he's knocking his wife about, what is he capable of doing to the child."

"It's not the same. I've seen plenty of cases where the wife is being beaten, yet the husband dotes on his children."

Arthur stopped preparing the tea and turned wide eyed on his friend. "And if you believe Mr Jessop is one of those men you're a fool, George. That man hasn't a decent bone in his body and he wouldn't think twice about hurting the girl."

"Even if you're right, Arthur, what do you expect us to do, kidnap the girl until her mother comes home?" He sighed again and went over to give his friend a reassuring pat on the shoulder. "I'm sure everything will work out OK."

"And what about last night? Why did she run out of the house in her night clothes unless something had frightened her?"

"I really don't know, Arthur. She may have had a nightmare and run out of the house without knowing what she was doing." George spread his hands and shrugged. "Who knows what goes through a child's mind."

"I wouldn't mind betting it wouldn't have happened if her mother had been there." Arthur emptied the kettle into the teapot and placed the cups on the tray before carrying them through to the living room where George was settling into the armchair. "I just think we should make sure she is all right, we owe it to her mother."

"And how do you propose to do that, go knocking on the door and ask her father?" Even sharing his friend's concern for the child, George knew their interference would probably do more harm than good. "Mrs Jessop will be home in a few days, so just let sleeping dogs lie until then, Arthur. Don't you agree?"

Arthur clearly didn't as he poured the tea, although he said nothing, deferring to the doctor's professional logic. But for Arthur, logic and emotion made poor bedfellows and a few days were a long time in a child's life.

Chapter Twenty-Six

What had driven Arthur to leave his cottage the following morning was still unclear in his mind. He had tried to persuade himself he was simply going for a walk, some gentle exercise, but he knew that was a lie. George had declined the offer to join him, saying he had to speak to Mrs Gulliver about her husband's condition, which was a relief to Arthur as the invitation was made purely out of courtesy.

Even as he approached the school an attack of nerves almost forced him to turn back towards home, because he had no plan, no idea what he would do once he reached the school gates. The only thing he did know was that he needed to be there.

It was morning break and the sound of children shouting and screaming excitedly as they played only added to his fears. He stopped at the end of the lane that led down to the school entrance, close enough to see the children through the railings, but far enough away to change his mind. He could also see the headmistress, Mrs Sawkins, talking with the teacher on playground duty and it was then that the idea came to him. But as he gave it more thought it became less of a solution and more a suicidal folly. Immobilised by indecision he stood staring at the children until he was shaken from his stupor by a shout.

"Mr Mulrooney!"

It was only when it was repeated did he react. Mrs Sawkins had her arm through the railings and was waving at him and he found himself drawn towards her.

"Were you coming to see me?" she asked expectantly. "You've changed your mind about giving another talk to the children?"

"No. Yes. I'm not sure." The vague notion that he could use that premise as his excuse for being there now seemed to be a very real option. "I thought we might talk about it, when you have time."

The Headmistress beamed invitingly. "There's no time like the present. I've got a class in half an hour, but I'm free until then." She waved a hand in the direction of the gate. "Come on then, Mr Mulrooney, let's have a chat."

There was no going back and Arthur found himself following the Headmistress across the playground with several pairs of young eyes watching him suspiciously. He glanced back and forth at the sea of inquisitive faces for a chance of seeing Rosie Jessop, but there were so many children, most of whom were running back and forth that it was impossible to distinguish any individual.

Inside her office Mrs Sawkins directed Arthur to the chair in front of her desk. "Well, I must admit, I'm a little surprised." She leant back in her chair and clasped her hand across her chest. "Surprised but delighted."

"I'm just as surprised myself," mumbled Arthur which was more of an aside than a response. "And now that I am here I'm not sure it's such a good idea."

She cocked her head to one side and studied him carefully. "You don't strike me as a man who does anything on impulse, Mr Mulrooney, so you must have given it some thought before you came here." She leant forward across the desk. "So, what will be the subject of your talk?"

Arthur had no idea since he had no intention of putting himself through another terrifying ordeal. "I haven't really got that far yet. I just wanted to know if you would agree to it."

"Why wouldn't I agree?" She smiled encouragingly. "It's not often we get the opportunity to benefit from someone with so much first-hand experience of the world."

"It's just that…" He stared down at the worn carpet beneath his feet. "It's just that what happened to that poor girl the last time I felt so guilty. I'm not sure I would want to chance that again." He slowly looked up. "How is she, by the way?"

Mrs Sawkins pondered the question for a moment. "I spoke to her mother afterwards and explained what had happened and that was the end of it, but having said that…"

Arthur waited apprehensively through an awkward silence. "Has something else happened?" he asked, trying not to sound too interested.

"I shouldn't really be discussing individual pupils with you, Mr Mulrooney," said the Headmistress distractedly, "but I'm trusting you are not a person given to gossip. The truth is I'm a little worried about Rosie. I believe her mother has been taken into hospital and she is being looked after by her father, if looked after is the right expression." She noted the change in Arthur's expression. "You think I've said too much,"

He shook his head and smiled bleakly. "I know a little of her father, he's not the friendliest of men. What has his daughter said?"

"That's just the trouble, Rosie's not the most outgoing of children. She does very little to engage with her teacher or her classmates." She sat back and stared thoughtfully up at the ceiling as she decided whether to say more. "It may be just an oversight on his part," she began hesitantly, "especially if he's not used to looking after her on a regular basis. But if her mother is perhaps a little overprotective that certainly doesn't apply to her father. Rosie usually goes home for her lunch and I understand that her father probably works during the day so she has to stay in school during the break. But to send the child to school with nothing to eat seems to me to be a little more than forgetfulness."

Arthur bit back on the sickening anger that churned his stomach. From what he knew of Stan Jessop it was unlikely that forgetfulness had anything to do with failing to provide his daughter with her lunch, and it was equally unlikely that work prevented him from taking care of his child. The man had no conscience. "So she's been going hungry," he muttered bitterly.

"Not exactly, some of the teachers have been sharing their lunch with her, but it's far from ideal." The Headmistress opened her hands expressively. "Anyway, we've departed from the reason you are here, Mr Mulrooney. I should never have involved you in school matters when you only came here to discuss your next attempt to give the children the benefit of your worldly experience. So, what have you in mind?"

With his thoughts fixed firmly elsewhere Arthur struggled to find a reply. "Well, I haven't thought that far ahead, I just wanted to know what you thought about it in principle."

Mrs Sawkins stood. "Well, now that you know what I think you had better go and prepare something," she smiled encouragingly, "and I'm sure this time it will all go swimmingly."

As she opened her office door the children were streaming in from the playground. Arthur pressed himself against the glazed-tiled wall as they pushed past on their way to the various classrooms.

"Quiet," shouted the teacher as she ushered them through the door, but the order had little effect. "Quiet."

Unable to move, Arthur studied the faces, hoping for a glimpse of Rosie, but, despite the pleading of her mother, he knew he could do nothing to intervene in her plight. The vengeful thoughts that had occupied his mind were suddenly converted to sympathy when he spotted Rosie's sad little face appear in the doorway, and the misery reflected in her pale blue eyes tore at his heart. She looked alone and friendless, in stark contrast to most of the other children who surrounded her, jostling each other and generally acting like children. Rosie just seemed afraid and cowed by the antics of her peers, and if her demeanour went unnoticed by the teachers it was painfully obvious to Arthur.

Despite the demands of the teacher for quiet the children continued with their noisy chattering and laughter and it would have been impossible to distinguish any individual voice until one raised itself above all the others and made Arthur start with alarm.

"Grandad!"

For a single moment all the other voices were extinguished and all Arthur heard was that one solitary word. Even if there had been another dozen men squeezed into that corridor he knew it was aimed at him and he knew from where it had come, but still it shocked him. And it shocked the Headmistress too because she looked first at the source of the voice and then at Arthur.

"Grandad!" It was repeated louder and with more passion.

Many of the children closest to Rosie turned to stare at her before focussing their curiosity on Arthur, which only served to make him twitch with greater discomfort, and as the children surged past, Rosie pushed her way towards him. He could feel the searching gaze of the headmistress on him and tried to imagine the awkward questions that would follow.

"Get the children to their classrooms, Miss Pickering," the Headmistress said, making it clear the order included Rosie Jessop, although her questioning expression softened as the child was swept along in front of her. "Go to your class, dear, and I'll be along to see you shortly." She turned to the teacher. "Ask Mrs Tate to keep an eye on year four and I'll be there as soon as I can."

As the corridor cleared of children Arthur shuffled nervously, trying to assemble something that would sound like a credible explanation.

"Shall we go back into my office, Mr Mulrooney?" said Mrs Sawkins, interrupting his thought process. She pushed open the door and stood aside to allow Arthur to go in before her. Once she was seated behind her desk she stared up at him with a look that left him in no doubt that she was at best confused. Recognising the anxiety in his face she waved him towards a chair as she continued to study him in silence until finally she spoke. "That poor child, I can't begin to think what must be going on in her mind. Her mother being in hospital and her father forgetting to feed her must really have disturbed her."

Even in his anxious state Arthur recognised that she was giving him a reason for the child's confusion regarding their relationship and it was easier to agree. "You're probably right. Perhaps I remind her of someone else, her real grandfather."

The Headmistress nodded thoughtfully. "But she seemed so sure, don't you think?"

Arthur flushed with guilt, despising himself for the deception and knowing he should have been honest from the start. The longer he prevaricated the more difficult it would be to explain. He found it impossible to meet her gaze. "The fact is," he began ponderously before faltering. "The fact is, I have bumped into her, and her mother, once or twice in the village since that unfortunate episode. I don't think Mrs Jessop blames me for what happened,"

"I'm sure she doesn't, but a few chance meetings wouldn't explain why young Rosie should call you her granddad."

Arthur shifted on his chair. "There was another occasion," he said reluctantly. "The child had fallen and hurt herself. Her mother took her down to see my friend Doctor Wallace but unfortunately he was away and I did what I could to help." He paused, appearing to recall the moment. "I seem to remember her asking if I was her grandfather, she doesn't have one apparently. But that was all there was to it, I had almost forgotten about it," he lied.

Mrs Sawkins smiled benignly, apparently satisfied. "Well, that would explain it," she said, getting up from her chair, indicating the meeting was over. "I'll pop along and see her, make sure she's all right, and you can go and prepare your next talk." She squeezed his arm. "I'm sure it will go perfectly to plan this time."

Her words offered Arthur no reassurance or comfort. Dishonesty did not sit happily with him, and now he had trapped himself into the ordeal of another talk. And as he walked away from the school the thought of Stan Jessop's neglect of his daughter only served to add to Arthur's sombre mood.

***

Mrs Sawkins held on to Rosie's hand as she led her across the playground, not because she was afraid the child would run off but rather to protect her from the spiteful ribbing of the other children. It was no secret that children can be particularly cruel towards those they perceived as being in some way different, and Rosie was an easy target. There was also another reason the Headmistress wanted to accompany the girl to the school gate, she was hoping to have words with her father.

Having spoken to Rosie in the classroom Mrs Sawkins had reached the conclusion that sending the child to school without her lunch was more than just an oversight. She felt an obligation to remind Stan Jessop of his responsibilities, if he bothered to turn up to collect the child.

"Can you see your daddy?" They stopped just outside the gate and the Headmistress picked the girl up for a better view. "Is he here?"

Rather than scanning the crowd outside the gate for any sign of her father, Rosie kept her head tucked into her chest and looked only at the ground. After asking again with the same result Mrs Sawkins resorted to asking one of the mothers if she knew Mr Jessop.

At first the woman appeared suspicious at the question but after recognising Rosie she smirked. "Oh, I know him," she said with a knowing nod. "But not as well as some of them here. Bit of a ladies' man by all accounts." She looked about her before pointing over to the fringe of the crowd. "That looks like him there, talking to Betty Baker."

The Headmistress thanked the women and with Rosie still held in her arms she weaved her way through the throng to where Stan and the woman seemed to be sharing a joke. Stan had his hand on the woman's shoulder while she giggled and pushed him playfully away. Stan had his back to Mrs Sawkins, but Betty saw her coming and immediately stepped away, any sign of familiarity leaving her face.

Noting the sudden change in her expression Stan glanced over his shoulder, recognising his daughter in the arms of the Headmistress, whom he didn't recognise. "What's wrong with her," he asked gruffly as she set Rosie down, "can't she walk?"

Mrs Sawkins glared back at him, untouched by his reputation. "She can walk perfectly well, Mr Jessop," she snapped back, unwilling to explain. "I wonder if I can have a word with you." She gave Betty Baker a sideways look. "In private."

Stan shrugged and gave Betty a wink. "Maybe I'll see you tomorrow, love, if you're lucky." Betty tossed her head back and sniffed haughtily before turning away to seek out her own child. "So, are you her teacher?" he asked, taking Rosie roughly by the arm and pulling her to his side. "What's she done now?"

"I'm Mrs Sawkins, the headmistress, and Rosie hasn't done anything, Mr Jessop, much like yourself."

Stan's eyes narrowed. "What's that supposed to mean?"

"It means that since your wife has been in hospital Rosie has had to stay in school during lunch break instead of going home as she normally would, and…"

"Of course she has." he interrupted. "I can't work and see to her at the same time. What am I supposed to do?"

"You're supposed to send her to school with something to eat, instead of leaving it to us to feed her." She gave Rosie a pitying look. "Some of the staff have been sharing their own lunch with her, otherwise she would have gone hungry."

For a moment Stan appeared to be lost for an excuse before sighing deeply. He pulled Rosie closer. "Are you married?" he asked the Headmistress, his face a mask of exaggerated sorrow. "Do you have children?"

"I don't see that has anything to do with you forgetting to feed your daughter," she replied with clear irritation.

He gave her a sad smile, allowing his lower lips to tremble with emotion. "Because if you was you would know how hard it is to be separated from someone you love." He sniffed and ran a cuff across his eyes. "When I came back from the war I vowed to my wife we wouldn't be apart any more, and we never have been, until now. I feel ashamed to admit it but I miss her and I'm lost without her. I never realised what it is to be a mother. I've never had to, and I'm struggling to cope." He gave her a pleading look. "You can understand that, can't you?"

Mrs Sawkins stared back at him, assessing his sincerity. "I sympathise with your situation, Mr Jessop, and I can understand how hard it must be for you, but taking care of your daughter ought to be your priority, however much to feel out of your depth,"

"You're right," he said, nodding his head, his voice heavy with contrition, "especially after what's been happening." He looked anxiously about him.

"And what is that, Mr Jessop?"

He sighed again. "I shouldn't really say. It's something and nothing."

"Well, if you're sure." She went to turn away.

"It's just that..." He clamped his big hands protectively on Rosie's narrow shoulders. "I don't think it's right when some old geezer's been sniffing round my wife and had his hands on my little girl." There was a hint of a sob in his voice.

"What is it you're suggesting, Mr Jessop? What man?"

He shook his head, his expression one of forlorn reluctance. "I've probably said too much, but she's my little girl and I can't help being worried about her." For several seconds he stared down at his daughter before jerking his head in the general direction of the harbour. "He lives down there with all the other old 'uns. He's always hanging around my missus and the other night..." He allowed his voice to falter. "I don't know how he managed to get her out of the house, but I found him with Rosie in his arms. He could have done anything to her."

Mrs Sawkins let out a low gasp. "Are you talking about Mr Mulrooney?"

Stan shrugged. "Is that his name? He's a friend of the old doctor, that's all I know."

"But I know Mr Mulrooney. I can't believe he would be capable of anything..." She struggled to find the right words as an element of doubt crept into her mind. "I was only speaking with him a short while ago."

"What, in the school?" He glared accusingly at the Headmistress. "He didn't get near my Rosie?"

"Not exactly," she said hesitantly. "But she did seem to know him."

"What do you mean?" he demanded,

"They passed each other in the corridor and she seemed to recognise him, that's all." She was reluctant to say more. "If you're that concerned you should speak to him, make sure he understands how you feel. I can't believe he means Rosie any harm."

"Well, you're not her father and it's up to me to look out for her." He jabbed out a threatening finger. "You make sure he don't get near her when she's in your school, and I'll do what I have to do." Without another word he gripped Rosie's arm and marched away across the green.

Chapter Twenty-Seven

Daisy stood by the side of the road as the bus pulled away, staring longingly in the direction of the village school. For the whole time she had been confined to the hospital she had been beside herself with worry, and now that she was back home all she wanted was to be reunited with her precious little girl. It had only been days, but it felt like a lifetime. Now she was barely able to resist the temptation to rush up to the school, take Rosie from her class and lavish on her all the love and affection that had built to overflowing during her absence.

It was an agonising decision, but Daisy reluctantly concluded that Rosie had probably been exposed to sufficient upset during those days and needed to slip back into her comforting routine as quickly as possible. With a heavy heart she trudged towards home to face whatever awaited her there and, glancing back towards the public house, wondering if Stan was inside. It did not take long to decide that she no longer cared where he was, or what he did, provided he did nothing to harm her or Rosie, although she was not so naive to believe in such a fantasy. Everything Stan did, especially his drink fuelled moods, impacted on their lives.

If spending time in hospital had achieved anything it was the time to allow Daisy the opportunity to assess her life away from her daily routine and the constant threat of her husband's aggressive behaviour. Unfortunately, the only conclusion she came to was no different from the one she had reached so many times in the past. Nothing would change for either her or Rosie while Stan remained part of their lives.

That depressing thought was still alive in her mind as she cautiously opened the back door to her home and ventured into the cold, damp atmosphere of the kitchen. The stove that she would normally keep alight all day as soon as the weather turned cool stood cold and uninviting in the corner and there was no evidence that it had been lit while she had been away. *If Stan had not bothered with that what else had he been neglecting?* A new flood of concern afflicted Daisy as she stared about her at the general lack of any housekeeping.

Dirty dishes and pans filled the sink and were strewn about the kitchen, and upstairs was just as untidy with neither bed being made. The damp mustiness of the house was masked by the heavy smell of stale tobacco smoke. It was probably no worse than it ever was, but her senses were more acute after days of breathing the sterile hospital air. It caught in her throat and made her cough, another reminder of how much she despised her husband, and that memory made her shudder.

With more than an hour to kill before she had to meet Rosie from school Daisy set about cleaning and tidying the house and after days of brooding inactivity it was strangely comforting to be engaged in something so familiar, until she heard the kitchen door slam shut. She was upstairs making her bed when the sudden noise reverberated around the house, shattering her calm and churning her stomach. For several seconds she stood frozen by a fearful stupor before finding the strength to go to the top of the stairs. The last thing she wanted was to be trapped in the bedroom, especially if Stan had been drinking, which he almost certainly had.

She was about to go down when he appeared in the hallway, his foot on the bottom step. He smirked smugly when he saw her. "So, you're back then."

Daisy made no reply. There was nothing she wanted to say to him that could lessen the loathing she felt. Instead she went slowly down the stairs until she reached the bottom where she waited for him to move aside.

He stayed where he was, baring her way. "What's the matter," he hissed through stained teeth, "nothing to say to me?"

Up to then she had refused to meet his malevolent gaze, but now she found the courage to raise her eyes and look him in the face. "Is Rosie all right?" she asked quietly but firmly. "You haven't done anything to hurt her?"

He gave a cynical chuckle. "I might have known the first thing you asked about was her, that you wouldn't be bothered about me. Why don't you ask how I've been, having to do everything while you've been lazing in some hospital bed, making eyes at the doctors and getting up to God knows what."

Daisy felt her anger and hatred rising and fought to hold it in check. "And whose fault was it that I was in hospital in the first place?" she said defiantly. "I didn't want to be there, and I wouldn't have been if you hadn't pushed me down the stairs."

His dark eyes flashed threateningly and he wrapped his fingers tightly around her forearm. "You fell down the stairs." He spat the words into her face. "That's what you told them, isn't it? I never touched you, and you make sure you remember that."

"Tell me you didn't touch Rosie while I've been away," she repeated more forcibly.

"I never touched her, but if I find out you've opened your mouth it's going to get a lot worse for both of you."

"I told them I fell." Daisy shook her arm free and tried to push past him. "Now, leave me and Rosie alone."

In response Stan took hold of her again, this time holding both arms. He pulled her close, his face thrust into hers. "You're still my wife, and you and that brat are mine to do with what I like, so don't you forget that." He gave her a menacing grin. "Next time it might be her that has an accident."

Although she tried to maintain an outward calm, inside Daisy was burning with rage. "I hate you, Stan Jessop," she breathed through gritted teeth.

Stan simply threw back his head and laughed, his hot, foul breath wafting over her. "Of course you do, sweetheart, but you're still my girl and you always will be. Remember the vows we made, until death do us part." Those last words struck Daisy like a judge pronouncing a life sentence with no chance of parole, except one. Then he pushed her away like a discarded toy. "So now you're home you can start being a wife again, we've got a lot of catching up to do."

Daisy understood his meaning perfectly and her whole body stiffened with revulsion. "I don't want you touching me anymore. You can get everything you want from those other women. I don't care anymore as long as you leave us alone,"

He bent forward to cover her neck in wet, slobbering kisses before whispering in her ear, "I will for now, but tonight…"

***

Daisy stood on the fringe of the gathered mothers around the school gate. She had pushed any thought of Stan to the back of her mind and now waited with excited anticipation for the school doors to swing open and for the children to spill out into the playground. She felt a touch of nervousness as she waited, longing to see her daughter again, to touch her soft skin, run her fingers through her hair and hug her to her breast. She could barely contain her eagerness, and even Stan's leering promise of what she could look forward to later could fail to dampen her spirits at that moment.

Finally the bell rang and seconds later the children fought and jostled their way through the confining doorway, their shouting and shrieking filling the air in their eagerness to escape.

Despite being taller than most of the other mothers Daisy stood on tip toe and craned her neck for an early view of Rosie. The child would be unaware that her mother would be waiting for her and Daisy tried to picture the wild excitement when they caught sight of each other. She shuffled forward impatiently as the crowd of women in front of her thinned, scrutinising every face as it appeared through the school gates, and when the flood dissipated into a trickle her excitement turned to anxiety. Finally she was left standing alone.

She was close to panic and began running across the playground when Rosie appeared in the doorway, hand in hand with the Headmistress. Relief mingled with a fear that something bad had happened to her daughter, but all that was wiped away as Rosie broke free of the Headmistress and ran headlong into her mother's arms.

"Oh, my darling girl!" Daisy sobbed with unrestrained joy as she crushed Rosie to her chest. "I've missed you so much."

Rosie simply cried into her mother's shoulder and clung to her neck as if her life was threatened.

"I'm pleased to see you are home from hospital, Mrs Jessop." Mrs Sawkins was standing over them as Daisy rose to her feet with Rosie in her arms. "I hope you are fully recovered."

Daisy nodded and fixed the Headmistress with a questioning look. "Why did you keep Rosie back and not let her out with the rest of the children?"

Mrs Sawkins took a moment to consider her reply. "It was just a precaution. I wasn't sure who would be collecting Rosie and I didn't want her waiting out here on her own." She gave a thin smile. "Your husband wasn't too dependable in that regard."

It was nothing more than Daisy had expected and readily accepted the reason. "Thank you." She was about to turn away when a mother's intuition told her there was more to it than that. "Has anything else happened that I should know about?" she asked nervously.

"No... nothing I'm aware of," she said with a vagueness that raised some doubt in Daisy's mind. "Have you spoken to your husband since you came home?"

"About what?" she demanded anxiously.

Mrs Sawkins was beginning to think she had already said too much. She shrugged. "Nothing in particular, perhaps you should just talk to him."

Daisy was getting agitated. "Look, if something has happened then I would prefer to hear it from you, so please, just tell me."

The Headmistress shook her head. "I don't know that anything has happened, you really should speak to your husband. It was just something he said to me, but I may have misunderstood. It's probably nothing." She reached out and patted Daisy's arm, giving her a patronising smile before turning away and marching back into the school.

Daisy was tempted to run after her and demand an explanation rather than talk to Stan. She had no wish to speak to him at all, and besides, she doubted that anything coming out of his mouth would be close to the truth. But Rosie's welfare remained her priority and if that meant questioning Stan then she had little choice.

She carried Rosie across the playground and set her down outside the gates, stooping down to speak to the child. "I've missed you so much," she said, combing her fingers through Rosie's unkempt hair. "Has daddy been looking after you?"

Rosie lowered her big blue eyes and nodded uncertainly. "But he forgot to give me my lunch."

Daisy sighed sympathetically. "Oh dear, you poor thing, naughty daddy." She stroked her daughter's cheek encouragingly. "But there's nothing else? You know you can tell mummy anything, don't you?"

Rosie pressed her lips together and shook her head, unable to look her mother in the face, forcing Daisy into the frightening conclusion that it was more than just a missing lunch and that she would only discover the whole story from her husband. She had known that little in her life would have changed during her short stay in hospital, although she had prayed that it would be no worse. But as she took Rosie's hand and headed towards home she accepted the futility of prayers.

Stan was asleep in the armchair when they arrived at the house, his loud snoring greeting them as soon as they entered through the kitchen door. Daisy indicated that they should do nothing to disturb his sleep and Rosie was more than happy to oblige, going up to her bedroom while her mother made them something to eat.

For an hour the pair tip-toed around Stan's slumbering body, only daring to whisper to each other when it was absolutely necessary. Daisy was desperate to question her daughter further, but the child seemed happy back in her mother's company and it would achieve little by upsetting that rare and precious moment of calm.

Stan was still sleeping when it was time to take Rosie up to bed so at least the child had been spared the risk of her father's spite. But as Daisy came down the stairs she was greeted by the disgusting sound of her husband coughing up the phlegm that had settled on his chest while he slept. She shuddered as she went straight through to the kitchen to make his tea. She detested the thought of doing anything for him while not wanting to give him any cause to provoke an argument.

She had barely begun when she heard the grunt that accompanied his hauling himself out of the armchair followed by his heavy tread on the bare floor.

"Where's my fags?" His voice was thick and offensive, so far removed from the smarmy charm he had used to woo her all those years ago. If only she had heeded her parents' warning.

"I expect you've smoked them all," she replied without looking at him.

"And you didn't think to get me some while you were out? You were gone long enough."

That last remark was an accusation but Daisy let it pass. "I've made you a sandwich. There was nothing else in."

She couldn't see him yet she could visualise the contemptuous expression on his face. "Not a very good start, is it," he sneered. "Still, it can only get better, can't it."

They were not questions, simply Stan's view of a wife's duties. "I'll go shopping tomorrow, if you leave me some money." She placed the sandwich on the table in front of him and turned back to the washing up she had already started, carefully avoiding the sullen, dark eyes that followed her every move.

"And where would I get money from? I couldn't work while I was looking after your kid, could I?" The chair scraped on the stone floor as he dragged it closer to the table. "And while I think of it, you owe the old biddy over in the shop for some sausages, although if it were up to me I'd make her whistle for it, the sausages were mostly gristle."

"But you had money enough for drink." It had only been a thought, but it burst from her mouth with no help from her brain.

Behind her she could sense him glowering with anger and she tensed, waiting for her reward. "So what if l did!" He almost choked on the mouthful of bread that caught in his throat as he spoke. "Haven't I earned it after what I've had to put up with while you've been lying in bed?" The chair scraped again as he got to his feet, announcing the menace Daisy had expected. Next she felt his fingers biting into her shoulders as he spun her round to face him. "You've no idea what's been going on while you were away, have you?"

Defiant, Daisy glared back at him, barely able to disguise the fear she felt. "How could I know anything, no one came to see me."

"What, not even that boyfriend of yours?" He sniggered as a humorous thought occurred to him. "Hardly a boy though, is he."

"That's a stupid thing to say. I've no idea what you're talking about." She tried to turn away, but he held her fast. "You've got an evil mind, Stan Jessop; you think everyone is as vile and deceitful as you. I wish I did have someone else, I wish I had never married you because then I wouldn't have had all these years of misery."

He let out a harsh, cynical laugh. "And you wouldn't have that brat you care so much about, would you? You've got her, but what have I got out of this marriage, a sour-faced wife and a kid who's got no respect for me."

"And whose fault is that? All you've ever done is hurt and bully us, and I can't leave the house without you demanding to know where I've been and who I've spoken to." She could see the rage growing in his eyes and braced herself against the expected response.

With one hand still clamped to her shoulder he used the other to grip her chin, painfully pinching her cheeks between his strong fingers. "You're my wife, I've a right to know what you get up to, but it still hasn't stopped you from running off to that old geezer every chance you get. What's he giving you that I can't?"

Unable to turn away Daisy flinched as the flecks of spittle and bread crumbs sprayed her face as he spoke. "Friendship," she said through pursed lips, "he gives me friendship."

"And that precious daughter of yours, what's he giving her?"

As much as she wanted to stay strong Daisy was close to tears and despair. Words were wasted on her husband, and rather than appealing to any humanity he may have they only served to provoke him into further hurt and abuse. But without any other means of hurting him words were all she had. "I don't know what you're talking about," she said, wondering if his question was in any way related to the worrying conversation she had earlier with the headmistress. A stab of anxiety shot through her. "What about Rosie, has something happened to her?"

He smiled, recognising with some pleasure the alarm on her face. "I thought that might get your attention. You might not care what I get up to as long as it doesn't concern your little girl."

"She's our little girl, Stan, it's just a shame you can't be the father she deserves." Daisy took hold of the hand that gripped her chin and wrenched it away. "If something happened to Rosie while I was away you have to tell me."

He made no effort to restrain her again, he had no need to, she was already under his emotional control and he delighted in the power held over her. With his hand free to roam over her body he took full advantage. "You need to start being nice to me if you want that kid to stay safe, after all I'm all you've got to protect her." He cupped her breast in his hand and squeezed hard, making her wince. "If you want me to be a proper father to her then you've got to learn to be a wife to me, not carrying on behind my back,"

"I still don't know what you mean." She began to sob with frustration, closing her eyes and tensing as his hand released her breast and slid down over her stomach and groped between her legs. "I'm not carrying on with anyone, and the only person Rosie needs protecting from is you." She tried to back away from his probing fingers, stretching out her arm to steady herself against the draining board. The tips of her fingers nudged the wooden handle of the knife she had used to cut the cheese for his sandwich. For a fleeting moment she was flushed with an almost overwhelming desire to pick up the knife and plunge the blade into his neck, and it was only the thought of Rosie, and what would happen to her, that held Daisy back. Anger and loathing turned briefly to despair. "Take what you want from me Stan Jessop, but please, tell me what happened to Rosie."

"I'll take what's mine by right," he hissed, thrusting his hand deeper between her legs to prove the point. "And as far as the kid is concerned, you'll have to ask your friend about that." He laughed brutally as he took hold of her arm and dragged her towards the stairs.

***

The bedroom was in total darkness when Daisy sat up in bed. Her head was throbbing painfully; she had been plagued with headaches ever since Stan had thrown her down the stairs, a legacy she thought would stay with her for the rest of her life with him.

She had managed only a few brief spells of restless sleep since Stan had finished with her, the despair and anger she had felt earlier returning with a vengeance. Next to her Stan snored contentedly which only served to heighten her contempt for him, the sound of him sleeping rubbing more salt into her emotional wounds. How easy it would be, she said to herself, and not for the first time, to go down and fetch the knife and free both herself and her daughter from their suffering. But she thought again of Rosie, although that thought went only a small way towards stemming the urge to end his life.

Quietly she climbed out of bed, even though nothing short of an earthquake would disturb him once he was asleep. Gathering up her clothes she crept from the bedroom and out onto the landing where she quickly dressed.

Rosie was still fast asleep, almost hidden from view beneath the covers when Daisy entered the room. It seemed a shame to wake her, but sacrifices had to be made and a broken sleep seemed a small price to pay at the time. Gently she shook the child awake and placed a finger lightly on her lips as she stirred.

"You have to get up, my darling," Daisy whispered, bending close to her daughter.

Rosie started, but made no sound. She rubbed her eyes open and unquestioningly obeyed her mother, and when she was dressed they made their way silently down the stairs and into the kitchen. It was only then that Rosie became aware that it was still dark outside.

"Am I going to school now, Mummy?" she asked, peering out through the kitchen door.

"No dear," Daisy replied, her voice shaking with uncertainty. For a moment it seemed she was unsure of what they were going to do. She looked about the night-shrouded kitchen as though seeking some inspiration from her surroundings. It was too dark to see very much, but familiarity can be a good friend and Daisy went over to the draining board where she picked up the knife. "Wait here darling, I won't be a moment." She caringly stroked Rosie's hair on her way towards the stairs.

Chapter Twenty-Eight

Arthur picked up his watch from the bedside table and blinked bleary eyed at the dial. He rubbed his eyes and tried again. As far as he could tell it was nearly four o'clock, almost dawn in summer, but in late autumn it was still the middle of the night. And what a night it had been, all because of that infuriating woman and her strange behaviour. He wanted to sleep. He needed to sleep, because of late he had been feeling more tired than usual and nowhere near as fit as he used to be. Now, as if that was not enough, his normal equilibrium had been further unbalanced by her.

A few days after his meeting with the Headmistress at the school was a Thursday, library day, and, as usual, Arthur had awaited its arrival with the usual mix of trepidation and eager anticipation, hoping for much but expecting disappointment and embarrassment.

As soon as the charabanc had slid to a halt opposite the pub Arthur had been gripped with a sense of foreboding that eclipsed his normal nervousness. Perhaps it was the way Florence Merryweather had stared stony faced at him through the side window before easing her bulk out from behind the steering wheel and opening the door. There were neither booming words of greeting as she placed the steps on the road, nor any insensitive innuendoes as he offered up the book in exchange for his library ticket. There was no lecherous intent in the look she gave him, and instead of the stage-managed touching of fingers when she handed over the ticket she simply threw it down on the counter. No words were spoken, but what she failed to say had unsettled him far more than anything she had uttered in the past.

He went to find a book, yet he was so distracted by her odd behaviour and his anxiety to leave that he had selected a book at random, one he had read at least twice before. "Thank you," he muttered when she had date stamped the fly sheet and slid the book back across the counter with a cold, steely-eyed stare. "Good day to you."

"And pleasant day to you, Mr Mulrooney," she returned sourly, her florid face turned distractedly to one side.

Arthur was about to go down the steps when nagging curiosity compelled him to stop and look back over his shoulder. "I apologise for asking, but have I done something to offend you?" He knew it had been reckless to ask but not to would have gnawed at him for days.

She gave a sort of half smile that suggested sarcasm, the corner of her mouth disappearing into crease of her cheek. "I don't think the Mr Mulrooney I knew would be capable of offending anyone," she replied, her voice unusually muted and tinged with emotion. "The Mr Mulrooney I knew was a gentle and, dare I say, honourable man, not a geriatric Lothario." The trilby hat slid from her head as she again tossed her head to one side. "I've nothing more to say."

"I'm sorry, but I've no idea what you're talking about," said Arthur, baffled by her remarks.

"I'm sure you don't," she retorted sharply, "men like you never do."

It was mostly her last words that had kept him awake as he questioned himself endlessly, trying to establish exactly what kind of man he was. He thought he knew, after all he had lived long enough to find out all by himself without the need to be told by someone else. And if the need should arise then the only opinion he valued was George's. That is why he had simply tucked the book under his arm and left the library without pursuing the matter further. He could have mentioned it to George, and George would have rebuked him for not asking, so he did what was natural for him to do. He brooded and went without sleep.

He sat up in bed, trying to decide if it was really worth making another attempt or to get up and start the day a few hours earlier than usual. In the silence that usually surrounded the harbour he could hear the rain. The light wind blowing off the sea swept it against his bedroom window making a familiar, comforting rattle. For a few seconds he just sat there listening, hoping to free his brain for other, more pleasant, thoughts. There were none, and he was about to get up when the noise of the rain was interrupted by something else, something unfamiliar at that time of the morning. *Footsteps?* It sounded as though someone was hurrying along the harbour which, to Arthur's mind, meant only one thing, trouble.

He jumped out of bed and went to the window, expecting to see his friend scurrying along on another mission of mercy, but it wasn't George, and even though he couldn't quite make out who it was, they were coming to see him, and that alone filled him with a sickening dread. Pulling on his trousers over his pyjamas he rushed downstairs in time to hear an urgent rap on the door.

"Mrs Jessop!" He stood in the doorway staring past her and down along the harbour without knowing what he expected to see. Perhaps Mr Jessop in pursuit!

Daisy stood at the bottom of the steps holding Rosie by the hand. They were both rain sodden and looking pathetic in the dull yellow glow of the living room light.

"I'm sorry, Mr Mulrooney, I had to leave the house and this is the only place I could come to." Her voice was laden with a frightened weariness and her face looked drawn and lined.

It explained nothing, leaving Arthur just as confused and uneasy. "Has something happened?" He knew enough of her domestic circumstances to be aware that something must have happened for her to force herself and her daughter out of the house at this hour and in this weather.

"Can we come in?" she asked imploringly.

Arthur realised he was still blocking the doorway and quickly stood aside. "I'm sorry, of course." He ushered them inside, still nervously aware that whatever had brought them to his door had undoubtedly left trouble in its wake.

Daisy stood in the tiny living room dripping water onto the floor and looking even more anxious than Arthur had first thought, with Rosie still clinging to her hand. "I'm so sorry," she said again. "I know I shouldn't have come here, but I didn't know what else to do and I really needed someone to talk to and you're the closest thing I have to a friend."

Her last words added both responsibility and intrigue to Arthur's trepidation, which he tried hard to disguise. "Let me take your coats and make you a cup of tea." He waited as Daisy helped Rosie off with her coat before removing her own which she handed to Arthur. "I've got some cocoa, if your daughter would prefer that."

Daisy shook her head: flicking off drops of rain as she did so. "I would like a cup of tea, thank you, but Rosie needs more sleep." She pulled the child in close and Rosie clung to her leg. "Would you mind if I lay her down on the settee?"

Arthur looked down at the pathetic sight of the child. "Take her up and put her on my bed. She'll be more comfortable up there and we won't disturb her when we are talking."

She gave him a nod and a thin smile of gratitude before picking up Rosie and carrying her up the narrow staircase. A few minutes later she was back down and stood in the doorway to the kitchen as Arthur boiled the kettle. "She went straight to sleep," Daisy said wearily. "The poor mite doesn't know what's going on."

Arthur was thinking the same himself. "Why don't you go and sit down. I'll be in shortly and we can talk… if that's what you want."

It was exactly what Daisy wanted, although she was afraid that what Arthur had to say might be far from what she wanted to hear. Without responding she turned away and sank into the soft embrace of the old armchair that felt strangely comforting. She laid her head back and closed her eyes but, unlike her daughter, she was so very far from sleep. Only when Arthur placed the tray down on the table did she open her eyes again, yet she was unable to meet his enquiring look, feeling she had been too rash in imposing herself on someone who was, after all, barely more than an acquaintance.

An embarrassing silence followed, broken only by the sound of Arthur pouring the tea, and it continued until he could bear it no longer and found the need to speak. "I've put some extra sugar in it," he said softly, handing her the cup and saucer. "I thought it might help."

She took the saucer in an unsteady hand, the china rattling to the uneven beating of her heart. "You're very kind, Mr Mulrooney," she struggled to say, still unable to look him in the eye, "but I feel foolish now that I'm here, like I'm taking advantage of you." She rested the saucer in her lap and let out a heavy sob. "I had to get out of the house and there was nowhere else I could go, not with Rosie."

Arthur busied himself with a teaspoon as he fretted over how to open the conversation, "I take it you are fully recovered from your accident?" he asked cautiously, "It must have been hard for you, being separated from your daughter." All he got in reply was a vague nod of her head. "You said there was something you wanted to talk to me about. Did something happen while you were in hospital?"

Daisy took a few gulps of the hot, sweet tea before she was able to raise her head to look him in the face. "I was rather hoping you could tell me," she said nervously. "Stan said there was something, but he wouldn't tell me what it was." She was now fixing Arthur with an enquiring stare. "He said I should ask you."

It sounded to Arthur so much like an accusation that for several seconds he stared back at her, unable to speak. Of course he had not forgotten that night on the village green, but he had not thought to worry Daisy with it, especially when the responsibility to tell her lay with her husband. "There's only one thing I can think of," he said, and then went on to recount how he had found Rosie and returned her home.

When he had finished she shook her head and placed a hand over her face. "She was running away from him," she said in a muffled voice. "I can't bear to think of what might have happened to her if you hadn't been there." She began to sob as the horror of that prospect hit home. "I hate him, Mr Mulrooney, I really hate him and I wish he was dead."

Arthur could easily understand her distress, and her extreme sentiment. "I know how you must feel, and we all say things in the heat of the moment that we don't really mean," he said quietly, trying to defuse her anger.

Her eyes were red and watery but there was no hiding the fury as she glared back at him. "But I do mean it," she breathed, "and I nearly did it."

Arthur nearly choked on the mouthful of tea he was about to swallow. "You nearly did?" he blurted out. "Does that mean…? Is he hurt…? Should I go and fetch George?"

He was about to scramble to his feet when Daisy waved him back down. "No, he's not hurt," she said regretfully. "I couldn't do it. I tried, but I couldn't, that's one of the reasons I had to get out of the house, because I couldn't trust myself not to try again." The cup and saucer were shaking violently in her hand and she put them on the table before the rest of the tea spilt into her lap. "I'm so sorry," she sobbed, "I don't know what you must think of me."

Arthur put his own cup down and leant forward with the intention of giving her leg a reassuring pat, but such familiarity did not sit easy with him and he pulled away. "What exactly did you do?" he asked instead.

Daisy's lip trembled and her shoulders rose and fell as she tried to curb her sobbing. "Nothing," she said after a lengthy pause. "Nothing, really." She paused again until her breathing became more controlled. "He was in bed asleep when I got up and got Rosie up. I don't know why, I just knew I had to. We went down to the kitchen and there was a knife on the draining board, and that's when I most wanted to kill him, to make him suffer the way he's done to us." She stopped and stared past Arthur as though she was reliving that moment. "I took the knife and went back up to the bedroom. It would have been so easy, he wouldn't have known anything about it, and me and Rosie would have been free of him." Her whole body was now shaking as she continued to stare at something over Arthur's shoulder; her future perhaps. "But we wouldn't be free, would we?" she went on in a more distant tone. "What would become of Rosie if they locked me up, or worse? No, I just stabbed the knife into the pillow so he would see it when he woke up and know that I could have done it if I had wanted to. After that we came here."

Whatever emotion Arthur was feeling was mostly hidden behind his thick beard, only his eyes betrayed the shock of her admission. "But what are you going to do now?" he asked, unsure if he really wanted to hear the answer. "Surely you will have to go back to him sometime. You said yourself you have nowhere else to go." He stopped abruptly, realising that nothing he had said was in any way helpful or encouraging. Despite that he continued in much the same vein. "I hope you won't mind my saying, but I don't think it was a good idea to leave the knife where you did. What I've seen of your husband he doesn't strike me as a man who responds kindly to threats."

Whether it was brought on by Arthur's negativity or not, Daisy was reduced to another bout of sobbing until he handed her back the tea she had left. "I realise that now," she said. "I wasn't thinking, and now I feel ashamed and stupid and I don't know what to do."

Arthur had no idea either, although he was reluctant to admit as much. He knew what George's advice would be, to return home and make the best arrangements she could with her husband. But George was a doctor and reasoned with a logical, medical mind that had little room for sentiment. But no amount of medical knowledge could cure what afflicted Daisy Jessop and her daughter and, Arthur knew, neither could he. But despite everything he knew he had to try. "I think I should go and speak with your husband, try to reason with him," he said hesitantly, as though it was merely an ill-considered thought.

Daisy's mouth dropped open with horror as she tried to picture the meeting. "No, you can't," she gasped. "It will only make things worse."

Arthur couldn't imagine how her situation could be made any worse, certainly not by his hand. "I just thought if I pointed out to him how much distress he's causing you and your daughter you could go back and…" His words tailed off as he realised that Stan Jessop probably cared little for the feelings of others.

"No," she said again, more forcibly this time, before realising that she was probably directing her anger at the wrong person. "I'm sorry, I didn't mean… You've been so kind to me and Rosie and I know I've taken advantage of that kindness by coming here." She looked up at him through eyes filled with sadness and despair. "I've got no right to put on you like this and as soon as Rosie has had some sleep, we'll go."

Filled with pity Arthur studied her tired, drawn face. "Go where, back home?" he asked.

"What choice do I have," she replied, resignedly.

With a suddenness that almost frightened him Arthur was struck by an idea. "You and your daughter could stay here and I could bunk down with George," he said optimistically. "It's not ideal, but it would give you time to find something more permanent."

Touched by his generosity Daisy began to cry as she shook her head. "No, I couldn't possibly," she said firmly. "It wouldn't be fair on you or the Doctor, and besides, Stan would soon find out where we were and it wouldn't just be me and Rosie he would take it out on." She clasped her hands over her mouth as she considered her husband's reaction. "No, it was stupid of me to come here in the first place, but it's helped having someone to talk to and I know I have to go home." A glimmer of hope showed in her eyes. "Perhaps he'll still be asleep and won't even know about the knife, or that I've been here." She looked Arthur in the face. "If I could just ask you for one more thing? Could I leave Rosie here while I go? It's best she's not with me, just in case, and, besides, she needs her sleep. I'll come and fetch her in time for school."

Arthur's face was creased with worry. "No," he said sharply, "I can't allow you to do that, it's too dangerous. You can stay here until it's time to take your daughter to school and I'll come with you. Once we've dropped her off we can either face your husband together or I'll wait outside in case you need me." He saw that

Daisy was about to protest and held up a hand. "I won't hear any argument, I'm coming with you."

Too tired to offer any resistance Daisy nodded and a few minutes after that she was asleep.

Chapter Twenty-Nine

It seemed to be raining harder than ever, Arthur noticed as he peered from his living room window at Daisy Jessop hurrying along the harbour dragging her daughter by the hand. Despite what had been agreed earlier that morning Daisy had begged him to allow her to take Rosie to school without him, pleading that she had spent little time alone with the child since returning from hospital, although Arthur knew as well as she did that she feared them meeting Stan before they reached the school and the consequences that might entail in front of the girl.

So Arthur had conceded the point and arranged to meet Daisy at her house once she had dropped Rosie off, but the pair had not even reached the bridge by the time Arthur had put on his raincoat and pulled his cap down hard over his thick tonsure. He hated the idea of deceiving the woman who had shared with him personal details of her life that had remained hidden to everyone else, and even as he left the cottage he was not fully convinced of his course of action.

The rain swept in off the sea, driven by spasmodic gusts of wind, soaking one side of his body more than the other. He looked forward to reaching the hill when the force of the wind would be at his back, helping him along. By the time he crossed the bridge he could only just make out the two of them in front of him, the rain acting as a shifting mist that blurred his view and helped to keep him hidden.

The roadway was becoming slippery as mud from the river bank had started to leak onto the tarred surface, and more than once he almost lost his footing. It was like walking on ice and before he was even halfway up the hill his breathing was laboured and his chest burned with pain. He thought of George and how he had chivvied his friend when he struggled to keep up during the countless times they had made that journey, and now he realised how unsympathetic he had been. A few times he stooped to recover his breath and ease the sharp pain that stabbed at his heart, before gingerly taking a few more steps, and when he finally reached the top he sank gratefully onto the rickety bench. There was now no sign of Daisy and her daughter.

Mrs Metcalfe nudged Queenie Butler with her elbow and jerked her head towards the shop window. Through the rain-spattered glass they watched as the woman and child half walked and half ran along the road past the shop on their way towards school.

"Where could she have been coming from at this time of morning?" wondered Queenie. "There ain't nothing down there."

"Only the old Doctor Wallace. Perhaps one of them was taken bad," commented the shopkeeper.

"She's just come out of hospital, so I hear."

"She owes me one and tuppence," said Mrs Metcalfe indignantly, "for some sausages her old man had while she was there."

"I've not seen much of her, but when I do she never looks happy," said Queenie before smiling at a sudden thought. "If my old man looked like hers I'd have a smile on me face all bleeding day."

"Looks aren't everything, they can be a curse sometimes, and I should know." Mrs Metcalfe gazed wistfully out of the window even though the object of their original attention had passed by. "My husband was a handsome devil when he was young and I was always looking for any sign that he'd been... you know."

"I never had that trouble with Joe; he's always been a fat, ugly bastard. Can't even remember why I married him." She shrugged her shoulders. "I suppose there must have been a reason."

She was still trying to remember when Mrs Metcalfe stabbed a finger at the window. "Here, Queenie, look!"

Queenie looked and saw Arthur as he left the road and started across the green. "Ain't that the doctor's friend," she said, pressing her thin face against the glass. "I wonder where he's going. The only time he ever comes up is for the library, or to come in here. He comes in the pub sometimes, when the doctor forces him to but he ain't no drinker."

The shopkeeper's mind was going in a different direction. "It seems strange, don't you think, first her and the girl, and then him." She dragged her gaze away from the window to fix Queenie with a wide-eyed questioning look. "You don't think she's spent the night down there with him?"

It was certainly what Queenie wanted to think, that sort of gossip only occurred once in a blue moon and was to be cherished. "I wouldn't dream of thinking such a thing," she lied, licking her thin lips. "He's old enough to be her father, what could she possibly want in someone like him?" then added with a mischievous glint in her eyes, "but you know what they say, there's no smoke without fire and it does all seem a bit of a coincidence."

Both women nodded sagely as they watched Arthur disappear from their view across the far side of the green.

Unaware of the eyes that had followed him, Arthur slowed his pace as he reached the rows of houses. His chest was still hurting which only added to his overall feeling of deep anxiety. He began to question why he was there and whether he was capable of salvaging something from a potentially explosive situation. He had arranged to be there just to lend his support to Daisy when she confronted her husband, yet here he was now outside her house with some half-baked notion of placating a man who had made no secret of his dislike for him and was more disposed to using his fists than his ears.

Arthur stood in the shelter of the alley as he shook the water from his raincoat and tried to marshal his frayed nerves. He attempted to formulate some kind of plan which was impossible to do since he had no idea if Stan Jessop was still asleep in bed and had not yet discovered the knife or was up and waiting for his wife to return. Either way involved him in some considerable risk, and the sensible thing to do was to wait for Daisy. So why did he wrap his raincoat around him, brave the rain and knock on the front door? He did it in a moment of recklessness and regretted it immediately afterwards as he prayed there would be no reply.

His prayer was answered, even when he dared himself to knock a second time, and a few seconds later he was back in the alley and having to make another difficult decision. But this time it was a little easier, Stan must either still be fast asleep or out of the house and Arthur went round the back and cautiously opened the kitchen door, although his caution was brief as a broken gutter channelled a small waterfall from the roof onto his cap which was already soaked through.

He entered the kitchen, took off his cap, wiped his face and listened. Except for the sound of water on the yard outside all was quiet, yet Arthur found it impossible to venture any further into the house. It was wrong, and the longer he stood there the more wrong it felt, but having ventured this far there could be no turning back and if he could recover the knife before Daisy returned there was hope of achieving some small victory. All those thoughts consumed him, deafening him to the sound of the door being pushed open, and he was only aware of the other presence when he felt the sharp prod in the small of his back.

"I could kill you and no one would blame me. It's a man's right to protect his own home and his family."

"I knocked on the door, there was no answer," replied Arthur, shocked by his own steadiness. "I came here to talk to you, that's all."

"Not to get hold of this?" The point of the knife dug deeper into Arthur's back, making him flinch. "Isn't that what she sent you here to get?"

"She didn't send me, she doesn't know I'm here," said Arthur, although it was only partially true. "She's taken your daughter to school, she'll be here soon."

Stan kicked a chair away from the table. "Then we might as well sit down and wait for her," he said, pushing Arthur before sitting down himself, "and you can tell me why you're here and what you've been up to with my wife and kid."

Arthur did as he was told. He had no appetite for a confrontation if it could be avoided, although that likelihood seemed remote. "I wanted to speak to you before she got here," he said, sitting back in the chair and resting his hands on the table in a manner he thought would not provoke. "I wanted to let you know that whatever you might think is going on between me and your wife is simply not so." He eyed the knife that Stan was toying with in front of him. "She knows what she did with that was wrong, but I also understand why she did it."

The corners of Stan's mouth twitched and he raised his eyes to glare across at Arthur. In a blur of movement he raised the knife and plunged the point deep into the table's wooden top, making Arthur throw his hands back out of the way. "You don't know bugger all, you interfering old bastard. You don't know anything about what goes on between me and her, and it's none of your bleeding business." He levered the knife out of the table and jabbed it at Arthur's face. "So why don't you piss off out of here and leave the two of us to get on with it before I use this on you."

"Not before I say what I came here to say," replied Arthur, leaning back as far as the chair would allow. "Your wife only did what she did because of the way you treat her and your daughter.

She would never have done anything like that if she wasn't provoked, if she wasn't desperate to make you see what you're doing to the two of them.

He wanted to say more, but was interrupted when the back door opened and Daisy stepped into the kitchen, her face, framed in the sodden headscarf, a disturbed picture of fear and shock. Without speaking she untied the scarf from under her chin and shook her hair free which fell in a soaked, lacklustre tangled mass that made her appear ten years beyond her age.

"Mr Mulrooney, I didn't expect you…" she started to say before Stan swung round on the chair and she saw the knife in his hand. "I wouldn't have used it, Stan, I just wanted to scare you."

Stan's lips curled into a callous sneer as he jerked his head in Arthur's direction. "That's what he reckons, but I expect he believes everything you tell him." He tapped the blade of the knife against the palm of his hand. "It makes me wonder what lies you have been telling about me, what things I'm supposed to have done."

"She hasn't told me anything that I haven't already guessed for myself," said Arthur.

"You shut your bleeding mouth," hissed Stan through clenched teeth. "This is between me and my wife, so why don't you do what I said and piss off out of here." He stood and went over to Daisy, putting a hand round the back of her neck to stop her from pulling away. "I'm sure we can sort everything out between the two of us, can't we, my love?"

Daisy squirmed under his grasp, shaking her head as she tried to avoid his piercing stare. "It's too late. I'm not going to let you hurt us anymore. I'd rather be homeless than carry on like we are." She tried to shake herself free but he tightened his grip and brought the knife up to her throat. From somewhere she found the strength to defiantly meet his eyes. "You'll have to use that before I give in to you anymore."

He let out a mocking laugh. "And leave that precious daughter of yours without a mother. You'll do what I want because you care more about her than what happens to you,"

The truth of that hurt and Daisy dropped her head in shame. "I just want to be treated like a wife," she muttered more to herself, knowing the words meant nothing to him.

Sensing her submission Stan took the knife from her throat, then turned when Arthur got to his feet. "And where do you think you're going?" he demanded. "You haven't told me yet what's been going on between you and my missus."

"There's nothing going on, Stan," pleaded Daisy, her voice weak with exhaustion. "There's never been anything going on. Mr Mulrooney is a friend, that's all, someone to talk to."

Stan waved the knife at Arthur. "You sit down," he said before turning back to his wife. "And what do you need to talk to him about that you can't say to me? What have I ever done to you that every other man doesn't do with his wife?" He glared at her, demanding an answer. "You tell me that."

What could she say? A kaleidoscope of abuse and misery flashed around in her head as she thought of all the things he had done to her, and only the probability of being overcome with grief prevented her imagination conjuring up all the terrible things he had done to Rosie. How could she speak about any of that to a man without an ounce of compassion, let alone in front of someone who was still a virtual stranger?

The hopeless resignation that Arthur saw etched into every line in her face tore at his heart and he could no longer hold his tongue. "She's frightened of you," he said, standing again, "anyone can see that. And before you start accusing her, she hasn't said anything to me about what goes on between the two of you, and I think I would rather not know." He ignored the rising rage that was so clear in Stan's face. "But for your wife to resort to such drastic measures then I can only imagine how used she must feel, and if you think that is normal then I pity you for the brutal fool you are."

Surprised by the vehemence and presumed honesty of his outburst Arthur clutched at the back of a chair for support as he was overtaken by a wheezing fit of coughing, and was in no position to defend himself when Stan flung Daisy to one side and lunged at him. Instinctively Arthur held up a hand to protect his face, anticipating the blow which never came. Instead, he felt the prick of the knife in the side of his neck.

"It would be so easy to kill you now," Stan hissed, "and it wouldn't bother me one little bit." He jerked his head towards his wife who stood hunched in fear, her hands clasped in front of her. "She never had the guts to do for me and I'm going to make sure she remembers it every day, but, like I say, it wouldn't bother me to stick you with this and tell the police you broke in and attacked me." He let out a vicious chuckle. "And she would be my witness, because if she said anything else she knows what would happen to that daughter of hers."

Arthur was too preoccupied with gulping down mouthfuls of air to concern himself with any other threat to his life. Through glazed eyes he stared back at Stan. "Do you think I'm frightened of anything you can do to me?" The words were punctuated with long wheezing gasps. "But you're just a loud-mouthed bully, and bullies pick their victims carefully."

The effort of speaking left Arthur close to collapse and it took all his strength and both hands on the back of the chair to stop himself from falling onto the floor. Seeing there was little sport to be had from the old man Stan turned his venom back onto his wife.

"I'll get rid of him and you and me can go upstairs." He wiped away the drool of lust that had collected in the corner of his mouth. "You've got a lot of apologising to do."

Watching Arthur's pathetic attempt to hold himself upright seemed to break through Daisy's lethargy of fear and she pushed Stan to one side as he tried to grab hold of her.

"He needs an ambulance," she said, rushing to Arthur's side and taking hold of his arm to ease him onto a chair.

His patience pushed beyond its endurance Stan threw his wife to the floor and yanked Arthur to his feet. "What he needs is to get out of this house," his voice seething with anger. "If he's going to die he can do it outside; he ain't our concern."

As he dragged Arthur forcibly towards the back door Daisy scrambled to her feet, incensed by Stan's total disregard of her friend's condition. Stan had left the knife on the table and in a blind conviction that she needed to save Arthur's life she picked it up and lunged at her husband. There was no conscious intent to use the knife on him, but in those few brief moments of madness and confusion the blade became buried in the side of Stan's neck and he sank to his knees, clutching at the wound as blood pumped through his fingers. Before his eyes glazed over and he lost consciousness, he stared up at his wife with a look of surprise and incomprehension on his face.

It took some time for Daisy to take in what had happened as she looked down at her husband who had rolled onto his side as the pool of blood surrounding his head spread wider across the floor. But when reality did finally dawn she let out a sharp, horrified screech. "I've killed him," she whispered, which was as much a question as a statement of fact. "I don't know how, but I've killed him."

While Daisy stood trance-like over the body it was Arthur who was forced to take some kind of control over the tragic scene. He was still breathing heavily, but strength was returning to his legs and he was able to release the hold he had on the door frame. Like Daisy he was unable to make any real sense of how Stan was suddenly lifeless at his feet, but the fact was clear enough and the man was dead.

He carefully stepped round the body and now it was his turn to sit Daisy down on a chair. "It was an accident," he said in a shaky, uncertain voice. "You never meant to harm him, I'm sure of that."

Daisy was staring unfocussed at the floor. "But I did it," she whimpered, her whole body trembling. "I killed him."

There was no denying that, yet Arthur was loathe to tell her so. "No one will blame you. When you tell the police what he was like they'll understand." There was as much conviction in his words as his faith that the justice system would believe them.

"The police!" She looked up at Arthur, her eyes wide with the sudden realisation that she was now in a situation that couldn't be stopped.

"We have to call them," Arthur said quietly. "The sooner the better."

She pointed vaguely down at Stan's body. "But he might not be dead. We should check."

Arthur was no medical expert, but he understood enough of the human anatomy to know that no one could lose that much blood and still be alive. "I'm sure he is dead, but I'll check if you like."

As Daisy nodded he bent over the body and with two fingers gingerly felt for a pulse, at the same time pulling away the knife and laying it on the floor. He looked up at her and shook his head.

As another thought struck Daisy she began to sob. "What am I going to tell Rosie? She'll be coming out for her lunch and I don't know what to tell her."

"Don't worry about that now." He tried to add some assurance to his words. "We'll call the police first and then decide what's best to do."

She clutched at Arthur's sleeve. "Can you call them, I don't think I can."

He patted her shoulder. "Wait here then, I'll be as quick as I can."

Faced with the prospect of being left alone with her dead husband Daisy leapt to her feet. "No, I'll come with you," she said, her voice laden with dread.

Chapter Thirty

George was puzzled. In fact he was much more than that, he was in a state of some perplexity. A few minutes after he had seen from his bedroom window Mrs Jessop with her daughter scurrying along the harbour, and had hurried downstairs to find out what was going on, Arthur was also seen going in the same direction. He had rushed to the door to call after his friend and had promptly been accosted by Enid Gulliver who had pirouetted up the steps to his front door with a raincoat pulled over her head.

"Going up top this morning are you, Doctor?" She had skipped past him to take shelter in his living room.

He allowed his gaze to linger on Arthur before following her inside. "I wasn't going to, but I think I might now. Was there something you wanted?"

"Wouldn't be asking if there wasn't," she said in her shrill voice and emerging from under the cover of the raincoat. "Milk and bread," she pressed a half crown into his hand, "and the change. Would have asked your friend, but I missed him."

"Me too," he muttered under his breath. "I don't know how long I'll be. Are you sure there's nothing else you need, only with this weather I don't know when we'll be able to get up there again."

"Would have said if there was," she replied, hopping from one leg to the other as she turned to leave. "Saw the woman with the young mite. Strange goings on if you ask me. Anyway, can't stand here jabbering. Going soon, are you?"

"As soon as I've got my coat on, Mrs Gulliver," George said distractedly. "As soon as I've got my coat on."

A dozen or more unanswered questions rattled around inside his head as he set off up the hill, and mingling with the confusion was a degree of anger. Something had clearly happened to bring Mrs Jessop and her daughter down to the harbour, and given the harshness of the weather it could only have been something serious. Why, he thought moodily, had Arthur not seen fit to seek his counsel?

Although the hill was now slick with red mud, he attacked the climb with more vigour than his short legs were accustomed to, and it was not too long before they began to rebel against the task, forcing him to proceed at little more than a laborious crawl, his feet slipping on the precarious surface. He had not even reached half way when he began to question the logic of the undertaking, and had it not been for the needs of Mrs Gulliver he would have turned back and leave Arthur to his intrigues.

After what seemed like an eternity, and several stops to catch his breath, George finally reached the top of the hill and dropped gratefully onto the rickety bench. He sucked in the fresh, damp air until he felt able to continue on, at least as far as the village shop where he hoped to kill two birds with one stone. If anyone knew what was going on it would be the shopkeeper, and at the very least she would have seen in which direction Arthur had gone.

Mrs Metcalfe barely raised an eyebrow when the new customer entered her shop, being deep in conversation with Queenie Butler, at least until she realised who it was and abruptly transferred her interest to the doctor. "Nice weather for ducks, Doctor," she commented, "but not for the rest of us."

George tipped his cap to the two women who looked at him expectantly. "Well, I certainly wouldn't have ventured out if it wasn't for old Mrs Gulliver," he replied guardedly. "I suppose you could call it an errand of mercy." He went over to the shelf where the bread was usually kept. It was empty and he looked enquiringly at the shopkeeper.

"The baker hasn't been yet," she said in response to the unasked question. "The weather I expect. Should be here any time now, if you want to pop back."

He went over to the counter. "Well, I don't know what I'm supposed to do until then," he said, giving Queenie a sideways glance, "unless Joe wants to open his door a bit early."

Queenie raised an indignant eyebrow. "It's more than his licence is worth, Doctor, you know that." She exchanged a knowing look with Mrs Metcalfe. "You could always go and meet your friend."

"Arthur? Why, is he up here?" George commented with a casual air of surprise. "Did he say where he was going?"

"Oh, he never came in," replied the shopkeeper sharply. "We only happen to notice him." She pointed across the green. "He went in that direction, soon after that Mrs Jessop went past with her daughter. We thought they'd been down to see you, what with her just coming out of hospital and that."

George made no reply. He had no intention of contributing to whatever speculative conversation had passed between the two women before he arrived.

"Doesn't Mrs Jessop live over that way?" prompted Queenie as George stared through the rain spattered window to the green beyond. "Just seems strange that he went over that way when Mrs Jessop went straight up the road towards the school. Don't you think it a bit strange, Doctor?"

Whatever George was thinking he was certainly not going to share it with two gossiping women to be spread around the village like a contagious disease. But he had to agree, it did seem strange. He pulled the peak of his cap further down over his eyes. "Put me a loaf by when it comes in, Mrs Metcalfe," he said as he made his way to the door, "and a pint of milk. I'll be back for them shortly."

When he had left the shop the two women gave each other a smug self-satisfied nod.

***

George had reached the front gate just as Arthur ushered Daisy through the narrow alleyway between the houses. With his head bent against the rain he failed to notice them until they were on top of him and he started with a surprise, a surprise that quickly turned to concern when he saw the taut distressed expression on each of their faces.

"George!" was all Arthur could utter as he automatically stepped back into the dark shelter of the alley, taking Daisy with him.

Recovering some degree of composure George turned his attention on Daisy who appeared to be on the verge of collapse as she sagged against the wall. "What's going on, Arthur?" he demanded as he lifted Daisy's head for a better look. "What's wrong with Mrs Jessop?"

"There's nothing wrong with her, George," Arthur replied weakly, "at least nothing you can help her with." He jerked his head towards the far end of the alley. "It's her husband, he's dead."

For a second George thought he had misheard. "Dead! What do you mean, dead?"

"He's dead, George, stabbed. It was an accident. We were just going to call the police."

George said nothing, staring at the two of them with numbed disbelief. Then he pushed past them to go and see for himself. A few minutes later he was back, a horrified expression on his blood-drained face.

"What have you done?" he gasped.

"It was an accident," Arthur repeated blandly.

"So you said," George snapped angrily, "but he was stabbed in the neck. How could that have been an accident?" He looked from one to the other, seeking an answer to his confusion. "Which one of you did it? The police will want to know when they get here."

There were several seconds of tense silence before Daisy's weak and trembling voice broke the deadlock. "It was me, I did it. He was attacking Mr Mulrooney, I just wanted…"

"Then it wasn't an accident," said George flatly. "Not as far as the police are concerned."

"You weren't there, George, you don't know what it was like," said Arthur defensively as Daisy shrank further into the shadow of the alleyway. "Can't you see how upset she is?"

"I'm only saying what the police will say," replied George, softening his tone. "Anyway, you had better go and call them, the longer you leave it the worse it will look."

Arthur nodded his agreement. "I'll do it," he said. "There's no point the both of us going. Will you look after Mrs Jessop while I'm gone?"

"We should go back inside," George said, doing his best to sound sympathetic once Arthur had left. "It could be some time before the police get here, and you look as though you could do with a cup of tea,"

Daisy stiffened at the thought of going into the house. "I can't," she sobbed. "I can't bear to see him. Besides, I need to go to Rosie. I can't let her find out about this from a stranger."

George sighed heavily. He had allowed his curiosity to draw him into a situation from which he could see no easy escape. "All right," he said after giving the matter some lengthy thought. "Go and fetch your daughter from school. Tell them her father is ill, or whatever you think best, and then take her down to my cottage. I'll wait here with Arthur for the police to arrive. They are still going to want to question you, but at least it will give you time to think carefully about what you say to them."

She gave him a questioning look. "I can only tell them what happened," she said. "What else can I say?"

Knowing something of the life she had with her husband George felt some pity for the woman, but it was a pity he knew would not be shared by the police. He knew enough of the law, and how it worked, to understand that there were very few grey areas when it came to an unlawful killing. A man was dead under violent and suspicion circumstances for which they required a culprit, and if they had one offering up a confession it would suit their purposes perfectly. In their eyes it would be case closed with a swift and inevitable outcome.

"Say as little as possible until you've spoken to a lawyer," he advised, placing a hand gently on her shoulder. "Now go and fetch your daughter. Spend as much time with her as you can before the police get here."

When Arthur returned to the house he found his friend sitting in the living room. At first it seemed he was asleep, but as he entered George glared up at him. "You're a bloody fool, Arthur," he said, "getting yourself involved in something like this. What were you thinking?"

Too agitated to sit, Arthur paced the floor. "It wasn't like that, George, she turned up at the cottage early this morning." He went on to relate what had passed between him and Mrs Jessop right up to the time when George had arrived at the house. When he had finished he finally sat, exhausted.

George sat in thoughtful silence, digesting what had been said. "Is that what you will tell the police when they question you?" he asked finally. "If you tell them that Mrs Jessop wanted her husband dead a few hours before she actually killed him it's hardly going to help her defence."

Arthur had already reasoned that much out for himself. "I'm not that much of a fool; besides, they'll only be interested in what went on here and how that poor man got killed."

George peered at his friend over the top of his glasses. "You do understand, Arthur, that when the police get here they are going to treat you either as an accessory or a witness. You haven't got long to decide which one you are going to be."

It was a harsh choice, a choice that Arthur had not even considered. It brought his involuntary involvement in the life of Daisy Jessop and her family into a nightmarish reality, and George's words of warning rang like a death knell in his ears.

***

The police arrived almost an hour after Arthur had made the telephone call to the local station which was no more than five miles away. The young constable who had taken the call had at first questioned the validity of the caller before reluctantly accepting it was no hoax, and then had a similar problem convincing his sergeant. It was now the two of them who arrived to see for themselves and not the dour men in shabby suits with trilby hats pulled low down over their cold, suspicious eyes that George had expected.

It was the Doctor who opened the door to them and the sergeant stepped inside without waiting for an invitation. "Are you the one who called us, a Mr...?" He looked to the constable for confirmation,

"Mulrooney," the constable said. He was tall with an unnaturally thin body topped off with a small head almost entirely invisible beneath his helmet.

By comparison the sergeant was a squat, rotund man with a round florid face and walrus moustache. "So, you're Mr Mulrooney?"

"No, I'm Doctor Wallace, a friend of Mr Mulrooney." He ushered the two officers into the living room where Arthur got to his feet to meet them. "This is Mr Mulrooney."

"Right." The sergeant took off his helmet, unbuttoned his raincoat and shook off the rain onto the floor. "And where's the body, if there really is one?"

"He's in the kitchen," replied George, acidly, "and I can verify that he's definitely dead."

George showed the sergeant through to the kitchen where the officer bent over the wax-faced body of Stan Jessop. "Stabbed in the neck," he said, straightening up with a pained expression on his face. "Hard to see how it was accidental."

"No one intended to kill him," said Arthur who had joined them in the kitchen while the constable hung back, reluctant to confront his first experience of death.

"Were you here when it happened?" The sergeant looked at Arthur before turning on George. "What about you?"

"It was just me and Mrs Jessop, the man's wife," replied Arthur cautiously.

The sergeant made an exaggerated show of looking around the room. "I don't see anyone else, why isn't she here?"

"She went to fetch her daughter from school. I didn't think it was a good idea to bring the child back here so they've gone to wait in my cottage." With the kitchen becoming crowded George tried to ease all of them back into the living room, which suited the constable. "So, what happens now, Sergeant?"

The sergeant gave the body a final lingering look before following the other three. "I need to ask Mr Mulrooney here exactly what happened and then speak to the woman, before the smart arses in CID come and ask them all the same questions over again." He sighed loudly as though the whole thing was an inconvenience. "Parkinson, get yourself over to the phone box and call division. Tell them we've got a suspicious death here. It should make their day."

As Arthur responded to the sergeant's questioning with vague, non-committal answers George could not help noticing how tired and aged his friend appeared. It was as though ten years had been piled onto his life in just a few days. At one stage he was on the verge of asking the officer to stop for a few minutes, but Arthur sensed the intervention and shook his head. By the time he had finished, it was clear that Arthur was exhausted and the sergeant was no nearer to an explanation.

"We had better go and speak to the woman," he said when Parkinson returned to say that the CID would be there within the hour. "You'd better stay here until they arrive," he told the constable, "if I'm not back by then."

"On my own, sergeant?" he asked nervously.

"You won't be on your own, son, you'll have the dead gent for company. Just don't touch anything." He glanced at George and shook his head despairingly. "A few years in the ranks would have done them the world of good."

George was relieved to be out of the house as he and Arthur climbed into the back of the police car. Arthur too seemed revived by the cold rain that was still falling heavily onto the great pools of water that had formed in the poorly repaired roads as the sergeant drove slowly towards the top of the hill.

"Bloody weather," he muttered every few seconds as the windscreen wipers struggled to cope with the torrent of water that flooded down the glass. "Damned bloody weather."

They reached the top of the hill and George leant forward to point out the road ahead. "Watch how you go, Sergeant," he cautioned, "the road is treacherous when it's been raining this hard,"

"I think I know what I'm doing, Doctor," the sergeant replied, but as the car started down the hill and gathered speed he touched the brake pedal and the old Wolesley slewed sideways across the road. "Bugger this," he cursed, frantically swinging the steering wheel to bring the vehicle under control and sighing with relief when it came to a halt on the grass verge beside the river.

"Even if you get down you'll never get back up again until the road clears," advised George.

The sergeant had no option but to agree. "Then I'll walk down and bring the woman back up." He turned in his seat to face the two men in the back. "You two can wait here until I get back. If you just tell me where I can find her."

"No, I'll come with you," said George. "Mrs Jessop will have her daughter with her and I don't think she'll want her taken up to the house, not with her dead father there." He patted Arthur's knee. "You can stay here, old chap, I don't think you're up to the task."

"I'm coming," retorted Arthur indignantly. "I don't want the sergeant here confusing Mrs Jessop with his questions and putting words into her mouth."

"It won't be me asking the awkward questions," the officer said. "They'll most likely send Inspector Beamish and by the time he's finished with her she won't know what day of the week it is." He climbed out of the car and the others did the same, holding onto the door for support. "We'll pick this up on the way back."

Walking in single file they made slow progress down the hill, finding the going easier on the grass than on the road. It was a relief to reach the bridge, and a few minutes later they were at George's cottage, and it was only then that the doctor considered the possibility that Daisy might not even be there. There had never been any doubt in his mind that she was responsible for her husband's death, whatever the circumstances might have been, and that the law was heavily weighted against her. With the prospect of a lengthy prison sentence, or worse, hanging over her there was a strong chance that she would have taken the opportunity to prolong her freedom, however brief that may have been. It was with a mix of disappointment and relief that he glimpsed her peering out of the window as they walked up the path to his door.

She eyed the sergeant nervously as they all entered the cottage and divested themselves of their rain-sodden raincoats which George collected and hung up in the kitchen.

"This is Mrs Jessop," George said when he returned. He looked around the room. "Where's your daughter?"

"I took her upstairs when I saw you coming. She's having a lay down. I didn't want her in the room while we are talking about... She doesn't know yet."

The sergeant took out his notebook and settled himself in an armchair, indicating that Daisy should sit. "Perhaps you'd like to tell me your version of what happened to your husband,"

Daisy sat, glancing anxiously up at Arthur. "What has Mr Mulrooney told you?" she asked in a whispered voice.

"It doesn't matter what he said, I'm only interested to hear your side of the story," the sergeant said impatiently.

Daisy clutched her hands to her chest as her eyes flicked between the three men who were all staring intently back at her. "I can't really remember much about what happened. I'm sorry, but I really can't."

George went over to her and sat on the arm of the chair. "She's in shock, Sergeant, which is hardly surprising considering everything that's happened this morning."

"Well, in that case there's little point in us wasting any more time down here," said the sergeant, clearly annoyed at having made the unnecessary journey down the hill and the prospect of the trek back up again when he could have sent the constable down to fetch her. He got up and turned to George. "I'll take her and Mr Mulrooney back up. There's no point in you coming."

A look of panic swept across Daisy's face. "What about Rosie, I can't just go and leave her without telling her something. She's going to be so upset." Tears rolled down her cheeks. "I don't know what to say to her."

"Whatever you tell her," George said, sharing in her emotions, "won't stop her getting upset. You still have to go and you can't take her." He stopped short of telling her that she would probably not be returning any time soon. "It might be best just to go and say nothing."

Daisy's mouth dropped open at the unimaginable thought of leaving without saying goodbye to her beloved daughter. She looked to Arthur for some kind of guidance or reassurance, but he could offer none and he turned away guiltily. He knew as well as George that the day would not end well for her, even under the most benevolent of police questioning.

It was left to the sergeant to take the decision out of Daisy's hands. "Well, we can't wait while you make up your mind, we have to go now." To reinforce his order he went through to the kitchen and collected the raincoats. "Get your coat on, Mrs Jessop. I don't want to be stuck down here if the weather gets any worse."

As she put on her coat Daisy's gaze lingered on the bottom of the stairs. It took all of her restraint to stop herself from rushing towards them, and even as the sergeant opened the front door she was rooted to the spot. Seeing the agonised look on her face Arthur gently took her by the arm.

"The sooner we go the sooner we'll be back," he said in a low voice that was full of encouragement but lacking in any truth.

Daisy was sobbing quietly as the three of them scurried back along the harbour. A cold wind blew the rain and salty spray off the sea and Arthur again took some small comfort that the weather would be at their backs when they tackled the hill. The events of the morning had taken their toll on him, both emotionally and physically, and he was struggling to keep pace with the sergeant, despite the advantage of his long legs that had served him so well in the past. He had a foreboding sense that his usefulness was coming to an end.

The mud that covered the road had washed slowly down during the morning, accumulating into a thicker layer towards the bottom of the hill where it was now a few inches thick, enough to cover the top of their shoes. It was going to be a long, energy-sapping journey to the top.

Chapter Thirty-One

"So, where are they?" demanded the inspector.

Detective Inspector Beamish had arrived at the house to find the constable and a dead body, neither of which could answer his many questions or dilute his foul mood. Only a few months before he had been transferred from the busy and career-making potential of the police station in Exeter to some backwater where the pinnacle of excitement had been the theft of a sheep. Now he had arrived at a house in a village he had never heard of to be told that a suspicious death having all the prima facia attributes of a murder was simply accidental.

Now he wanted to know why, if the body lying at his feet was really the result of an accident, there was no one in the house who could explain how it had happened. "So," he said again, "where are they?"

Constable Parkinson felt an irritation at the back of his neck; it was fear. It had been bad enough being left alone with the body, but Inspector Beamish was a far more frightening proposition. "The sergeant went to fetch the woman," he mumbled.

"But if she was a witness to the death why was she allowed to go in the first place?" His thin weasel-like face twitched with uncontrolled irritation. He paced the floor of the kitchen; carefully avoiding the bloody patch that had dried to a red-brown colour. He raised his eyes to the ceiling as if seeking something more inspiring than the constable's blank expression. "Well, you'd better go and find them, and if you can't don't bother coming back because you're no use to me here."

Parkinson was about to enquire how he was to do either on foot but felt the answer would be no more useful than his own initiative. So he went out into the pouring rain, almost pleased to be away from the creeping coldness of the deceased and the even colder opinion of his superior.

He turned up the collar of his raincoat and crossed the green, the rain dripping off the pointed rim of his helmet and dropping onto his nose. It was times like this that he questioned the reasons why he had joined the police when he could have been earning more money sitting in a warm dry office drinking cups of tea.

He reached the road, wiped the rain from his nose and stared forlornly in both directions, willing the sergeant and the witnesses to miraculously appear. Through the window of her shop Mrs Metcalfe watched him, just as she had watched the comings and goings of the police for most of the morning, raising her curiosity levels to explosive proportions. But now, at last, she had someone within her grasp who could supply all the answers to the questions that had been brewing since Arthur and Daisy had passed by her shop first thing that morning.

The constable seemed to be stuck on the horns of a dilemma and it was her moral duty to offer what help she could. She rapped on the window, startling the young officer out of his apparent stupor, and when she had caught his attention she beckoned over, going to meet him at the shop door.

"Is there anything I can do, Officer?" she enquired evenly, hiding the desperation in her voice, "Only you seemed a little lost." She stood aside and waved him in. "You don't want to be standing around outside, not in this weather."

He nodded his thanks and took off his helmet. "I don't suppose you saw which way the police car went about an hour ago?"

Mrs Metcalfe's face creased into a thoughtful frown. "Well now, let me see. I do remember seeing it arrive some time ago and thought to myself, 'Wonder where that's going'." She gave him a look of pure innocence. "We don't often see the police around here, that's why I noticed, so I knew it had to be something serious." She stared up at him encouragingly and only continued when nothing was forthcoming. "Yes, and then it came back and went that way." She pointed towards the top of the hill. "I assume it was going down to the harbour. Would there be any reason for it to be going down there, only it does seem odd?"

Not as gullible as Mrs Metcalfe hoped, Parkinson refused to be drawn. "Down to the harbour, you say. Thank you." He nodded again and left, leaving the shopkeeper wringing her hands in frustration.

He strode towards the top of the hill and then stopped dead when he saw the police car parked at an odd angle a short way down on the grass verge, but any hope that his sergeant and the two men were still inside was soon dispelled when he found it empty. He stared bleakly into the rain-shrouded distance and sighed at his misfortune. Two choices faced him: he could go back to the inspector and report that the sergeant was down at the harbour and would return shortly with all the witnesses, and pray for that to be the case, or he could brave the elements and risk pneumonia by staying out of the inspector's way for as long as possible. Suddenly pneumonia seemed the more attractive.

The small party had made slow progress in their assent, held back mainly by Arthur whose long legs where disadvantaged on the slippery surface. Also, the pain in his chest that had subsided while they had been at the cottage was now reinvigorated by the exertion and every deep breath made him wince.

They were only about a quarter way up the hill by the time the constable met up with them, the back of his raincoat thickly smeared with the red mud where he had twice fallen over.

The sergeant gave him a questioning look. "What are you doing here, Parkinson?" his anger partly diluted by his breathlessness. "I thought I told you to wait at the house for the CID."

"I did. The inspector told me to come and look for you. He's not very happy that these two weren't there."

"Well, now you're here, make yourself useful." The sergeant nodded at Arthur who was bent double over the grass verge. "See if you can help the old gent."

With the sergeant and Daisy taking the lead and Arthur leaning heavily of the constable's shoulder they set off again, but had gone no more than twenty paces when Arthur let out a low groan and sank to his knees into the glutinous mud. Not recognising the seriousness of his charge's condition Parkinson tried to lift Arthur to his feet but the dead weight was too much for him, and with no purchase beneath his feet he allowed Arthur to slide onto his back where he lay, his breath laboured and rattling.

"Sergeant!" Forgetting the first aid he had learnt in training, Parkinson reacted with panic. "The old man's passed out; it looks bad."

Daisy was the first to Arthur's side and she knelt down in the mud to cradle his head in her arm. "I think he's having a heart attack," she said, looking imploringly up at the sergeant. "We have to get him help."

"His mate's a doctor, isn't he? Go down to the harbour and fetch him," he ordered the constable. "It's the fourth cottage along, and be quick."

There was little either Daisy or the sergeant could do for Arthur as they waited for the constable to return with George. It was probably no more than ten minutes, but as the colour drained from Arthur's face Daisy grew more and more concerned. The relief she felt when George arrived was driven to greater heights when she was reunited with her daughter who ran precariously through the mud to be at her mother's side.

It took George only moments to arrive at his diagnosis. "We have to get him to hospital," he said gravely to the sergeant. "Your constable will have to go up and call for an ambulance."

The sergeant waved a hand at the road. "You've seen the state of that; they'll never get an ambulance down here."

"I know that," George snapped impatiently. "Tell him to call the ambulance and for it to wait up the top of the hill, then he can go to the pub." He ignored the incredulous look on the sergeant's face. "There's bound to be a few farmers in there on a day like this. One of them will have a tractor somewhere close by. It's the only thing that can get down here."

The sergeant nodded and passed on the instructions to Parkinson. "And there's nothing I can do down here either," he said to George. "I'll carry on up with Mrs Jessop before the inspector sends anyone else to look for us." He tipped his head towards Rosie who was still huddled by her mother's side. "What about her, can she stay with you?"

"I don't think there's any choice," George replied resignedly as he drew the sergeant a few paces away. "I don't suppose there's any chance your inspector is going to accept that it was an accident and just let her go."

"You saw the body, Doc, what would you think?" He gave a sigh. "I think the best she can hope for is manslaughter, but my money would be on something worse."

He had said no more than George already feared, but for the time being he had no choice but to appear optimistic as he went over to Daisy. "I'm sorry," he said as she got to her feet, Rosie clinging to her arm, "you have to go with the sergeant, but I'm sure everything will be all right. I'll keep your daughter with me until you get back, so try not to worry."

It was a pointless suggestion. Having forced herself to leave Rosie in the doctor's care just a short time before she now had to do so again, only this time it would be far worse. She picked the child up, almost slipping over in the process, and kissed her on the forehead. "Be a good girl, darling, and stay with Doctor Wallace.

Mummy has to go with the policeman for a little while but I'll be back soon, I promise."

Rosie's little face creased with anguish and she burst into tears. "Why mummy? Why can't I come with you?"

It was heart-breaking to watch for George and he reached out to take the child. "You stay with me, my love," he said in his soft comforting voice. "I need you to help me look after Mr Mulrooney. He's very poorly and I don't think I can manage on my own, and when the ambulance comes you can help me look after him until we get to the hospital. It will be quite an adventure for both of us. What do you think?"

At first it seemed there was nothing on earth that could compensate Rosie for being separated from her mother, but little by little her sobbing subsided and she turned to face the doctor. "Is Mr Rooney going to die?"

George forced a reassuring smile. "Not if you're here to help me look after him."

It took a few more encouraging promises from both Daisy and the doctor before mother and daughter could be prized apart as the sergeant grew more and more impatient. The constable was already halfway up the hill and he was anxious to be on his way as well. "We have to go," he said, taking Daisy by the arm.

She gave her daughter another kiss as she was dragged away. "Be a good girl, darling, and I'll see you soon."

George kept a firm hold on the child as she watched her mother go. A lump formed in his throat as he focussed his attention back onto the care of Arthur, at the same time wondering when and where mother and daughter would see each other again.

Chapter Thirty-Two

The rain was a minor inconvenience to Florence Merryweather in a life that had been plagued by inconveniences, like the death of her husband. In the years since the war ended she had suffered the solitary existence of a widow, not through grief but because most of those she came in contact with were frightened of her, especially men. She had successfully disguised her fragilities behind a façade of bluster and verbal assault. It was an act she was beginning to regret in one particular respect, until the object of her interest seemed to be placing his affections elsewhere.

Now she negotiated the country lanes as though the flooded surfaces were mere puddles and no challenge to her determination. She was making the unscheduled journey to Little Bridge to see her friend, Dorothy Sawkins, after the two had spoken on the telephone the previous evening, after which Florence had brooded over the conversation, debating whether or not she cared before deciding she did; enough to make the hazardous journey.

"I think you're over reacting, Florence." The headmistress had run across the playground with a raincoat pulled over her head and was now leaning heavily against the library counter recovering her breath. "He's old enough to be her father, they're just friends."

Sitting in the driving seat Florence snorted with derision. "There's no such thing as just friends where single men and married women are concerned." She turned to face her friend. "Why else has he shown no interest all this time? It all makes sense now."

Dorothy Sawkins resisted the urge to laugh, although she did allow herself a wry smile. "From what I've seen and heard you haven't exactly gone out of your way to woo the man. I imagine he's more terrified of you than harbouring any feelings of affection." She gripped the edge of the counter as Florence brutally forced the charabanc into gear and the vehicle lurched forward. "I only told you what I did because I knew you liked him and I thought you should know. You shouldn't take any notice of what Mr Jessop said, and I wish I hadn't told you."

"Well you did, and after that other business at the school there must be something in it."

It took only a few minutes to drive the short distance to the Dun Cow, but it was too far to walk in the rain, and Florence's spirits had been dampened enough already. The pub would not have been her usual choice of hostelry, but she was in desperate need of a gin and tonic, and even if a few cubes of ice and a slice of lemon were out of the question it was a sacrifice she was prepared to accept.

The bar was far busier than would normally be the case for a weekday lunch time, the usual clientele boosted by farmers and labourers driven from the fields by the bad weather. As the two women entered there was a brief, but noticeable, lull in the various conversations as several pairs of eyes turned in their direction. While the Headmistress had the feeling of unwelcome conspicuousness Florence glowered back at them with open contempt. As all the customers were men they were no more than an irrelevance in her mind. She elbowed her way to the counter, daring anyone to object.

Joe Butler abruptly ended the discussion he was having with his wife to serve them. "Good day, ladies, we don't often have the pleasure of your company."

Florence wiped a finger across the counter top as she looked about her disdainfully. "And why do you think that is, not exactly the Savoy, is it?"

Dorothy Sawkins gave her friend a sharp nudge. "I apologise for her, landlord, she's not in the best of moods today."

Joe shrugged off the criticism with a smile while behind him his wife was less inclined to accept the slur on her establishment. "It suits our customers," she commented sourly. "They come in here for the beer and the company, not for fancy trappings and cherries on sticks.

"So I expect an olive or a slice of lemon in a couple of gin and tonics is out of the question then," said Florence sarcastically, "but we'll have them anyway."

"We don't get a lot of call for lemons in here," said Joe apologetically, giving two glasses an extra polish with a tea towel, "but we can certainly manage the gin and tonic." As he prepared the drinks Queenie continued to stare down her long nose at the two women. He leant over the counter as he took Florence's money. "Don't mind her," he said with a surreptitious twitch of his head. "She sees other women as a bit of a threat."

Florence looked the landlady up and down. "And it's plain to see why." She sniffed at her drink. "You did put some gin in here, didn't you?"

"Florence, that's enough," said the headmistress sharply. She looked around the bar. "You're just miffed because your fancy man isn't here to feel the rough end of your tongue."

Florence peered through the blue haze of tobacco smoke that hung in the room, although she knew Arthur Mulrooney would probably be engaged elsewhere. "He can do as he pleases," she said dismissively, "and with anyone he likes."

Dorothy pulled her friend into a quieter corner of the bar. "I don't imagine he's with Mrs Jessop," she said. "She came to the school earlier to collect her daughter. It seems her husband is unwell. I must admit she looked pretty upset, so it must have been serious. She didn't look like a woman who is having an affair."

"And what do those women look like?" scoffed Florence, rejecting the reassurance with a curt wave of her hand. "He's bound to be with her, offering his shoulder for her to cry on." She went back to the counter and banged down her empty glass. "Put another one in there, landlord."

Fifty yards away from the public house Constable Parkinson put down the receiver in the telephone box, picked up his helmet and prepared himself for the dash along the road. The ambulance, he was told, could be some time. The weather had put a severe strain on their resources and if any other arrangements could be made to get the patient to hospital that would be advisable. Without the gift of initiative there was little room in the constable's imagination for other arrangements. He had been tasked with getting the old bloke to the top of the hill and it was there his responsibility would end, and with that fixed firmly in his mind he pushed open the door of the telephone box and ran towards the pub, where at least he would be out of the rain.

The reaction of the customers to his appearance in the bar was of significantly less surprising than that created by the two women a little earlier, a clear indication that his authority mattered less to the clientele than the presence of two women in their pub.

The landlord regarded him with an amused expression. "Come in out of the rain, have you constable?" He gave a wink to the nearest customers. "Only if you want a drink I'll have to ask you for proof of your age."

There was a small ripple of laughter as Parkinson opened his raincoat and shook it over the floor. "I've come for a tractor," he said blandly, looking around at the grinning faces. "Have any of you got tractors?"

There was another round of humorous remarks before someone in the crowd piped up. "Most of us have tractors, constable, but we don't generally bring them into the pub with us."

"All right, gents," shouted Joe, holding up his hand for silence. "If the constable wants a tractor then I expect there's a good reason for it." He looked at Parkinson, inviting him to explain.

"There's an old bloke down the hill by the harbour, had a heart attack or something and we can't get him up, what with the mud. His mate reckons the only thing that can get down there is a tractor."

A hum of muttered comments surrounded the constable, most confirming that a tractor was the only vehicle for the job, although there was a conspicuous lack of offers to provide one. The community spirit, it seemed, that had got them through six years of war had now passed.

The landlord looked round at his customers, a little surprised by their reaction. "Come on now lads, there must be at least one of you who's got a tractor handy?"

The embarrassing silence that followed was quickly broken as Florence barged her way through the throng and poked the constable vigorously in the back. "The man who had the heart attack, what's his name?"

Parkinson turned and gave her a look that suggested the question was irrelevant under the circumstances. "A big bloke with a beard, Muh-ooney I think. Why, have you got a tractor?"

"Idiot," she said, taking him by the lapel of his raincoat and dragging him towards the door. "I've got something better than that." As they reached the door she glanced over at her bemused friend. "I'm sorry, Dotty, but he's going to have to take notice of me now."

Still holding firmly onto the constable's coat she hauled him across the road to the parked charabanc. As she opened the door he shook his head, bracing his feet firmly on the ground.

"You're not going to try and get down the hill in that, are you?" he stuttered, a look of terror peering out from under the rim of his helmet. "You're mad."

"Quite possibly," she snapped back, using her considerable strength and determination to haul him inside the library. Having shut the door behind her she squeezed into the driving seat. "You had better hold on to something, I don't want two invalids on my hand."

The rain had eased a little but the road through the village was still awash with water and as Florence ploughed through it waves spread out on either side. She only slowed when they had reached the top of the hill and she saw the danger that lay on the road ahead. As soon as she put her foot on the brake pedal the vehicle began to skid on the slippery surface and the constable let out an involuntary groan of terror, his knuckles white as he clung to one of the shelves, convinced he was going to die.

The charabanc slewed round until it was sideways on to the road and facing the river, and even Florence thought her rescue mission was over before it had barely begun. She cursed loudly, stamping down harder on the pedal, and then cursed again at her own stupidity as the training she had been given and the lessons she had learnt during the war came flooding back. She released the brake, spun the steering wheel to the right and rammed the lever into first gear with an ear shattering protest from the engine. Finding some purchase on the grass verge the vehicle began to respond to her efforts as it slowly swung round to face down the hill. She beamed with smug satisfaction as all she had to do now was to control the decent over the mud covered surface of the road.

Constable Parkinson had groped his precarious way to the back of the library, assuming it offered him the best chance of survival, while at the front Florence gritted her teeth, gripped the steering wheel and jammed her foot back onto the brake pedal, releasing it just enough to allow the charabanc to move slowly down the hill an inch at a time. Their progress was painfully slow and all the while she had the vivid image of Arthur fighting for his life with her as his only chance for survival. She began to question her right to an opinion of him. In the time she had known him all she had ever done was to heap one humiliation after another on his innocent shoulders, expecting that he would accept it for what it was, a childish attempt to endear herself to him, which had spectacularly backfired. No, he owed her nothing, and now it could be too late to make amends. But she had to try, while the constable cowered in the back.

Further down the hill, and out of sight of Florence, George cradled Arthur's head in his arms, silently willing his friend to keep breathing until help arrived, whatever form it took. Now wrapped in the blanket that George had sent Rosie to collect from his cottage, Arthur's breath came in short shallow gasps, and now the child crouched by their side staring down at Arthur with sad pleading eyes. No longer was she the only child in school without a grandparent, and when she returned she would be sure to let the other children know of her part in saving her grandfather's life.

George was beginning to despair of any rescue attempt, after all what farmer would want to risk such a valuable asset as a tractor to go to the aid of a stranger. There was a limit to the price of any act of mercy after all, and the price for Arthur's life was more than the residents of Little Bridge could afford.

He was about to accept that Arthur's chances lay in his hands alone when he thought he heard the sound of an engine and he said a silent prayer. It was answered seconds later as the incredible sight of the mobile library edged into view round a bend in the hill.

It took several more agonising minutes before the charabanc slid to a halt just yards from where Arthur lay. Florence, rigid from the intense concentration it had taken to get down the hill, stayed in the driving seat and it was the ashen faced constable who was the first to leave the vehicle, clutching at its side to support his fear weakened legs.

"You could have bloody killed me," he shouted at Florence as he passed in front of the windscreen.

Shaken from her temporary stupor she jumped up, her face stricken with alarm at the sight of Arthur lying in the mud, starkly bringing home to her the seriousness of his condition. Cautiously she left the charabanc and made her precarious way to his side.

"Don't just leave him lying there," she said, her booming voice hiding her fear, "let's get him out of the mud and inside." As she bent close to George she whispered, "Am I in time?"

George raised a speculative eyebrow. "It pretty much depends if you can get that thing back up the hill." He jerked his head at the library. "He's very weak and I'm worried about pneumonia."

"I got down here, didn't I?" She looked round for the constable and found him leaning against the charabanc wiping mud from his raincoat. "Get over here you useless article and give me a hand with him," she ordered before turning to the doctor. "You'd better get yourself home and take the girl with you before you both end up in hospital with him."

"I'm coming with you, and so is she," George replied firmly. He took Rosie by the hand and together they walked unsteadily round to the door. "Be careful with him, please."

Between them Florence and the constable eased Arthur away from the cloying grip of the mud, and whatever benefit the blanket had served now proved to be a hindrance, its sodden weight making it more difficult to lift the patient. Florence pulled it away, throwing it to one side before the two of them took an arm each and dragged him across the road, the heels of Arthur's shoes forming furrows through the mud. By some miracle and extreme effort, they managed to get him up into the library and lay him down in the space between the shelves. Beneath her tweed jacket her heavy breast heaved with exhaustion and emotion as she gave Arthur a long lingering look before turning away and climbing into the driver's seat. She wiped a tear from her cheek as she started the engine.

"How are you going to turn this thing around?" The constable was leaning across the counter, his tone, unhelpful, mocking even. "There's not enough room, we'll end up in the river. I think I'd rather walk."

But before the officer could make good his escape there was a loud grinding of gears and the charabanc lurched in its effort to move backwards. "Stop whining, Officer," she hissed over her shoulder, "and make yourself useful." She made another attempt to reverse the old vehicle up the hill but the back wheels simply spun on the mud. "Get your coat off and put it under one of the back wheels and put that blanket under the other." She turned and glared at him, defying him to object. "Go on, move yourself, we haven't got all day, a man's life is at stake."

Parkinson hesitated long enough to consider how he would explain the ruination of his uniform to his superiors, but the threat delivered by Florence's expression convinced him not to protest.

When everything was ready he thumped the side of the charabanc and was about to climb back in when she stopped him. "Get round the front and be ready to push," she ordered.

The engine screamed, and at first it appeared that nothing more would happen, but as Florence deftly juggled the clutch and accelerator there was a sudden shift backwards and the constable went sprawling onto the road. By the time he scrambled to his feet the library was making slow, but steady, progress up the hill and his shouted imprecations were lost in the roar of the engine.

Between the shelves of books George sat on the floor supporting Arthur's head in his lap while Rosie sat opposite sobbing softly. She had spoken hardly a word since her mother had been taken away by the sergeant, and it was impossible to guess what was going on in her young mind. It must have seemed to her that no one gave any thought to her plight, that the only one in the world who cared for her had left for no apparent reason and she was now alone. Even the grandfather who had so recently entered her life was about to desert her.

Less than a half mile away Daisy was feeling equally alone and afraid, having arrived back home to be confronted by a belligerent Detective Inspector Beamish whose mood had blackened with every minute he had been forced to wait to question the pair who between them were clearly responsible for the body lying on the kitchen floor.

He looked aggressively from the sergeant to Daisy then back to the sergeant. "There's supposed to be two of them, where's the other one?" he demanded before they were barely inside.

The sergeant held the inspector's fierce gaze. There was no love lost between the two officers, in fact, as far as the sergeant was concerned, the whole of the CID were a load of self-absorbed morons. "The old chap, Mr Mulrooney, had a heart attack or something. We had to leave him with his mate waiting for an ambulance." He waved a hand at Daisy. "This is Mrs Jessop, the dead man's wife."

They were all standing in the hallway where the inspector looked Daisy up and down through narrow accusing eyes. "So, you're responsible for this mess?" he said, jerking his head in the direction of the kitchen. "Do you want to tell me how it happened?"

Daisy's expression was blank. She felt as though she was living through a bad dream, that she would soon wake to find that none of it was real. On top of that she was cold and wet, the rain had soaked through her coat into her dress and through to her skin. She began to shiver and the sergeant felt a wave of sympathy, recognising that she was in no condition to answer the inspector's questions.

"I think we should let Mrs Jessop dry off, sir," he said, placing a disrespectful emphasis on the last word. "It's been quite a morning for her and I think she's suffering a bit from shock."

Beamish let out a short, mocking laugh. "It's been quite a morning for that poor bastard in there as well, and it's a bit more than shock that he's suffering from." He stared long and hard at Daisy before giving a curt nod. "All right, she can go and change, but I want the clothes she's wearing for evidence."

It took Daisy a moment to understand what had been said, but with some gentle encouragement from the sergeant she went upstairs. "I'll wait outside the bedroom," he said to her. "Pass your clothes out to me when you're ready."

When they came back down Beamish was pacing the living room, irritation and impatience etched into his narrow face. He slapped the back of an armchair, indicating that Daisy should sit. "Now," he said emphatically, "perhaps you can tell me exactly what happened here."

Getting out of her wet clothes had helped Daisy feel more comfortable but her mind was still awash with vague recollections of events, as though it was trying to shield her from the reality of Stan's death. The intimidating presence of Inspector Beamish looming over her did little to assist her memory and she gazed down at the floor in despair.

"Well," demanded Beamish, breaking a long and tense silence, "I'm waiting."

"I'm sorry," she mumbled, "I know I must have done it, but I can't remember much."

Beamish stood in front of her, his hands on his hips as he shook his head. "Is that it, Mrs Jessop, are you saying you killed your husband?"

She supported her head in her hands and sobbed. "I was holding the knife, I must have done it." Her words were muffled and barely audible. "I think he was attacking Mr Mulrooney."

"And you were trying to protect him?" the inspector prompted. "He was attacking your friend and you stabbed him?"

Daisy's sobbing increased in its intensity as she forced herself to remember. "Yes… I don't know… I suppose so."

Sensing he was close to a confession, and a major boost to his stagnating career, Beamish stooped down until his eyes were level with Daisy's face. "Either you did or you didn't, Mrs Jessop. Which was it?" he asked, his patience finely balanced.

Daisy slowly lifted her head out of her hands and fixed him with red, vengeful eyes. "I hated him. For what he did to me and Rosie, I hated him," she hissed through gritted teeth.

That was enough for Beamish. He stood up and gave the sergeant a satisfied nod before returning his attention back on Daisy. "Mrs Jessop, I'm charging you with the murder of your husband." He paid lip service to her rights, knowing they meant nothing to her. "We'll do the rest of this at the station." He went over to the sergeant who was less enthused by the outcome of the questioning. "Once we get the corroboration from that Mulrooney chap I think it'll be pretty much cut and dried. Get that constable of yours over to the hospital to take a statement, if it's not too late."

Chapter Thirty-Three

Backing the charabanc up the hill tested Florence's nerve and skill to the limit. Several times the tyres on the old vehicle threatened to lose their grip on the road and send it careering down the hill, but by careful management of the controls she kept it moving. By the time they reached the top her whole body ached from the tension and concentration.

The sergeant caught up with them as she was turning the charabanc round to face in the right direction. He was on his way to retrieve the police car from the river bank and he waved at her to stop.

"How is he?" he asked as he opened the door and peered down to where Arthur was lying on the floor,

"You can see how he is," snapped Florence, "and he's not going to get any better with you holding us up."

"I just need a word with my constable," he said apologetically, beckoning Parkinson outside.

George wanted to ask after Daisy, but felt it unadvisable in front of the child. The less she knew for the time being the better. He would find out soon enough.

The constable was barely back inside the library before Florence accelerated along the road and out of the village. In the failing light of the autumn afternoon and with the rain still falling steadily Florence drove the charabanc at a frantic pace through the Devon lanes, sending surges of water across the road and into the fields and ditches beyond.

In the back of the library George did his best to protect Arthur, Rosie and himself from the books that cascaded off the shelves and onto the floor. He knew it was pointless demanding that Florence slow down; she would ignore his order and had every right in doing so. He feared for his friend's life far more than the harm caused by a few flying books.

Rosie huddled against the back of the library, her arms wrapped round her knees that were drawn up tight to her chest.

George's concern was as much for her as for Arthur, and he could only guess at what terrifying thoughts were going through her mind. Everything in her life that made her feel safe had been taken from her and he could give her no reassurance that it would ever return.

At the front of the library Constable Parkinson clung to the edge of the counter, his knuckles white as he was thrown from side to side. Any hope he had of escaping the vehicle had been dashed by the sergeant when he was ordered to accompany the witness to the hospital. As if the journey wasn't harrowing enough he was now burdened with the responsibility of taking a statement that would condemn a woman charged with murder. It was not the day he envisaged when he began his shift that morning.

Ignoring the incessant pleadings of the constable to slow down Florence stared intently at the road ahead, her only concern to help save the life of the man she was now prepared to accept she had wronged. Whatever his relationship with Mrs Jessop had been was of no consequence now and had probably only ever existed in her head. Had she not been such a fool in her embarrassing treatment of Arthur Mulrooney perhaps the situation they all found themselves in could have been avoided. Wracked with guilt she urged more speed from the charabanc as they sped through the encroaching darkness.

As they skidded to a halt outside the hospital, after a journey they all thought would never end, the constable, on the forceful order of Florence, dashed inside. Seconds later, he returned with a porter pushing a trolley.

It was just a small cottage hospital, catering for the needs of the local population providing those needs were nothing more serious than broken bones and non-threatening illnesses. George knew that Arthur's condition came within the scope of neither category but, despite that, the hospital provided him with the best chance of survival, even if that chance was slight. He had not been retired from medical practice for so long not to know that the prognosis was bleak.

The doctor who examined Arthur was an acquaintance of George and the news he had for his colleague was nothing more than George expected. "You were right to worry about pneumonia," he said in a low voice as they stood next to the bed. "Combined with the weakness of his heart…" He patted George on the shoulder. "We should really transfer him to the County Hospital, but it looks like he's been through enough already and I can't see it making any difference to the outcome. I'm sorry, Doctor Wallace, we'll do everything we can but I think it's only a matter of time."

George nodded his acceptance as he reached out to take Arthur's hand. Given the few years difference in their age he had always worried that Arthur would have been the one left behind and how he would have coped. Although he never told his friend as much he was a little comforted by Arthur's friendship with Daisy Jessop and her daughter and that he would not have been entirely left alone. But now it seemed that very friendship may have contributed to his present condition.

"Thank you, Doctor Purcell," he said, his voice cracking with emotion. "At least he's comfortable, and I agree he shouldn't be moved. You don't mind if I stay with him, he doesn't have any other family."

Doctor Purcell assured him he could stay as long as was necessary. "What about the constable and the other two, do you want me to say anything to them?"

George had almost forgotten about them. While Florence and Rosie sat waiting in the corridor outside the ward Constable Parkinson paced up and down, irritated that his shift had already ended. He cornered Doctor Purcell as he left the ward.

"When can I talk to him, doc?" he asked, peering over his shoulder at the patient. "I need to take a statement."

The doctor drew him to one side, away from the other two. "Not today and quite probably not at all." He turned his back on Florence who was taking an interest in what was being said. "I doubt if he will recover sufficiently to answer any questions, and even if he does it will be some time. I don't see any point in your waiting here."

The information placed Parkinson in something of a dilemma. He was told to stay at the hospital until he could take a statement, but surely no one expected him to wait around until the patient died. After several minutes spent mulling over the situation he went to look for a telephone.

George was sitting at Arthur's side when Parkinson returned. "I've just phoned the station and told them what the doctor said about him." He nodded down at Arthur. "They're going to send a car to pick me up seeing as there isn't much chance of him saying anything."

George let go of Arthur's hand and got to his feet. "He might just be a witness to you, constable, but he's still a human being.

Imagine if he was your father or grandfather, wouldn't you want him treated with a bit more respect." He prodded Parkinson in the chest. "You run along, and if he is able to say anything I'll be sure to pass it on to your superiors."

"I'm sorry," he replied with genuine apology, "but I've never had to deal with anything like this before. I really am sorry." He turned away and started towards the door before stopping. "By the way, I thought you ought to know, they've charged the woman with the murder of her husband."

As the constable left the ward George slumped back down onto the chair. His first thought was what he should say to Rosie. How could she possibly understand any of this? Perhaps it would be kinder to say nothing. If the unthinkable happened and Daisy Jessop was found guilty of murder then it would be up to others to decide what Rosie ought to know.

***

Night had descended over the hospital adding to the Stygian gloom in the corridor outside the ward. Thankfully Rosie had fallen asleep a few hours earlier, laying across two chairs and covered by a blanket provided by a nurse. George had divided his time between sitting beside Arthur and keeping company with Florence. He had tried to persuade her to go home, but she was adamant she wanted to be there when Arthur awoke, convinced that he would despite all the medical opinion to the contrary.

"He's stronger than you give him credit for," she told him with some conviction. "And when he does come to I want to be here."

George was reluctant to argue with her. The truth was he was pleased she was there, saving him from the loneliness of a long vigil. He gave her a weak smile. "He was always frightened of you. I just hope he doesn't relapse when he sees you."

She let out a throaty chuckle. "He had better not or he won't hear the last of it."

After that they both sat in dispirited silence and George finally slipped into a light sleep, until just after midnight when he was woken by Florence shaking him by the shoulder. The nurse on duty in the ward had come out to tell them that Arthur was stirring and she thought they would want to know. Florence was already on her feet, anxious to see for herself, but George placed a restraining hand on her arm.

"Let me go in first to see how he is. He won't know where he is and I'd like the first person he sees to be me. I'll call you in if I think he's up to it."

She nodded. "Just make sure you do."

George found his friend awake and turning his head from side to side to take in his strange surroundings. When he saw George his mouth opened to speak, but his gasping breath made it impossible to find the words.

"It's all right, Arthur, don't try to speak. You're in hospital." As Arthur tried to sit up George gripped his shoulder. "Lie still. You've had quite an adventure and you need to rest."

Arthur continued to look about him, trying to make sense of the lost hours. "How long have I been here?" he asked in short, laboured breaths that were further impaired by his obvious agitation. "How long?"

"That doesn't matter. All you need to worry about is getting well, so just lie still and try to rest." It was clear to George that something was troubling his friend that went deeper than his chronic condition. "I'll send for Doctor Purcell, he can give you something to help you sleep."

Before George could call for the nurse Arthur took hold of his friend's arm in a grip that belied the weak state of his health. "No," he gasped emphatically, his watery eyes looking up pleadingly. "Mrs Jessop."

"Don't worry about Mrs Jessop, just concentrate on getting yourself well again." It came as no surprise to George that his friend's first thoughts would be for the woman and her daughter, but even if he were up to making a statement George doubted it would help her cause. "You need to rest, Arthur, and we'll see how you are in the morning."

It was stubborn determination that stopped Arthur from giving in to the fatigue that ravaged him. He pulled on George's arm to lift himself off the pillow. "I need to tell you something," he said, the strain twisting his face into an agonised mask.

"Not now, Arthur, you really do need to rest." He tried to free his arm and force his friend back down but he resisted forcibly. "This won't help you, or Mrs Jessop, so get some sleep and we'll talk about it in the morning."

"It will be too late, George, I'm dying." He fixed George with a resigned look. "Please don't lie to me, I know how bad it is but I can't go until I tell you something." He sank down onto the pillow, exhausted, his hand slipping from George's arm.

Behind him George heard movement, and when he looked round he saw Florence standing in the doorway holding Rosie by the hand. They crept silently over to the foot of the bed.

"She woke up and started crying," whispered Florence by way of explanation. "She wanted to see him and it was the only way I could mollify her." She peered over at Arthur. "How is he?"

George shook his head. "He's awake. He's more worried about the girl and her mother than himself and says he wants to tell me something."

"What are his chances?" she asked, leaning close to George who shook his head again.

"Does he know?"

"I haven't told him, but he knows."

"Then you should let him speak before it's too late. If it's that important then he'll only have peace when it's out."

George had never credited Florence with such a sensitive perception; perhaps there was more to the woman than he thought. It was a shame that it surfaced too late to benefit Arthur. He nodded. "Maybe you're right, after all, what harm can it do."

While they had been talking Rosie had slipped her hand free of Florence's hold and had climbed up onto the bed next to Arthur who had managed a thin smile as the child lay her head on his shoulder. Florence was about to lift her away but was stopped by George.

"That can't do any harm either," he said, a lump catching in his throat.

"I didn't expect to see you here," Arthur said as Rosie gazed closely at him.

The child smiled. "We've been on an adventure, haven't we, Mr Rooney?"

Arthur managed a nod. "We certainly have, and I think I'm about to go on another one."

Rosie's blue eyes widened expectantly. "And can I come?"

Arthur did his best to hide the sadness that showed in his eyes. "I'm sorry, Rosie, this is one adventure I have to go on alone."

Arthur closed his eyes, missing the disappointment on Rosie's face. A stab of panic bit into George as he bent over the bed, fearing his friend had gone without the chance of saying goodbye. Then he heard the rasping sound as Arthur sucked in another mouthful of air and he breathed a sigh of relief.

"I think we had better let him rest," he said to Florence, lifting Rosie from the bed. "I'll sit with him, but I promise I'll call you if anything changes."

Florence gave him a look that threatened consequences if he failed in his promise as she led Rosie from the ward. George settled himself on the chair for a long night watching over Arthur as he slept. He was hoping to pass some of the time catching up on the sleep that he so desperately needed; the day had taken its toll on him, both physically and emotionally, and it was only all the disturbing thoughts that ran through his mind keeping him awake. He closed his eyes, letting his head drop onto his chest and crossing his arms, but before his tiredness swept away his consciousness he was suddenly dragged back to reality.

"George?"

George sat bolt upright and stared through the dim light of the ward at his friend.

"I'm here, Arthur, I thought you were asleep." He leant in close, finding Arthur's hand.

"Have they gone?" Assuming he referred to Florence and Rosie, George nodded. "I have to tell you something and you have to listen." The insistence in Arthur's voice overcame the struggle to force out the words, although each one left him breathless.

"You don't have to say anything," insisted George, even though he knew his objection was pointless. "It can wait until you are stronger."

Arthur's hand tightened around George's fingers, demonstrating his agitation. "Please George, tell me the truth. Am I dying?" He lifted his head and fixed George with a penetrative gaze. "I have to know."

During his years as a doctor there had been so many times when he had been forced to tell his patients the last thing they wanted to hear. It had never been easy and he had often marvelled at the stoicism with which many had accepted the news, but never had any of them begged to be told. Why was it so important to Arthur?

"It's not looking good, old chap," he said, avoiding the inevitable truth. "We just have to wait and see. Doctor Purcell is looking after you, he'll be round in the morning and you can ask him anything you need to know."

"I need you to tell me, now, George." There was an urgency that baffled George, but the look on Arthur's face was indisputable. "The truth George, please."

George let out a long, plaintive sigh. "Doctor Purcell thinks it's unlikely you will recover and I agree with him." The admission almost choked him and he bit back on his sentiments. "It seems you have pneumonia and your heart is failing. I'm sorry, Arthur, but there's very little that can be done. I wish I could promise you more, but I can't."

He thought he caught the flicker of a smile cross Arthur's face. "It's quite all right, George. I need to tell you something, but I had to be sure first." He lay back on the pillow as though the confirmation he was looking for had settled his mind. "What's happened to Mrs Jessop, do you know?"

There seemed no point in keeping anything from his friend. "I understand she's been charged with murder. I don't know any more than that."

Arthur turned his head and there was intensity in his expression that George had often seen before. "I'm going to tell you something in case I go before the police can get here. If I do then you have to promise to tell them exactly what I say. You promise me." He waited for George to nod his agreement. "I don't know what Mrs Jessop has told them, but she didn't kill her husband, I did." As George stared at him in disbelief Arthur fought to recover his breath. "She might have thought she did but it was me. She had the knife and she was going to stab him to save me." There was another lengthy pause as his chest heaved beneath the bed covers, although the intensity remained in his eyes. "I stopped her because I knew what it meant, and I took the knife from her and stabbed him in the neck." He gripped George's arm with a strength he had found from somewhere. "I did it, George, and you have to tell the police that. I know I'm dying and I know what I'm saying, they have to believe you." His grip tightened. "You tell them, George, you promise me."

Those last words were spoken with such vehemence that George had no choice but to nod his agreement. "I promise, Arthur, I'll tell them."

Satisfied his friend would carry out his wishes Arthur fell back down onto the pillow, the strain of the past few minutes draining from his face. His breathing, although now more shallow, settled into an even rhythm. George reached over and felt his brow, which was cold and clammy, but there was calmness to his friend that George had seen in many of his patients over the years, just before their lives slipped peacefully away. He crept away from the bed and returned a few seconds later with Florence Merryweather.

"Is it nearly time do you think?" she whispered, her voice wavering as she looked down at the man who had been driven from her affections by her own stupidity. "I've been such a fool, Doctor."

George gave her arm a comforting squeeze as he smiled reflectively. "Arthur always was blind to subtlety. He was frightened of anything that deviated from his idea of the obvious. I don't know if you could have made him happy, but it would have been interesting to find out."

As the pair of them watched over him he suddenly stirred, his eyes wide open and his head twisting as if looking for something until his gaze fixed on George. "It's all right, George," he said weakly. "It's all right, I'll cheat him again."

Florence looked quizzically from Arthur to George. "What did he mean by that?"

George waited for something more from his friend, but Arthur had sunk into another peaceful slumber from which he never recovered. A tear trickled down the Doctor's cheek as he placed two fingers against Arthur's neck and Florence sobbed gently for the man who had stirred emotions she thought were long dead.

"I think I know what he meant," said George as the two of them stood in solemn vigil by the bed until Rosie came to join them.

With Florence's help the child climbed up onto the bed and kissed Arthur on the cheek.

"Night, night granddad," she whispered.

Chapter Thirty-Four

A pale grey dawn was creeping over the eastern horizon as the three of them left the hospital. The rain had finally ceased, to be replaced with a thin mist that spread in from the coast. As one they all shivered as the fresh cold air engulfed them after the oppressive warmth of the hospital. Perhaps it was more than just the cold that affected them as they walked to where the charabanc had been left the day before. None of them had spoken much since Arthur had died, each of them dealing with the loss in their own way.

For Florence there was regret, tinged with guilt for the torment he must have endured at her hands. From the moment he had passed she had not stopped telling him how sorry she was and how inconsiderate he had been in leaving before she could explain. Selfish man!

George probably felt the loss the most. Arthur had filled his hours with pleasure, despite his infuriating little ways and his lack of interest in chess. Walking across the hospital car park he fought back the tears and an overwhelming feeling of despair, and it was only Rosie walking beside him that stopped him from giving in to his emotions.

And Rosie! Who knew what was going through her mind. Her whole life had been ripped apart without her even knowing why, and no one had given a thought to what would happen to her now that her father was dead and her mother was facing an uncertain future.

"I have to go to the police station," George said quietly to Florence as they entered the library. "There's something I need to tell them."

"Is it something that's going to help her mother?" enquired Florence after making sure Rosie was sufficiently out of ear shot.

George shrugged. "I don't know, but I have to try."

"I have to ask, what did he mean when he said something about cheating him again?" She started the engine, allowing it to idle before pulling away. "Obviously there's something I don't know about the man."

George resisted a coarse laugh. "There's a lot about Arthur you don't know, that nobody knows." He gripped hold of the counter as the charabanc lurched forward. "And I'm not sure anyone has the right to know."

"But I'm not just anyone, Doctor," Florence said, guiding the vehicle out onto the road. "I wronged him when I should have realised he felt humiliation at what most would have recognised as flirting. He was sensitive in a way I never thought any man could be, and now it's too late for either of us." She sniffed loudly, wiping a tweed cuff across her face. "I'm guessing he was never in the navy?"

"I'm fairly certain Arthur never set foot outside of England," George said with a rueful smile, "except in his head. That's why he read so much about far flung places, to make up for all the years he missed."

Florence negotiated the still flooded road at a more sedate speed than the day before, allowing much of her attention to be diverted from the driving. "Tell me about him, Doctor, it can't do any harm now, surely. How long have you known him?"

George gave her request a lengthy consideration before replying. In his life Arthur had been such a private person that to talk about him now seemed like a betrayal. He looked down the library to where Rosie sat with her back resting against a shelf, she seemed to be sleeping. If Arthur had been her grandfather how much of his past would she want to know? He took a deep breath and let it out in a long sigh.

"I don't know if I have the right to tell you, or anyone else, but keeping it to myself all these years hasn't been easy, especially when I've had to listen to folk telling me what an odd fellow he was." He sighed again. "It would be less of a strain for someone else to share the burden, so I'll tell you and trust in your discretion."

With her eyes fixed on the road Florence nodded solemnly. "It would comfort me to know."

"As you already know, he was never in the navy." George chuckled, making Florence glance round. "It's a bit ironical but he was a librarian in Torquay. That was before I knew him." He paused, knowing what came next would come as a shock to the woman who had set her cap at a man she never really knew. "His name is not Mulrooney, and the first time I met him was in a cell in Datirnoor Prison before the war." A loud gasp of disbelief escaped from Florence and the charabanc swerved erratically across the road, almost throwing George off his feet. "I was doing some locum work as prison doctor and I was attending the man sharing a cell with Arthur. The man died, and his name was Patrick Mulrooney."

"So he assumed the dead man's name?" questioned Florence, recovering some of her composure. "And why was he in prison?"

"His real name was Brewer, Arthur Brewer, a name he tried hard to forget."

"But why was he in prison?" pressed Florence when George appeared reluctant to continue.

"You probably won't remember the case," George began reflectively, "the war made us forget much about what went on before it started." He rested his weight on the counter, relieving the strain on his tired legs. "Like I said, Arthur was a librarian in Torquay and he was married to a woman called Alice, who couldn't have been more different from Arthur if she tried. A harridan, I suppose you would call her, who made Arthur's life a misery. Anyway, that's bye the bye, the real issue was that she was having an affair with the man who lived next door to them and neither of them made any secret of the fact. Alice, it seemed, used to taunt Arthur about his inadequacies as a husband, comparing him to her lover.

"From what I could find out the man was a brute, in the habit of beating his wife and young daughter." He stopped abruptly as he was suddenly struck by the sickening similarities with Daisy Jessop and her family. "One day, apparently, it all got too much for Arthur, he just snapped. It's hard to believe, isn't it, that Arthur should have a temper. Anyway, he confronted the man and a fight broke out and the man died. I don't know any more than that,

"Arthur never said. Alice, however, claimed that Arthur had told her he was going to kill the man and it was mainly on her testament that he was convicted of murder. It was only after the trial that a witness came forward to say what had really happened, placing doubt on the verdict which was changed to manslaughter and Arthur served ten years,"

"Otherwise he would have hanged," said Florence, horrified by the thought and realising that George had nothing more to add. "So, who was the witness, do you know?"

George breathed heavily. "It was the little girl, the man's daughter."

A light flashed on in Florence's brain. "He cheated the hangman, and now he's done it again. That's what he meant. He's confessed to killing this man to save the woman, knowing he would never live to stand trial." The charabanc slowed to a gentle halt outside the police station. "And now you have to convince them. Do you think they will believe you?"

George opened his hands and puffed out his cheeks. "They might, if they find out who he really is." He looked down the library to where Rosie was still sleeping. "I don't know what's going to happen to her."

Florence eased herself out from behind the steering wheel. "Don't worry about her, Doctor, she's coming home with me."

Epilogue

Four months later
Spring bloomed in the gardens surrounding Luxford House, although the new buds and fresh growths were lost on the weed strangled flower beds and bramble entwined shrubs. The gravelled drive leading up to the house crunched under the slow tread of his brogues as George made no attempt to keep pace with Florence Merryweather, her enthusiastic curiosity driving her to lengthen her stride.

"Magnificent," she said, her hands on her hips as she stared up at the crumbling façade of the old building. She turned as George caught up with her. "Just the ticket!"

George nodded, while gasping for breath. "I thought you would approve, given everything that's happened." He fished in his pocket for the key. "I suppose you want to look inside while we're waiting."

Florence was already heading for the imposing doorway beneath the portico. "Well, I haven't come all this way just to stand outside."

Everything inside was exactly as George remembered from when he was last there with Arthur, and the memory of that moment sent a chill of remorse through his body. There were some signs of other visitors, surveyors and builders sent by the county council as a prelude to implementing the plans that had changed slightly since George had first approached them.

While George waited in the hallway Florence explored the house before announcing that the house would suit its new role perfectly.

She had not long joined him in the hallway when the sound of voices outside drew their attention away from magnificent potential of the house.

"All the years I've lived here this is the first time I've been here." Daisy Jessop peered in through the doorway before stepping inside, pulling Rosie by the hand. "It's such a lovely old building, what a pity it's been left to rot like this."

"Not for much longer," said George, his old watery eyes twinkling behind his glasses.

"They're not going to pull it down, surely," gasped Daisy, staring about her at the grand staircase and ornate cornices. "That would be such a shame."

George shook his head, smiling with a little self-satisfaction. "On the contrary, it's going to be turned into something that I think will be of great benefit to a lot of people." He exchanged a knowing glance with Florence. "I suggested to the county council that it would make an ideal home for elderly folk when they were no longer able to look after themselves. They agreed, and that was going to be the plan. Work was due to start any time now."

"That's a wonderful idea," said Daisy smiling with agreement until a frown creased her face, "but you said 'was', have they changed their mind?"

George couldn't resist puffing out his chest. "Well. I'd like to think that I played some small part in changing their mind, me and Mrs Merryweather here." He paused, taking some pleasure at Daisy's confusion. "It was decided that this house was a bit too remote for old folk, or more especially for anyone wanting to visit them. They have found somewhere more fitting. But its location is perfectly suited to another use; something that I think will appeal to you, Mrs Jessop."

"But I don't understand." Daisy continued to look around, seeking a solution to George's tantalising conundrum.

George's smugness changed to something more serious as he considered the rawness of the subject he was about to broach. "I think you mentioned to Arthur on more than one occasion that you would have left your husband if it wasn't for the fact you had no nowhere else to go." He swept his arm dramatically around the vastness of Luxford House. "The council have agreed with us that there are probably many women in your situation, a problem that has increased since the end of the war. They agreed that this house would be suitable as a temporary refuge for women, and their children, until the difficulties at home can be resolved. What do you think?"

If he was expecting a euphoric and immediate response from Daisy he was to be disappointed. She gazed around at the accumulated rubbish in the rooms that adjoined the hallway, only her eyes betraying a feeling of sadness. "I'm surprised they agreed that there was a need for such a place," she said after a lengthy and thoughtful silence. "I'm surprised they thought this was a cause worthy of spending money on. Oh, I know they gave us the vote, but it's still very much a man's world, Doctor Wallace."

George sighed, finding it hard to disagree. "Perhaps the world is changing Mrs Jessop. Perhaps the war has taught us that woman are equally as valuable as men." He glanced across at Florence whose expression left no doubt that she agreed. "It might be just a small step, but it's one in the right direction."

Conceding the point, Daisy granted him a thin smile. "I'm sorry, I didn't mean to sound ungrateful." She looked about her again, as though trying to imagine how it might look in the future. "It's a wonderful idea, I'm just sorry it will be too late to help me. Stan might still be alive and Mr Mulrooney…" Her words tailed off, choked by the reminder of the sacrifice her friend had made. "It's a shame it couldn't be called Arthur Mulrooney House."

The reporting of Arthur's confession had left many of the villagers of Little Bridge with the smug conviction that they had been right in their opinion of the strange new comer all along. In particular the landlady of the Dun Cow and her friend Mrs Metcalfe who feasted on the gossip for weeks on end.

Not given to outward displays of emotion Florence found herself fighting back some tears. "It's a shame he will only ever be a hero in the eyes of us four, that the rest of the world will only know him by what they have read in the newspapers. But I don't think that will trouble him too much." She held out a hand to Rosie who readily went to her. "And you two have a home with me for as long as you want." George was wiping the back of his hand across his cheek when she turned her attention on him. "And you too, doctor. I've plenty of room if that hill gets too much for you."

George smiled, shaking his head. "It's a kind offer, Mrs Merryweather, but the council have promised that us old folk down at the harbour will be a priority as soon as the property is ready. Until then I've still got some use."

They were all silent as they walked slowly away from the house, deep in their own sombre thoughts, although there was little doubt they were all focussed in the same direction, the adventures of Arthur Mulrooney, wherever he was.

THE END